Divas in the Convent

Divas in the Convent

Nuns, Music, and Defiance in
Seventeenth-Century Italy

CRAIG A. MONSON

The University of Chicago Press   Chicago and London

CRAIG A. MONSON is professor of music at Washington University in St. Louis and the author of *Nuns Behaving Badly: Tales of Music, Magic, Art, and Arson in the Convents of Italy,* also published by the University of Chicago Press.

The University of Chicago Press, Chicago 60637
The University of Chicago Press, Ltd., London
© 1995, 2012 by Craig A. Monson
All rights reserved. Published 2012.
Printed in the United States of America
21 20 19 18 17 16 15 14 13 12   1 2 3 4 5

ISBN-13: 978-0-226-53519-7 (paper)
ISBN-10: 0-226-53519-3 (paper)

Library of Congress Cataloging-in-Publication Data
Monson, Craig (Craig A.)
    Divas in the convent : nuns, music, and defiance in seventeenth-century Italy / Craig A. Monson.
        p. cm.
    Revised edition of Disembodied voices
    Includes bibliographical references and index.
    ISBN-13: 978-0-226-53519-7 (paperback : alkaline paper)
    ISBN-10: 0-226-53519-3 (paperback : alkaline paper) 1. Music in convents—Italy—Bologna—history—17th century. 2 Santa Cristina della Fondazza (Convent : Bologna, Italy) 3. Church music—Italy—Bologna—17th century. 4. Church music—Catholic Church—17th century. 5. Vizzana, Lucrezia Orsina, 1590–1662. Componimenti musicali. I. Title.
    ML3033.8.B65M66 2012
    780.88'2719004541—dc23

                                                           2011036603

♾ This paper meets the requirements of ANSI/NISO Z39.48-1992 (Permanence of Paper).

Alla Mafia Monacale Internazionale

(you know who you are . . .)

Contents

Illustrations

MUSICAL EXAMPLES

Preface to the New Edition

When *Disembodied Voices: Music and Culture in an Early Modern Italian Convent* appeared in 1995, it was the first book-length study of sixteenth- and seventeenth-century music and female monasticism, a field then largely unexplored. In the subsequent fifteen years, additional monographs, numerous articles, a few dissertations, and one very good novel on the subject have found their way into print.[1] The year before the book's publication the Bolognese ensemble Cappella Artemisia recorded three motets from *Componimenti musicali*, composed by the book's heroine, Bolognese convent composer Lucrezia Orsina Vizzana. The British ensemble Musica Secreta recorded the complete *Componimenti musicali* not long thereafter, prompting the *Observer* to comment that "Vizzana's 20 motets are historical treasures," the *Sunday Times* to describe the music as "admirably wrought and certainly worth discovering," and the *Times* to laud Vizzana's "exceptional musical talent." (These reviewers were all equally enthusiastic about the performances on the CD as well.) Musicians apparently took note. For Vizzana's motets now turn up remarkably often, at least in early-music concerts—and not just those single-mindedly promoting "music herstory."

The publication of many Vizzana motets in modern editions has facilitated their being heard—though performers still must work reasonably hard to lay hands on the music. In addition, a substantial body of other music composed by and for nuns, some of it directly related to Vizzana's convent of Santa Cristina della Fondazza, has become available in print, on recordings, or online. And more is on the way.[2]

Thanks to recordings, a few dramatic productions, film documentaries, and published studies aimed at wide audiences, the world of nun composers and musicians is increasingly familiar beyond the field of academic music history. Hildegard of Bingen has even achieved cult status (though this may say as much about twenty-first-century fashions as it does about the twelfth-century nun and "Renaissance women"). Many music lovers now realize that convent music did not simply involve Gregorian chant; some may even recognize that in the 1600s a good deal of the best sacred music resounded within convent chapels.

When *Disembodied Voices* appeared, the convent of Santa Cristina della Fondazza stood abandoned and in a perilous state of decay. Within the last decade, it has become a showplace for the city of Bologna, restored as nearly as possible to its original form. The former nuns' cloister serves appropriate feminist, artistic, and scholarly uses, while the church has been transformed into an attractive, popular concert venue. But one wonders whether the spirits of the sisters who once sang and prayed here might note the considerable irony that a favorite of Italy's ecclesiastical old-boy network arrogated the inaugural performances at the restored church on 21 August 2007. For the Cappella Musicale Pontificia "Sistina" made the journey up from the Vatican especially for the evening.

For all these reasons the time has come to reintroduce *Disembodied Voices*, which has been out of print throughout most of these developments, and to recall Lucrezia Orsina Vizzana, who figures so prominently in the story.

Originally I conceived *Disembodied Voices* as a work of academic music history. Given the unfamiliarity of convent music at that time, the earlier edition therefore incorporated a wealth of information that would prove useful to the wider scholarly community and especially to individual scholars attracted to the then comparatively new aspect of music history unfolded in the book. Although one reviewer claimed the author's "seventy-five pages of notes, largely transcriptions of archival materials, alone constitute a valuable historical resource,"[3] only the most determined nonspecialist would likely care to follow every historical thread unraveled in those notes and elsewhere in the earlier version.

This new, abridged *Disembodied Voices*, retitled *Divas in the Convent: Nuns, Music, and Defiance in Seventeenth-Century Italy*, focuses directly on the story of an extraordinary century at the convent of Santa Cristina della Fondazza in Bologna, but it leaves out the extensive ancillary information from the original edition. The tale begins shortly before 1600 with the arrival of the eight-year-old Lucrezia Vizzana, who not only learns music there but becomes Bologna's only published convent composer. It attempts to describe the convent as a girl growing up there might have seen and experienced it. Documents may not confirm how and when Vizzana may have seen what I have her see, but they do confirm what she saw. Similarly, some of her childhood experiences here are based on documented incidents in the lives of other, similar girls and women from comparable convents, in which case relevant documentation appears in the notes.

The narrative describes the convent's musical heyday, which took place during Vizzana's formative years and, thus, allowed her creativity to flower. It follows crises and disasters that erupted at Santa Cristina in the early 1620s, at the pinnacle of Vizzana's career. These were provoked in part by that same, singular musical tradition and by the overabundance of talent that made the convent a local musical attraction.

Ecclesiastical and secular politics eclipse music in the nuns' subsequent eighty-year struggle to undo the damage of the early 1620s—to reassert their good name and to maintain some independence from the usurping authority of the archbishop of Bologna. Extraordinary confrontations, including physical, as well as verbal, conflicts between the nuns and their superiors, overcome the imaginative but frail composer Lucrezia Vizzana, who, after having retreated from music into private spirituality, is driven literally mad by the turmoil.

Despite a further fifteen years of research, Santa Cristina's defiance of archiepiscopal authority for generation after generation still seems as largely unparalleled in convent history as it did in 1995. After testing less direct confrontational strategies against an unassailable ecclesiastical system, by 1700 the women of Santa Cristina finally emerge with some measure of renewed self-esteem and autonomy (more apparent, perhaps, than real). Music and ritual again play leading roles as the nuns act out their allegiances to time-honored traditions and a somewhat equivocal independence from the Bolognese church hierarchy.

Acknowledgments

My sense of indebtedness to many institutions and individuals singled out in the acknowledgments of *Disembodied Voices* (1995) only grew in the course of this revision. I regret that in too many instances our paths have not recrossed since the publication of that original version. The institutions include the Archivio Segreto Vaticano and the Biblioteca Apostolica Vaticana; in Bologna, the Archivio di Stato (dottoressa Carmela Binchi), the Biblioteca Comunale dell'Archiginnasio (dottoressa Anna Maria Scardovi, dottoressa Anna Manfron, and dottoressa Cristina Bersani), the Biblioteca Universitaria, the Archivio Generale Arcivescovile (dottore Mario Fanti), the Archivio Isolani-Lupari (dottore Francesco Cavazza), the Archivio Opera Pia Davia-Bargellini (dottoressa Luisa Laffi), the Pinacoteca Nazionale (Giampiero Cammarota); the monastery of Camaldoli (A. Ugo Fossa); in Wrocław, Biblioteka Uniwersytecka (Professor Miroslaw Osowski); and in St. Louis, Washington University Library. I also acknowledge with regret the passing of some who initially had a hand in the project, whose generosity and friendship I fondly recall and greatly miss: Susan Porter Benson, Franca Camiz, Donna Jackson Cardamone, Dafne Dickey, William Mattheson, Oscar Mischiati, and Giorgio Piombini.

An especially happy aspect of my return to *Disembodied Voices* has been the opportunity to renew old connections and to create new ones (these days, as often via virtual reality as face-to-face). These include most notably the institutions connected with the restoration and reoccupation of Santa Cristina della Fondazza: the Fondazione Cassa di

Risparmio di Bologna (dottoressa Annalisa Bellotti); the Centro delle donne di Bologna (dottoressa Annamaria Tagliavini); the Dipartimento delle Arti Visive of the University of Bologna (Professore Daniele Benati); and the parish of San Giuliano in Bologna (Monsignor Niso Albertazzi).

Many have contributed in diverse ways to the revival of this endeavor since I got the idea in January 2011. For two decades, Candace Smith has shared not only knowledge and enthusiasm but also a "git 'er done" attitude rarely equaled when it comes to matters of convents, music history, and performance. The ensemble she directs, Cappella Artemisia, continues to restore to life sixteenth- and seventeenth-century music composed by and for nuns. As in the past, Luca Salvucci brought imagination, enthusiasm, and resourcefulness to the creation of many of the illustrations that represent an especially attractive feature of this revision. Kaye Coveney, from the wider world beyond the academy, contributed salutary writing strategies, both general and particular. Steve Smith did what he could to help unravel a more accessible narrative thread out of the original, sometimes tangled academic prose.

The University of Chicago Press endorsed my vision of creating a svelte version of a zaftig, aging, assiduously scholarly original. As always, its staff made the pursuit of that and other goals entirely too much fun. Randy Petilos, who acquired my earlier book *Nuns Behaving Badly* for the Press, promoted the process for this new book with salutary encouragement, essential wit, and judicious realism. Pamela J. Bruton addressed editorial issues with reassuring authority. Other Press staff—Joan Davies, Micah Fehrenbacher, Mary Gehl, and Natalie Smith—brought boldness and imagination to design and production, getting noticed, and garnering praise. I also want to thank the people who worked on *Nuns Behaving Badly*, my last book with Chicago, since I didn't think to at the time: Alice Bennett, Erin DeWitt, Natalie Smith, Joan Davies, and Stephanie Hlywak. Micah Fehrenbacher, after leaping into the publication process for *Nuns Behaving Badly* in midstream, has remained unfailingly patient and solicitous in the face of streams of pestering e-mails. I hope he will welcome the chance to work on another book about these courageous Italian nuns.

The many others who generously and variously lent a hand include Antonia Banducci, Philip Barnes, Jane Bernstein, Sarah Dunant, Jonathan Glixon, Bonnie Gordon, Kelley Harness, Tomasz Jez, Robert Kendrick, Kelsey Klotz, James Ladewig, Lucia Marchi, E. Ann Matter, Magda Mazur, Katrina Mitchell, Kimberlyn Montford, Karen Olson, Dolores Pesce, Colleen Reardon, Deborah Roberts, Anne Jacobson Schutte, Pamela Starr, Laurie Stras, Carolyne Valone, Elissa Weaver, Gabriella Zarri, and Carla Zecher. Most figure in the collective dedication.

Dramatis Personae

Italian family names for early-modern women sometimes end in *a* (e.g., Lucrezia Vizzana) instead of the usual, modern *i* (e.g., Ludovico Vizzani, Lucrezia's father). For the entries in the following list, I have used an *i* ending for both males and females.

ADDA, FERDINANDO D' (1650–1719). Cardinal, official protector of the Camaldolese order, papal legate in Bologna (1698–1707). Interceded on behalf of the nuns of Santa Cristina in the suit regarding the Sacra (1698–99).

ALLÉ, MARIA CATERINA (1624–1707). Mother superior at Santa Cristina. Rallied noble support to the nuns' cause in the suit regarding the Sacra (1698–99).

AZZOLINI, MARIA ELISABETTA ERMENEGILDA (1637–1708). Abbess at Santa Cristina during the suit against Giacomo Boncompagni in 1704 regarding nuns' music.

BARDELLONI, DESIDERIO. Camaldolese visitor who participated in the first pastoral visitation at Santa Cristina (1622–23).

BIANCHI, CECILIA (c. 1576–c. 1630?) (*al secolo* Irenea). Emilia Grassi's musical rival and chief fomenter of the crises at Santa Cristina in the 1620s.

BOLOGNETTI, LUCIDARIA (d. c. 1662). Cecilia Bianchi's ally in the struggles of the 1620s at Santa Cristina.

BOLOGNETTI, COUNT PAOLO. Particular advocate to the nuns of Santa Cristina in the suit regarding the Sacra (1698–99).

BOLOGNINI, MARIA GIUDITTA GINEVRA (1680–1762) (*al secolo* Teodora Maria). Nun at Santa Cristina; was consecrated in 1699 and sang on the feast of Saint Christina in 1704, in violation of Archbishop Giacomo Boncompagni's ban on convent music.

BOMBACCI, CAMILLA (1571–1640) (*al secolo* Laura). Nun at Santa Cristina; served as organist, mistress of novices, and abbess during the struggles of the 1620s; led the revolt against Archbishop Ludovico Ludovisi; Lucrezia Orsina Vizzana's maternal aunt.

BOMBACCI, FLAMINIA (1563–1624) (*al secolo* Lodovica). Nun at Santa Cristina; served as abbess at least twice and as the convent's spiritual leader in the early 1620s; Lucrezia Orsina Vizzana's maternal aunt.

BOMBACCI, GIOVANNI DI ANTONIO (d. 1604). Father of Isabetta, Camilla, Flaminia, and Ortensia; Lucrezia Orsina and Isabetta Vizzani's maternal grandfather.

BOMBACCI, ISABETTA (1560–98). Wife of Ludovico Vizzani; mother of Lucrezia Orsina and Isabetta Vizzani.

BOMBACCI, ORTENSIA (1565–1631) (*al secolo* Isabella). Nun at Santa Cristina who became a recluse in later life; Lucrezia Orsina Vizzana's maternal aunt.

BONCOMPAGNI, GIACOMO (1653–1731). Second in succession to his uncle Cardinal Archbishop Girolamo Boncompagni as archbishop of Bologna (1690). His reforming interests included substantial restrictions on convent music and at least two clashes with the nuns of Santa Cristina.

BONCOMPAGNI, GIROLAMO (1622–84). Cardinal Archbishop of Bologna (1651–84).

BONDINI, GIOVANNI (known as "don Gioanino"). The apparently corrupt Bolognese vicar of nuns under Archbishop Ludovico Ludovisi.

BORDINO (OR BARDINO), GIUSTO. Camaldolese monk. Mauro Ruggeri's successor as confessor at Santa Cristina in the 1620s. Allegedly infatuated with Isabetta or Lucrezia Orsina Vizzana.

BOVIO, CARLO. Suffragan bishop of Bologna under Archbishop Ludovico Ludovisi. Led the second pastoral visitation to Santa Cristina (1626) and the subsequent takeover of the convent.

CAPRARA, ALESSANDRO (1626–1711). Bolognese prelate in Rome who surreptitiously supported the nuns of Santa Cristina in the suit over the Sacra (1698–99); made a cardinal in 1706.

CAVAZZA, CHRISTINA TERESA PRUDENZA DEODATA (c. 1679–1751). Music-loving nun at Santa Cristina; consecrated in 1699; sang in violation of Archbishop Giacomo Boncompagni's ban on convent music in 1704. Caught leaving the cloister in disguise to attend the opera in 1708.

COLLOREDO, LEANDRO (1639–1709). Cardinal appointed *ponente* for the suit regarding the Sacra (1698–99) and for the suit regarding nuns' music (1704).

FABBRI, LUDOVICA (d. 1633). *Conversa* at Santa Cristina; Cecilia Bianchi's below-stairs ally in the troubles of the 1620s.

GOZZADINI, ANGELO. Suffragan bishop of Bologna under Archbishop Ludovico Ludovisi; led the first pastoral visitation to Santa Cristina (1622–23).

GOZZADINI, ULISSE GIUSEPPE (1650–1728). Bolognese professor of canon law, papal secretary of briefs, and eventually a cardinal and titular archbishop of Imola; supported the nuns of Santa Cristina in the suit regarding the Sacra (1698–99).

GRASSI, EMILIA (d. 1633). Leading musician, patron of the arts, twice abbess, and a protagonist in the intramural rivalries at Santa Cristina in the 1620s; Cecilia Bianchi's chief enemy; illegitimate offspring from the Grassi family.

LEONI, ADEODATA (d. 1655). Important mediator, political figure, abbess in the 1640s, and patron of music and art at Santa Cristina.

LUCHINI, CAMILLA (d. 1612). Wife of Giovanni Bombacci; grandmother of Isabetta and Lucrezia Orsina Vizzani.

LUDOVISI, LUDOVICO (1595–1632). Cardinal nephew to Pope Gregory XV and cardinal archbishop of Bologna (1621–32); took the convent of Santa Cristina from Camaldolese jurisdiction and subjugated it to archdiocesan control.

LUDOVISI, NICCOLÒ ALBERGATI (1608–87). Cardinal archbishop of Bologna (1645–51); opposed the nuns of Santa Cristina in the matter of secular confessors (1646–47).

MALATENDI, FRANCESCA (d. 1643). *Conversa* at Santa Cristina; confessed to having spread rumors about another *conversa's* possible pregnancy in the 1620s.

MALVASIA, MARIA GENTILE (d. 1647). One of the three troublemakers who fomented the crises of the 1620s at Santa Cristina; Cecilia Bianchi's chief ally.

MUZZI, MARIA DILETTA VITTORIA (1678–1748) (*al secolo* Livia). Nun at Santa Cristina; was consecrated in 1699; sang in violation of Archbishop Giacomo Boncompagni's ban on convent music (1704).

ORSI, LUDOVICO MARIA. Prior of the Camaldolese hermitage of San Benedetto di Ceretola; a primary mediator for the nuns of Santa Cristina in the suit over the Sacra (1698–99); brother of Luigia Orsina.

ORSI, LUIGIA ORSINA (1632–1720). Bursar, prioress, and abbess at Santa Cristina; oversaw the suit over the Sacra (1698–99); sister of Ludovico Maria.

PALEOTTI, ALFONSO (1531–1610). Distant cousin, coadjutor, and successor to Gabriele Paleotti as archbishop of Bologna (1597).

PALEOTTI, GABRIELE (1522–97). Cardinal, bishop (1567), and first archbishop of Bologna (1582); strongly committed to the implementation of the decrees of the Council of Trent.

RUGGERI, MAURO (d. 1660). Prior general of the Camaldolese order in the 1630s; confessor to the nuns of Santa Cristina in the early 1620s; eyewitness to the convent's struggles, described in his manuscript "Caduta di Santa Cristina di Bologna."

SABBATINI, GIOVANNI BATTISTA. Protégé of Ludovico Maria Orsi. Served as procurator in Rome for the nuns of Santa Cristina in the suit over the Sacra (1698–99).

VIZZANI, ANGELO MICHELE DI DIONIGIO (b. 1620). Natural son of Dionigio di Ludovico and Anna Veneta; legitimized in 1628 and made heir to the estate of Ludovico di Obizzo; nephew of Lucrezia Orsina and Isabetta.

VIZZANI, DIONIGIO DI LUDOVICO (1584–1628). Brother of Lucrezia Orsina and Isabetta; father of Angelo Michele.

VIZZANI, ISABETTA (1587–1653) (*al secolo* Verginia). Nun at Santa Cristina; political leader at the convent from c.1624 to 1653; daughter of Ludovico Vizzani and Isabetta Bombacci; sister of Lucrezia Orsina.

VIZZANI, LUCREZIA ORSINA (1590–1662) (*al secolo* Lucrezia). Nun at Santa Cristina; composer of *Componimenti musicali* (1623); daughter of Ludovico Vizzani and Isabetta Bombacci; sister of Isabetta.

VIZZANI, LUDOVICO DI OBIZZO (d. 1628). Father of Lucrezia Orsina, Isabetta, and Dionigio.

VIZZANI, MARIA CLORINDA (1618–95) (*al secolo* Valeria). Nun at Santa Cristina; illegitimate daughter of Dionigio di Ludovico, sister of Angelo Michele, and niece of Isabetta and Lucrezia Orsina.

VIZZANI, TERESA POMPEA (1618–84) (*al secolo* Elena). Abbess and important patron of music and art at Santa Cristina; distant cousin of Isabetta and Lucrezia Orsina.

ZANELLI, SCIPIONE. Roman lawyer of the nuns of Santa Cristina in their suit over the Sacra (1698–99).

Abbreviations

AAB	Archivio Generale Arcivescovile, Bologna
ASB	Archivio di Stato, Bologna
ASV	Archivio Segreto Vaticano
ASV, VR	Archivio Segreto Vaticano, Sacra Congregazione dei Vescovi e Regolari
BAV	Biblioteca Apostolica Vaticana
b.c.	basso continuo
BCB	Biblioteca Comunale dell'Archiginnasio, Bologna
BUB	Biblioteca Universitaria, Bologna
CDSC	Camaldoli MS 652, "Caduta di Santa Cristina di Bologna," by Mauro Ruggeri
CNC	*Canti nel chiostro* (compact disc)
Gozz.	Gozzadini
JAMS	*Journal of the American Musicological Society*
ks	key signature
MS	manuscript
posiz.	posizione
processo	ASB, Demaniale 48/2909 (Santa Cristina), no. 3/L (processo 1622–23)
processo 2	AAB, Misc. Vecchie 820, 2 (processo 1622–23, excerpts)
prot.	protocollo
reg. batt.	registro battesimale
reg. episc.	regestum episcoporum
reg. monial.	regestum monialium
reg. regular.	regestum regularium
SACDOC	ASB, Demaniale 49/2910 (Santa Cristina)
SED	*Songs of Ecstasy and Devotion* (compact disc)
sez.	sezione

SMSM   *Soror mea, sponsa mea* (compact disc)

  ten. tenor

  < > enclose words omitted in a redaction of preexistent text

  £ Italian lire (1 scudo = approximately £5 in seventeenth-century Bologna)

Praeludium: Putting Nun Musicians in Their Place

The Singing Nuns of Bologna

What shall I say of the virgins of Bologna? At one time they resound in spiritual song, and at another they provide their sustenance by their labors and seek similarly to provide the material of their charity with the work of their hands. (Saint Ambrose, c. AD 392)[1]

Moved by perpetual excesses, innumerable as the sands, which constantly erupt in the convents of our city of Bologna because of the music they unfittingly perform, I tearfully plead, prostrate at the feet of Your Most Illustrious and Reverend Lordship, that you get the Sacred Congregation to ban this music. You know that men flock much more than is respectable to nuns' churches as if to plays and other frivolous, unholy places. As a confessor at many convents, I know for certain that there is so much contention and such warfare among them because of their musical rivalries that sometimes they would claw each other's flesh if they could. (don Ercole Tinelli, 1593)[2]

Twelve hundred years after Ambrose's encomium to Bologna's convent singers, at a time when nuns' music more regularly offered cause for comment, clerical reaction to it had taken quite a negative turn. Had don Ercole lived another thirty years, he might have expired from a paroxysm of schadenfreude masking as indignation in the face of the unparalleled warfare at Bologna's most musically illustrious convent. How might he have pled for a ban on convent music had he witnessed the following scene?

Finally the episcopal auditor arrived with his many yeomen to put them to the test. The nuns immediately and with one accord climbed up high and, throwing down tiles and stones, forced his retreat out of range with his squadron. Then, as the bell sounded the alarm and crowds flocked there, donna Isabetta Vizzana, crucifix in hand and with her head veiled, made the convent's case so passionately that she moved her audience to pity and indignation. Not a few were weeping, and many called out rebelliously, "Long live the nuns of Santa Cristina," threatening insurrection. Meanwhile, children were gathering up lots of stones and tossing them into the convent through the small gateway to ensure the nuns would not run low on ammunition. And surely the uproar would have ended in a bloodletting if the curia and their supporters had not beaten a hasty retreat. (Gasparo Bombacci, c. 1640)[3]

What follows is, from the Catholic hierarchy's point of view, a story of decades of discord echoing within what should have been a realm of celestial harmony: the convent of Santa Cristina della Fondazza in Bologna. At least one disgruntled convent insider agreed with her masters, alleging that these conflicts all "began because of music." Most others from within the convent walls saw and heard things differently. Theirs was a story of often independent-minded women, who brought with them from the world to the more private sphere of Santa Cristina incongruous, often less sacrosanct conventions about sacred and secular, about social hierarchy, and (of course) about gender. It is a tale of these women's attempts for most of a century to maintain some autonomy and some room to maneuver within an often-conflicting religious conformity imposed from the outside by the external, patriarchal Catholic hierarchy. To that hierarchy it became—and perhaps still is—a story of willful defiance.

It may come as something of a surprise that nuns' music loomed as large as it did in the minds of many nuns, their religious superiors, and the public beyond the convent wall. Nuns of that era represented the prime example of women making music within a private sphere, one that the church authorities strove through the enforcement of unbreachable cloister to keep as private—and as religious—as possible. It should not be surprising that until quite recently we remained largely unaware of nun musicians and their accomplishments. As Elissa Weaver once put it, "Among the nuns only the saints have been remembered."[4] After roughly 1550, hundreds—perhaps thousands—of organists, singers, and composers can be traced within the records of Italy's nunneries, records that largely remain unavailable to the general public. The more talented of these sacred divas may have kept out of sight, but in their own times, they were regularly on the minds of music lovers.

For young women musicians of the 1500s and 1600s, the cloister remained the obvious milieu in which to practice that profession respectably. When accepted as convent organists, these women saved their parents hundreds—indeed, thousands—of lire. For her family, the development of a daughter's musical gifts with an eye toward the nunnery proved a very sound investment. Parents could send their daughters there with a much smaller dowry than a potential husband would require, and if the convent accepted a young woman as their organist, they might reduce her nun's dowry by 25 to even 100 percent. Especially for a poor or orphaned girl, musical talent offered a means to rise above the convent servant class (the *converse*), which she might enter with a very modest dowry, to the upper, governing class (the *professe*), generally reserved for affluent women from elite families.

Once on the job, convent musicians who pled overwork might receive special privileges. Rome granted sor Giovanna Tavora in Braga, Portugal, her own, private servant after she complained, "I am always so busy with public functions that I can't take care of the necessities in my cell, and what little time I have left barely frees me long enough to finish the Divine Office."[5]

For nun musicians, a convent musical career provided opportunities to perform and to rise to a certain azimuth of "star" stature in a realm associated with celestial harmony but having none of the taint commonly attributed to the public stage. Convent musicians could reach an appropriate "public" and still retain respectability—at least in the eyes of the nobility and upper classes that the nuns courted as audience, if not in the eyes of their ecclesiastical superiors. A wall divided a convent's inner chapel, reserved for the nuns, from an outer, public church (fig. 3 A and B), accessible to the world. The nun musician, who performed behind grated windows from within the pseudoprivacy of the inner church, "spoke" to the worldly audience in the adjoining public church. In doing so, she not only surmounted the constraining walls but found a way around genteel suspicions of musical professionalism and public performance that extended from Aristotle to Castiglione and beyond.

Most Bolognese convents practiced music to some degree. San Lorenzo, Santi Naborre e Felice, Santi Vitale et Agricola, San Guglielmo, Santa Margherita, and especially Santa Cristina della Fondazza fostered notable musical traditions, which attracted audiences from Bologna and farther afield. At least a dozen composers dedicated published collections of music to Bolognese nuns, testifying both to the nuns' musical talents and to their ongoing interests as patrons of the arts.

The city's nun musicians are particularly interesting because they maintained their musical traditions in the face of strong and persistent opposition from the local episcopate. The restrictions on Bolognese convent music, enacted by the reforming archbishop Gabriele Paleotti, continued unabated under the comparably antipathetic Alfonso Paleotti and Ludovico Ludovisi. In the last decade of the 1600s, Archbishop Giacomo Boncompagni revived his predecessors' earlier severity. Even in intervening periods of less strict enforcement, Bologna's singing nuns never enjoyed the artistic encouragement of a pastor such as Archbishop Federico Borromeo of Milan. The history of the musical nuns of Bologna is thus a history of artists working against the odds yet discovering ways to maneuver around barriers regularly erected by their diocesan superiors.

The Historical and Social Background

Bolognese convent music came to prominence at a time of comparative peace, prosperity, and tranquility, following centuries of disruptions. On the other hand, before 1500 Bolognese history gives the impression of nearly perpetual political ferment.

The Bolognese liked to date the first of half a dozen periods of their city's republican government to about the time Saint Ambrose remarked upon the singing of the city's sacred virgins, twelve centuries before the period of this story. The last republican era began in 1276 and coincided with a time of prosperity and commercial expansion. Bologna's situation at the intersection of routes to Rome, Florence, Milan, Ravenna, and Venice made the city a major commercial center. Its leading families grew wealthy in banking and trading, particularly in hemp. The city also specialized in finished wool and silk goods. In fact, Bologna claimed to have few rivals in the spinning and weaving of silk. More than three hundred silk mills, staffed by some three thousand laborers, lined the city's canals by the late 1500s, and as many as six thousand other silk workers wove the thread into fabric.

Bologna's other primary economic resource was, of course, its famous university, which attracted numerous foreign students to the city. A favorite explanation for the characteristic, deep porticoes that shade the sidewalks in Bologna was the influx of thousands of these university students, who supposedly found in the abundant arcades along the city streets a useful public extension of the tiny living spaces above their heads, garrets that commonly protruded out over the sidewalks.[6]

During the same period Bologna gained increasing significance as a focus of devout Catholicism. Saint Dominic, who resided in Bologna off and on in 1219–21, made the Bolognese Dominican monastery one of the two principal houses of his order of friars-preachers. At his death in 1221 Dominic was interred in the church of San Domenico, where he draws pilgrims to this day. Shortly thereafter, another friar saint, Anthony of Padua, founded the Franciscan *studium* in Bologna. Not long after midcentury, the Augustinians and Servites joined the burgeoning Catholicism of thirteenth-century Bologna.

Women's religious orders also achieved their greatest expansion in the city during the spiritual renewal of the thirteenth century. Scarcely more than half a dozen Bolognese convents date from before 1200, but by the late thirteenth century the number reached three dozen, the highest of any period.[7]

Bologna became definitively Catholic in 1506, when Pope Julius II, Giuliano della Rovere, a former bishop of that city, entered it in full armor at the head of his troops to claim it for the papacy. After a final paroxysm or two, papal rule settled in firmly and to stay by 1526. "Recognizing that [papal rule] permitted it to live merrily and pleasantly, without the disruptions of war or sedition, [Bologna] dedicated itself to it completely, valuing life in the lap of the church as a true and steady liberty, as in effect it is"—thus the Bolognese academic Camillo Baldi, writing in the early 1600s, rather cynically characterized Bologna's abandonment of republican aspirations for a comfortable papal domination.[8] In any case, subsequent Bolognese historiography suggests that the city's acceptance into the bosom of Holy Mother Church ushered in a relatively trouble-free period that contrasted pleasantly with the regular disruptions of earlier centuries.

After the establishment of papal control, the rare occasions when international events directly touched Bologna arose from its ecclesiastical role, eclipsed only by that of Rome. One can come away from reading Bolognese historians with the impression that after 1550 little happened in the second city of the papal realm for two and a half centuries. In Camillo Baldi's view, the Bolognese happily pursued wealth, comfortable living, and self-interest, relatively unscathed by the world around them:

I do not deny that now this people may not be rather soft and timid, and disaffected to work, fickle, contentious, and divided and very hostile to discomforts. This has all been increased by the fact that an extended tranquility has settled upon Italy and this city. Thus, a people dispirited in an extended peacetime, and grown enamored of comforts, rarely and with great difficulty stirs itself to take offense and easily puts up with every discomfort, however great, in civic affairs.[9]

In sixteenth-century Bologna, increasingly powerful papal legates, whom the pontiff appointed to govern the papal state, controlled the oligarchy of leading families that constituted the Bolognese senate. Senatorial rank left economic power chiefly in the hands of the forty or fifty most important Bolognese families, whose dependence upon and allegiance to the papacy were reinforced by substantial privileges and grants of regular city revenues. This administrative system remained in force until Napoleon's arrival in 1796.

The 1500s and early 1600s also brought an era of expanding convent populations to the city, second only to the late-thirteenth-century boom. For the women involved, the period of growth was chiefly driven by families' coercive practices when it came to their daughters' futures. Rather than squander the family patrimony on the rising cost of dowries demanded by husbands of their own class, patrician families dispatched their daughters to convents in increasing numbers—with or without their consent.

Women religious thus played a perhaps unwilling but prominent part in the increasingly constrained life of late sixteenth-, seventeenth-, and early eighteenth-century Bologna. Because the church hierarchy largely succeeded at confining them within their cloisters after the 1560s, convent women played an even less visible role than they may have done in earlier times. Of Bologna's 59,000 male and female inhabitants in 1595, 2,480 (4.2 percent) were nuns, even then more than twice the number of friars. In little more than two generations, the percentage of the city's total *female* population who lived behind convent walls in 1631 had climbed to 13.8 percent.[10] The ratio among daughters of Bolognese noble and upper-class families was considerably higher. Thus, expanding Bolognese monastic populations came to control larger and larger sections of the city until, in 1705, when the number of women taking vows had actually begun to ebb, city officials complained to the archbishop that, with one-sixth of the city area already occupied by religious corporations, further expansion had to stop.

Santa Cristina and Convent Women's Culture

If it is true that women musicians throughout history have generally been accorded no more than a marginal place, which, in turn, governed their musical development, this is nowhere truer than in nunneries. A clearer example of male domination that devised a sexually segregated, constricted sphere for women, where they were locked away to preserve the family patrimony and protect family honor, would be difficult to find. Within the cloister women interacted almost exclusively with one another, "protected" from men and kept subordinate.

Once confined and separate within the women's sphere created and enforced by the church hierarchy, the impenetrable walls—both physical and social—allowed women to interact with men hardly at all, and then only under strictest control, through veiled windows protected by grates and shutters. Any unauthorized contacts between the genders were almost invariably described in overtly or implicitly sexual language.

Yet in a time when many—and in some cities, most—upper-class women from an early age had no other destiny than the cloister, this must have seemed the "natural" life option. Although the number of authentic religious vocations may have been limited, many cloistered women found the life tolerable, or at least never thought to question whether such a system was right or wrong. For the numerous widows and abused wives who sought refuge there in later life, the cloister probably represented the preferable choice, or certainly the lesser evil, among such women's meager life options. For the artistically creative, the cloister provided a wider, if imperfect, space in which to exercise their talents than was readily available to them in the world.

Though often forcibly enclosed within this imperfect, socially ambivalent "women's sphere," nuns also found means to manipulate it. Although the convent's indoctrination encouraged passive, unquestioning acceptance of authority, many nuns developed a kind of agency, a little room for maneuver, by evolving informal rules and customs that interpreted, challenged, and subverted the formal prescriptions imposed upon them by the church's external hierarchy.[11]

Thus, nuns might choose to miss parts of the daily round of services in order to prepare musical or dramatic performances—or merely to make sweetmeats in the kitchen. Some modified their convent's dress code by adorning their habits with jewels, ruffles, and other bits of finery. To achieve a little freedom from the more austere realities of convent life, many found diversion as often as possible in the public *parlatorios*, or parlors, even while religious services were going on in chapel. These sites of distraction and temptation, where nuns visited with family and friends, separated from them by a wall pierced by grated and shuttered windows, rivaled convent choir lofts as targets of clerical disapproval.

Ecclesiastical superiors' constant stream of prohibitions directed at these convent infractions reveal what the sisters must actually have been doing—not behavior that they dutifully and obediently avoided. Church authorities' attempts to cover every contingency in their repeated rulings reveal that the sisters were past masters—or mistresses—at discovering loopholes in restrictions, even though rule breaking for nuns carried a heavy psychic burden, laden with guilt, sin, and potential violation of their vow of obedience. Church authorities persistently employed a vocabulary that harped on the women's childishness and sinful disobedience as they condemned what prelates perceived as nuns' repeated backsliding. But the complexities of ecclesiastical bureaucracy mediated against fully effective enforcement and, in turn, provided nuns with ample and diverse opportunities to fragment authority and counter the dint of authority.

Prelates who met off and on at the Council of Trent between 1545 and 1563 to promulgate wide-ranging Catholic reforms only got around to convents toward the end of their final session. By then many in the hierarchy were literally packing their bags to go home. The resulting reform decrees, hastily drafted, hurriedly debated, and ratified at the last minute, dramatically altered the character of female monasticism, most notably in the matter of strict monastic enclosure. After 1563 nuns who had taken final vows faced excommunication if they set foot outside the cloister wall. Any who crossed the wall in the other direction without special permission incurred similar penalties. After the council, the physically enclosed space of the convent thus came to define an archetypical "women's sphere" having both positive and negative aspects. To the favor of those enclosed within them, cloistered spaces, while conceived to promote separation and subordination, could be shaped advantageously at least to some degree. Nuns found ways to render their spaces somewhat less private; that is, they opened windows (sometimes metaphorical) in convent walls without demolishing them. At the hands of talented women, music could and did become a powerful tool partially to de-privatize architectural spaces. Further, nuns employed it to forge affective and, in the broad sense, political links with networks in the external, public sphere.

Convent women's culture also extended outward through intertwining social networks that constituted a particularly vital aspect of life inside the convent. In this way, a complex web linked convent with parish, neighborhood, and kin. Nuns, whom the world and society had set apart, came to depend for any agency in the world on their successful social use of influence on such networks. These networks included not only men (members of nuns' families, class, and sympathetic religious orders) but also other women: female members of their own families or of the Bolognese patriciate, nuns of the city or of their own religious order further afield, and even such female saints as Catherine Vigri of

Bologna. The nuns of Santa Cristina even invoked the influence of the mothers of cardinals in distant cities—with some success, apparently. Such effective agency suggests that wide-ranging informal bonds of solidarity, friendship, and shared expectations based on class and gender existed between the convent and the outside world. Since women did not employ these bonds for thoroughgoing critiques of the patriarchal system and concrete plans to change it, they cannot properly be termed "feminist." Nevertheless, they testify to the existence of a "female consciousness" in their day.

The story of Lucrezia Orsina Vizzana and her music, which occupies our attention in early chapters, shifts from everyday social interactions to singular events around the publication of her *Componimenti musicali* in 1623. Not long afterward, Vizzana's modestly flourishing musical career withers at its height. The nuns of Santa Cristina move from the relatively ordinary world of women's culture into a contrasting world of dramatic events, crises, and direct action. Their struggles, beginning internally and possibly because of music in the early 1600s but chiefly precipitated by Archbishop Ludovico Ludovisi and the Bolognese diocesan hierarchy, expand outward to involve the diocesan curia, various congregations of cardinals in Rome, and even the pope himself. Lucrezia Vizzana is caught up, swept along, and lost in political events within the convent walls and across them. The resulting crises, which one disgruntled sister claims "began because of music," change the convent of Santa Cristina decisively and quite literally overwhelm its composing nun.

I intended originally to write a history of music at Santa Cristina and of the composer Lucrezia Vizzana, but when I encountered the era of crisis at the convent, I was compelled to redirect my narrative away from music, which becomes a minor motif during the turbulent 1620s, 1630s, and 1640s, when the other nuns hijack the narrative in different directions. As I examine the sorts of strife that arose among ambitious, talented, and frequently creative upper-class women, conscious of their abilities and their station, others eclipse Lucrezia Vizzana and emerge as complex, strong, but not always sympathetic personalities. Yet, despite deep differences, the nuns were able ultimately to unite when it became necessary to oppose threats to what they valued in their way of life.

What started as the story of a "great woman" composer of the 1620s ended as the history of families that reappear in successive generations. In the hope of unwinding some sense of order from the confusing tangle of Bombacci, Boncompagni, and Vizzani family relationships, I have placed a list of dramatis personae at the beginning of the book. To forestall some additional and, for some readers, inordinate explanation in the text, a glossary of Latin, Italian, religious, and musical terms appears at the back of the book.

Finding Convent Women's Voices

The fact that the post-Tridentine Catholic hierarchy intended nunneries to be completely private habitations for women compounds the challenge of rediscovering convent music and of re-creating its place in the life of Santa Cristina della Fondazza. One must rely on fleeting and often disconnected glimpses, drawn from widely scattered and fragmentary information. Among the most important sources are the convent archives. Santa Cristina's archive, long kept in a locked chamber near the convent's main parlatorio, was transferred after the Napoleonic monastic suppression to the Fondo Demaniale in Bologna's Archivio di Stato. Amid hundreds upon hundreds of legal contracts concerning nuns' dowries, transfer of property, loans, and the business of running a convent, we discover, often by accident, more personal details such as inventories of nuns' property, informal chronicles of the most important (and many unimportant) events, necrologies (memorials to deceased members), and so on. These reveal the institution's more private face. Unfortunately, the Demaniale records have been to some extent dispersed, pilfered, and misplaced. And so, for example, Santa Cristina's most significant archival sources about music, cited in their own seventeenth-century inventories, have completely disappeared.

Although the impersonal and formal nature of much convent archival material creates a barrier between modern observers and the historically distant nuns, some of the documents from Santa Cristina's archive permit us to approach them more directly. The lengthy transcript of the pastoral visitation to the convent in 1622–23, when a notary took down the nuns' comments largely verbatim, provides a wealth of information about convent life in the nuns' own words. It permits us to hear some echo of the nuns' own voices, including Lucrezia Vizzana's. In dozens of private letters between the nuns and their advocates written between 1696 and 1705, during subsequent struggles with the diocesan curia, my protagonists speak much less guardedly than in more official documents.[12] Here we may catch glimpses of wit, humor, and affection.

Given the important control over convents exercised by the Catholic hierarchy, its archives have proved particularly useful. The Archivio Generale Arcivescovile in Bologna contains a small but significant collection of documents related to reforms under Archbishops Gabriele Paleotti and Alfonso Paleotti. Here we encounter primarily the official view of convent life, created and promoted by the male professional clergy. The archive also preserves many bureaucratic records of Santa Cristina's prolonged struggles with the archbishopric that appear nowhere else.

Of the congregations of the Roman curia, the Sacred Congregation of Bishops and Regulars was clearly the most important for convent government, for it had the final word on every aspect of monastic discipline and conduct. Because music was suspect and frequently the subject of disagreement between nuns and their diocesan superiors, the archive of the Congregation of Bishops contains thousands of pages of petitions for dispensations and judgments related to music. These are interspersed among hundreds of thousands of documents from throughout the Catholic world, contained in some two thousand cartons in the Archivio Segreto Vaticano.[13] The records of the Congregation of Bishops are a chief witness to the struggles between Santa Cristina and the diocesan hierarchy from 1620 to the early eighteenth century. But amid the records of major events documents may occasionally surface to elucidate the lives of individual nuns such as Lucrezia Vizzana.

Some of the large gaps left by these sources can be filled by documentary materials preserved chiefly in the Archivio di Stato, the Biblioteca Comunale dell'Archiginnasio, and the Biblioteca Universitaria in Bologna. These include notarial acts plus jottings and records from various chroniclers and diarists—often usefully recording history from the viewpoint of the nobleman on the street. Although no formal history of the sort created in other convents[14] survives for Santa Cristina, the convent necrology transmits details about individual nuns, recorded at their deaths. For Santa Cristina the previously unexamined "La caduta di Santa Cristina di Bologna" (The fall of Santa Cristina in Bologna) by the Camaldolese monk Mauro Ruggeri—which survives in the archive of his order's mother house at Camaldoli—offers an extraordinary and richly detailed behind-the-scenes eyewitness account of the turmoil during the 1620s through the 1640s, turmoil that had barely concluded when Ruggeri, who had served as convent confessor at the start of the turbulence, put pen to paper.

Only a few hundred of Lucrezia Vizzana's own words survive: from testimony before episcopal investigators and a few personal petitions to the Congregation of Bishops. As we shall see, they are anything but candid. A second, perhaps more revealing window into her life and worldview can be found in her music. Of course, given music's ineffable nature, using it as biographical evidence risks going astray. But the texts of Vizzana's *Componimenti musicali*, especially as highlighted by music of particular boldness and expressivity, offer hints about the composer's character that are hard to ignore. Her motets suggest that Lucrezia Vizzana spoke the language and shared the cosmology of imaginative, gifted women religious over several centuries. It is also possible that they reflect her view of the crises that dominated convent life in the decade before she ventured into print and that seem, in the end, to have silenced her altogether.

I shall therefore examine some of Vizzana's music in detail. I shall do so, however, with a minimum of music theory or specialized vocabulary. While the analyses may require a reader's patience, they will not demand greater musical sophistication than Vizzana might have expected from her seventeenth-century audience. Fortunately, all the motets from *Componimenti musicali*, as well as music by other composers discussed here, are now readily available in excellent performances on compact disc and downloadable versions. The reader who wishes to hear her music will find the most important CD titles and track numbers indicated at relevant points in the text.[15]

In the wider perspective of church history from that time, struggles with diocesan superiors were hardly unique to Santa Cristina. More unusual—at least given our present understanding of the time—is the indomitable persistence, for generation after generation, of nuns at Santa Cristina in refusing to submit to the will of the local archbishop or to relinquish their liberty, as represented through their religious links to the Camaldolese order. Do the attitudes and actions of the sisters of Santa Cristina contrast, then, with Camillo Baldi's assessment of the tepid political commitment of the Bolognese upper classes at that time? In these nuns' struggles, music and particular rituals emerge as central. Like many other tactical weapons that women with little direct power have utilized over the centuries, music and ritual provided the nuns of Santa Cristina with indirect, somewhat ambiguous, but potentially effective means of working toward goals and facilitating their agency in the world.

ONE

Donna Lucrezia Orsina Vizzana of Santa Cristina della Fondazza

In 1598, probably in late spring or early summer, two little girls left the world to enter the convent of Santa Cristina della Fondazza in Bologna. We don't know the exact date, but documents tell us that their mother, Isabetta Bombacci Vizzana,[1] had died on 19 April of that year. The following November their father, Ludovico Vizzani, loaned the convent a sizable sum, most likely to secure places for the girls. The older girl, Verginia, had recently turned eleven; the younger, Lucrezia, was barely eight.

At such a tender age, Lucrezia had no idea about what the future held for her, let alone that she might become an accomplished musician. But, out of more than 150 women musicians rediscovered in Bolognese convent archives in recent years, Lucrezia would be the only one whose compositions would find their way into print. Her *Componimenti musicali de motetti concertati a una e più voci* (Musical compositions in the form of motets in consort for one or more voices), published in Venice in 1623, assured her a modest renown in her day. She has not quite been forgotten in our own, even if the definitive modern dictionary of music managed to get her name wrong as recently as the 1980s. When in 2001 she made it into the standard college music history textbook, Lucrezia Orsina Vizzana achieved "real composer" status.[2]

Like most nuns of her time, Lucrezia Orsina Vizzana

long remained little more than a name to us. Although the seventeenth-century Bolognese historian Gasparo Bombacci carefully set down the exemplary life of his and Lucrezia's aunt Flaminia Bombacci of Santa Cristina (Bologna's only Benedictine nun to have died "in odor of sanctity" before 1650), he makes no mention at all of his distinguished musical cousin, Lucrezia. By contrast, an elegantly decorated necrology from Santa Cristina, now lost, which extolled both the pious ends of sisters who achieved "good deaths" and others' artistic and intellectual accomplishments, afforded its longest encomium—longer even than Flaminia Bombacci's—to Lucrezia Orsina Vizzana.[3] Perhaps among her sisters in religion Lucrezia's star burned a little brighter than elsewhere in the world because they were the audience who knew her work first and best.

We can only piece together Lucrezia Vizzana's life from scattered scraps of information. Her father, Ludovico di Obizzo Vizzani, hailed from an old, distinguished family, active in the city since the 1200s (see fig. 1). Various Vizzani distinguished themselves on the battlefield, in scholarship, or in the church. Carlo Emanuele di Camillo Vizzani, Lucrezia's distant cousin, became rector of the Sapienza in Rome (now Sapienza—Università di Roma) in the mid-seventeenth century, for example, and inaugurated the Vatican Library in its modern form.

Since the late 1300s the family had lived on via Santo Stefano, not very far from the convent of Santa Cristina, at the site where in the 1550s and 1560s the imposing Palazzo Vizzani rose at via Santo Stefano 43 (fig. 2, near no. 87). This branch of the Vizzani line allied itself by marriage to the highest Bolognese elite: the Bentivogli, the Malvezzi, and the Ludovisi.

In the 1500s, Lucrezia's father, Ludovico, and his less preeminent branch of the family lived farther downtown, near the corner of modern via d'Azeglio and via de' Carbonesi, south of the basilica of San Petronio (fig. 2, no. 3). Even so, Ludovico's father had been illustrious enough to merit interment in an extravagant, pyramidal tomb raised on marble columns (fig. 2, visible to the left of no. 76, between the two columns), which still draws tourists to Piazza San Domenico outside the basilica of the same name. Though Ludovico's brother served a term among the *anziani* (aldermen), who administered the city, as his father and grandfather had done before him, Ludovico di Obizzo apparently achieved no such distinction and also goes unmentioned in Pompeo Dolfi's "Who's Who" of the Bolognese élite, *Cronologia delle famiglie nobili di Bologna* (Chronology of the noble families of Bologna; 1670).[4]

Given his less elevated position within the Vizzani clan, Ludovico Vizzani could not expect to find a wife among the Bentivogli, Malvezzi,

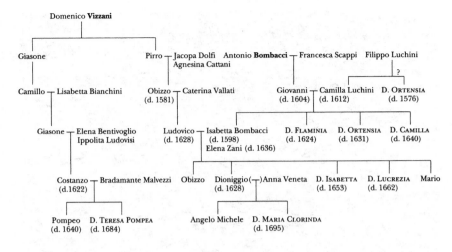

FIGURE 1. THE VIZZANI AND BOMBACCI FAMILIES (ABBREVIATED)

or Ludovisi. His future wife, Isabetta di Giovanni Bombacci, came from an upwardly mobile family of slightly lower patrician status locally than her future husband's. The marriage contract describes Isabetta's father as *mercator* (merchant), the lowest of the city's three governing ranks. Despite Gasparo Bombacci's special pleading in his family history that "in Bologna trading still remains highly honorable and has been practiced by nobles without losing their claim of nobility," we may safely assume that these Bombacci represented the sort of family to which more illustrious Vizzani than Ludovico were unlikely to turn at that period "if not for reasons of wealth or love," as a seventeenth-century Bolognese social commentator put it.[5] All the same, the Bombacci traced deep and ancient roots within the Venetian nobility and maintained venerable links to the Camaldolese order, for whom they had helped to build the Monastery of San Michele di Murano in the Venetian Lagoon. Isabetta's father, Giovanni di Antonio Bombacci, had achieved greater civic distinction than his future son-in-law would ever manage, for he served among the *gonfalonieri del popolo* (people's standard bearers), who represented Bolognese society's lower ranks, and later in his life among the *anziani*, where Ludovico's brother also served.[6]

Isabetta Bombacci, born in 1560, was the eldest survivor among Giovanni Bombacci and Camilla Luchini's twelve daughters. Such an impressive brood was not extraordinary for upper-class Italian families.

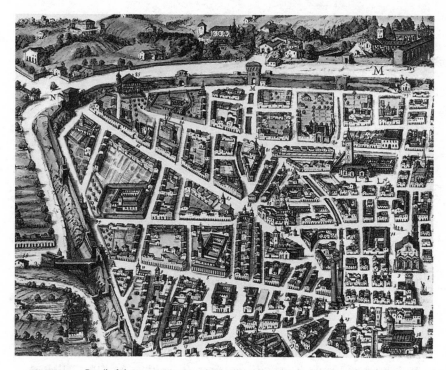

FIGURE 2. Detail of the eastern quarter of Bologna, showing Santa Cristina c. 1590. After Joan Blaeu, *Theatrum civitatum et admirandorum Italiae* (Amsterdam, 1663). Reproduced with permission of the Biblioteca Comunale dell'Archiginnasio, Bologna. A = Porta and strada Maggiore; N = Porta and strada Santo Stefano; no. 93 = Santa Cristina; near no. 87 = Palazzo Vizzani; no. 5 = Santa Maria dei Servi; no. 3 = basilica of San Petronio; no. 38 = cathedral of San Pietro; no. 76 = San Domenico.

Isabetta's paternal great-grandmother, for instance, had borne no fewer than twenty-four children, who (just as amazing and perhaps more so) had all lived past infancy. The fates of Isabetta and her eleven sisters were more typical for sixteenth-century families. Half died within two days to three years. At age twenty-seven, one married rather late and quite modestly but soon died in childbirth. By then Isabetta Bombacci had also married; after bearing at least five children, she expired before age forty. Isabetta's four remaining sisters all became nuns, three at the convent of Santa Cristina—where the trio outlived all their other siblings by ten to thirty years.[7]

On 12 May 1581 Ludovico Vizzani and Giovanni Bombacci agreed to Isabetta's dowry, most of which was to be invested in Bologna's thriving silk trade. Although the Bombacci were active in banking and finance, some of their money came from the silk business, as their name suggests (*bombice*, "silkworm grub"). Ludovico and Isabetta's marriage was recorded on 19 October 1581 in the Bombacci family's parish church.[8]

Their first son arrived within a year but must have died in infancy or early childhood since he promptly disappears from the written record. After a fourteen-month respite, Isabetta was pregnant again. Dionigio was born in 1584. A third son, Mario, followed much later, in 1593. We know that he lived long enough to witness his mother's death, but he followed her to the grave not long thereafter (no record testifies to exactly when). By 1593 Isabetta had also borne two girls. Verginia arrived in March 1587. Lucrezia, the future composer, entered the world three years later, on 3 July 1590.[9]

Verginia and Lucrezia later claimed to have lived in the convent of Santa Cristina della Fondazza since earliest childhood. Lucrezia's convent memorial confirms that she sought refuge there "at an age when she thereby avoided the world's swelling tides and sandbanks" (presumably a refined way of suggesting a time before puberty).[10] Only a little over five minutes' brisk walk from their maternal grandparents' home on strada Maggiore—but quite a long way from their father's house—Santa Cristina was the obvious choice for offspring of the Bombacci family.

Having entered Santa Cristina in early childhood, Lucrezia Vizzana scarcely knew the wider world beyond the convent wall, and not at all as an adult. Yet, as constricted as the monastic world she had entered might have been, it was eminently one of the best of all possible worlds of its sort in Bologna. By the early 1600s Santa Cristina, the second-oldest female house of the Camaldolese order (a relatively recent branch of contemplative Benedictines), had become one of the wealthiest, most exclusive, and most artistically distinguished of Bologna's monasteries for women. In 1574 its yearly income had tied for fourth place among the diocese's twenty-eight convents. By 1614, when its social and political fortunes had begun to decline, Santa Cristina still ranked a very respectable sixth.[11] Catering to Bolognese noble and patrician families, Santa Cristina hovered above the reach of what the nuns called "ordinary" women. Members of the community tended to call each other *donna* (lady) or, for the most senior nuns, *madre donna*, rather than *suora* (sister, a name reserved at Santa Cristina for the servant nuns). They referred to the convent as the *collegio* rather than as the *monastero*. Some aspired as much, perhaps, to arts and letters as to religious life or, at the very least, saw nothing incongruous about intermingling arts and religion, exactly as various male members of their order had done for centuries. (Perhaps the most obvious examples are Guido of Arezzo in music, Lorenzo Monaco in art, and Niccola Malermi, first translator of the Bible into Italian.)

In convents of that time, a separate class of servant nuns known as *converse* looked after the governing class of professed nuns, thereby leaving the latter free to pursue the higher callings of prayer, contemplation, and chapel. The servant class usually comprised simple, illiterate country girls, who came to the convent with much smaller dowries than future professed nuns. The *converse* had no serious chapel responsibilities and no voice in convent government. They performed all the menial tasks within the convent—cleaning, cooking, gardening, tending the animals. In addition, each saw to the personal needs of a few *professe*, or professed nuns—much of the time, the three Bombacci sisters at Santa Cristina shared a single *conversa* with just one other *professa*. For a community theoretically governed by a vow of poverty, the extent of individual attention lavished on each of the *professe* would eventually strike ecclesiastical authorities of the 1620s as inappropriately luxurious.[12] But in 1598, when Lucrezia Vizzana entered Santa Cristina, the convent's opulent style of monasticism had yet to catch their attention.

Despite their mother's recent death and their father's virtually abandoning them at the convent gate, the little girls may have felt less forsaken than we might imagine. By 1598 the Bombacci had established such strong ties at Santa Cristina that the girls' arrival there seemed inevitable. Three Bombacci aunts were already waiting there to receive them. Flaminia Bombacci had been accepted in 1578, Ortensia in 1580, and Camilla in 1588. Verginia and Lucrezia's acceptance and socialization at the convent were thus due primarily to matrilineal connections. Flaminia and Camilla Bombacci would become the convent's spiritual and political leaders of the 1620s.

Ranging in age from twenty-seven to thirty-five, these three maternal aunts, whom the little girls had probably visited since babyhood in frequent company with their mother, very likely cared almost maternally for the orphaned girls and perhaps doted upon them. In any case we know more generally that the reassurance and encouragement of sympathetic aunts commonly served as a gentle form of persuasion at the same time that it may have figured as something of an antidote to the socially forced confinement of an extraordinary percentage of upper-class girls of the day in convents. Although the Council of Trent had forbidden parents to force their daughters to become nuns and required bishops to be sure that every girl entered of her own free will, families developed subtle, effective means of encouragement. The typical practice of depositing the very young in the care of cloistered relatives ensured that after such an early entry into the cloister, by the time their sojourn there became permanent it would seem like the "natural" order of things for these girls. They would scarcely have had time to learn about the other meager options life might have offered them beyond the cloister's arcades. As history would have it, the Vizzani girls were in fact among the last children accepted for education by close relatives at Santa Cristina, because the church hierarchy would explicitly prohibit this time-honored practice at the convent on via Fondazza a few years later—but for punitive, not humanitarian, reasons, as we shall see.[13]

Verginia had no sooner reached novice age (twelve) than Ludovico Vizzani increased his earlier loan to Santa Cristina and extended its term for four more years following April 1599. At that time the nuns voted whether to accept Verginia as a novice, with the assumption that she would go on to take final vows at the appropriate time. After the count at her formal election revealed that the white balls outnumbered the black more than two to one, Verginia received her novice's habit in a clothing ceremony customarily attended by family and friends (as many as the bishop and the budget would allow). Fairly transparently, her father's loan increase was meant to guarantee her place until she reached the legal age of profession in 1603. For her part, Lucrezia became a novice in 1601—a year short of the minimum permissible age and after the enactment of similar rites.

Almost like clockwork, five months after Lucrezia turned sixteen, Ludovico Vizzani reappeared in the parlatorio at Santa Cristina on 4 December 1606, together with his daughters' maternal uncle Antonio Bombacci, in order to cancel repayment of all his loans to the convent. The very next day the nuns absolved him of his daughters' dowries and the cost of their convent furnishings. By then the young women had long fixed firmly on their life's course. The contract between their father and Santa Cristina lists Verginia among the professed nuns, who by then had voted a second time to accept her into the choir. Only then did she profess final vows of poverty, chastity, and obedience. In return she received the professed nun's veil in another elaborate ceremony at her family's expense. In the contract Verginia appears with her religious name Isabetta, clearly a "remaking" of her late mother's name. Her sister, whose profession the document claimed was imminent, became Lucrezia Orsina.[14]

Having settled his daughters at Santa Cristina, sorted out their dowries, and agreed to provide them with the requisite yearly stipends for their upkeep, Ludovico Vizzani had discharged his paternal obligations quite as far as custom and family required. Antonio Bombacci may have appeared in the parlatorio in December 1606 just to make sure he did so. Isabetta and Lucrezia probably saw little of their father after that, as life took him in other directions. By 1610 he had married Elena Zani, from a rich and noble family who were neighbors to his illustrious cousins on via Santo Stefano, a match that probably represented an improvement on Ludovico's original Bombacci alliance. Their brother Mario's early death further weakened Lucrezia and Isabetta's remaining links to their father, who quite understandably ignored them in disposing of his own estate in September 1628. They were women, after all, within an alternative convent family of their own by then. Since Elena Zani had produced no male heir, and since Ludovico's sole surviving son, Dionigio, lay near death, the mortally ill Ludovico Vizzani hastily legitimized Angelo Michele, Dionigio's son, born out of wedlock and raised by his mother, "Anna Veneta" (possibly a servant), in his grandfather's house. Ludovico died barely two weeks later; Dionigio followed him to the tomb a week after that. Eight-year-old Angelo Michele inherited everything. It took six years of litigation before Lucrezia Orsina and Isabetta managed to recover the two-thirds of their mother's dowry that they claimed as an inheritance through their late brother Mario.[15]

It may strike modern readers as surprising, or at least ironic, that in short order teenaged Angelo Michele would think of his aunts and Santa Cristina when the time came to sort out his sister Valeria's future. But to Angelo Michele (or perhaps Anna Veneta), as well as Lucrezia Orsina and Isabetta Vizzani, it probably made perfect sense. There was little point in squandering the family patrimony to find Valeria a husband in the world, particularly since her illegitimacy could complicate matters. So she entered Santa Cristina, where she took the name Maria Clorinda Vizzana and professed in November 1639. Just as the Bombacci sisters had followed a maternal aunt, Ortensia Luchini, and the Vizzana sisters had joined their maternal aunts—Flaminia, Ortensia, and Camilla Bombacci—some forty years later Maria Clorinda Vizzana now followed her *paternal* aunts to Santa Cristina and continued into a further generation the once common method of maintaining family ties within convent walls. Maria Clorinda and her aunts then played out another common reality of cloistered women's lives. They struggled for decades to obtain the yearly support rightfully due them from Angelo Michele as titular head of their family. As late as 1662, when Lucrezia Orsina died, the matter still remained unsettled.[16]

A few years before their niece joined them, other distant family ties combined with Lucrezia Orsina and Isabetta's presence at Santa Cristina to draw another, notably preeminent Vizzani relation there. In 1634

Teresa Pompea, daughter of Senator Constanzo Vizzani (d. 1622), Knight of Savoy, left behind the very illustrious side of the family at Palazzo Vizzani and came to dwell alongside her cousins at the convent. Although Teresa Pompea Vizzana possessed musical gifts, Santa Cristina benefited chiefly from financial gifts that she lavished on its musical and artistic pursuits. After the early death of her brother Pompeo in 1640 and in the absence of any male heirs, Teresa Pompea and her three blood sisters (all nuns) shared equally in their brother's sizable estate. In the manner customary for nuns, Teresa Pompea Vizzana spent this inheritance on convent improvements and adornments, including an opulent new altarpiece for the external church.[17]

Before the Vizzani sisters first arrived, the convent had already achieved—and even surpassed—the architectural form commemorated rather tardily in Joan Blaeu's *Theatrum civitatum et admirandorum Italiae* (Amsterdam, 1663; fig. 2, no. 93). Through the convent's great double gateway in the wall facing via Fondazza, which the nuns draped with Arras tapestries on feast days, the little girls would first have entered a courtyard with access to the external church straight ahead. They would have passed through an elaborate stone archway at the right, perhaps glimpsing the public parlatorios, where nuns conversed with visitors through grated windows (fig. 3, M), and then entered the external reception room (E), with its own elaborate stone portal. Leaving their father and the world outside the interior porter's lodge (E), which was always kept carefully locked and diligently guarded by the nun porter, they would first have met their aunts face-to-face.

Although it is the idlest sort of speculation, one wonders about the reception the little girls received at that meeting. Though their senior aunt, donna Flaminia, is remembered even today for religious devotion, her brand of piety tended to unfold as generosity toward others, reserving austerity and severity for herself. She probably extended the sort of warm welcome one would like to imagine for the little girls. Donna Ortensia, the middle aunt, with eighteen years in religion behind her, may already have started to assume the role of self-styled recluse that she would adopt in earnest by the early 1620s. Ortensia perhaps remained as much a nonpresence in her nieces' lives as convent documents suggest she was in the life of the house as a whole. Twenty-seven-year-old Camilla, known for her generous and outgoing personality, may have served most actively *in loco matris*. In addition, her musical enthusiasms may soon have rubbed off on the younger of her nieces.

Turning from their aunts' greeting in the reception room, the girls would have progressed through a second set of newly installed, ornate

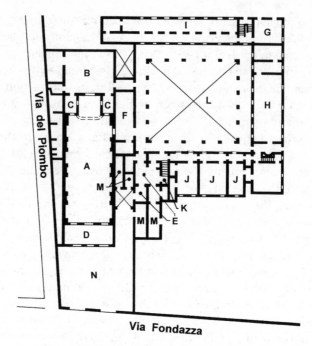

FIGURE 3. Plan, Santa Cristina della Fondazza. Based on Ugo Capriani, "Chiesa e convento di Santa Cristina della Fondazza: Ipotesi di ricerca e recupero" (degree thesis, University of Bologna, 1987–88), reproduced with permission.

terra-cotta or sandstone doorways[18] and gained access to the northwest corner of the spacious cloister (fig. 3, L) with its wellhead in the center of the courtyard. Perhaps curious *converse* on laundry duty there paused a moment to inspect the new arrivals. Around the courtyard, deep and lofty arcades, decorated on the outside with additional fine terra-cotta ornament, rose from sandstone columns with simple, leafy capitals. For the rest of their lives, these cloister arches would protect the two Vizzani from inclement weather in winter and oppressive heat in summer. Above the cloister arcades rose the new second story, completed less than twenty years earlier to house nuns' individual cells, since every professed nun at Santa Cristina had a room of her own. The cloister (fig. 4) survives to this day, much as the Vizzani sisters first saw it, though later occupiers modernized the upper-story windows, and much of the elegant, painted filigree that once adorned the plaster has vanished now.

When Lucrezia and her sister had time to continue exploring, they might have peered into another parlatorio (M) through doorways on the north side of the cloister; then they would have passed remains of the

FIGURE 4.   Santa Cristina della Fondazza, the cloister (2011), photographed from the southwest corner, near the kitchen and refectory. Photograph: Luca Salvucci, Bologna.

chiesa vecchia (old church, F) on their way to the nuns' inner chapel (B). In this lofty, vaulted chamber with double rows of walnut choir stalls standing opposite each other, they may initially have joined their aunts along the higher row, reserved for professed nuns. Before long, though, once they grew used to the place, they would have moved to the lower stalls, appropriate to lesser members of the community. The young Lucrezia probably took to chapel as quickly as did other musically precocious girls of earlier generations. After a visit to Santa Cristina in 1433, an entranced Ambrogio Traversari, Camaldolese prior general, recalled, "It was most delightfully pleasing to admire a little girl about six years old in choir, reciting chapters, verses, prayers, responsories from memory, so well that she made not one mistake, and likewise another girl, ten years old." Perhaps those two had also been sisters, with aunts observing proudly from the back row.[19]

In the late 1590s, when the Vizzani girls came to live there, all the convent spaces would certainly have been in disarray. To concentrate on the Divine Office must have been hard enough for professed nuns, much less little girls, for work progressed on the new church just the other side of the wall to the nuns' chapel. By the time Verginia and Lucrezia arrived, the old campanile visible in Blaeu's engraving had already been pulled down to make way for the expanded new church. The elegant new campanile by a member of the Bibiena family still graces the city's eastern skyline, but it would not rise until thirty years after Lucrezia's death. Then the nuns' perennial nemesis, Archbishop Giacomo Boncompagni, fretted that the gilded figure of Santa Cristina atop its pinnacle flew in the face of monastic humility. Perhaps Boncompagni was right, but it took God a while to notice, because lightning did not strike the tower until the 1740s. In Lucrezia Vizzana's day a more appropriately modest, even stunted little tower accommodated three bells; yet one of them was so large that women could not ring it without assistance—of burly men, some naturally assumed. That dangerous prospect may well have caused earlier watchdogs of monastic propriety than Boncompagni to fret.[20]

Back in the cloister, each of its wings incorporated broad interior galleries, where the nuns could exercise when bitter winter cold drove them indoors. Some wings also housed ancillary chapels (fig. 3, G), with occasionally lavish decoration to inspire a nun's mental prayer. Off the passage along the east wing the *converse* toiled at the nuns' laundry, and the professed nuns gathered in common rooms (I) for more refined pursuits such as needlework. In these rooms, Lucrezia and Verginia probably first heard singing and other informal music making, for they were far enough from the dormitories across the courtyard not to disturb other sisters. Novices' quarters were upstairs in the east cloister wing, though the practice of segregating novices had apparently fallen into disuse by the late 1500s at Santa Cristina. For that reason Lucrezia may very well have kept close company with her aunts right through to the time of her profession.

Most of the southern wing of the cloister consisted of an imposing refectory (H), which must have inspired as much awe in an eight-year-old as the nuns' chapel. Walnut paneling completely covered the four walls of its spacious interior. Seated at table, Lucrezia's gaze would frequently have been drawn to a large, beautifully sad fresco of the Crucifixion above the door, near the vaulted ceiling (fig. 15). In the intense calm of this scene, already almost a century old when Lucrezia first saw it, the Blessed Mother, Saint John, a monk all in white, and an elegant lady look on in quiet, almost dispassionate resignation while Mary Magdalene clutches the foot of the cross.

Perhaps Lucrezia struggled initially to keep still and silent at table, as her legs still dangled from hard benches constructed without regard for a little girl's diminutive stature. Her aunts would have stressed that she and Verginia must not disturb the sister sonorously intoning church fathers' edifying words from an impressive pulpit that protruded from the refectory's south wall. Within a year or two Lucrezia may even have begun to read from the pulpit herself. After all, what *professa* would not prefer to hear a precocious ten-year-old, even if she mispronounced the occasional biblical tongue twister, as a novel change from the usual routine?[21]

In the adjoining atrium Lucrezia occasionally must have paused before a mysterious landscape, painted in a concave niche opposite the refectory door. Through what resembled a tall archway she stared into a distant landscape with azure hills and a pale sky across which different sorts of birds wing their way. A river flows and broadens into the distance on one side, and an imposing walled city rises on the other, where a few robed and bearded men gather outside. Our Lord sits to the left of the shallow opening, his rosy-cheeked, softly bearded face luminous in haloed light. His right hand stretches outward across his body toward a beautiful lady in iridescent yellow silk and a diaphanous veil over chestnut hair, who gazes back at him across the landscape. Lucrezia's aunts explain that the resurrected Christ is cautioning Mary Magdalene, "Noli me tangere." But as Lucrezia lingers before the image, she knows that this fresh-faced Lord is welcoming one of his chosen brides to join him within an earthly paradise.

But as she gazes at the one who one day will choose her as his bride, she realizes that she, too, is being observed. Between forked branches in the tree behind the lady in yellow, a cat sits watching her. Though its tawny fur blends into the mottled green of surrounding foliage, its pointed ears, grizzled jowls, enigmatic grin, and wide eyes slowly emerge from the tree's shadowy recesses. From then on, whenever Lucrezia hastened past, she automatically searched it out. It always waited patiently for her, quietly staring back.

Over the decades, as Lucrezia regularly passes this romantically depicted couple on her way to and from meals, a host of other Christian heroes join them as the atrium walls grow full with images of Saint Lawrence, Saint John the Baptist, Saint Andrew, Saint Antony Abbot, Saint Luke painting the Madonna's portrait, and a giant Saint Christopher bearing the Christ child on his shoulder (and, thus, the saint most likely to speak to children's imaginations). Eventually a comparable assembly of saintly female worthies—Saint Catherine, Saint Barbara, Saint Gertrude, Saint Scholastica, Saint Francesca Romana, Saint Veronica, and (of course) Saint Christina—looks down from trompe l'oeil galleries as Lucrezia and the other nuns hasten to meals. These paradigmatic women will not join all the paradigmatic men, however, until Lucrezia draws close to her final years.

In an alcove around the corner from the welcoming Jesus Lucrezia must have happened upon a dark, narrow flight of stairs, rising steeply between walls that press in on both sides toward small windows high above, where the steps turn and disappear (fig. 5). Curiosity eventually overcomes trepidation, and she tests these stairs, narrow and already so

FIGURE 5. Santa Cristina della Fondazza, the back staircase near the southwest corner of the cloister (2011). Photograph: Luca Salvucci, Bologna.

precariously worn that she must cling with both hands to a rounded banister carved deeply into a groove in the right wall. It takes forever to reach the landing and the light, and as long, perhaps, to muster courage enough to turn the corner. There, a further flight, even more scarred and worn than the first, disappears above into narrow darkness.

After initiation into the mystery of these stairs, Lucrezia may have found in them a favorite retreat, at least until she grew older. The elder nuns never took them—for the infirm or overweight, they would be impassable. This dark passage remained the domain of the *converse*, who were content to share it with an occasional youngster, especially one who did not put on airs.

Any eight- or ten-year-old would also be lured to the land of the *converse* by odors emanating from behind the mysterious frescoed landscape and the shadowy staircase. The cloister's southeast corner housed the kitchen, with its great hearth. Wintertime made that part of the house even more alluring, for its common fire was the convent's primary source of heat. Without doubt, Lucrezia and Verginia stopped there regularly during their daily rounds; alluring smells must have frequently signaled the possibility of a tasty handout at the kitchen's pass-through window. Ecclesiastical superiors habitually grumbled about wasteful amounts of oil, sugar, eggs, and flour that disappeared into this corner of Santa Cristina's cloister, where the nun cooks transformed them into delicious treats such as biscuits flavored with musk and rose water, a specialty of the house.[22]

Upon reaching the far end of a nearby, lengthy interior corridor that ran to the west, past the infirmary (J), the sisters would take a left at the main staircase (K) ascending to the upper floor. Perhaps they averted their eyes from the painful depiction of the crucified Christ here, high above them on the wall to the right (fig. 16). As in the refectory, the Magdalene again hugs the cross, but here his mother's sorrow and the Beloved Disciple's profound grief intensify the anguish of the scene. Without a doubt, Lucrezia clambered up those broader steps soon after she came to live at the convent, for she would share her first cell with one of her aunts. When she first climbed the stairs, she may have puzzled over a large disk painted on the opposite wall. Framed in the archway above her was a blue center ringed by a broad white band, outlined with a narrow gold band. As she came and went at various times of the day, she would soon learn that light and shadow passing across Roman numerals encircling the blue disk marked the quiet but ceaseless progression of the hours of each day.

On the upper floor, doorways lined a lofty central corridor, opening into the nuns' individual cells (fig. 6). The pious donna Flaminia's

FIGURE 6.   Santa Cristina della Fondazza, a nun's cell on the upper floor, west wing of the cloister (c. 1988). Photograph courtesy of Ugo Capriani.

ascetic cell must certainly have surpassed what Lucrezia probably had heard about convent austerity before her arrival. So she may have been surprised to discover that Aunt Camilla's was little different from rooms at home. A great, welcoming bedstead of wood or iron, outfitted with a straw mattress, various linens, bed hangings, and a cover (a different one for winter and summer) dominated the room, while a large walnut armoire against one wall vied with the comfortable bed for space and attention. Before long Lucrezia would probably discover that in the fanciest of Santa Cristina's accommodations the armoire might open into a tiny, hidden staircase that led to a second, but somewhat cramped chamber at mezzanine level.[23]

Her aunt Camilla's cell was very likely also richly appointed with other furnishings, such as a small table, a poplar chest for covers and blankets, a walnut inkstand, the odd chair or bench, an iron tripod with a majolica basin, plus various copper and brass vessels, basins, and kettles. Lucrezia might also have spotted a shelf of books, which would have meant little to her until later: a breviary, a missal, a psalter, a martyrology, an office of the Blessed Virgin. The windows were hung with heavy curtains and a Venetian shutter for the exterior, while a heavy, leather curtain covered the doorway. Sisters from the very best families sometimes decorated the door cover with their family coat of arms.

What may have struck Lucrezia most oddly was the private altar in her aunt's room—certainly, there was nothing like that at home. In addition to the inevitable crucifix, the altar held candlesticks, a holy-water vessel, a few small paintings in gilded frames, and her aunt's certificate of profession. Some nuns' private altars rivaled those in modest parish churches. Her aunt's wealthy contemporary Colomba Glavarini had an altar that had cost as much as it would take to feed eight nuns for a year—or so some said. Even though Lucrezia was probably unaware of the fact, her father certainly knew that the majority of all these furnishings, particularly those involving sewing and decorative needlework, were created in the convent and then charged to a postulant's parents. The fitting out and provisioning of new members thus constituted a modestly lucrative convent cottage industry.[24]

What made the cells more personal were decorative items recorded in nuns' personal inventories: a "small painting with San Francesco di Paola," a "miniature altar with a Madonna," "five little paintings of saints," an "Annunciation with its frame." In addition to other common personal items such as bed warmers, foot warmers, sewing baskets, and pin cushions, the number of looking glasses listed in such inventories would surprise any who take the church hierarchy's prohibition of such "vanities" at face value. When Lucrezia Orsina moved into a cell of her own, it might eventually have accommodated a small harpsichord as well, possibly handed along from donna Camilla.

One especially lavish list of a nun's more precious possessions from the Bolognese convent of Santa Margherita includes all those that commonly turn up elsewhere individually: "two thimbles, one of silver and one of ivory, a pick ornamented with silver and one with scissors, a compass and a pen of silver, a little silver box, four rings of gold, six pairs of silver buckles, a silver cup, two pairs of silver candlesticks, a silver fork and spoon, a silver reliquary cross, a golden inkwell with the stamper and seal of silver, six keys on a silver chain, a rosary and two chaplets decorated with silver." Among the most noteworthy of such personal possessions (particularly if its owner happened to be a singer) was "a goldfinch in its cage." Clearly, in affluent, unreformed convents such as Santa Margherita or Santa Cristina the nuns still managed to surround themselves with many of the comforts of home.[25]

Splashes of color may also have helped cheer Lucrezia and Verginia's initial introduction to cloistered life in the late spring or early summer of 1598. Nuns attempted to brighten the cloister's spacious interior by balancing pots of flowers on cell window ledges, even going so far as to pry loose the grilles on outside windows to make room for them. The girls must eventually have wandered into the sizable gardens and fields, totaling some six and a half acres, which surrounded the cloister proper. In Lucrezia Vizzana's time the private gardens featured rosemary bushes, vines, roses in prolific supply, the odd walnut tree and mulberry bush, and cane breaks. The sisters might once in a while have filched a treat from small orchards of peaches, pears, and figs. Two pergolas ran outward, one from a door in the east wing and the other from a door in the south wing of the cloister, all the way to the convent's outer wall. Scattered across the grounds were holy sites and small chapels, including a *campo santo* (burial ground) to explore. Lucrezia and her sister would have visited a chapel dedicated to Our Lady of the Snow in procession with the other nuns, who carried the image of the Madonna.[26]

The property's more utilitarian farm outbuildings included a chicken house, dovecote, and a stall for the father procurator's horse, which he rode during his requisite visits to the convent's properties outside Bologna. Remains of a convent icehouse survived even into the 1900s. Although orchards and gardens were intended to be held in common, by the early 1600s several nuns had expropriated specific portions of the grounds for themselves. Lucrezia and Verginia must have been delighted to discover potential pets in the chickens, sheep, one cow, and, not to overlook it, a donkey kept out back by their paradigmatically pious aunt, Flaminia Bombacci, for personal use—in spite of the church's rules to the contrary.[27]

Back inside the cloister, up the main staircase (K), near the northwest corner, Lucrezia and Verginia would eventually have discovered a large, lofty, and airy choir, also known as the Cappella della Beata Vergine del Rosario. This chapel, above the arcaded gallery shading the public church's triple portals, had grated windows facing east into the public church and others looking west into the public courtyard out front. Twenty-five years later, Isabetta Vizzana would gain a certain celebrity—or notoriety—by her audacious behavior at these windows. Not long thereafter, this chapel would become Lucrezia Orsina's special refuge from an increasingly unbearable world.

The Vizzani sisters' socialization began immediately upon their arrival at Santa Cristina, even during their first tour of the premises. They learned, both formally and informally, not only the obligations of the Camaldolese order that they would officially enter in good time but also—and just as important—their convent's venerable history and prestigious position in the city. By 1598 that illustrious history stretched back half a millennium. The original convent's earliest history is shrouded in uncertainty, but some claimed it had been founded as early as 1097. The Camaldolese order had grown out of the reforms of Saint Romuald (c. 952–1027) earlier in that century. Santa Cristina was established at Settefonti (or Stifonte) in inhospitable, rugged terrain about twelve miles from Bologna. The earliest surviving documents suggest that papal recognition came sometime around 1125.

In 1245 the nuns of Santa Cristina di Settefonti received the bishop of Bologna's permission to find more hospitable quarters closer to town. The site they chose stood on via Fondazza east of downtown (fig. 2, no. 93), halfway between strada Maggiore (fig. 2, A), the main thoroughfare to Romagna and the city of Rimini, and via Santo Stefano (fig. 2, N), the route to Tuscany and Florence. At that time, the location was still relatively remote and open, for it stood outside the original wall that enclosed the congested old city but in the shadow of sections of a new wall running outward from Porta Maggiore. These wall segments that then existed near the site for Santa Cristina would, by 1400, be incorporated into a second wall encircling the expanding city. One can still see a stretch of the fourteenth-century wall behind Santa Cristina today.[28]

By the late 1400s portions of the monastery yet recognizable in 2011 had begun to take shape. On the south wall of the cloister Lucrezia and Verginia would have been shown a memorial and coat of arms dated

1494, marking the completion of the convent's ground floor. The nuns' sanctuary may also have been remodeled in those years. About two-thirds of the so-called *chiesa vecchia* (old church) survives today, although it is cut off by the late-sixteenth-century wall of the new church. The vaults of the ancient sanctuary, which eventually became the nuns' chapter house for conducting formal meetings, retain vivid decoration along their ribs and fine frescoes of Saint Romuald, Saint Christina, and Saint Benedict, attributed to Lorenzo Costa, already nearly a century old when the Vizzani girls first saw them.[29]

In the late 1550s, as Bologna expanded outward to meet the new city wall, the convent's own encircling wall rose around it, not so much to keep the nuns inside (the Council of Trent's severe restrictions were still a dozen years off) as to keep undesirables out, to judge by a ban in 1552 forbidding prostitutes to live anywhere along the length of via Fondazza or via del Piombo, which bounds the convent to the north. The nuns had in fact been complaining about the number of prostitutes who had set up shop in the neighborhood for decades. They remained an abiding problem, apparently. In the 1580s elite visitors to the convent of San Lorenzo, a few blocks southwest of Santa Cristina, complained about such disreputable women frequenting the parlatorios. When the Vizzani sisters arrived at their convent, the archbishop was still busily slapping broadsides on the walls around town in an effort to prohibit prostitutes from living within a mile of any convent gate.[30]

A notable expansion got under way at Santa Cristina after 1570 and continued down to Verginia and Lucrezia's arrival. During an apostolic visitation in 1573 to implement the decrees of the Council of Trent, the visitor discovered construction on the new buildings in full swing. His insistence that the convent either acquire more of the surrounding property or increase the height of its wall to thwart the curious gaze of the public suggests that by then the rural landscape at the city's far reaches was becoming heavily populated.[31]

When the Vizzani sisters arrived in 1598, Santa Cristina's outer church must have been a busy work site, surrounded in scaffolding. In March of that year twelve workmen had fallen from that building scaffold, five to their deaths. By then, the nuns were already embarking upon an ambitious program of chapel decoration under the patronage of individual sisters. Significantly, Santa Cristina is the only convent for which Carlo Cesare Malvasia's guide to Bolognese artwork, *Le pitture di Bologna* (1686), specifically singles out the nun patrons of virtually every altarpiece in the external church.[32]

The convent's older paintings, awaiting transfer from the old church to the new, may for a brief, rare period have been visible inside *clausura*. Francesco Salviati's *Madonna and Child with Saints* (fig. 7), donated by the convent's father confessor back in 1540 for the high altar of the old church, would find its way to the chapel at the left of the new church's main entrance. Perhaps the Vizzani girls studied it before its removal outside *clausura* and once more out of view, for the painting had much to teach future postulants. Among the saints crowded around the Madonna and child, Lucrezia would have spotted Saint Christina, easily recognizable by the fatal arrow protruding from her forehead (though she looks remarkably cheerful nonetheless). Saint Romuald, founder of the Camaldolese order, is there too in his telltale white monastic habit and with an emblematic ecclesiastical edifice on a tiny mountain sitting in front of him (representing either Camaldoli or the old church in Settefonti).

Lucrezia's teachers—certainly donna Flaminia—would be sure to point out Blessed Lucia of Settefonti, the convent's much-venerated, aristocratic twelfth-century abbess, kneeling at the front in a Camaldolese nun's habit. Lucia, as Lucrezia would learn, had resisted the perpetual threat of importunate male amorousness with resolute female chastity. Faced with a young knight's persistent attentions, Lucia retreated to her convent cell, closed its window, and never reopened that window for the rest of her life. Blessed Lucia's subsequent compassionate intercession from beyond the grave for her jilted ex-suitor-turned-Crusader, by then languishing in an infidel prison, resulted in the knight's miraculous liberation and transportation in a trance some fourteen hundred miles, from the Holy Land all the way back to Settefonti. Though Lucrezia never saw his fetters, which were carefully preserved at Blessed Lucia's tomb in the country church, she could still find them depicted in Salviati's painting, beside the virtuous Camaldolese nun who had resisted all fleshly temptations. Twenty years later Aunt Flaminia would successfully campaign for the translation of Blessed Lucia's relics to Santa Cristina. During the same period, a less benign, tattletale nun would allege that one of her nieces had failed to heed Blessed Lucia's example.

One would hope that Lucrezia and Verginia also set eyes on Giacomo Francia's *Nativity* (fig. 8; c. 1552) before it was moved from the *chiesa vecchia* to the chapel immediately to the right of the new church's doors and directly across from Salviati's altarpiece. After all, Malvasia claimed that the artwork had been commissioned by a nun from the Vizzani family. Perhaps Ludovico Vizzani's loan from 1598 helped pay for an altar to

FIGURE 7. Francesco Salviati, *Madonna and Child with Saints* (c. 1540), public church of Santa Cristina della Fondazza. Reproduced with permission of the Biblioteca Comunale dell'Archiginnasio, Bologna.

FIGURE 8. Giacomo Francia, *The Nativity* (c. 1552), and the so-called Vizzani altar, public church of Santa Cristina della Fondazza (2011). Photograph: Luca Salvucci, Bologna.

FIGURE 9. Ludovico Carracci, *Ascension of Our Lord* (installed 1608), high altar of the public church of Santa Cristina della Fondazza (2011). Photograph: Luca Salvucci, Bologna.

house it, and one of the little girls thus unwittingly became the convent patron whom Malvasia memorialized.

The theme of this painting required no explanation, of course. Lucrezia's teachers probably pointed out the sole female onlooker, in convent garb, and identified her as Saint Scholastica, the very first Benedictine nun, whose feast the nuns celebrated every year. As a child, though, Lucrezia was probably more taken with the rather comical ox and ass staring amiably back at her and calling to mind Aunt Flaminia's menagerie out back.

The Vizzani girls arrived in time to get a look at Ludovico Carracci's monumental *Ascension of Our Lord* (fig. 9), which Malvasia declared had been commissioned by a nun from the Bottrigari family in 1597 for the *chiesa vecchia*. In fact, Lucrezia would have known well this contemporary of her aunts, Maura Taddea Bottrigari (1581–1662), for she hailed from a local musical family. Maura Taddea's dowry must have paid for Carracci's painting, which seems not to have been finally transferred to the new church's main altar until 1608, when the bursar paid a metalworker for "nails and brackets for the altarpiece on the high altar."[33]

Lucrezia and her sister would never have had a chance to study carefully or perhaps even to look upon the other, newer altarpieces for the
external church. Also commissioned by various nuns whom Malvasia
memorialized, these works contrast with the style of the older altars
flanking the doors. Costanza Duglioli (d. 1614) and Ottavia Bolognetti
(d. 1612) donated Lucio Massari's *Visitation* (fig. 10; 1607) for the second
chapel on the right. Mary's reception by her older relative, a popular
convent subject that turns up in at least half a dozen Bolognese convent
chapels, usefully affirms that time-honored convent tradition recently
reenacted when the three Bombacci aunts received their Vizzani nieces
into Santa Cristina. The same scene would eventually adorn the end of
the refectory antechamber's frescoed ceiling (fig. 30).[34]

Tiburzio Passerotti's *Annunciation* (c. 1603), third on the right, was
provided by Angela Maria Zambeccara (d. 1645), whose religious name
reflects the protagonists of the painting: the angel and Mary. Margherita Glavarini (d. 1619, an older relation of the wealthy nun whose
cell contained its own especially opulent private altar) commissioned
Passerotti's *Christ's Fall beneath the Cross* (1603) for the front chapel
on the left. The donor's name saint, Saint Margaret, appears prominently in the painting. Bernardino Baldi's *Coronation of the Virgin* (fig.
11), for the third altar on the left, was financed by Emilia Grassi—a
key player in the story that only begins to unfold with the arrival of
the Vizzani girls at Santa Cristina's doors; by the early 1600s she was
already a dominant musical figure in the convent as both a performer
and a patron.[35]

Between the new church's altars six monumental stucco statues,
also provided by the nuns at their own expense, soon stood solemnly
in elaborate niches with sculpted decoration largely completed by the
time the Vizzani girls arrived. Nearest the church doors two important
female saints received pride of place: Saint Christina, the convent's
matron saint, and Saint Mary Magdalene, not only the first to testify
to the Resurrection and a paradigm of the contemplative life but also a
female saint closely linked to music. Ahead of these figures stood statu-
ary showing the chief saints of the Camaldolese order, Saint Benedict
and Saint Romuald. Nearest the high altar were the chief heroes of
the early church, Saints Peter and Paul, both statues attributed to the
young Guido Reni, rapidly becoming one of Bologna's most distinguished artists.[36]

Thus, the decade after Lucrezia Vizzana's arrival must have been an
artistically exciting time for the imaginative novice, for Santa Cristina

FIGURE 10. Lucio Massari, *Visitation* (1607), public church of Santa Cristina della Fondazza. Reproduced with permission of the Biblioteca Comunale dell'Archiginnasio, Bologna.

FIGURE 11. Bernardino Baldi, *The Coronation of the Virgin* (before 1615), public church of Santa Cristina. Reproduced with permission of the Biblioteca Comunale dell'Archiginnasio, Bologna.

underwent a transformation from a relatively modest chapel into one of Bologna's three or four most elegant and opulent convent churches.[37] Before long, its artistic distinction would be matched by comparable musical renown that burgeoned during that same period, at least in part because of the developing talents of the little girl who entered in 1598.

TWO

Lucrezia Vizzana's Musical Apprenticeship

"Music Here Is Presently Quite Destroyed"

How could young Lucrezia Vizzana, who entered a tightly cloistered monastery at the tender age of eight, not only learn music but learn it so well that she came to compose striking motets and even to publish them in an era when few women did such things? The times might appear inauspicious for an illustrious monastic musical career. Bologna's musical nuns had to contend with a string of church decrees against their music, stretching back to Gabriele Paleotti's time as archbishop of Bologna. In January 1567 Pius V promoted Paleotti to be bishop of the city, stressing as he did so Paleotti's commitment to implementing reforms of the Council of Trent. Gregory XIII elevated Paleotti to archbishop when Bologna became an archdiocese in 1582. Bologna's convents and the music within them became an important object of Paleotti's reforming zeal.

As a student, Paleotti had shown considerable musical aptitude himself, even composing and singing to his own accompaniment on the lute, a diversion he continued into adulthood. His personal musical interests notwithstanding, Paleotti felt no sympathy for those of nuns in his charge. As early as March 1569 Paleotti forbade all vocal music except plainchant and banned any singing with organ accompaniment in the church of the nuns of Santi Vitale et Agricola,[1] a decree that probably applied to other convents as well. The severity of Paleotti's attitude in this decree in fact closely resembles a preliminary proposed crackdown on convent music that delegates at Trent had earlier judged too severe and rejected.

During the 1570s, the archbishop's minions diligently cataloged perceived monastic laxity—musical and otherwise—and pondered how best to combat it. One don Leone offered the archbishop a list of common abuses in Bolognese nunneries. Besides keeping dogs and birds, reading vain literature "such as [*Orlando*] *Furioso*, Petrarch, Boccaccio," and playing cards and even dice at Christmastime, "They spend feast days in idle songs to the organ and in frivolous music; they carry on conversations and friendships with male singers. They spend too much time singing and playing. Some singers and organists have too much freedom, and sing and play vain pieces. Sometimes male singers sing with the nuns. They invite the magistrates for Holy Week and to their Easter compline service."

Another report also inveighed against imagined intimacies with male singers, either religious or secular professionals, and reasserted that on feast days these outsiders joined forces with the nuns, who also lavished presents upon them. The accounts continued with more detailed allegations that raise familiar issues of time-wasting and the enticement of dangerous and distracting crowds. One indictment also suggests music's potential utility as a means of convent communication with the world, despite the physical walls that closed nuns in:

Experience demonstrates that the excessive study that nuns devote these days to their songs not only fails to serve the end to which music was permitted them—to praise God and be aroused to the contemplation of celestial harmony—but instead also impedes them from greater goods and encumbers their souls in perpetual distraction. It causes them vainly to expend precious time that they could use more fruitfully. And while they stand with their bodies within the sacred cloisters, it causes them to wander outside in their hearts, nourishing within themselves an ambitious desire to please the world with their songs.[2]

Typically, behind the regular echoes of distraction and time-wasting, the churchman's paranoid fear of sexual contact on the nuns' part also resonates.

Interim measures came together in the seven rules of Paleotti's "Ordine da servarsi dalle suore nel loro cantare e musica," published in 1580. This order set the standard in Bologna for at least the next century and a half, with periodic swings both to the liberal and to the more conservative directions:

ORDER TO BE OBSERVED BY THE NUNS IN THEIR SINGING AND PLAYING

1. Nuns' music should be performed down below in the chapel where the other nuns stand. It is permissible, however, for a solo voice to sing to the organ at the times permitted—not vernacular pieces, but Latin, ecclesiastical ones having to do with religion.
2. The Divine Offices for Holy Week are to be recited as if spoken, that is, in simple chant; and finally it is permitted to sing the Benedictus and Miserere in song, which should be *falsobordone* [a simple, hymnlike style].
3. On the feast of the Resurrection it is not permitted to sing the psalms in polyphony, neither at vespers nor at compline, but only in plainchant; but it is permissible to play the organ between the psalms, with a solo voice that sings to the organ without any other *concerto* [i.e., musical interaction with instruments].
4. On their feast day, that is, once a year, it is permitted to sing the psalms in polyphony without any sort of *concerto*, and similarly the Mass.
5. During the rest of the year, on all solemn feasts, when Mass is celebrated, it is permitted to sing a sacred song once or twice, and similarly at the end of vespers.
6. No type of musical instrument should be used except the viol for the bass part where necessary, with the permission of their superiors, and in their cells, the harpsichord.
7. It is forbidden for any sort of music master to go to teach the nuns, also to rehearse any of their music, whether on the organ or in song.[3]

Four years later Paleotti further intensified his campaign against convent music as a centerpiece of his monastic reform program. He not only banned performances by secular musicians in the convents' outer chapels but also required the removal of convent organs to the nuns' inner chapels and the walling up of windows into the outer churches that formerly accommodated organs.

Shortly before Lucrezia Vizzana entered Santa Cristina, Gabriele Paleotti's distant cousin and former coadjutor, Alfonso Paleotti, succeeded him in the diocese of Bologna. A comment in 1607, from the last years of his reign, aptly sums up the latter archbishop's particular antipathy to convent music: "Throughout the time that I've been coadjutor and archbishop, from my experience I've felt that what removes the spirit, devotion, and peace within the nunneries is music, which they compete to perform in the choirs of their convents." In 1598, 1603, 1604, and 1605 Alfonso Paleotti reiterated earlier decrees forbidding outside musicians in the convents, thereby provoking a stream of petitions to the Sacred Congregation of Bishops and Regulars in Rome for exemptions to the rule. But between 1598 and 1610 the uniform response "Nihil" (nothing) awaited petitions to permit outside music teachers, however aged or god-fearing, from various convents and from at least one music teacher himself, a "Geronimo del Trombone," who vainly pleaded for special dispensation because "my household is burdened with four female offspring."[4]

Eighteen months before Lucrezia Vizzana's *Componimenti musicali* appeared in 1623, Bologna's latest archbishop, Cardinal Ludovico Ludovisi, renewed the antimusic campaign, forbidding all outside musicians to sing, play, or teach in the city's convents. A few months later, after Ludovisi's suffragan bishop Angelo Gozzadini took things a step further and banned all music but plainchant, all musical instruments but organ or harpsichord, all performances by outside musicians, and any music lessons by outside music teachers, an anonymous nun lamented:

In all the cities of Italy nuns sing and perform *concerti* in their churches, with the sole exception of the city of Bologna. Music here is presently quite destroyed, to the great detriment of the [convent] *virtuose*, and especially of the most eminent among them, who had spent their lives acquiring such a noble talent to praise His Divine Majesty. And it's not right that they should suffer such mortification, and, above all, those who entered the convents to practice their talent, given us [*sic*] by Divine Goodness for his praise.[5]

On paper, at least, the barrage of decrees creates the impression that Bologna's convents became pious musical wastelands. This clearly was not the case. Nuns did not take long to find ways to work within and around these restrictions. They would interpret such formal prescriptions, in which they had had no say, in informal ways that suited their own purposes and, in their eyes, were justified by circumstances. Much of what Paleotti and the church hierarchy saw as "abuses" had represented the normal way of life at convents for a good century and a half before Trent. The council's imposition of sweeping monastic reforms had abruptly overturned upper-class social systems and the basic assumptions under which many nuns had entered convents. In 1601 a nun from Udine remarked quite matter-of-factly to her bishop, "I was fifteen or sixteen when I became a nun and I entered the convent willingly. For, because I had lots of sisters, it seemed necessary to me that I come here. And when I took the veil, I never thought that act obligated me to anything at all, if not to live with the freedom one had at that time to come and go; and my family could also come inside."[6] During Paleotti's particularly strict Bolognese reforms, the nuns of Santi Naborre e Felice cried out to the pope in words vehemently expressing the reaction of those women whose way of life had been doubly disrupted against their wills:

The nuns of the Monastery of Santi Naborre e Felice in Bologna express to Your Holiness with all humility their miseries and misfortunes. Notwithstanding that their relatives shut most of them in here against their wills, for all that they have borne it with considerable patience, and during a time when they have been so tormented with various statutes and orders that they no longer have the strength to endure it. Most recently, besides requiring the organ's removal from here, now the doctor has been denied them, so that nobody except their father and mother can see and speak to them. Their old servants who were accustomed to serve them in the convent cannot speak to any nun, and should they speak they incur excommunication reserved to the Apostolic See. Likewise, any little children who climb inside the *ruota* and any four- or five-year-olds who set foot inside the doorway without permission immediately incur that same excommunication. Wherefore we fear that, deprived with such strictness and abandoned by everyone, we have only hell in this world and in the next.[7]

Such cloistered communities represent one of the most compelling examples of how male domination challenged women to discover some measure of autonomy and solidarity. Nuns developed their own informal rules and customs to interpret and subvert the formal prescriptions that external ecclesiastical authority imposed upon them.

Within the convent, a polyvalent medium such as music, in which the same words could convey different meanings in different contexts, proved to be a valuable and persuasive tool of convent women's culture. Given music's normal place in liturgy, nuns' musical performance could be justified—and often was—as a natural part of the professed nuns' sanctified work: the recitation of the Divine Office, prayer, and intercession. Post-Tridentine restrictions, particularly the nuns' total banishment from the public gaze, made their "angelic voices" an even more powerful and affecting means of influence beyond the convent wall, especially when resounding from behind grates high up in such walls.

It is interesting how frequently outside ecclesiastical authorities afforded music pride of place in their lists of convent "abuses," and how their condemnations help us to perceive music's usefulness in establishing patterns of socialization, clientage, and influence that remained important strategies in a world otherwise dominated by male clerics. Nun musicians' methods of resistance to clerical prohibitions directed at their art reflect the same patterns of response apparent in other aspects of convent life and convent women's culture.

Thus, in December 1584, the nuns of Sant'Omobono were among the first to subvert Gabriele Paleotti's decree against convent organs while still observing it to the letter. They did indeed remove the organ that protruded into their external church and walled up the opening as required, "to the entire satisfaction of our illustrious Archbishop Paleotti." But once the organ had been enlarged and made more powerful, they had it reinstalled in their inner church six months later and positioned it so that "resounding excellently well, it still creates delightful harmony for those outside."[8]

The Sant'Omobono example illustrates a common strategy of taking episcopal decrees absolutely literally, observing them to the letter—but no further. Indeed, writers of episcopal pronouncements wracked their brains to anticipate every possible loophole that nuns were sure to uncover, as Archbishop Ludovisi's decree of 1621 demonstrates:

We expressly command that in future every person, whether ecclesiastical or secular, regardless of their state, rank, or condition, neither dare nor presume to go near monasteries of nuns, both those of the city and those of the diocese; neither [should anyone visit] their parlors, grates, doorways, *ruote*, or their exterior churches to sing or play or to teach the same nuns or lay students living in the convents, even though they may be subject to regular orders; [nor should anyone] listen while they rehearse their music, on any occasion, on church festivals or for funerals in those churches annexed to them for the care of souls; nor [should anyone] perform there any sort of music, even though they may have been summoned by confessors, chaplains, or any other sort of person, despite the fact that they may have had a license to do so.

Such a litany of prohibitions offers a tacit admission of failure, a response to subversion that was sustained and fairly often successful. Lest any convent claim unfamiliarity with such decrees, authorities required that they be read at least twice a year in the refectory or in chapter "so that their observance remains alive, so that no one may plead ignorance."[9] All the same, pleas of ignorance on the nuns' part would continue into the eighteenth century, as we shall see in chapter 11.

In the absence of much real authority of their own, nuns also exercised various indirect means to influence the church hierarchy, chiefly by exploiting the tangled lines of ecclesiastical authority, represented by archbishop, suffragan bishop, vicar general, nuns' vicar, papal legate and vice-legate, secular clergy, regular clergy, convent confessor, convent chaplain, and curate, not to mention civil authorities and the city's patriciate. Monastic reforms represented only one area in which fragmented and inconsistent authority or opposition from elsewhere in the chain of command thwarted Gabriele Paleotti's efforts. A century and a half later the same problems still plagued Archbishop Giacomo Boncompagni. Such difficulties characterized attempts at convent reform within the post-Tridentine church generally. Sixteenth- to eighteenth-century attempts to separate convents from upper-class lay society, with its own secular assumptions and conventions, and to subsume them into a hierarchical and professional church, with opposing nonsecular and archaic conventions of its own, could never entirely succeed.

In the first wave of convent reform, nuns and their families turned for support to the Bolognese papal legate, who governed the city. Several letters from 1584–85 between Rome and the legate were clearly intended, for example, to firm up the legate's apparently wavering support for Paleotti's efforts, including the archbishop's removal of convent organs (which, according to the legate, occurred "not without great lamentation"). One Roman letter to the legate reveals that some nuns had sought sympathy among another important source of support, the citizenry of Bologna, "to [whom] it seems harsh that there should be this penalty of excommunication [for infractions]."[10] The church hierarchy's normal reticence about exercising authority in ways their city perceived as unreasonable or overly severe also encumbered church efforts and embroiled clerics in attempts at self-justification. Since some in the church hierarchy, civil government, and other segments of the intelligentsia saw nuns, enclosed within convent walls, as mediators for the city before a heavenly authority and as sacrificial victims to their families' long-term financial security, ecclesiastics' overly dictatorial actions could also quite easily tip the balance of public sympathy in the nuns' favor.

In 1585 nuns inaugurated another primary method of exploiting the conflicting lines of ecclesiastical authority: direct recourse right over the archbishop's head, to Rome. This strategy had its unpredictable side, for Rome's administrative congregations routinely turned around and requested the local bishop's opinion. The phrase *Episcopo pro informatione et voto* ([send to] the bishop for information and his vote) appears on petition after petition that went directly to Rome. Nevertheless, congregations of cardinals weighed factors such as tradition, local custom, and political lobbying on both sides often enough to afford convent supplicants some measure of hope in the outcome.

Within months of Paleotti's ban on organs, for example, the Congregation of Bishops granted the nuns of San Pietro Martire in Bologna special license to use their organ, "walled up as it is," on Easter and the feast of San Pietro Martire. The nuns of Santissima Trinità got wind of their sisters' success via the convent grapevine and also petitioned the congregation, citing the earlier concession to justify their cause. The congregation instructed Paleotti to satisfy "these poor little ones, who, closed up forever within these walls, deserve to be permitted some further relief." A month later a defensive Paleotti had to reassure the congregation that he had never intended to deny the nuns the use of convent organs entirely and was willing to come to some accommodation with the nuns of Santissima Trinità. Another month or two later Paleotti was suggesting that after their initial agreement with his terms of concession, "I see that they are now going around looking for new avenues to achieve what suits them," implying that Santissima Trinità should have been quicker to obey.[11]

Lobbying for small concessions that they could parlay into further advantages when circumstances permitted remained a convent strategy for centuries. Convent gossip traveling through family networks (since a single family might have daughters in two or three different institutions) permitted one religious house to exploit concessions granted to another. Such tactics did not escape the attention of Bologna's ever wary archdiocesan curia. One cleric put it rather extravagantly, "One must be strong in not licensing music masters to teach the nuns. Otherwise, if the tiniest path is opened, it will be the ruin of these convents, which will never again be well governed."[12]

So the hierarchy stood firm to avoid setting dangerous precedents. Once Gabriele Paleotti died, the nuns of Santa Margherita thought his passing made it worthwhile to petition to move their convent organ back to the outer church. The Congregation of Bishops denied the petition with the comment that "to concede this to these and not to the other nuns could provoke dissatisfaction among them and also set a bad precedent."[13]

The nuns also worked the conflicting lines of authority to their own advantage by concentrating on persons invested with intermediate authority. These ranged from powerful patrician patrons to members of senatorial government, from their own father confessors to local curates, who could sometimes serve as buffers between the nuns and the ecclesiastical hierarchy. To forge and strengthen such alliances, nuns brought diverse influences to bear. Their strategies included promises of prayers, willingness to sing masses on request, plates of toffee, or other little gifts on feast days. Prelates repeatedly decried these gifts as a useless squandering of convent resources, but nuns regarded this medium of exchange as important and a sound investment in public relations.

Noble intercession on nuns' behalf represented another time-honored practice, as is revealed by a letter of 1512 from Isabella d'Este to convent superiors, requesting that certain nuns be permitted an outside music teacher since their singing was so bad that "when we visit the said convent and hear such discord, our ears are deeply offended and scarcely consoled." A century later, one exponent of nuns' music suggested that if the nuns hoped to overturn Archbishop Ludovisi's latest musical pro-hibitions, "it is necessary that some important prince demand the grace most efficaciously, because Monsignor Ingoli [Ludovisi's secretary] is very tough and makes the excuse that this is the particular view of His Holiness and of Lord Cardinal Ludovisi." This is exactly what the nuns of Corpus Domini did in similar circumstances forty years later, after the Congregation of Bishops rejected their initial request to admit a new organist in 1662. They turned to one of Bologna's most powerful bank-ing families, who had supported them in musical matters for decades. Vittoria, daughter of Marquis Cesare Pepoli and wife of Count Odoardo Michele Pepoli, wrote politely but firmly to the secretary of the congre-gation:

I know that if you wished to grant me this grace none of the others will dispute it by saying the Sacred Congregation should be of a mind to remove all the organs from the nuns. I know that in Rome all convents sing and play and I know of no scandal arising there. But, rather, devotion increases, as everything is done in God's honor. And for this reason I know the fulfillment of such sophistical opinions will not follow. Forgive me, Your Eminence, if I speak too freely.

Vittoria Pepoli's mediations were irresistible. The suit was granted, and the organist accepted within the month.[14]

An agreement between the Bolognese nuns of Sant'Orsola and their new father confessor and curate, drawn up in 1684, not only reveals exactly how the fragmented hierarchical system could be turned upon itself, but also how informal rules and customs, worked out privately by the nuns, subverted the prescriptions of both the diocese and Rome:

On the feast of Saint Catherine, the curate sings the mass and the nuns respond in plainchant, which is against the decrees of both the Congregation of the Council and the Congregation of Bishops and Regulars. Nevertheless, to please the nuns who wish it, with the consent of the ordinary he [the confessor] shall permit it, with the approval of the ordinary, as appropriate. And although the curate should not sing the solemnities with the nuns, since abuses were introduced long ago without the confes-sor pro tempore's objections to the curate's singing with the nuns, who would go up to the organ loft [in violation of Paleotti's first rule of 1580!] to sing the Magnificat in plainchant, in order to please the nuns who wish it, the confessor shall permit it.[15]

Clearly, nuns turned confessors and curates into accomplices to sub-vert higher authority. Recognizing that father confessors could be the weakest link in their chain of command, the church hierarchy required that they rotate every three years, and that their appointment be subject to the local bishop's final approval, though these rules, too, were inevitably interpreted flexibly. As we shall see, the interposition of confessors would become a key factor in later struggles between the nuns of Santa Cristina and the church hierarchy.

Convents like Santa Cristina, which were under the jurisdiction of regular monastic orders—Dominicans, Benedictines, Franciscans, Lateran canons, Camaldolese, or others—and therefore not directly subject to the local archbishop's authority, found in the precedential relationship another especially useful method of mediation. Given traditional rivalries and antagonisms, especially in matters of jurisdiction, between regular orders and secular clergy affiliated with the diocesan curia, nuns in regular orders found naturally sympathetic ears among their male monastic superiors. The following letter from the general of the Lateran canons to a subordinate who governed the Lateran canonesses of San Lorenzo in Bologna provides an excellent example of how the nuns could evade the letter of episcopal law and benefit from flexibility that superiors of their own order were prepared to introduce:

It's true that a few days ago donna Gentile as organist petitioned in great humility for permission to perform a *concerto* on the organ on their feast day. In light of the humility of her request and recognizing her and her companions as good and obedient daughters, I was inclined to grant her that on the feast day she could have some motets sung with one or two voices at most, forbidding every sort of musical instrument, and not extending the license beyond the feast day of San Lorenzo.

I gave this license because I could give it—I make the laws; I can make exceptions to them. I took a look in the Illustrious Paleotti's decrees, where he permits nuns to sing with one voice to the organ. If I was content with two voices, it is not a sin in the Holy Spirit. I also deemed this grace reasonable, thinking thereby to relieve in part these embittered souls. Nor does it seem to me a good idea to revoke it; nor do I believe further confirmation is required [i.e., from the diocesan curia].[16]

The general's liberal reinterpretation of Paleotti's decree also illustrates why archbishops perennially distrusted the regular clergy's rule of nunneries, for it undermined their own authority and uniform implementation of curial policy. These factors, in their turn, explain why the hierarchy battled to wrest nunneries from the control of regular orders. Indeed, as we shall see, Santa Cristina della Fondazza figured in just such a battle in spectacular form.

From time to time, nuns also quite cavalierly disobeyed decrees they found simply unreasonable. In this way they interpreted the 1580 prohibition against all convent instruments except the organ, harpsichord, and bass viol with considerable flexibility or flatly ignored it, depending on their purposes. In 1602, for example, the nuns of Santi Vitale et Agricola purchased five viols of different sizes for their *scola da cantare* (singing school) although only the largest bass was fully legal. Inventories of nuns' personal property at Santa Margherita in the early 1600s reveal that one nun still owned a lute and its case, another owned an archlute, yet another owned "a spinet harpsichord, a guitar, and a lute," one more owned "1 clavichord, 1 lute, an archlute, 1 violin," while two nuns each owned a trombone. Theoretically forbidden trombones continued in use at Santa Caterina, Santa Cristina, and San Giovanni Battista as well.[17]

To control such cascading infractions required a level of vigilance that a diocesan curia with two dozen convents in its charge could scarcely manage. Moreover, that cornerstone of post-Tridentine reform, the system of strict enclosure, exacerbated the problem. For higher cloister walls not only kept the nuns in and hidden from view but also very effectively kept their overseers out. After Trent, it was certainly more difficult than before for male ecclesiastics to maintain a clear sense of what was going on inside convents without co-opting someone within the convent community to work on the hierarchy's behalf, as would happen at Santa Cristina in the 1620s. The Tridentine management policy simultaneously brought other unintended effects, for segregation bred solidarity as well as marginality. The internal community of every convent socialized its members virtually from childhood, first at the hands of their cloistered aunts, then under the novice mistress, but also informally through the community as a whole. Quite unsurprisingly, these women who lived together accepted their group's solidarity with few second thoughts—especially when someone from outside the group attacked their own collective and traditional prerogatives. In such a situation they might put aside internal rivalries or minor disagreements in order to face down the perceived common enemy, exactly as the nuns of Santa Cristina would demonstrate during the course of the seventeenth century.

"A Divine Office Nowhere Celebrated More Diligently"

Because the nuns of Santa Cristina were variously successful at implementing any number of these strategies, Lucrezia Vizzana's musical reality was considerably less grim than the plethora of ecclesiastical prohibitions suggests. She could count herself lucky to have entered one of the best of all possible worlds in Bologna for a budding female musician. Bolognese noble and patrician families shared a view of music with their peers in other Italian cities, an attitude reflected in and shaped by Castiglione's *Book of the Courtier.* Given this perspective, worldly musical training for young women concentrated on singing or playing and placed little or no emphasis on composition.[18] A handful of late-sixteenth- and early-seventeenth-century women composers have come to light among the women who found increasing musical opportunities in the secular realm of the court, or as professional actresses or courtesans—though no Bombacci or Vizzani would have allowed his daughters to associate with any but the first of these options. Laywomen such as Maddalena Casulana and Barbara Strozzi, whose musical careers most closely resembled those of their male counterparts and who may have been trained explicitly for composing careers, represent obvious exceptions to the general rule.

Lucrezia Vizzana entered Santa Cristina at such a tender age that she is unlikely to have had much, if any, prior musical knowledge. Her education in music must have been almost entirely a product of the monastic environment and traditions. As far back as the fifteenth century Santa Cristina's nuns had a reputation for music. In 1433 Camaldolese prior general Ambrogio Traversari lauded the nuns for "a divine office that is nowhere celebrated more diligently in common; its psalmody is nowhere more expertly and more melodiously sung. As far as a monastery of virgins is concerned, nowhere was I so delightfully moved."[19]

Even though the curia had banned outside music teachers before Lucrezia Vizzana arrived, there was no shortage of musical talent inside Santa Cristina, on which the young Lucrezia must have relied. As a rule, *educande* received their first instruction from a cloistered aunt. Subsequent training within the institution, including instruction in how to sing the chants of the Office and Mass, fell to the novice mistress. Lucrezia's most probable mentor was one of her mother's three sisters, who looked after her upbringing. The youngest, Camilla Bombacci, was in fact a musician. At her death in 1640 the convent necrology remembered donna Camilla as "first organist, three times mistress of novices, and subsequently abbess." In 1623 the current abbess suggested Camilla Bombacci for choir mistress, but donna Camilla ultimately became abbess instead.[20]

The relationship between Lucrezia and Camilla Bombacci was probably akin to a case described a century later in a petition to the Congregation of Bishops from the Monastery of Santa Caterina da Siena in Catanzaro: "The noble maiden Lucrezia Vigliarolo, eight years old, desires to remain under the care and direction of suor Margarita Almirante, her maternal aunt, in which she has made such progress that she now sings the Office with the nuns in choir and reads at table." Such musical precocity was not particularly unusual. In 1668, for example, a ten-year-old singer being educated at the Bolognese convent of Santi Gervasio e Protasio received special permission to sing a duet at Mass with an older nun (her aunt perhaps?) on the feast of the patron saints. And, as mentioned in chapter 1, Lucrezia Vizzana was hardly the first musically precocious preteen at Santa Cristina.[21] Lucrezia Vizzana's early studies must have resembled those described by Paula Dorothea Vitali of Santa Cristina in the early 1620s: consisting of reading and singing plainchant. Lucrezia was probably taught in the domain of the novice mistress, which, according to Vitali, was located "in the rooms up above, in the middle"—near the large storage area under the roof—"to be separated from the convent and not disturb the nuns."[22]

The likely student-teacher relationship between Lucrezia Vizzana and Camilla Bombacci suggests the beginnings of a modest musical dynasty within the walls on via Fondazza. In fact, Lucrezia Vizzana later acted as novice mistress. Lucrezia's relative Teresa Pompea Vizzana, who entered Santa Cristina in the 1630s, may have been trained by donna Lucrezia Orsina, for the convent necrologist memorialized the younger woman as having musical gifts of her own. Quite possibly the mentorship within the family therefore extended to a third generation.

The apparent Bombacci-Vizzana-Vizzana musical relationship suggests that the search for musical talent within families should not overlook the probably common though elusive strictly female lines of musical kinship within cloisters of the age, where we can find nieces instructed in the art by their musical aunts. Such intergenerational musical ties turn out to have been reasonably common in Italian convents.[23] These generations of musical nuns may often be overlooked in worldly family trees, but they were carefully remembered for their artistic gifts in the sisters' necrologies.

Yet Lucrezia Vizzana's most probable teacher, Camilla Bombacci, was only one of several capable musicians at Santa Cristina during her niece's formative years. Chief among the others was the formidable Emilia Grassi, clearly the dominant musical force—for better or worse—in the early 1600s. Lucrezia had scarcely arrived when, in 1599, Grassi received the dedication of Adriano Banchieri's *Messa solenne a otto voci* (Solemn Mass for eight voices), presumably because it was underwritten by her or her family. The garrulous composer and Olivetan monk's dedication warrants a closer look for what it reveals about the lavishness of music at Santa Cristina and about Emilia Grassi's role in it:

On the day when the feast of the glorious Saint Christina was solemnized, I found my-self in the church of Your Reverence while first vespers was being sung and heard with great pleasure the harmonious *concerti* of voices, organs, and various musical instru-ments, directed with most exquisite sentiments of devotion. I endeavored to discover from a musician, my particular friend (who was present there), who led these *concerti;* and from him I learned it was Your Reverence. And justly he further added that in addition to your other most honorable qualities you are highly skilled in both singing and playing, using all these talents for the praise and glory of our Blessed Lord. I desire no other reward but that on occasions when you perform these *concerti* you and your dear sisters would remember to pray to God for me in your devout and holy prayers.[24]

Emilia Grassi served as choir mistress from around the time when Banchi-eri heard the choir and off and on into the 1620s—she even refused later on to relinquish the post when the abbess wished to replace her. Af-ter her death the convent reconfirmed Banchieri's description of donna Emilia as one who "above all, so excelled in playing all musical instru-ments that she was second to none." Don Mauro Ruggeri, her former confessor, also singled out donna Emilia for her vocal abilities and for her talents on the organ, harp, and other instruments.[25]

Two years after Banchieri's collection appeared, another nun from Santa Cristina, Adeodata Leoni, received the dedication of the *Secondo libro de mottetti* (Second book of motets) by the Camaldolese monk Ga-briele Fattorini, sometime *maestro di cappella* (choirmaster) of Carceri Abbey (Veneto) and later of Faenza cathedral. The dedication—actually penned by the Camaldolese monk don Donato Beroaldo, who assembled the collection—suggests that the compilation had been put together spe-cifically at donna Adeodata's behest. Soon thereafter the whole group of singing nuns at Santa Cristina became the object of a third dedication, when Giovanni Battista Biondi, alias Cesena, published his *Compieta con letanie* (Compline with the litany; 1606). Like the two earlier imprints, it consisted of works for eight voices. Venetian publisher Giacomo Vincen-ti's dedicatory letter marvels at the divine *concerti* at various Bolognese convents and singles out those at Santa Cristina in particular.[26] Finally, in 1613 Ercole Porta, organist of the collegiate church in San Giovanni in Persiceto, dedicated to Cleria Pepoli of Santa Cristina his *Vaga ghirlanda di soavi e odorati fiori musicali* (Charming little garland of sweet-savored musical flowers), a diverse collection of motets, psalms, and simply har-monized settings for one to five voices and basso continuo.

Surely it must signify the status of Santa Cristina as Bologna's premier convent for music that among some ten musical publications dedicated to convent women in Bologna between 1582 and 1675, no fewer than

FIGURE 12. Angelo Michele Cavazzoni, interior view of the public church of Santa Cristina (ink and watercolor, eighteenth century). An organ window facing the high altar is visible at the right. The chapel above the church portal is at the left. Reproduced with permission of the Soprintendenza delle Belle Arti and the Archivio Opera Pia Davia Bargellini, Bologna.

five (counting Lucrezia Vizzana's own) were dedicated to nuns from Santa Cristina. The testimony of these imprints suggests that the nuns' own music must have been decidedly more lavish than archiepiscopal prohibitions would sanction.

Architectural evidence points in the same direction. Santa Cristina's new church included two raised organ rooms, one on each side of the high altar, only accessible from the nuns' inner chapel, and each containing an organ (fig. 9 shows the high altar and the location of the raised choir rooms on each side of the altar recess; fig. 12, at the right, shows one of the organ windows facing the high altar, in the external church; fig. 31 shows the catwalk connecting these two organ rooms in the inner church and a loft window facing the inner chapel). In 1607, the convent organ builder indicated that Santa Cristina's instruments and choir lofts were arranged to permit double-choir singing by the nuns, whose voices carried through different windows into both the inner church and the public church.[27] An additional pair of smaller windows in the outer church faced directly toward the nave. Although the organ loft windows had screens in front of them, some of these could be removed

FIGURE 13. View through a perforated screen in one of Santa Cristina's choir lofts at the front of the church (2011). Photograph: Luca Salvucci, Bologna.

during performances, enabling the singing nuns to see each other and to coordinate their actions as one choir responded to the other. Members of the curia were appalled when they eventually discovered that the loft screens were perforated and allowed Lucrezia and the other musicians to peer out into the public church without being seen (fig. 13).

Musical coordination would have been much easier in the nuns' large chapel at the rear of the external church and above the church doors, for its three grilles right at floor level could easily have accommodated double choirs that would remain invisible to the external church but have full view of one other (fig. 12 shows this choir at the far left; fig. 24 shows the interior of this chapel). Don Mauro Ruggeri, Santa Cristina's father confessor during the early 1620s, claimed that the nuns performed "choirs of music" there on feast days. Ruggeri further indicates that they accompanied themselves, not only with the two organs, but also "with various instruments, violins, trombones, harps, and such like."[28] This fairly substantial evidence suggests not only that the archiepiscopal decrees from 1580 onward had limited effect at Santa Cristina but also that the descriptions of lavish music at the convent by Adriano Banchieri and others represented more than mere hyperbole.

Music from the collections dedicated to the nuns at Santa Cristina must have been conceived at least partly with the singing nuns of that house in mind and must also offer some measure of their skills. Adriano Banchieri's *Messa solenne*, for example, includes a few pieces that meet Gabriele Paleotti's old rule permitting the nuns "to sing once or twice a sacred song when Mass is celebrated, and similarly at the end of vespers." Nothing in the collection, however, comes close to approaching the limit of a single voice with solo organ accompaniment. Two pieces—*Laetamini et exultate quia surrexit Christus* (Rejoice and be glad for Christ is risen; *CNC*, track 16), clearly intended for Easter, and *Adoramus te dulcissime Jesu Christe* (We adore thee, sweetest Jesus Christ), meant for the Elevation of the Sacrament—are scored only for four high voices, with the lowest part in the tenor rather than the bass range, as would have certainly suited the nuns. The self-contained *Crucifixus* from the creed of Banchieri's Mass is likewise for four voices that descend no lower than the two motets. The motet *Decantabat populus Israel* (The people of Israel sang), too, employs only four higher voices, though the lowest part here drops into the baritone range for half a dozen notes, which could easily have been transposed up an octave without marring the harmony.

The remaining items in Banchieri's collection largely feature eight voices: two contrasting four-voice choirs. The composer juxtaposes the higher-voiced choir against the second, lower choir. Indeed, in the so-called Concerto at the Offertory, *Beata es tu Sancte N.* (*CNC*, track 15; "Blessed art thou, Saint X"—an appropriate saint's name could be inserted in this multipurpose piece), the upper choir stays higher than in any other work in Banchieri's collection and appears particularly prominently on its own in the opening section. This certainly suggests that Banchieri had the singing nuns of Santa Cristina in mind. The second choir, however, here and in the other double-choir pieces, tends to descend to masculine depths where the nuns could rarely follow. Thus, the musicians may have relegated the lower parts for the second choir of Banchieri's double-choir pieces to the bass viol that Paleotti permitted them or to the trombone—forbidden, but apparently still in use at some Bolognese convents. They may also have intabulated the pieces for the organ, a practice documented in Bolognese convents since the mid-sixteenth century. The organ would have filled out the lower harmonies while the nuns sang those upper parts they could manage.

The Fattorini and Cesena musical collections, on the other hand, are more uniform and traditional in their contents, making less obvious provisions for the special circumstances of convent singing. Nonetheless, like a good deal of the Banchieri *Messa solenne*, both of these collections consist entirely of works for two four-voice choirs. And the full vocal ranges within them suggest that some works would have been difficult or impossible for nuns to perform without relegating some lines to instruments.

Some of Fattorini's motets, however, would have been especially effective if sung by hidden double choirs of nuns. *Audi coelum* (Hear, O heavens) employs especially striking and witty echo effects, with the second choir jumping in fleetingly to repeat a fragment of the first choir's last word, yet still making verbal sense. Within the context of the words in this motet, as they would be performed by two hidden choirs, the convent choir loft becomes the angelic realm within, from which singing angels, intimately in touch with celestial realities, respond to one another, interpret signs, and prophesy.

[choir 1:] Hear O heaven, hear my words, full of longing and pervaded with joy [*gaudio*]. [choir 2:] *I hear* [*Audio*]. [choir 1:] Tell me, I pray, who is she that shines like the dawn, that I may bless her [*benedicam*]? [choir 2:] *I will tell* [*Dicam*]. [choir 1:] Say, for she, fair as the moon, radiant as the sun, fills with joy the lands, heavens, and seas [*maria*]. [choir 2:] *Mary* [*Maria*]. [choir 1:] Mary, that same sweet virgin foretold by Ezekiel, the prophet, the portal of the east [*orientalis*]? [choir 2:] *That very one* [*Talis*]. . . .

Likewise, the question-and-response formula of Fattorini's *Himnum cantate nobis* may have been especially telling when sung by cloistered nuns, who occasionally used their incarceration as a means to arouse sympathy in the world. The first choir's fifteen-measure introduction, "Sing unto us a hymn," is answered by the second, "How shall we sing the Lord's song in a foreign land?" As the motet continues it is the higher, second choir of "captives" that pointedly introduces the rest of the text: "Those who led us captive into that place asked of us the words of our songs. Sing unto us a hymn. How shall we sing the Lord's song in a strange land?" At least some hearing those words in Santa Cristina's outer church, particularly as disembodied echoes from behind barred windows, would have recognized the analogy to the nuns' own life situation: they had been led into the captivity of the cloister by their own families and by the community outside their walls, who, like Babylon, could not decipher the language of the nuns' simultaneous longing and acquiescence to their state.

Resonating from within cloisters such as Santa Cristina in the years when Lucrezia Orsina Vizzana was growing up, such echoes, whether the clever single-word fragments of *Audi coelum* or the calls and despairing responses of *Himnum cantate nobis*, represented an especially effective conceit. For, just as the sad mythological figure Echo, after her rejection by Narcissus, went to live in hidden, lonely caves, whence she tossed back sounds to the world, nuns had been compelled to withdraw since the 1560s into enforced seclusion behind convent walls raised around them. As Ann Rosalind Jones has observed, Echo became a symbol that women writers of the period commonly employed to represent the silence imposed upon them. Indeed, male writers on female conduct made Echo a paradigm for women. In 1552 Alessandro Piccolomini urged wives to be the echoes of their husbands. In 1588 Robert Cleaver affirmed "as the echo answereth but one word for many, which are spoken to her, so a Maid's answer should be a single word."[29]

The female voice echoing from behind the convent grate plays upon the Echo metaphor in an especially telling spiritual mode. Despite fifty years of Bolognese churchmen's efforts at control so strict they amounted to silencing, the songs of the nuns in Bologna during Lucrezia Vizzana's time, like the voice of Echo, lifted up in a hauntingly mysterious call to the world beyond the convent walls.

THREE

Musical and Monastic Disobedience in Vizzana's *Componimenti musicali*

Despite episcopal prohibitions, music in the convents of Bologna managed to hold its own in the decades after Trent. As one of the city's most musical convents and especially well supplied with talented performers, Santa Cristina della Fondazza had long fostered a lively musical tradition, one that could inspire the young Lucrezia Vizzana and impart to her many details of her art. There is a problem, however: Vizzana's compositions partake of the novel development in seventeenth-century music termed the *stile moderno* (modern style), a new, demonstrative style that often incorporated musical gestures that violated sixteenth-century compositional rules in order to express the text. This "modern" musical idiom, first associated with secular music around 1600, quickly found its way into Bolognese sacred music created outside the convent: it was published in collections such as Adriano Banchieri's *Nuovi pensieri ecclesiastici* (New musical ideas;1613) and Ercole Porta's *Sacro convito musicale* (Sacred musical banquet; 1620).

Many works in the *stile moderno*, whether secular or sacred, were printed in the twenty years before Vizzana's motets appeared in 1623. All but two of the twenty motets in her collection are for one or two soprano soloists accompanied by basso continuo (simple, discrete chords improvised on the organ), a characteristic musical idiom of the *stile moderno*. A number of Vizzana's solos seem especially self-conscious in their adoption of novel, expressive stylistic traits that took hold in the solo musical idiom of the early 1600s.

Her acutely affective *Usquequo oblivisceris me in finem?* (*SED*, track 6; example 1) speaks that stylistic language with quiet intensity. It offers examples of all her favorite musical gestures drawn from the *stile moderno* and always calculated to heighten details of the verbal language:

How long will you forget me? Forever? How long will you hide your face from me? How long shall I take counsel in my soul, having sorrow in my heart daily? How long will my enemy be exalted over me? Have regard for me and hear me, O Lord my God. Lighten my eyes in death, lest my enemy say, "I have prevailed against him."

The voice's delicately virtuosic ornamentation, in no way a gratuitous show, first conveys the opening line's restless unease and also the conclusion's broader, more languid resignation. Repeated phrases, transposed upward to higher pitches, serve a rhetorical purpose, most notably at the opening, where the restatement of the first line at a higher pitch heightens the sense of questioning and underlying anxiety. The disjunction between phrases caused by beginning a new line of text on a chord not directly related to what went before and effectively canceling the previous tonal center by slipping downward, seems to undercut the earlier moment of musical repose that concluded the setting of the previous line of text. This happens most clearly at the break between the end of the first phrase (bar 5) and the musical continuation and also after the cadence at "sorrow in my heart daily" (bar 19).

Two other gestures are particularly arresting as well. The first involves the expressively jolting juxtaposition of two major chords with bottom notes a third apart: obvious at bars 25–26 (B-flat major versus G major, where the bottom note of the first chord jerks up a half step to become the middle note of the second chord), and possibly also at bars 6–7, which can be harmonized C major versus E major (contrasting the G-natural of the first chord with a G-sharp in the second). Such immediate harmonic contrasts momentarily trick the ear in order to arouse through a slight harmonic confusion a feeling of disorientation at one point, and at another a sense of quiet wonder or transformation.

More unusual still, and most striking of all, is the bold leap away from a high note, held over in the voice, clashing sharply against the bass note for expressive effect at bar 14. Vizzana's unusual resolution of such dissonant clashes represents a notable violation of time-honored rules of sixteenth-century compositional practice, which required that the upper voice resolve its clash with the bass by descending quietly,

EXAMPLE 1. Lucrezia Vizzana, *Usquequo oblivisceris me in finem?*

smoothly, and logically to the adjacent lower pitch, to form a sweeter, purer consonance. The attentive ear, even if untutored in music theory, still senses a momentary disruption at Vizzana's skip away from the dissonance. For Vizzana that illicit leap away from the clash between voice and bass aptly captures the mood of momentary despair.

These musical features, particularly the boldest of them, were carefully conceived to convey directly, forcefully, and rhetorically the moment-to-moment implications of the text. All of them reappear in greater or lesser profusion throughout Vizzana's collection.

How could Lucrezia Vizzana have learned this particular modern idiom? She and her potential nun music teachers left the musical world

EXAMPLE 1. *(continued)*

outside the cloister at the crucial time when music was beset by significant changes. Ludovico Viadana's immensely popular *Cento concerti ecclesiastici* (A hundred church *concerti*), that landmark of the new texture for solo voice and basso continuo in sacred music (though his work's musical idiom commonly remained more traditional than Vizzana's would turn out to be), first appeared in 1602, for example. By then, Lucrezia had already been behind the convent wall for at least four years, while her probable music teachers, Camilla Bombacci or Emilia Grassi, had been cloistered for at least fifteen. One must wonder when and how distinctly they first heard echoes of the newer style that reecho in Lucrezia Vizzana's motets.

The church hierarchy discouraged any attempts by convent women to keep up with changing musical styles, at least to judge by the Congregation of Bishops' response to a petition dated 1606 from three modern-minded singing nuns at the convent of San Biagio in Cesena, sixty miles from Bologna: "Sister Felicita Stellini, Sister Anna and Sister Armellina Uberti, all considerably versed in music, wish to study how to sing some spiritual motets in the Roman style. They humbly request that you permit Canon Manzini to come once or at most twice to the public parlatorios to explain and teach to the above-mentioned nuns the way to sing them, in the presence of the abbess and the appointed chaperones." This petition met with the inevitable response when it came to outside music teachers: "Nihil" (nothing).[1]

Even the laity could be comparably suspicious of convent musical innovation, judging by one nobleman's complaints in the diocese of Acqui (Monferrato) in 1652. Not only were the local Benedictine sisters causing scandal by their inordinate familiarity with the laity and by installing the equivalent of picture windows in the wall bordering the public street, but "now they are being taught polyphony by their confessor, and on this pretext they are using the musical scale with other key signatures besides the one with .b. flat and .b. natural, acceptable to nature." It is not clear what unorthodox scales the outraged (and musically unsophisticated) count was trying to describe— they presumably introduced unusual chromatic pitches, similar to those in Vizzana's juxtaposed chromatic chords. But they obviously shocked him.[2]

Yet, despite similarly severe restrictions in Bologna, music from the outside world found its way inside the walls of Santa Cristina, thanks largely to nuns' reinterpretation of the rules imposed upon them and thanks to their indefatigable petitioning to Rome. In 1605, for example, over Archbishop Alfonso Paleotti's strenuous objections, the Congregation of Bishops finally began to relax its prohibition concerning performances by outside musicians at Bolognese convent festivities.[3] After initial success by the nuns of Corpus Domini in 1605, the convents of Santa Caterina, San Guglielmo, San Bernardino, Sant'Orsola, Santi Vitale et Agricola, and Sant'Omobono, one after the other, all clamored to receive permission to bring musical outsiders into their external churches for feast days and funerals.

By 1607 even Bolognese secular musicians were petitioning the Congregation of Bishops for permission to sing and play in nuns' external churches. Despite Alfonso Paleotti's repeated predictions of "indecencies, scandal, and secret practices," recalling the sexual paranoia of post-Tridentine diocesan pronouncements, the congregation overruled him.

Outside musicians also came to perform at Santa Cristina, enabling the nuns to experience the newer musical styles of the early 1600s. The echoes of such new music ought to have reached their ears only faintly: through various grated windows. But musical nuns contrived ways not only to hear better but also even to see outside performers. Pastoral investigators in 1623 reported that the raised organ rooms flanking Santa Cristina's high altar not only had windows facing one another across the high altar (fig. 12, right) but also contained other windows that faced directly into the external church. Although the nuns covered these windows with movable screens, the coverings were perforated so that they could see through them and down into the nave (fig. 13). Furthermore, the large grated windows of the spacious choir above the doors at the far end of the public church (fig. 12, left) had similar screens and grilles through which nuns could view the entire external church.[4]

Nuns also managed to study the scores of newly published music. It is hard to imagine that the dedicatees of the musical prints of Banchieri, Fattorini, Cesena, and Porta never set eyes on the collections dedicated to them, publications that they or their families had probably paid for. Nuns from other Bolognese convents definitely owned volumes of music at exactly this time. An inventory from the convent of Santa Margherita reveals that in 1613 one nun owned seven books "to sing and play." In 1617 a benefactress left the nuns of San Guglielmo a whole trunkful of vocal music.[5]

Furthermore, although musicians and music teachers may have been repeatedly forbidden to visit convent parlatorios, nuns' parents were not. Therefore, little would have prevented the Bolognese composer, wind player, and esteemed music teacher Alfonso Ganassi from visiting his daughter donna Alfonsina, who had entered Santa Cristina around 1591. Perhaps he presented her with musical scores or merely recounted the latest musical news. The introduction of such musical information or music books at Santa Cristina probably came quite easily. In 1623 several nuns admitted that the abbess no longer always bothered to examine incoming and outgoing mail, and she appointed no chaperones to keep watch in the parlatorios.[6]

All of which suggests that after Alfonso Paleotti's death in 1610, vigilance concerning the introduction of music into convents probably relaxed, at least temporarily. In 1616, for example, Paleotti's successor licensed local composer Ercole Porta to visit the convent of San Michele in San Giovanni in Persiceto two or three times to teach the nuns music for Rogation Days. At Santa Cristina, the most telling witness of all to this new laxity was the fact that from around 1615, at the instigation of donna Emilia Grassi, abbess at the time, the convent surreptitiously employed a regularly salaried, if illicit, *maestro di musica*, Ottavio Vernizzi, organist of the basilica of San Petronio. The prioress explained in 1622 that such a regular salary was necessary because there were three organists needing lessons,[7] one of whom was certainly Lucrezia Orsina Vizzana. Church authorities promptly put a stop to that practice—in 1623—when it finally came to their attention. Despite many and varied episcopal prohibitions concerning music, ways could nonetheless be found to nurture Lucrezia Vizzana's talent.

So, for Lucrezia Vizzana and her sisters in religion monastic enclosure may have been less musically restricting than episcopal prohibitions intended it to be. Can one go far enough with this speculation as to suggest what music may actually have reached our young musician? Given music's natural elusiveness, one can scarcely hope to recover Vizzana's musical world with much certainty from the musical language within her own works. Nevertheless, the distinctive musical gestures in Vizzana's motets offer intriguing clues.

Banchieri's *Messa solenne* of 1599, dedicated to Emilia Grassi, provides a plausible starting point, since Banchieri assumed that the nuns of Santa Cristina would perform his works. It is intriguing to encounter in the opening bars of one of those motets scored only for high voices, presumably with the nuns in mind, the expressive juxtaposition of two major chords a third apart (G major versus E major, with G in the first chord shifting to G-sharp in the second). Vizzana particularly favored this very harmonic contrast, sometimes to heighten the meaning of individual words but equally often to intensify the prevailing mood of a passage. Indeed, she employs it in at least half of her own motets, occasionally several times in a single piece.

By 1599 this musical device had entered the general language of secular music, of course, particularly for expressive ends. We need not look far to find it in the later madrigal repertory, for example. In the sacred repertory of the early 1600s, which Vizzana is more likely to have known than secular madrigals, the gesture appears somewhat less commonly. Banchieri introduced it only three times in the whole of his 1599 *Messa solenne*, for example. He came to use it a little more liberally in his more diversified collections containing new-style motets for one or two soloists and basso continuo, which are more closely akin to Vizzana's motets.

Of these collections, *Nuovi pensieri ecclesiastici* strikes the listener as most self-consciously modern, both by its title and by its contents, which employ many of the contemporary devices common in Vizzana's works. This collection also happens to include a so-called *ghirlandetta* (little garland) of motets by other local organists, whom Banchieri describes as "the author's friends and loving companions." Two of the names are already familiar to us. Ercole Porta dedicated music to Cleria Pepoli of Santa Cristina in 1613. The other is Ottavio Vernizzi, whom Banchieri singles out as "the author's most cordial friend." As we have seen, Vernizzi served as the unauthorized *maestro di musica* at Santa Cristina and therefore probably as Lucrezia Vizzana's teacher. In the years when Banchieri was experimenting with the modern sacred style, Vernizzi published three collections that include several works for a few soloists and basso continuo, which further corroborate these two men's mutual artistic influence.

Thus, we find three musical friends (Banchieri, Vernizzi, and Porta), all connected to Santa Cristina, who between 1604 and 1613 were all experimenting with the *stile moderno*, exchanging motets in that style, and publishing one or more collections containing such works. Of the three, Vernizzi can most easily be placed on the musical scene at Santa Cristina over a period of years. In 1623 the abbess of Santa Cristina remarked that as part of Vernizzi's duties the *maestro di musica* also "composes some pieces to play, that is, songs [*canzoni*] and the like."[8] He might have been the one to extend this musical circle to include, indirectly, his probable pupil, the talented student composer from Santa Cristina, who was trying her hand at similar works during those same years.

The motets of Vernizzi and Banchieri could not have represented the farthest boundary of Lucrezia Vizzana's musical world, however. Vizzana's most strikingly expressive motif—that leap in the vocal line away from a dissonance against the bass—was apparently too bold for the sacred works of this pair of Bolognese organist-composers. Her notable leaps away from dissonances remained much less common in the sacred repertory generally than the juxtaposed major chords mentioned earlier. Yet the device appears in as many as six of Vizzana's twenty motets.

Such expressive setting of text inevitably calls to mind Claudio Monteverdi, the most distinguished composer known for untoward dissonances in his works. Monteverdi's *Vespers* (1610) offers some precedent for Vizzana's attempts at expressivity, including one identical use of her favorite leap from a dissonance in the opening section of his *Audi coelum*.

Another example appears at the opening of Monteverdi's five-part *Christe, adoramus te* (1620). But even in Monteverdi's sacred works this technique of leaping away from dissonances is rare. His more common uses of this gesture occur, not in the sacred works from the early 1600s, but in his madrigals and in the extremely influential *Lamento d'Arianna*.

The possibility of tracing Monteverdi's influence becomes problematic when the proposed imitator is a woman immured behind a Bolognese convent wall. Could the cloistered Lucrezia Orsina Vizzana have learned this expressive language from Monteverdi? Could the unusual idiom of his madrigals somehow have intruded as a source for her dissonant leaps?

Monteverdi was obviously well known to Bolognese musicians. Indeed, his irregular dissonance treatment drew the fire of the old-fashioned Bolognese music theorist Giovanni Maria Artusi (as every music history student knows). Adriano Banchieri, however, in his *Conclusioni nel suono dell'organo* (Conclusions on organ playing; 1609), commented that "when the words in compositions call for breaking the rules, this must be done in order to imitate the word"; he then singled out "the most gentle composer of music, Claudio Monteverdi, with regard to modern composition. His artful sentiments in truth are worthy of complete commendation, uncovering every affective part of perfect speech, diligently explained and imitated by appropriate harmony."[9]

More significant for our purposes, when Banchieri founded his musical Accademia dei Floridi in 1614, he stipulated that the motet or sacred madrigal by Lassus or Palestrina, whose performance he required at each weekly meeting, could be replaced by "one of those madrigals by that most gentle of composers, Claudio Monteverdi, *which have been changed into motets* by Aquilino Coppini, by request of the Most Illustrious Cardinal Federico Borromeo."[10] Thanks to Coppini, many of Monteverdi's most renowned madrigals were sanctified by replacing their original and occasionally notoriously secular Italian texts with sacred Latin words ("Ah kisses, ah mouth, ah tongue" from *Si ch'io vorrei morire* thus became "O Jesus, my light, my hope" in the textually purified *Iesu mea vita*).

Something that began as a madrigal—even a rather racy one—was thus not necessarily beyond a nun's ken. Some of Coppini's pious retextings were in fact conceived with nuns in mind, for one volume was explicitly dedicated to a Milanese nun.[11] Virtually all the Monteverdi madrigals-made-motets, heard at the musical gatherings of Banchieri and his friends, came from Monteverdi's experimental madrigal books 4 and 5, particularly notorious for their dissonant transgressions against contrapuntal rules.

Monteverdi himself also had ongoing personal contacts within Bologna during the years we are considering. Not only did his sanctified madrigals have an honored place in Banchieri's weekly academies, but their composer was feted at a meeting of the group in 1620. The year before Banchieri's academy honored him he had also visited the city to settle his musical son, Francesco, as a law student in the city. In late January and early February 1619 father and son stayed at the monastery of Santa Maria dei Servi (fig. 2, no. 5), a little over five minutes' walk around the corner and up the street from Santa Cristina della Fondazza. During that time the nuns might well have been preparing with Ottavio Vernizzi the music for the feast of the founder of their order, Saint Romuald, celebrated on 7 February.[12] Perhaps Monteverdi might even have attended.

It is very tempting to suggest that Banchieri's or Vernizzi's greatest musical gift to Lucrezia Orsina Vizzana, who obviously could not have joined the group of men at the Accademia dei Floridi, was not to present the convent with their own attempts at the *stile moderno* but to introduce Vizzana to the music of Claudio Monteverdi. At this point, however, that second of Banchieri's Bolognese "friends and loving companions" steps forward to provide the closing link in the chain of influence: Ercole Porta, who had also dedicated his *Vaga ghirlanda* (1613) to a nun at Santa Cristina, despite his primary employment farther afield in the Bolognese suburb of San Giovanni in Persiceto. In 1620 Porta published *Sacro convito musicale*, in which several compositions suggest a particular fascination with Monteverdi's music. The works in this collection turn out to be more self-consciously modern in their musical detail than Banchieri's or Vernizzi's. The solos and duets reveal a boldness of harmony and flights of ornamentation that must reflect Porta's own encounters with the works of Monteverdi. In six of these motets Porta experiments with the boldest musical gesture also employed by Vizzana: that leap away from a suspended dissonance in the voice. Unequivocally confirming his debt to Monteverdi, Porta actually borrows, reworks, and resets one of the same Latin texts that Coppini had created for a Monteverdi madrigal: *Ure me Domine amore tuo.*

Unfortunately for us, no comparable musicological "smoking gun" emerges to demonstrate without a doubt whether it was the Monteverdi madrigals made into motets by Coppini or the Monteverdi style as filtered through Ercole Porta that most directly shaped Lucrezia Vizzana's musical choices. But clearly, Bolognese experiments in the *stile moderno* were not limited to the better-known, more regularly studied male musical preserve around San Petronio and the cathedral. They were also pursued more discreetly behind the cloister wall on via Fondazza, where they have long been overlooked and until recently forgotten. Indeed, we discover intriguingly that some of the boldest attempts to adapt the gestures of the *stile moderno* for sacred use came out of the aesthetically "marginal" environment of a convent and were composed by a Bolognese woman whose only exposure to that style would have occurred indirectly, illicitly, and at a considerable distance.

Lucrezia Vizzana's *Componimenti musicali*, published early in 1623, was the fifth and final musical collection dedicated to the nuns of Santa Cristina and effectively marks the close of the most musically illustrious period in the convent's history. After 1623, though Vizzana lived another forty years, this imaginative and, as it turns out, notably bold composer never again published any music. Whether she continued to compose is impossible to say—the remnants of Santa Cristina's archive offer absolutely nothing to enlighten us. Indeed, not a single word in surviving, original convent documents testifies to Lucrezia's musical talents.[13] Still, we are lucky to glimpse as much as we can of her musical world, a world that its regulators did their best to keep so emphatically private. On 1 January 1623 Lucrezia Vizzana dedicated her *Componimenti musicali* to her fellow nuns at Santa Cristina. It was a fitting choice, for the special nature of the hidden world they shared helped her creativity to flower in ways that would have been largely impossible for her beyond the convent walls on via Fondazza.

FOUR

Hearing Lucrezia Vizzana's Voice

"Sponsa Verbi"

"In the beginning was the Word. . . . And the Word was made flesh and dwelt among us." The opening of John's Gospel remained at the heart of both Lucrezia Vizzana's artistic creativity and her spirituality. Daily, weekly, and yearly repetitions of scripture, liturgy, the words of the church fathers—and, if the ecclesiastical hierarchy had its way, very little else—marked the rhythms of a nun's life. Vizzana must have found in these words a living vocabulary in a way that composers simultaneously active in both the church and the world would not have done. Nuns lived their lives with a restricted repertory of verbal and intellectual stimuli. Although Santa Cristina perhaps did not exactly fit the pious ideals of either Saint Romuald or the post-Tridentine hierarchy, most of Vizzana's experience of art, music, and life must have been constructed around and filtered almost exclusively through the language of scripture and the liturgy. This *sponsa Christi* (bride of Christ) might, in the words of the eleventh-century Jean de Fécamp (addressed to another nun), also be called *sponsa Verbi* (bride of the Word).[1]

Rhetorically heightened by her musical language, the texts of Vizzana's *Componimenti musicali* reveal connections with female spirituality, Santa Cristina's monastic environment, and the cultural flowering that occurred there during the early 1600s. Little concrete evidence (e.g., archival documentation) survives to help us know Lucrezia Vizzana.

The best window into the spiritual world she inhabited, one that has practically vanished in later centuries, is therefore her music, which probably tells us more about her than any other available evidence.

Vizzana takes her texts seriously, and the music suggests that she accepted what they would have implied. If we are to discover something of her world, we must take her texts and their music as seriously as she did. She invites us (as, in fact, do other composers of her age) to pay attention to the wide resonance of those words as well as to the musical gestures that capture their affective spirit and bring them more fully to life. If we do not share for a few moments, at least, some measure of Vizzana's commitment to the enterprise of wedding music to words in order to uncover levels of musical and textual meaning, while we may still hear echoes of her voice, we will not hear her speak.

More than half the texts in *Componimenti musicali* have yet to come to light in other sources. Other motets reuse older texts in ways that suggest they bear specific relevance to Vizzana's life and/or the spiritual life at Santa Cristina. At least half a dozen of her works probably relate directly to the convent's liturgical life. As many as eight pose Jesus as listener, not surprising for a community of brides of Christ. Almost as many motets might relate to the precarious situation in which the convent was embroiled when *Componimenti musicali* appeared and which might even have partly motivated its publication.

Of course, it is perfectly possible that the unique texts that Vizzana sets may have been created within her convent's walls. Their rhetorical wordplay based on scripture would not have been out of place at Santa Cristina, which was among Bologna's leading convents in the cultivation of Latin. The most distinguished rhetorician at Santa Cristina was in fact Lucrezia Vizzana's aunt, the venerable donna Flaminia Bombacci, praised for "the fluency of her tongue and pen; for, having joined to the sincerity of her circumspect eloquence the knowledge of the Latin language, she spoke beyond the ordinary capacity of her sex and composed most learned sermons and spiritual discourses." The same was reputedly true of her niece, for Vizzana's memorial in the convent necrology records that "she was likewise so gifted in Latin and Italian that she won the admiration of most eloquent and learned men."[2]

"Cuius Mihi Organa Modulatis Vocibus Cantant"

There is something self-conscious about the frequency with which Vizzana's collection invokes the acts of singing and playing. Only one of the six texts for Vizzana's motets that refer to music is not rare and most likely unique to her collection. When Vizzana causes two sopranos to conclude *O invictissima Christi martir* with the words "Ut cantare possimus. Alleluia" (that we may sing. Alleluia), when the soloist of *Confiteantur tibi Domine* exhorts "cantate et psallite" (sing and play the psaltery), when sopranos sing "cuius mihi organa modulatis vocibus cantant" (whose instruments sing to me with harmonious voices) in *Amo Christum*, or when two sopranos open another duet with "Omnes gentes cantate Domino" (Sing unto the Lord all ye people)—in each of these cases, the composer highlights a widely recognized distinction of Santa Cristina, one that particularly set it apart from the twenty-three other convents in Bologna.

Vizzana's more general motets could have served on any number of liturgical occasions for rejoicing or expressing communal enthusiasm. One of them, *Domine Dominus noster, quam admirabile est nomen tuum* (O Lord, our Lord, how admirable is Thy name; *SED*, track 17), happens to be prescribed in the Camaldolese Breviary for the vigil of the Ascension. This is the scene commemorated in Ludovico Carracci's monumental painting that the young Vizzana possibly saw before its installation above the high altar of the new external church (fig. 9). Vizzana's relatively "monumental" setting for two sopranos, alto, and basso continuo accompaniment, the second-most elaborate motet in her collection, suggests that it was intended for an important context. So perhaps the feast of the Ascension, Carracci's painting, or even its installation on the high altar in 1608 could have prompted the motet's composition.

Other motets also appear to be specially conceived for particular feasts in the convent's liturgical life, and these, too, are reflected in visual art installed throughout Santa Cristina. Both musical and visual art link up most directly to the space where the convent met the world, Santa Cristina's external church, which during these years underwent dramatic expansion and artistic adornment. *O invictissima Christi martir* (O Christ's most invincible martyr; *SED*, track 9; *CNC*, track 11) addresses Saint Christina, who appears in numerous images in the church and cloister that bear her name (see figs. 7, 11, 25, 30, 32) and who was venerated in her own chapel in the external church. The great stucco statue of the saint must have been installed in its niche in the nave during the years when Vizzana was composing, and she obviously wrote this motet for the convent's matronal festival on 10 May, the most lavish feast of the church year for the convent and its parish.[3]

The more opulent scoring of *Protector noster* (Our protector; *SED*, track 4; *CNC*, track 13), Vizzana's only work for four voices, suggests its creation for another major festival. Vizzana might have intended it to honor either of the two most important saints of the Camaldolese order: Saint Benedict or Saint Romuald. The nuns of Santa Cristina likewise celebrated both founders' feasts with music. A pair of large stucco statues of these saints stood opposite one other in the external church. And just as Santa Cristina's image turns up at various places, these saints' images appear in the convent's oldest altarpieces, which were moved to the new church in the years after Lucrezia Vizzana's arrival: Saint Benedict figures prominently in Francia's *Nativity* (fig. 8), and Saint Romuald takes his place among the figures in Salviati's *Madonna and Child with Saints* (fig. 7).

In *Componimenti musicali*, *Filii Syon exultate* (Rejoice, sons of Zion; *SED*, track 1) immediately precedes *O invictissima Christi martir*, *Domine, Dominus noster*, and *Protector noster*. While this piece might seem to be a more generalized exaltation of saints ("for this day earth is made heaven for us, not by stars falling from heaven to earth, but by saints ascending into heaven"), the text's central theme recalls one of the most striking stories from Camaldolese tradition: "Saint Romuald's dream" of a ladder to heaven (fig. 14). Blessed Rudolph, prior of Camaldoli, described how Saint Romuald had come to found the hermitage there:

When he came to the region in the countryside around Arezzo, he wished to discover a suitable site. He encountered a man named Maldulus, who said he had a pleasant field, located up in the mountains. Once, as he [Maldulus] slept there, he saw a ladder like the one of the Patriarch Jacob, raised up so that its top almost touched the heavens, on which a host of people, resplendent and robed in white, seemed to ascend. When he [Romuald] heard this, the man of God, as if enlightened by a divine oracle, thereupon sought out the field, saw the place, and built the cells on that site.

Vizzana's *Filii Syon exultate* may well commemorate this important moment for her order, when "earth is made heaven for us."

The opening of *Ornaverunt faciem templi* (They decorated the front of the temple with wreaths of gold, and dedicated the altar to the Lord; *SED*, track 15) suggests that it was prompted by the building and decoration of the external church, which coincided with Lucrezia Vizzana's most musically productive years. Thus, this motet could fittingly have been performed a number of times during the twenty years before its publication, as the church of Santa Cristina was transformed into one of Bologna's most artistically distinguished convent churches.

Amo Christum (I love Christ; *SED*, track 13) must connect to the most lavish and rarest of all Santa Cristina's—and Bologna's—convent

FIGURE 14. Pseudo-Jacopino, *The Dream of Saint Romuald* (c. 1340). In the painting Saint Romuald receives credit for the dream. The painting quite likely originated at Santa Cristina. Reproduced with permission of the Pinacoteca Nazionale di Bologna.

ceremonies, the ritual consecration of virgins. The opening segment of its text clearly seems to suggest a nun's consecration:

Amo Christum in cuius thalamum introibo, cuius Mater virgo est, cuius pater feminam nescit, cuius mihi organa modulatis vocibus cantant, quem cum amavero casta sum, cum tetigero munda sum, cum accepero virgo sum; annulo suo subharravit me, et immensis monilibus ornavit me, et tanquam sponsam decoravit me corona. Alleluia.

I love Christ, whose bedchamber I shall enter, whose mother is a virgin, whose father knows not woman, whose instruments sing to me with harmonious voices, whom when I will have loved I will be chaste, when I will have touched I will be clean, when I will have received him I will be a virgin; with his ring he has betrothed me and adorned me with countless gems, and with a crown he has adorned me as a spouse. Alleluia.

The concluding phrases almost certainly confirm this likely purpose, for according to the Roman pontifical, "He has adorned me with countless gems" ends the Gregorian chant that a consecrand sings after receiving her crown. "With a ring he has betrothed me" and "with a crown he has adorned me as a spouse" both appear in the chant the nun sings with her hand raised high to display the ring she has just received (figs. 26–27).

The theme of this motet also resonates with the subject matter shown in an altarpiece installed in the external church at about the same time. Santa Cristina's prominent musician, Emilia Grassi, paid for Bernardino Baldi's *Coronation of the Virgin* (fig. 11). Depictions of the Virgin Mary's coronation were relatively uncommon in Bolognese convent altarpieces, yet the theme was particularly appropriate for nuns, as it exalts virginity and reveres the coronation of God's spouse. At the turn of the fifteenth century, theologian Jean Gerson had claimed that virgins "sing a new song. You will be singled out and crowned with a divine crown in paradise. You are queen of the earth and heaven by your ardent song of contemplation."[4] The theme that Gerson applied to all virgins would have been particularly apt to the musical nuns of Santa Cristina and especially to the composer of new music among them.

Santa Cristina's singularly lavish consecration rite, unlike any other Bolognese convent ritual, was also effectively a coronation. Santa Cristina staged this final rite of passage for its nuns only every ten years or so; ecclesiastical law permitted only women who had reached the age of twenty-five to attain the status. Its symbolic importance for the nuns of Santa Cristina will become especially apparent in later chapters. Apart from its other trappings, this sumptuous ceremony was particularly notable for music performed by the nun consecrands. At Santa Cristina their music could be especially elaborate. For the only time in their lives as nuns, the young women were not only heard but actually seen by others in the external church during the rite, which traditionally required them to leave the cloister and process through the public courtyard and down the aisle of the public church to receive their crowns.

Santa Cristina's rule required a nun to complete this ceremony before she could assume high convent office. Even so, the convent celebrated this ritual only twice between 1600 and 1620. For her part, Lucrezia Orsina had scarcely donned her professed nun's veil before she and her sister petitioned the Sacred Congregation of Bishops and Regulars in March 1607 for permission to participate in their convent's first enactment of this lavish rite since 1599. At the time of the petition, Lucrezia Orsina had not even turned eighteen, and Isabetta had barely reached her twenties. Nonetheless, Isabetta's request was granted. Lucrezia seems to have padded her age by over a year in the request, but the Congregation of Bishops deemed her simply too young. Refusing to take no for an answer, the younger sister promptly petitioned again and claimed that the consecration was "nothing else but a ceremony to confirm one's profession." Yet the congregation remained adamant, so Lucrezia languished for a while as Santa Cristina's only unconsecrated *professa*.

In the end, she had to wait six full years, until late in 1613, for the next consecration to occur. Because she still had not reached twenty-five, she petitioned the Congregation of Bishops once again for special permission to participate. Once again they denied her request at first. Unwilling to languish longer, Lucrezia quickly laid her complaint directly before the pope, suggesting that the congregation "did not wish to hear her and therefore forced her to seek refuge at the feet of Your Holiness." Her petition passed from the top of the ecclesiastical pecking order to Cardinal Antonio Zapata y Cisneros (Spain's protector general to the Holy See and sometime Inquisitor of Rome). Upon the cardinal's recommendation, the Congregation of Bishops finally relented on 15 October 1613, though even then Vizzana admitted that she remained twenty-two months shy of twenty-five.[5] We can be quite certain that the congregation heard *Amo Christum* at donna Lucrezia Orsina's ritual consecration not long thereafter, when she stepped for a few hours into the world outside the convent wall for the last time. As she received her crown or raised her hand to display her ring, the congregation not only had Vizzana's motet in their ears and Baldi's *Coronation of the Virgin* before their eyes but could also admire Vizzana and the other virgin consecrands face-to-face, a prospect that would vex Bolognese archbishops for generations.

"O Dulcedo Deitatis"

The primary subject that receives pride of place in *Componimenti musicali* is the human and divine person of Jesus. It should come as no surprise that the figure of Jesus as mediator/redeemer and spouse, present in the Sacrament or on the cross, would eclipse all other subjects in a nun's expression of her devotion, given the special relationship between Jesus and his chosen brides, a relationship enforced and reinforced on both sides of the convent wall.[6]

The composer attends especially to two closely related aspects of her relationship to her heavenly spouse: Christ as present in the Eucharist at the altar and Christ suffering on the cross. Vizzana's musical preoccupation with Jesus in the Sacrament figures particularly in *O si sciret stultus mundus* (Oh, if the foolish world knew; *SED*, track 14) and *Veni dulcissime Domine* (Come, sweetest Lord; *SED*, track 2). Each of these pieces resonates with one of the most important themes of post-Tridentine art, a theme particularly objectionable to Protestants and a topic debated extensively at Trent: the mystery of transubstantiation. Vizzana's preoccupation, however, also reflects the personal influence of her aunt Flaminia Bombacci, who was particularly devoted to the Sacrament. As abbess she inspired a renewed devotion to the Eucharist in many of her charges. In 1622 one nun from Santa Cristina commented that "at the present time the nuns frequent the Sacraments more than they ever have."[7]

Among the Jesus-centric motets, *Veni dulcissime Domine* ("Come, sweetest Lord, come immaculate sacrificial victim, come bread of fasting. . . . Behold, I come to you . . . whose body and blood I yearn to receive") almost certainly served as a motet for the Elevation of the Host, the moment during the Mass that commemorates the miracle of Christ become flesh in the Communion bread. As the priest raised the Host, which became visible to the nuns in their inner chapel through the window above the altar in the external church, the solo singer of Vizzana's motet reiterated the urgent "Come!" no fewer than eighteen times: the musical language and its message are direct and clear.

O si sciret (example 2), on the other hand, seems the most rhetorical and "artificial" exposition of the Eucharistic theme in the collection. It expresses a longing for the world's illumination, which could be obtained, in the author's view, only from Christ's nourishing flesh in the Sacrament.

EXAMPLE 2. Lucrezia Vizzana, *O si sciret stultus mundus*

O si sciret stultus mundus
Cibus quantus sit iucundus
Carnes mei Domini
Fatigatus non sederet
Panem sanctum manducaret
Cum fervore fervido.
Quaeret panem. Vinum mixtum
Aqua, Jesum Christum,
Non videtur quaerere.
Quaerat ergo quidquid placet.

EXAMPLE 2. *(continued)*

Meum cor solum delectet
Amor Jesu quaerere.

Oh, if the foolish world knew
What delightful nourishment
The flesh of my Lord is,
Though weary, it [the world] would not sit idle,

EXAMPLE 2. *(continued)*

But it would eat the holy bread
With burning ardor.
It seeks [earthly] bread. The wine mixed
With water, Jesus Christ,
It seems not to seek.
Let it therefore seek whatever pleases.
Let my heart delight only
In seeking the love of Jesus.

From the opening notes of her setting of *O si sciret*, Vizzana's music illuminates this text in her most rhetorical and artifice-laden manner. Let us consider how she accomplishes this feat.

Her first musical gesture is the most extreme. With an unorthodox leap away from the voice's first dissonance over the bass, the composer wittingly violates traditional rules of sixteenth-century counterpoint. Then the instrumental bass accompaniment refuses to descend a step from D to C, as the harmony predicts and as the listener expects. Instead, the bass leaps immediately upward to f-sharp, almost colliding with an f-natural that the singer has only just abandoned. Now launching itself through an octave run upward, the voice repeats its opening, unconventional leap from a dissonance; but the composer transposes the leap here onto a higher pitch. Vizzana usually associated this unorthodox melodic figure with anguish or longing for an absent object of desire. Here she uses it to make explicit a longing that reaches beyond the bounds of meaning implicit in the opening words alone, "Oh, if the foolish world knew."

The object of such intense desire becomes immediately apparent in the second line: there Vizzana's direct juxtaposition of two major chords with conflicting accidentals—a favorite technique—shows at once that this *cibus* is no ordinary food. The harmonic transformation, which in Vizzana's other works underlines various physical or spiritual transformations, becomes a momentary symbol for the miracle of transubstantiation, Christ becoming fleshly food, in anticipation of "Carnes mei Domini" (The flesh of my Lord) in the next line. The plethora of half steps in both voice and bass, urgently yearning to resolve at "Cibus quantus sit jucundus" (What delightful nourishment this is), likewise hints at pleasures of great intensity: this gesture seeks to transform itself from something often associated with secular longing into something sanctified.

The musical setting provides a moment-to-moment commentary on the text by making those words linked most intimately to Jesus as heavenly food and physical body stand out emphatically. After scrambling busily through quicker notes for "Fatigatus non sederet./Panem sanctum" (Though weary, it [the world] would not sit idle. But [it would eat] the holy bread), the voice pauses abruptly for three beats near the top of its range at *manducaret* (would eat), lending a moment of profound stillness before it launches into two and a half bars of ecstatic rapture, unparalleled in the piece thus far.

At "Quaret panem" (It seeks bread) Vizzana captures humankind's desperate search for earthly bread by making the bass frantically chase the voice. Then, at "Vinum mixtum/Aqua, Jesum Christum" (The wine mixed with water, Jesus Christ) musical time virtually stops again, this time for the mention of the Eucharist's second element. The composer delicately and languidly resolves another affective, sustained dissonance in the voice above the expressive descent by a half step in the bass. After a short, trickling melisma of several notes on *aqua*, the voice pauses at the bottom of its range this time, on the words "Jesus Christ," for two bars of a chord warmed by the singer's sweet major third above the bass.

Vizzana's noteworthy musical treatment of the word *manducaret*, meaning literally "would chew," reflects centuries-old emphasis in female spirituality on the earthly physicality of Christ's real presence in the Eucharist, described in earlier times as "eating God" by Mechtild of Magdeburg. Ida of Lovain experienced the taste and feel of Christ's flesh in her mouth just by reciting "Verbum caro factum est" (The Word was made flesh; John 1:14). She literally went mad for the Sacrament to the point where she had to be chained up. In Vizzana, the shift from one note per syllable to the ecstatic stream of notes on *manducaret* conveys a possibility of being caught up by the Eucharist into affectivity. Thus, this gesture strikingly recaptures late-medieval religious women's sense of release into mystical union with a human, literally "incarnate" Christ.[8]

Likewise, Vizzana's affectionate musical treatment of "vinum mixtum aqua" (wine mixed with water) highlights the priest's commingling of water and wine at the altar during the Mass. Here the music lingers reverently over the ancient sacramental connection to the physical mixing of blood and water that flowed downward (like the musical gesture itself) from Christ's wounded side at the Crucifixion (John 19:34). By musically emphasizing the word *aqua* Vizzana therefore hints at another traditional focus of female devotional intimacy with Christ: his side wound. The musical gesture of yearning that Vizzana sets for "wine mixed with water, Jesus Christ," echoes the intense preoccupation with Christ's blood and his side wound that regularly finds its way into the visions of earlier Italian mystics.[9] Angela of Foligno (1248–1309) not only reputedly drank from Christ's side herself but also witnessed his placing the heads of the friars who were her "spiritual sons" in his side wound. Early-modern artists depicted Catherine of Siena's "nursing" from Christ's side.[10] Through her musical gesture in this piece Lucrezia Vizzana renews the many resonances of this traditional symbol of female devotion.

One of Vizzana's most overt love songs to the heavenly spouse, *O magnum mysterium* (O great mystery; *SED*, track 16), intensifies and broadens our sense of the composer's preoccupation with this common theme of Christ-centered female spirituality. *O magnum mysterium* grows out of a quiet, meditative spirit (example 3).

O magnum mysterium, O profundissima vulnera, O passio acerbissima, O dulcedo deitatis, adiuva me ad aeternam felicitatem consequendam. Alleluia.

O great mystery, O deepest wounds, O most bitter passion, O sweetness of the Godhead, help me to the eternal happiness following therefrom. Alleluia.

This motet offers a meditative outpouring of the redemptive focus for women religious, Christ's suffering and the wounds of the Passion.

Within the cloister at Santa Cristina the nuns need not have looked far for iconographical images to encourage meditation on the Passion, which had recently assumed new significance in their devotions because of visual and ritual transformations there. The refectory, for example, had long displayed a compellingly beautiful fresco of the Crucifixion with saints at the foot of the cross. Art historians attribute it to the school of Francesco Francia (c. 1500), putatively to Timoteo Viti (fig. 15). In addition, every time the nuns turned left to ascend the main staircase near the parlatorios, an inescapable image confronted them. A starkly

EXAMPLE 3. Lucrezia Vizzana, *O magnum mysterium*

contrasting Crucifixion (fig. 16) of the same period as the refectory fresco imbues the scene with intense pathos rather than serenity.

According to records from 1634, there was also "a fair image of Our Lord that the nuns visit every Saturday for their regular devotions" in the cloister's upper gallery and a depiction of the Deposition within these same hallways. One of these works must have been the *Crocifisso di pietà* that the nuns claimed had "miraculously" appeared on Good Friday in 1613 or 1614, during Emilia Grassi's term as abbess. Lucrezia Vizzana would have gone in procession with the other nuns to visit it every Friday. There they recited three Our Fathers and three Hail Marys in remembrance of Christ's hours on the cross, and according to the church

EXAMPLE 3. *(continued)*

of their day, each of them gained an indulgence of a hundred days for every Friday that they did so. At the insistence of Emilia Grassi, it also became customary after meals to offer thanks in front of this image rather than in choir.[11]

As a potential source of other inspiration for Vizzana around this time, the tiny landing on the convent's narrow back stairs near the refectory and kitchen had been transformed into a little chapel in 1616 (fig. 23). A Man of Sorrows, possibly even older than that date, stands between two small windows. Below him and dated 1616, the Virgin of Consolation holds the baby Jesus close. A pedestal on each side of these figures depicts what appears to be Christ's Sacred Heart on display. Lunettes above contain scenes from the Passion. And above all these images, the dove of the Holy Spirit hovers on the vaulted ceiling.

The miraculous revelation of the *Crocifisso di pietà* in the cloister may have inspired Vizzana's *O magnum mysterium*, or the very affecting focus of devotion on the staircase landing (fig. 23) may have prompted its composition. Though a brief text, Vizzana clothes every phrase of *O magnum mysterium* in tropes from her most spiritually ardent musical vocabulary. She frames the triple invocation, "mysterium . . . vulnera . . . passio acerbissima" (mystery . . . wounds . . . most bitter passion) as a

FIGURE 15. School of Francesco Francia (Timoteo Viti?), *Crucifixion with Saints* (c. 1500), refectory of Santa Cristina della Fondazza (2011). Photograph: Luca Salvucci, Bologna.

study in cadential gestures that involve expressive melodic descents in the bass that are to some extent mirrored by similar descents in the vocal part. The triple invocation might possibly allude to the three Our Fathers and three Hail Marys and, thereby, recall the nuns' prayers on Fridays as they stood before the *Crocifisso di pietà*.

In any case, by comparable musical transformations Vizzana conveys urgency in the petition that succeeds the opening's contemplative stillness. The allusion to the "sweetness of the Godhead," which supplants

FIGURE 16. Anonymous, *Crucifixion with the Blessed Virgin, Saint John, and Mary Magdalene* (early 1500s), ground floor west corridor of the cloister of Santa Cristina della Fondazza (2011). Photograph: Luca Salvucci, Bologna.

the relatively static beginning with more forceful motion in both voice and accompaniment, also recalls one of the strongest images from the vocabulary of female mysticism regarding the Passion: "And then she was rapt in spirit before the Crucified, and looking on him, she immediately began to weep, sensing as a result of this sight extraordinary comfort and sweetness" ("Revelations and Miracles of Blessed Margarita of Faenza," c. 1300).

The taste of sweetness in the mouth was a standard motif of female spirituality that was obviously connected with receiving Christ's body in the mouth during the Eucharist. In the 1300s Agnes Blannbekin, for instance, assumed that all communicants tasted honeycomb.[12] In Vizzana's work, the word "sweetness" provokes almost inevitable upwardly resolving tones in the bass, a common musical trope of the day to signify amorous or ardent urgency.

The subsequent "adiuva me ad aeternam felicitatem consequendam" (help me to the eternal happiness following therefrom) overwhelms the listener, not only with Vizzana's boldest stroke of a supplicative leap away from a dissonant suspension in the voice for "help [me]," but also with juxtaposed chromatic chords at "happiness," all within the space of four bars. Only then does the motet dissolve and resolve into the ecstasy of "alleluia." The final burst of Vizzana's full expressive vocabulary in this motet thus seems to convey an intense desire to take on the sufferings of Christ's Passion.

"Quasi Cithare Citharizantium"

Surely Lucrezia Vizzana had some inkling about the singular nature of her musical talents and of her act of publishing her work. In the history of Italy to 1623, only ten other women composers (five of them nuns) are known to have published music.[13] In the second motet from Vizzana's collection, *Sonet vox tua in auribus cordis mei* (Let your voice sound in the ears of my heart; *SED*, track 10), she sounds the trumpet of music and focuses the listener's attention on it through the singer's "I," which must represent the composer herself as artist giving voice to this song (example 4). At some stage in the preparation of these pieces for publication, Vizzana may have conceived *Sonet vox tua* as the opening number. For in this exordium the poet-singer self-consciously justifies her act of composition and publication by invoking the source and inspiration of her art; her Muse is the "most beloved Jesus" himself:

Sonet vox tua in auribus cordis mei, amabilissime Jesu, et abundantia plenitudinis gratiae tuae superet abundantiam peccatorum meorum. Tunc enim cantabo, exsultabo, iubilabo, et psalmum dicam iubilationis et laetitiae. Et erit vox mea quasi cithare citharizantium et eloquium meum dulce super mel et favum.

Let your voice sound in the ears of my heart, most beloved Jesus, and let the abundance of your grace overcome the abundance of my sins. Then truly I will sing, I will

EXAMPLE 4. Lucrezia Vizzana, *Sonet vox tua*

exult, I will rejoice, I will recite a psalm of jubilation and rejoicing. And my voice will be like the striking of the kithara and my speech sweeter than honey and the honeycomb.

With words invoking any number of psalms, Vizzana calls directly upon Jesus to sing inside her, for from the time of Clement of Alexandria (d. c. 215) down to her own day, Jesus represented the new Orpheus, the singer of the "new song" of Christianity.[14] The speaker in Vizzana's text becomes the poet-singer as *sponsa Christi* (bride of Christ), who pleads to hear the voice of her beloved. Then, inspired by the abundance of Christ's grace, she can raise her own true voice to exult and jubilate.

Vizzana's concluding words, "dulce super mel et favum" (sweeter

EXAMPLE 4. *(continued)*

than honey and the honeycomb), resonate most sympathetically with Psalm 118:103, "How sweet are thy words unto my taste! Yea, sweeter than honey to my mouth." Literate in Latin, Vizzana might also have heard in such words the added play on *mellis* (of honey) versus *melos* (song). And it is *melos*, of course, that will make Vizzana's own *eloquium* (rhetorical eloquence) sweeter than honey and the honeycomb.

In her concluding emphasis upon *eloquium* (the word, speech, rhetorical eloquence), Vizzana leaves her audience's ears ringing with a

EXAMPLE 4. *(continued)*

theme that resonated sonorously for a self-aware, educated early-modern woman—particularly a cloistered one. The world had long regarded rhetoric and the art of oratory as useless, if not actually dangerous, pursuits for women. Francesco Barbaro affirmed in 1416 that woman achieved "eloquence" through silence: "Women should believe that they have achieved the glory of eloquence if they honor themselves with the outstanding ornament of silence. Neither the applause of a declamatory play nor the glory and adoration of an assembly is required of them, but all that is desired of them is eloquent, well-considered and dignified silence." Considerably more bluntly, yet perhaps in tune with his society's fears, Nicolò Barbo put it: "An eloquent woman is never chaste."[15]

These views of the larger society were especially important—and particularly constraining—for women religious. A mid-fifteenth-century English guide for anchoresses, *De institutione inclusarum* (On the instruction of enclosed women; c. 1162), proclaimed that chastity required the avoidance of "the conversation of the world."[16] Can it be anything other than just such an equation of chastity with silence that found emphatic reinforcement four centuries later in the post-Tridentine emphasis on the separation and silence of monastic enclosure?

In that climate and not long after Ludovico Ludovisi's explicit bans on music within convents, for Lucrezia Vizzana to publish her motets must have seemed an especially audacious act. Through publication, not only did her music breach the convent wall when it sounded from Santa Cristina's choir lofts, but now, in print, her motets could scale the walls of Bologna and the church itself.

Like other religious women bold enough to make themselves heard, Vizzana adopts a time-honored ploy. She begins with a textual conceit linked to the biblical metaphor of the heart, both as the internal center of what is most personally defining and as the seat of forces that come specifically from deep within rather than more superficially from without. The musician Vizzana calls upon her heavenly spouse to let his voice "sound in the ears of my heart." Like female mystics of previous centuries, she implies that her authorization to speak, and to speak rhetorically, thus derives from that divine inner voice, which sanctifies it.

Vizzana's trumpet-like musical setting of these opening words, in which the instrumental bass creates a fanfare of thirds, recalls the venerable belief that the prophet was the trumpet of God, a tradition that included Hildegard of Bingen (d. 1179; the mystic is like a trumpet that "merely produces sounds but does not cause them; someone else blows into it, so that it will produce sound") and Mother Juana de la Cruz (d. 1534; God "spoke in an audible voice, as when the musician plays, it is not his own voice that sounds, but the voice of the flute or trumpet by means of the breath that he blows through it").

Roused by this initial empowerment by the voice of Jesus sounding within, Vizzana has little choice but to respond both personally and affirmatively: "Then truly I will sing, I will exult, I will rejoice, I will recite a psalm of jubilation and rejoicing." Proceeding from this declaration of grace and intent, the text concludes with a clause in which the first words "Erit vox mea" echo the opening "Sonet vox tua," as donna Lucrezia's voice makes audible that holy and beloved inner voice, "quasi cithare citharizantium" (like the striking of the kithara).

The characterization "quasi cithare citharizantium" further illuminates Vizzana's awareness of her relationship to an older tradition. The prophet or mystic as a stringed instrument was as venerable a concept as the trumpet metaphor. As he did with the imagery of Christ as singer of the new song, Clement of Alexandria likewise expressed this image of the prophet fourteen hundred years earlier: "Let the kithara be taken to mean the mouth, played by the Spirit as if by a plectrum. 'Praise him on strings and the instrument' refers to our body as an instrument and its sinews as strings from which it derives its harmonious tension, and when strummed by the Spirit it gives off human notes."[17] It is possible that Vizzana came to the phrase "cithare citharizantium" via a commentator on this prophetic tradition. However, we can be almost certain that she heard the terminology in Giovanni Battista Cesena's *Compieta con letanie*, dedicated to the nuns of Santa Cristina. The text of the motet *Cantabant sancti canticum novum* (The saints were singing a new song; *CNC*, track 1) from Cesena's collection is based primarily on Revelation 14:2 and 3. But it employs language resonant with the same imagery Vizzana uses in *Sonet vox tua*, especially the mention of the kithara:

Cantabant sancti canticum novum, alleluia; ante sedem Dei et Agni, alleluia; et resonabat terra in voces illorum, alleluia. Et audivi voces illorum sicut citharedorum citharizantium in citharis suis. Alleluia.

The saints were singing a new song, alleluia, before the throne of God and the Lamb, alleluia, and the earth resounded with their voices, alleluia. And I heard their voices like the kithara playing of singers upon their kitharas. Alleluia.

The composite text seems remarkably apt for Cesena's dedicatees. Cesena focuses upon the acts of singing and playing, for which the nuns were renowned. By analogy with the apocalyptic singers of Revelation, those at Santa Cristina could not be defiled by that which came from their mouths; they were virgins and in their mouths no falsehood could be found, for they were without stain. This allusion to Revelation could only further affirm Vizzana's musical eloquence as well as that of the convent singers who performed her works, despite abiding suspicion of female eloquence and—within the Bolognese diocesan hierarchy—of any convent music and every convent singer.

But for Vizzana, "quasi cithare citharizantium" might also have represented an apt metaphor not only for her mind-body as composer-performer, played by the deity, but also for her own identification with the suffering Christ as kithara. For the body, particularly that of Christ, could displace the kithara as an instrument of spiritual melody, as Saint John Chrysostom (d. c. 400) observed: "Here there is no need of the kithara, nor taut strings, nor the plectrum and technique, nor any sort of instrument; but if you wish, make of yourself a kithara, by mortifying the limbs of the flesh and creating full harmony between body and soul. For when the flesh does not lust against the spirit, but yields to its commands, and perseveres along the path that is noble and admirable, you thus produce a spiritual melody."[18] In *The Mystical Vine* Saint Bonaventure (d. 1274) expressed this relationship between Christ's suffering body, the kithara, and the female monastic: "Your Spouse has become a Harp [i.e., kithara], the wood of the cross being the frame and His body, extended on the wood, representing the chords."[19]

Lucrezia Vizzana need not have looked outside the convent at all for a model for the imitation of Christ's suffering. She grew up in the shadow of her most obvious spiritual model, the venerable Flaminia Bombacci, who "subdued the rebellions of her body with sackcloth, with scourges, and with frequent fasting, so that its resistance to the number of such torments seemed marvelous." Vizzana was blessed with bodily sufferings that were not self-induced. In the year *Componimenti musicali* went to press, she claimed that "on feast days everyone gets up for matins, but I do not get up because I am unwell." The convent necrology also recorded that "she did not seek in vain from her immortal spouse the gift, the stone of purgatory in this mortal life. For afterward she endured infirmity and, in fact, the burden of greater misfortunes, with admirable patience, with a cheerful spirit, and virile fortitude, as if the burden had fallen straight from heaven." The necrologist further recorded that "increasingly severe illness deprived her of highest monastic office."[20] With the phrase "cithare citharizantium," perhaps Vizzana sought to affirm not only her musical gifts and divine inspirations but also the gift of lifelong earthly sufferings, her own *imitatio Christi* (imitation of Christ).

Finally, in *Sonet vox tua* Vizzana may have incorporated the personal significance of her response to a favorite text of convent spirituality, Song of Songs 2:14. There would have been special reasons why the first and only musical nun in Bologna ever to venture into print would be drawn to the whole of the verse from the Song of Songs where the phrase "Sonet vox tua" appears:

Columba mea in foraminibus petrae in caverna maceriae ostende mihi faciem tuam *sonet vox tua in auribus meis vox enim tua dulcis* et facies tua decora.

O my dove, in the clefts of the rock, in the hollow of the walls, show your face to me, *let your voice sound in my ears, for your voice is sweet* and your face is fair.

Vizzana's motet not only offers a ringing response to the first half of verse 14 but also a justification for her public voice. Her own musical rhetoric boldly reaches out to the world, while the singers of Santa Cristina present these words in a musical idiom, not merely sweet, but sweeter than honey and the honeycomb. Yet, while Vizzana's published music will meet the public gaze, her face and the faces of the other nuns remain unseen, as they sing, like the dove of Song of Songs 2:14, hidden "in the clefts of the rock, within the hollow of the walls."

Lucrezia Vizzana's *Componimenti musicali* thus reflects many of the most illustrious moments in the liturgical, artistic, and devotional life at Santa Cristina and also, perhaps, the composer's own, personal religious concerns. Other motets than those we have considered in this chapter may allude to a darker side of convent life and offer some of the first hints of decline at Santa Cristina. The illustrious musical tradition that helped Lucrezia Vizzana's creativity to flower in ways largely impossible beyond the convent wall may also be implicated in political conflicts festering within the convent for years, as well as in the world outside its walls. Such strife may have silenced Vizzana, and it certainly changed Santa Cristina forever. To the history of these rifts, music's alleged place in them, and their relationship to *Componimenti musicali* we turn in the next chapter.

FIVE

Troubles in an Earthly Paradise: "It Began because of Music"

On the vigil of the feast of Saint Thomas the Apostle, 20 December 1622, just a week before Lucrezia Vizzana signed the dedication to *Componimenti musicali*, at a time when the nuns should have been preparing to celebrate the feast of the Nativity, Bolognese Suffragan Bishop Angelo Gozzadini, Camaldolese visitor don Desiderio Bardelloni da Monza, Bolognese nuns' vicar don Giovanni Bondini, and the episcopal notary appeared at Santa Cristina on the direct order of Cardinal Ludovico Ludovisi. Twenty-seven-year-old Ludovisi had become archbishop of Bologna just the previous year, a month after his uncle, Pope Gregory XV, named him cardinal on the day after the pope's coronation.

Ludovisi's deputies were there on the gravest sort of church business. Four months earlier a letter had reached the powerful cardinal nephew in Rome. Devout, scandalized—but anonymous—nuns from Santa Cristina alleged that many sisters no longer bothered with services and ridiculed any who fasted and revered the Sacraments; several kept animals for personal gain; others, not content with their own cells, had expropriated the public rooms as their private quarters; the novices lived in fear of their mistress, who knew nothing of strict observance; the nuns in authority squandered communal funds, then refused to open the books for inspection by outside administrators; many flouted the dress code by wearing added frills and bits of finery and claimed that fasting would mar their complexions. Most troubling were the comments "Chastity—I would not speak of it out of respect" and "an investigation without the threat of papal excommunication will serve no purpose."[1]

Pastoral visitations customarily took place in a convent parlatorio, with interrogators outside the grates that marked the boundary of *clausura* and the nuns on the other side. But Suffragan Bishop Gozzadini claimed that "the nuns could not be properly and secretly questioned in the parlatorio" and therefore moved his entire party inside the cloister, where he commandeered the end of the infirmary (fig. 3, J) for his interrogations.

It was also customary to begin with the abbess and descend by seniority through the ranks to the novices and *converse*. But Gozzadini first summoned the most junior *professa*. Mauro Ruggeri, then the convent's confessor, later claimed that the suffragan bishop hoped that this maneuver would catch the nuns off guard. But the pastoral visitors could well have decided to begin with the nuns most likely to revere their authority—not an unreasonable strategy, for the senior nuns later showed little inclination to cooperate. The venerable madre donna Angela Cherubini's responses to thirty questions yield barely ten lines: "Everybody behaves well toward the senior nuns and our superiors, and I know of no one who does what she shouldn't. Everything is fine and well done, and I don't have anything to say to you." Madre donna Verginia Fuzzi offered only "Because I am an old sister I attend to my soul alone." Madre donna Ortensia Bombacci, Lucrezia Orsina Vizzana's aunt, justified her terse responses with "I live in seclusion and I don't know anything." The less senior donna Paula Dorotea Vitali even tried a passive-aggressive diversion: "So, should any reform be needed, let it be in the kitchen."[2]

Gozzadini's strategy proved almost as fruitless with the most junior nuns, whom the bishop called the first day. He did not bother with the customary, often disingenuous "Have you any idea why you have been summoned?" Presumably the answer went without saying. Although more respectful than their elders, the youngest generally offered little to pique the visitors' interest. Indeed, Giuliana Glavarini seems to have done her best to mislead: "I don't know of any dissension among them."[3]

In the waning light of the first day, after five previous witnesses, donna Lucrezia Orsina Vizzana finally entered the infirmary as the day's final witness. With twenty-five years of convent life behind her, Vizzana was no junior member. Her cautiously worded answers avoid both direct affirmations of leading questions and anything that could be cited as overtly misleading or outright perjury—in other words, the time-honored techniques for facing down inquisitors. "*I do not know* if there might be abuses in the convent, nor wicked practices. . . . *I have not seen* profane paintings, much less dogs. . . . *Nor do I know* if there could be any variety of dress among us, nor any vanities of lace or of other sorts" (emphasis added). But donna Lucrezia had also grown up at the center of Santa Cristina's musical establishment. So she was the first to acknowledge openly, but with characteristic understatement, what was on every nun's mind: the strife within the choir (fig. 17). "Nor do I know of any disagreements. And it merely seems to me that between suor Emilia and suor Cecilia there might be some rivalry that causes some modest disturbance within the convent" (original underlining).[4]

Donna Lucrezia was putting it mildly. The next day six of nine witnesses elaborated in detail upon problems with the two whose names Lucrezia had dropped: donna Emilia Grassi and donna Cecilia Bianchi. Lucrezia's older sister, Isabetta Vizzana (decidedly the more forthright of the two sisters), put it bluntly: "There's one donna Cecilia by name who is moved by a certain infatuation [*passioncella*] she had with donna Emilia. Between them there rages a rivalry, so that they put the convent in disorder. Donna Emilia observes the actions of donna Cecilia and, to be contrary, does something else, in such a way that even in reciting the Office in chapel they want to outdo one another with their voices; and each of them wants to get the better of the other."[5]

This may not have been the most important problem, as far as Ludovisi's emissaries were concerned, but most of the nuns seemed to think of little else. More than a dozen raised the issue, and usually in terms of the choir. Others who did not address the rift directly still complained about Cecilia Bianchi's behavior in chapel. The choir thus had become the central arena in which the rivalry was played out most overtly:

[Donna Cecilia] complains about everybody in choir, declaring that the Divine Office is not recited precisely and as it should be. And it's not for her to correct. It's the job of the abbess.

Especially in chapel donna Cecilia wants to direct the choir, and I believe she does it with good intentions, so the Office will be recited in an orderly way; that's how she feels if it's not recited her way.

If one could see to it that donna Cecilia conforms to everyone else in reciting the Divine Office, that would remove many difficulties from the chapel. Because she should

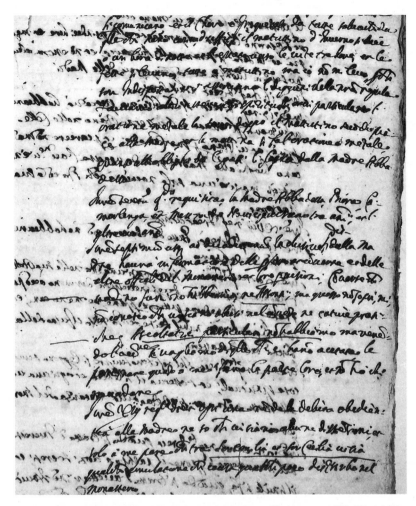

FIGURE 17. ASB, Demaniale 48/2909 (Santa Cristina), no. 3/L (processo 1622–23), fol. 10r. Lucrezia Vizzana's testimony acknowledges no abuses or evil practices (ten lines from the bottom) but offers the first hints of convent strife (four lines from the bottom). Reproduced with permission of the Ministero per i Beni e le Attività Culturali, Archivio di Stato, Bologna.

recite the Office with a voice matched to the others, and not cause confusion by one time reciting high and another low.

Sometimes donna Cecilia has words in choir because she wants us to follow how she recites, either fast or slow. I don't know of other dissension except some rivalry between donna Emilia and suor Cecilia, who each claims to direct the choir according to her taste. The running of it falls to donna Emilia as prefect.

And then there's the choir, which is a perpetual comedy theater, where they relate what they've seen and heard—especially the older ones. Between donna Emilia and donna Cecilia there's vehement and envious warfare, especially because donna Emilia pretends to be better than donna Cecilia and would like donna Cecilia to ask her permission. Donna Emilia wants all of us as her subjects.[6]

It did not take investigators long, therefore, to recognize who was at the heart of the problem (though most of them certainly had a good idea already). Months later, when the notary abridged the evidence for the ecclesiastical powers-that-be, only the testimony of Emilia Grassi and Cecilia Bianchi (plus the abbess's) seemed important enough to deposit in the archiepiscopal archive, while the original transcript, which he had hastily recorded on the spot, found its way in the end to the convent archive.

Eventually Cecilia Bianchi had her say (which took twice the time of anybody else's). She began her second day of testimony, "I have pondered what you sought from me; and to expedite matters I offer you the present page on which is written everything that I can say regarding this investigation and its causes." She handed her interrogators a document, which the notary dutifully recorded in the archbishop's copy of the proceedings but omitted from the copy intended for the nuns' eyes. It begins, "It has been eighteen years that I have endured this persecution, and it began because of music."[7]

Donna Cecilia left no doubt about the nature of the difficulties and who had caused them:

In the recitation of the Office and Mass there is tremendous negligence, because in the summertime at that hour the nuns are always being called to the doorways and the nuns' grates by gentlemen and ladies. So the chapel is unattended. Sometimes there are so few of us left that we cannot even recite the Office. As for the recitation of the Office, it is not said as it should be, following the calendar, because donna Emilia Grassi changed it when she became mistress of the choir—and this against the orders of our superiors. We have orders to recite the Office as if in song, but this is not done. They bring dogs and cats into the chapel. There is madre donna Emilia Grassi, who has a little cat who comes looking for her in chapel and she doesn't send it away as she should. There is also the prioress, donna Sulpizia Bocchi, who has a little dog which she sometimes carries into the chapel; but at present she has sent it home. And donna Pantasilea Tovagli keeps a little book while the Office is being recited and doesn't pay attention to the service as she should. The master of music has been receiving provisions, and the mother abbess has complained about it. It was madre donna Emilia who wanted him to receive them. We also have two organs, one of which could be sold. Furthermore, you should establish the way and time to recite the Divine Office and sing masses, etc., because, despite the fact that the mother abbess has ordered that they be performed in one way, suor Emilia does the opposite, which provokes disagreements and scandal.[8]

The testimony of the abbess, madre donna Lorenza Bonsignori, usefully balances Cecilia Bianchi's allegations, which Bianchi designed to reinforce church fathers' common view of independent, spirited nuns as disobedient, rebellious children. For her part, the abbess admitted that chapel could be better attended if nuns did not leave to answer summonses in the parlatorios or if they all attended services instead of sometimes making toffee in the kitchen—these were, in fact, perennial complaints lodged by superiors at any number of convents. From the nuns' point of view, meetings in the parlatorios and gifts of homemade sweets, a vestige of the much freer interchange between convent and city before Trent, served to maintain important ties to their families and to reaffirm their place in the community's social structure.

The abbess also acknowledged that dogs and cats, especially donna Emilia's cat, occasionally attended services in chapel, but she denied that there was any indecorous gossiping or giggling, as one of Bianchi's allies had claimed. But restrictions on convent pets were perpetually ambiguous, and pets' presence tended to be turned into a convent "abuse" when it served someone's political advantage.[9] It further emerged that donna Emilia's alleged changes in the calendar had involved nothing more important than the insertion of extra readings from the prophets, a practice that the Camaldolese father general had already put right. As for donna Cecilia, the abbess remarked, "She should be advised to be more circumspect about talking too much and being insulting to the sisters. Sometimes in chapel she goes around imitating those poor elderly sisters who cannot contribute to the choir, and who sing certain words either too high or too low."

The abbess did not, however, hide her resentment at Emilia Grassi's refusal to give up the position of choir mistress, which she had monopolized for more than six years, despite the fact that the abbess should have appointed the officeholder. Over the abbess's objections, Grassi also continued to insist upon a regular salary for a master of music, Ottavio Vernizzi, whom she had originally hired—in direct violation of archiepiscopal law. The abbess made it clear that by 1623 the appointment of a new choir mistress was long overdue and suggested Lucrezia Vizzana's aunt, the former organist Camilla Bombacci, for the position.[10]

By contrast, the shrewd donna Emilia, when her turn came, initially couched counterattacks much more evenhandedly. Her assertion (quite implausible by then) that "there is no dissension here within this convent" prompted the scribal aside "in response she said—she well and truly answered thus." Her initial description of her rival was comparably mild-mannered: "For the last six years I've been in charge of directing the choir. And in chapel there doesn't seem to be anything else to disturb our common peace except that donna Cecilia sometimes either goes too fast or recites more slowly than the others, reproving some of the nuns heartily and often, primarily those on the side where she stands—although one wouldn't expect her to criticize, since I'm in charge of the choir, as I said."[11]

She went on smoothly, and with surprising self-assurance, given that twenty-nine nuns, including donna Cecilia, had testified before her, to offer her own contradictory view. When the interrogators abandon their scripted thirty questions, hemming her in with accusations suggested by previous testimony against her, she holds her ground, responding with dazzling audacity that eclipses anyone else's feeble attempts at resistance.

"Is anything added or removed from the Office at the behest of the choir mistress?"

"It seems to me that when they began reading the history from some prophet something may have been added, but for about a year they've only recited what's permitted by their rule."

"Do you or others bring cats to chapel?"

"Sometimes my cat hears me in choir and comes in to find me, but it leaves right away."

"Does anybody keep books hidden in front of their body while reciting the Office?"

"No."

Before long donna Emilia launches verbal countermoves of her own, without further provocation:

I've discerned nothing inappropriate being done in choir. I'm unaware that the abbess has complained about what the organ tuner or music master get paid, and nobody's done any harm by having to go to the gallery for grace after meals before the crucifix. I don't like your question—if anybody gives me something, they say it's from their own share, and not from the convent's, and the convent has already had its share. I don't speak haughtily to demean our superiors. As for donna Cecilia, I don't know what to do about her, and I do her honor as I do every other nun and conversa in the convent. I'm not offended because the sisters study with suor Cecilia, and, sure, I've told the others in donna Cecilia's absence that she's a hypocrite, and I told others not to be taken in by her. As for claims that I make hateful gestures toward her in choir, sometimes I move about to be more comfortable and to enjoy the sunlight, but not out of hatred. As for my having told some nuns they needn't observe fasts and vigils strictly, it was when donna Giulia had a prolonged illness, and it was with the doctor's consent. Nor have I coached anybody on how they should answer in this visitation, and I didn't say I wanted to torment donna Cecilia. I never insisted that the abbess do things my way, any more than while reading in the refectory I added lessons at others' expense. As for wearing a hat, I admit I do it, for protection from the heat and the bad air. But it's the practice in the convent, and the mother abbess and the bursar wear hats too. And my shoulders are covered up by the scapular and everything else.[12]

(The last remark may be a subtle response to allegations that donna Emilia went around with her bosom uncovered.)

Clearly, then, by the 1620s the nuns' choir had become a major battleground, which helps explain donna Cecilia's cryptic line about music's role in her persecution. The first hints of these musical rivalries can be traced back to the turn of the century, around the time that donna Cecilia claimed her persecution had begun. In 1600 a petition had arrived at the Congregation of Bishops that suggested that an overabundance of musical talent, praised by Adriano Banchieri in 1599 and by Giacomo Vincenti in 1606, was already beginning to divide the convent from within:

Since time immemorial it has always been customary in the monastery of the nuns of Santa Cristina in Bologna, of the Camaldolese order, to elect an organist from among the nuns. And the election should always fall to the one who best knows how to play. And because ordinarily the number of those who knew how to play well was small, only once or twice was there strife in the election. Now that the number of those who seek the office has grown considerably, there is such discord that it is impossible to arrive at the election of the most talented, the one who most deserves the position. Therefore, on behalf of the abbess and nuns of the convent, Your Most Illustrious Lordships are humbly requested to deign to command that now and whenever the occasion for such an election should arise, the nun should be elected who best knows how to play and is most adept, talented, and qualified for such an office, ahead of any other claim or respect.[13]

The choir may have contained more than half a dozen rivals for the organist's post. In addition to Emilia Grassi, who, Banchieri indicates, was leading the choir in 1599, there would have been Camilla Bombacci, the sometime convent organist, and her talented niece, the young

Lucrezia Vizzana, who had recently entered the convent but had yet to profess. In 1601 Adeodata Leoni commissioned Gabriele Fattorini's *Secondo libro de mottetti*, which suggests her own strong commitment to the choir. Although the illustrious Cleria Pepoli apparently also took an interest in music, judging by the dedication of Ercole Porta's *Vaga ghirlanda* of 1613, she is likely to have presented a threat only as a patron and not as a performer, since she seems to have been a virtual invalid. Angelica Malvezzi, on the other hand, represented a serious rival, whose angelic voice was lauded at her death in 1615. The convent necrologist likewise remembered Giuditta Nobili for her musical talents. Alfonsina Ganassi, daughter of Bolognese musician Alfonso Ganassi, was very probably also a performer. And, of course, there was Cecilia Bianchi.

This sort of musical contention came as no surprise to church authorities, who had long cited such rivalries as a primary evil of convent music. A few years earlier, one convent father confessor had complained to the Congregation of Bishops, for example: "There is such wrangling and war among the nuns because of musical rivalries that sometimes they would claw each others' flesh if they could."[14] For him, as for many, convent music provided the spark to set off what they had long seen as female fury, smoldering beneath the surface, women's imagined irrational propensity for jealousy, leading to violence and the provocation of discord—an old, familiar theme.

Another anonymous, half-literate Bolognese complaint to the Congregation of Bishops in 1602 could well describe the continuing problem at Santa Cristina:

For many years I've been a laywoman in a convent and I've seen many occasions for sin, especially about playing the organ and making music. These singers and players harass one another and take sides. One side says, "Our group performs better," and the other side responds, "It isn't true. Our group sings and plays better." And this causes uproar, the greatest hatred, and such infinite animosity that the convents are afire and aflame.[15]

In November 1600 the Congregation of Bishops commanded the Bolognese vice-legate to undertake a "diligent and secret" investigation at Santa Cristina "regarding the government of the convent." The inquiry probably resulted from a combination of complaints, including a claim that the convent procurator came and went as if the cloister were his home and maintained an unseemly friendship with one of the nuns. Six weeks after the discreet investigation, the congregation issued several follow-up decrees chiefly concerning details of *clausura* (e.g., walling up windows, modifications to grates), with no specific mention of music. Such disorders have a familiar ring, however, for they represent the same sorts of abuses that Cecilia Bianchi would cite twenty years later, when her rivalry with Emilia Grassi reached its height.[16]

It is intriguing that Gabriele Fattorini's *Secondo libro de mottetti* saw the light in the immediate aftermath of the vice-legate's visitation. Adeodata Leoni, the dedicatee and probable patroness of the collection, was singled out twenty years later as one of the nuns enlisted to reconcile donna Emilia and donna Cecilia.[17] The dedication of the *Secondo libro*, dated 28 May 1601, raises the possibility that Leoni might have turned to music as a means of mediation during the earlier musical crisis. Some motets contain exhortations to repentance and amendment of life in time of catastrophe. *Impetum inimicorum* ("Do not be afraid of the attack of your enemies . . . and now let us cry to heaven, and our Lord will be merciful unto us") opens the collection in the heat of battle. Two choirs leap in and out of the fray, echoing each other in repeated trumpet calls before the texture broadens into the concluding calm assurance of God's grace, in eight parts. *Positis autem genibus* ("But kneeling, he cried in a loud voice, saying, 'Lord, reckon not this sin upon them'") and *Praeparate corda vestra* ("Prepare your hearts unto the Lord and serve him only, and he will deliver you out of the hands of your enemies. Return to him with all your hearts"; *CNC*, track 3) both reflect similar sentiments.[18]

Lucrezia Vizzana's *Componimenti musicali* appeared two decades later, at the climax of convent strife that had also begun because of music. Five motets, most of them intriguingly positioned early in the collection, reflect themes of penitence, abandonment, or vengeance:

1. *Exsurgat Deus et dissipentur inimici eius* (Let God arise, and let his enemies be scattered; *SED*, track 19)
3. *Ave stella matutina* (Hail morning star; *SED*, track 5; *CNC*, track 12)
5. *Domine, ne in furore tuo arguas me* (Lord, in your anger do not rebuke me; *SED*, track 18)
7. *Usquequo oblivisceris me in finem* (How long will you forget me? Forever?; *SED*, track 6)
15. *Domine, quid multiplicati sunt qui tribulant me* (Lord, how are they increased who trouble me!; *SED*, track 7)

Could these pieces have been heard in relation to conflicts and factionalism at Santa Cristina? One must be cautious about reading biographical implications into settings of such extremely common biblical verses.

Nevertheless, for those whose lives were regulated by the constant recitation of scripture, the language it speaks could come to be heard as the language of their own lives.

A number of anomalous features about Vizzana's printed collection and its publication strengthen the possibility that the current crisis within the cloister affected the print's appearance. The extreme austerity of the title page (fig. 18) is striking. It is devoid of all ornamentation, in contrast to the usual practice in sixteenth- and seventeenth-century music prints. More striking is the absence of any mention of a publisher, a feature rarely absent from music title pages. "Nella Stamparia del Gardano IN VENETIA Appresso Bartholomeo Magni" (at Gardano's printing house in Venice, in conjunction with Bartholomew Magni) only appears in the colophon at the end of the volumes. Neither is there any mention of a *privilegio* (copyright). Such evidence suggests that Vizzana's *Componimenti musicali* was probably a privately contracted job, in which the printer had no financial interest, that the convent of Santa Cristina had specially commissioned and underwritten.

Most intriguing, however, are anomalies between the two surviving copies. The title page of one, dated 1622, does not specify the nuns as dedicatees, whereas the second copy, dated 1623, does. Furthermore, the less precise salutation to the dedication on the overleaf to the first copy, signed 1 December 1622, "Molto R.R.[de] in Christo Giesu" (Very Reverend in Jesus Christ; fig. 19), has been expanded and made quite specific in the second, "Alle M. R. Monache di S. Christina di Bologna" (To the Very Reverend Nuns of Santa Cristina in Bologna), signed exactly a month later, 1 January 1623. The layout of the table of contents at the end of the prints also differs slightly in the two copies.[19] Clearly, these pages must have been recast during the printing process for some reason. Since title pages, dedications, and concluding lists of contents were often the last items to be printed, it is possible that the printing of the music text was already complete by late December 1622. These last-minute revisions, which called particular attention to the convent, were carried out right in the midst of the pastoral visitation in December 1622 and January 1623. The finished copies could have been delivered by February, before the matter had reached any sort of resolution.[20] *Componimenti musicali* might have been conceived as an instrument to influence the outcome of the crisis.

For the nuns of Santa Cristina, music had long been a means of clientage, of bridging the convent wall to influence those in the world. Given the rigors of post-Tridentine *clausura*, nuns' patterns of clientage were largely indirect, reinforcing links to their own families and fostering

COMPONIMENTI
MVSICALI

DE

MOTTETI CONCERTATI A VNA E PIV VOCI

DI

DONNA LVCRETIA ORSINA VIZANA
Monaca nel Sacro Coleggi o di
S ante

CHRISTINA DI BOLOGNA
Della Congregatione

CAMALDOLENSE

ANNO
M DC XXII.

FIGURE 18. Lucrezia Orsina Vizzana, *Componimenti musicali,* title page from the copy dated 1622. Reproduced with permission of the Biblioteka Uniwersytecka, Wrocław.

others with potentially powerful advocates in the world. There can be no question that Lucrezia Vizzana's *Componimenti musicali* was intended to enhance the luster of the convent that must have paid for it. The convent may have received most, if not all, of the copies to distribute to families, friends, and allies. The contents and organization of the collection, and the last-minute revisions of the front matter, suggest that Vizzana's volume may have been intended not only to call attention to the house, its venerable history, and its distinguished artistic tradition but also to arouse public sympathy and support for this honorable institution and its music, currently under attack, from both within and without.

The "quasi-autobiographical" *Sonet vox tua* is not printed first, but instead a motet beginning *Exsurgat Deus* (fig. 19; *SED*, track 19), in which a solo soprano invokes the Lord in rising trumpet calls (which recall

FIGURE 19. Lucrezia Orsina Vizzana, *Componimenti musicali,* dedication from the copy dated 1 December 1622 and the motet *Exsurgat Deus.* Reproduced with permission of the Biblioteka Uniwersytecka, Wrocław.

Fattorini's first motet *Impetum inimicorum)*, inaugurates the collection. There may have been a particular point behind the placement of this opening exhortation:

Exsurgat Deus et dissipentur inimici eius et fugiant qui oderunt eum a facie eius. Sicut deficit fumus, deficiant sicut fluit cera a facie ignis sic pereant peccatores a facie Dei. Et iusti epulentur, et exultent in conspectu Dei <> in laetitia. Alleluia.[21]

Let God arise, and let his enemies be scattered, and let those who hate him flee before him. As smoke dies out, let them die out; as wax melts before a fire, let the sinners perish before the face of God. And let the righteous be joyful, and let them exult in the sight of God in joy. Alleluia.

It is difficult to believe that Lucrezia Vizzana, her fellow nuns, and knowledgeable outsiders would not have read into such lines as "Let his enemies be scattered," "Let them flee before him," "Let them die out," and "Let the sinners perish" a special relevance to current political strife dividing Santa Cristina. Vizzana concludes her opening motet on a firmly positive note, "Let the righteous be joyful, and let them exult in the sight of God in joy," dissolving into a string of jubilant alleluias. Within six years Santa Cristina's troublemakers would indeed be scattered to other convents. The archbishop's yeomen would have fled before a hail of bricks and stones. But, as we shall see, by then this public show of optimism would have turned to sorrow.

As the collection unfolds, every other piece for most of the first half of the volume (nos. 1, 3, 5, and 7) insistently hammers home these themes. *Usquequo oblivisceris me* (*SED* 6; example 1), examined earlier, was a text set only infrequently in the early 1600s. A Bolognese listener, aware of recent goings-on, could have heard, even in its very first words, a communal cry of despair, leading to a final plea for deliverance:

Usquequo <> oblivisceris me in finem? Usquequo avertis faciem tuam a me? Quamdiu ponam consilia in anima mea dolorem in corde meo per diem? Usquequo exaltabitur inimicus meus super me? Respice et exaudi me Domine Deus meus. Illumina oculos meos <> in morte, nequando dicat inimicus meus prevalui adversum eum.

How long will you forget me? Forever? How long will you hide your face from me? How long shall I take counsel in my soul, having sorrow in my heart daily? How long will my enemy be exalted over me? Have regard for me and hear me, O Lord my God. Lighten my eyes in death, lest my enemy say, "I have prevailed against him."

The subtle alterations of the original psalm text must represent conscious artistic decisions. Most surprising is the suppression of any mention of the Lord in the opening phrase, "Usquequo [*Domine*] oblivisceris me." For a convent audience or anybody else who regularly ran through the Psalter like clockwork or regularly recited the penitential psalms, the suppression of the opening "Domine" could signal that the Lord was specifically *not* being addressed.

For quite some time, the nuns of Santa Cristina had had reason to claim such oppression and abandonment. Since 1616, at least, when the Congregation of Bishops had once again ordered diocesan ministers to gather "accurate, secret, extrajudicial information" about alleged financial irregularities at the convent, the nuns' relationship to outside authorities had been steadily deteriorating. In 1618 the congregation had denied the nuns' petition to accept an additional *conversa*, claiming that the ratio of servant nuns to professed nuns was already overly luxurious. In 1620 the Bolognese archbishop had rejected two postulants, proposed by the convent as replacements for two recently deceased sisters.[22] The altered psalm opening of Vizzana's *Usquequo oblivisceris me* could thus be heard as a plea, not only to the convent's ultimate superior, but also to the episcopal authorities, intended to arouse public sympathy at their hardhearted rebuffs.

It could be that Vizzana saw in these motets a way to touch the hearts of those beyond the wall, in the midst of a crisis that Cecilia Bianchi claimed "began because of music." A search back through other archival documents, widening out from Bologna, to Camaldoli, and to Rome, reveals, however, that although music had indeed been a significant element of discord, it was eclipsed by others more potent and elemental, likewise festering over two decades. These were the forces that would carry the convent to the brink of destruction.

SIX

Voices of Discord at Santa Cristina

There was a certain donna Emilia of the Grassi family, but a natural off-spring, a full-blooded woman and, as a result, merry, outspoken, and uninhibited. In her youth she was good-looking, eloquent, talented, a singer. She played the organ, the harp, and other instruments—and well. A lady bountiful and liberal so that she won to her the hearts not only of the nuns but of others too. She therefore wanted to have a hand in all the affairs and governing of the nuns and the convent.

The other nun (in her youth also donna Emilia's friend) was a donna Cecilia [Bianchi]. She had only one ally, donna Gentile Malvasia, who, had she not been corrupted, might have been as amiable as her name. But she consorted with the she-wolf and learned to howl. This donna Cecilia was melancholy, with a gloomy manner, dominated by irasci-bility and consequently spiteful, haughty, envious. She criticized the actions of others and retained a high opinion of herself. But above all she wanted to ape donna Emilia but lacked her manner and grace.

Don Mauro Ruggeri, former prior general of the Camaldo-lese order (d. 1660) drew up this sketch of diametrically opposed rivals in the late 1640s. Ruggeri knew what he was talking about, for he served as father confessor and titular abbot to the convent of Santa Cristina during the crisis and the years leading up to it. His manuscript "Caduta di Santa Cristina di Bologna" (The fall of Santa Cristina in Bologna), long forgotten in the monastic archive at Camaldoli, offers a detailed, firsthand account of the catastrophe to come, often from behind the scenes. Documents from the archives of

Santa Cristina, the city, diocese, and the Vatican generally confirm him in matters of fact, which enhances his credibility in the many instances where he remains our sole witness to what went on behind the walls along via Fondazza.[1]

Ruggeri apportions almost as much blame for the calamity that followed to Emilia Grassi as to the less sympathetic Cecilia Bianchi. But his chief villains skulk within the Bolognese episcopal hierarchy. Ruggeri does his best to hold himself and his fellow Camaldolese above reproach. The good-hearted, well-meaning, at times a little foolish Camaldolese monks who minister to the nuns appear at the mercy, on the one hand, of the infinitely more powerful Archbishop Ludovico Ludovisi—"The big fish eats the little one," as Ruggeri put it—and, on the other, of the deluded aspirations and subtle persuasions of Emilia Grassi and Cecilia Bianchi.

Ruggeri's Polonian advice to don Giusto Bordino, his successor as the nuns' confessor, was thus to keep his distance from Bianchi, humoring her with kind words and glossing over her errors. Above all he must elude Grassi, who, not about to be directed, "would have used every possible deceit to win him over." Ruggeri had barely left town after his term as confessor ended before the inexperienced Bordino, "an immature brain who presumed to know more than everyone else," promptly divulged every confidence to the forceful donna Emilia, who easily won him to her side with gifts that the needy monk found irresistible.[2]

Ruggeri weaves the details of his story into a parable to illustrate how the absence of the cardinal convent virtues of humility and obedience from a few hearts could undo the good work of many. To hear him tell it, his own beneficent ministrations could do little to control these irrational enemies, for, as he puts it, in words that echo and reecho at least as far back as Ecclesiasticus, "a woman's fury may certainly be covered up sometimes, but in fact it is never extinguished."[3] Ruggeri's gentle exhortations to patience and humility as a means to perfection had little effect on these implacable rivals, whose ways he contrasts with donna Laura Bocchi, known for her sweet manner and patience, and, above all, with those of Lucrezia Orsina Vizzana's aunt, the venerable donna Flaminia Bombacci.

As a foil to Grassi and Bianchi, Ruggeri offers donna Flaminia's brief, pious biography, which later helped win her a place in the Camaldolese calendar of the sainted and blessed down to the present day. Ruggeri leaves to others any mention of the "miraculous" side to donna Flaminia's history (a sort of testimony to sanctity then falling out of fashion, at least among clerical professionals). Her relative Gasparo Bombacci had no such qualms. He related that during a violent thunderstorm Flaminia three times started toward her cell and three times was distracted. Then, as she was diverted into her sister's cell instead, her own was struck by lightning—clearly, her guardian angels had been hovering above her.[4]

Ruggeri concentrates instead upon virtually every paradigmatic saintly attribute fostered by the post-Tridentine church. Indeed, he could have culled donna Flaminia's merits from the official life of such newly minted saints as Santa Francesca Romana, canonized in 1608: asceticism; regular discipline; years of dedication to constant prayer; exemplary piety that provided an effective model to others. Donna Flaminia overflowed with compassion—for a year she cheerfully tended to a dying nun with breast cancer, whose lesions leaked pus black as ink (a detail recalling the ministrations of Saint Catherine of Siena, who had sucked pus from the wound in a dying woman's breast). Donna Flaminia was charitable—she dedicated what money she had to the sacramental life of the parish and loaned her clothing to poorer nuns, while she wore sackcloth (a contrast with the illicit bits of finery in dress decried during the visitation of 1622–23). Above all, Flaminia Bombacci displayed perfect humility—even when other nuns verbally abused her, she patiently asked forgiveness for having offended. For Ruggeri, donna Flaminia's prayers had held the devil and disaster at bay.[5]

"I Called Her Misbegotten"

Donna Cecilia, seconded by Ruggeri, reveals almost in passing a primary force that provoked her original falling out with Grassi and set in motion the convent's decline. Bianchi's list of complaints to episcopal visitors in 1622 opened with "and it began because of music," then continued, "because we had words, I called her misbegotten, and she responded to me viciously."[6] Ruggeri, on the other hand, began his description with "there was a certain donna Emilia of the Grassi family, *but a natural offspring*" (fù una certa donna Emilia de' Grassi, *ma naturale* [emphasis added]). Emilia Grassi may have come from one of Bologna's oldest, most illustrious families, and also one of the most prominent at the convent (the Grassi had sent more novices to Santa Cristina during the last century than virtually any other family), but she was also known to bear the taint of illegitimacy, a blot her aristocratic peers were unlikely to overlook, and one she could not forget.

Thus, the probable scenario of the breakup of the two nuns becomes clearer. Back around 1600, Emilia Grassi, the domineering *maestra del coro*, must have tried to impose her will on the singer Cecilia Bianchi or to assert her superiority once too often. Bianchi hit back with a word Grassi could not tolerate: "bastard." In an earlier age, illegitimates—at least those of male family members—were widely accepted in noble households, though they were commonly married off to families of somewhat lower rank. But they were also morally and legally ambiguous and a potential threat to the family patrimony. By the 1500s an increased Italian preoccupation with proper birth brought a significant loss of status for natural children, who could be excluded from economic and political privileges and from family inheritance if not specifically singled out in wills or unless legitimized, as happened with Lucrezia Vizzana's illegitimate nephew, Angelo Michele.[7]

Illegitimacy's taint to noble blood might explain Emilia Grassi's presence at Santa Cristina in the first place. For when Renaissance nobles looked for wives, they wanted unsullied bloodlines. As Francesco Barbaro put it:

We know that many and indeed most superior species of vegetation and nuts will never grow if not in their own characteristic and superior locality. But if they migrate to undistinguished territory, they put off their innate dispositions, and the defiled fruit deteriorates the better sap. Also, outstanding young shoots, if grafted to poorer branches, yield inferior fruit. Wherefore it is also reasonable that human beings may hope for more illustrious children by far from distinguished women.[8]

Rather than find the illegitimate Emilia Grassi a socially inferior husband willing to take her, in return for an inordinately large dowry, her father chose the cheaper route: he sent her off to Santa Cristina.

Such a defect of birth also affected a woman's chances outside the marriage market. In the 1580s, gossip about the possible illegitimacy of the renowned convent-trained singer Laura Bovia, "niece" of Giacomo Bovio, chief canon of San Petronio, derailed negotiations for her acceptance as lady-in-waiting to the Duchess of Mantua. Cloistered nobles were as sensitive to this issue as their sisters at court. The Congregation of Bishops had to reassure Spoleto's diocesan curia in the 1590s that Sixtus V's bull *Contra illegitimos* (Against illegitimates) did not apply to convents, where bastards could still be elected as superiors, a point carefully noted in Bolognese curial documents.[9]

This aspersion helps explain Emilia Grassi's vengeful campaign against her ex-friend, "who she believed had undermined her reputation before our superiors and the laity, but I don't know the details," as the abbess put it. Grassi's obsession with her flawed origins also helps explain her

compulsive attempts to achieve and retain dominance within the cloister. Her natural musical talent initially helped her realize artistic distinction. Her lavish spending of her own private means, supplemented by
sizable amounts apparently drained off from the convent's own coffers
during her reign as abbess, looks like an effort to overcome the defect of
her birth through musical and artistic adornments: on the musical side,
Adriano Banchieri's *Messa solenne*; and on the artistic, Bernardino Baldi's
altarpiece, *The Coronation of the Virgin,* for the external church.

The title page and dedication to Banchieri's *Messa solenne* may speak
to the issue in revealing ways. Where the coats of arms of Adeodata
Leoni and Cleria Pepoli are emblazoned on the title pages of music imprints dedicated to them, Banchieri's title page substitutes instead the
Venetian music publisher's emblem. Banchieri's turns of phrase for his
dedicatory letter are equally noteworthy. Having lauded the music at
Santa Cristina under donna Emilia's direction, Banchieri continues, "Recalling the affection that I have maintained since my earliest years for
your most ancient and illustrious house, the Grassi, whence have come
cardinals, prelates, senators, and other personages who always have and
still reflect great luster on this our city of Bologna, I responded to my
friend that truly *from such a good tree nothing could issue but the most
excellent fruit*" (emphasis added). Banchieri's final phrase suggests that
perhaps this friend had not limited his comments to donna Emilia's
musical talents. Indeed, the composer's proclamation of Emilia Grassi's
good name and illustrious roots reads like a response to Francesco Barbaro's analysis of illegitimacy.[10]

To establish her position, Grassi also worked to win over the younger
sisters with special favors—she was "cunning and shrewd in gaining followers," as don Mauro put it. She escorted junior nuns to the gateway
she controlled as *portinara* (gatekeeper) to visit with relatives, and she
provided little tea parties at the gate for those who had been initially accepted for future admission (a useful means to win them and, more im-
portantly, their families to her side before their formal acceptance). One
such singular party occurred just the summer before the 1622 visitation.
Then Grassi arranged a long table across the cloister portal, with half
inside the convent for donna Emilia's cloistered allies and half outside
for their lay relatives—another fine example of how nuns observed the
restrictions of enclosure to the letter but no further. As it turned out, the
guest list included a brother to donna Claudia Gozzadini at Santa Cristina—who was also related to the chief interrogator in the investigation,
Suffragan Bishop Angelo Gozzadini. In the copy of testimony prepared
for the archiepiscopal archive the name of the bishop's male relative has

been discreetly scratched out and disguised with meaningless squiggles, rendering it illegible.

To consolidate her power during her term as abbess, Grassi had shrewdly appointed as bursar one of her cronies, "who didn't know how to write anything but her name," as the later abbess Lorenza Bonsignori alleged. Grassi thus managed to concentrate both executive and financial control in her own hands and presumably gained easy access to convent funds for her own pet projects.

The investigation of 1622–23 confirmed that Emilia Grassi and her immediate followers had even expropriated the convent's spacious common rooms, intended for the novitiate and infirmary, as their personal salons. Grassi offered the justification that there was currently but one novice, while in winter the sick found their own cells more comfortable than the drafty infirmary. Grassi even went so far as to expropriate a pair of silver candelabra and other altar furniture from the sacristy for personal interior decoration (though she claimed she took them only for safekeeping). As abbess she had finally become so domineering that the other nuns blackballed her at reelection time. But even after her demotion, she never lost her will to rule.

Donna Emilia's insecurities about the defect of her birth provoked the most damaging blow to Santa Cristina. According to Abbess Bonsignori: "Nor did Emilia Grassi fail to cause uproar at the time when some tried to reintroduce *educande* [lay students]. Also in 1604 she wrote a truly infamous petition against those who had kept lay students and sent it to Rome to the Congregation of Most Illustrious Cardinals. And to support her opinion she provoked the greatest tumults, so that lay students no longer returned here for their education." Don Mauro Ruggeri's explanation of her tactics makes perfect sense: "She observed that the convent was filled with nuns from Bologna's premier families, who kept their relatives there to be educated. Most of them then received the veil. As noblewomen, they consequently did not wish to be subject to donna Emilia's beck and call." Before 1604, no fewer than twenty-one of the convent's forty-two *professe* hailed from the first families of the Bolognese elite, and another eleven from patrician families of the second rank, while the remaining ten included two sisters related to the future Pope Gregory XV.[11]

In such illustrious company, the illegitimate donna Emilia might well feel eclipsed. Religious vows rendered cloistered nobility no less prone than their siblings in the world to "adopt with their inferiors a less civil manner," to be "severe with their inferiors if they do not give way to them at once," as one acerbic critic of Bologna's upper classes put it.

Shortly after 1600 Grassi had therefore complained to convent superiors that these noble *educande* distracted the nuns from strict observance of their rule and that the lay students were kept in virtual imprisonment and treated like slaves or servants. As a result, the Congregation of Bishops had forbidden the convent to accept *educande* in future.[12]

This meant, of course, that the natural flow of the bluest blood to Santa Cristina had been stanched, for girls tended to profess at the convent where they had been educated. This left Emilia Grassi and her contingent in a better position to blackball any undesirable prospects when the entire community voted on their acceptance; the prospective postulant would not have been raised within the cloister and would not have formed the necessary social alliances to ensure her election.

If this strategy failed at election time, the Grassi faction even scared some entrants off before their final admission. Ruggeri hints at this practice, but only the less credible Cecilia Bianchi suggests how it worked. When the mother of a girl from the illustrious Orsi family was fed tales of what supposedly went on inside Santa Cristina, "she claimed she wanted to make her daughter a servant of the Lord and not of the world" and enrolled her instead among the Discalced Carmelites of San Gabriele, just over the back wall from Santa Cristina. Another prospective postulant's treatment was even more extraordinary: "When she asked who her [novice] mistress would be and she was told she would get donna Giuditta [Nobili—one of Emilia's allies], the girl decided not to come—she rejected her. Apart from other offensive comments that scandalized those present, donna Emilia said that if the girl were in any other's hands, she would always persecute her. So the girl's mother said she no longer wanted her to be a nun and married her off instead."[13]

Whether or not the tales donna Cecilia carried were completely true, the impact of the Grassi stratagem was ruinous. In the eighteen years between the Congregation of Bishops' ruling on *educande* and the investigation of 1622–23, a mere six girls joined the *professe* at Santa Cristina. Only one of them hailed from a preeminent family. Four came from the second rank—lower down the social hierarchy than the Grassi. It is significant that when Lucrezia Vizzana's maternal uncle sent his own daughter to the cloister, it was not to Santa Cristina, which had received his aunts, sisters, and cousins.[14]

During the pastoral visitation of 1622–23 nine sisters lined up squarely behind Emilia Grassi, usually in words that echo her own so exactly that there may have been some advance coaching: "Educande non habbiamo et non ne voressimo havere" (We do not have *educande* and we would not want to have them). It is particularly interesting that these nuns who opposed *educande* included, along with Lucrezia Vizzana (probably the last to enter before the 1604 ban), every single postulant after her except the two most recent (who did not commit themselves for or against). Grassi's faction thus encompassed just about all those junior members of slightly more humble origins, by Santa Cristina's illustrious standards, whose entry she may have screened and whose favor she had presumably curried.

Lucrezia Vizzana's own opposition to *educande* suggests that class distinctions could also touch more established, presumably better integrated sisters. Her vote suggests that she had reason to share some of Grassi's sensitivity about her own status, in this case because of the mercantile origins of her own mother's family, which, as it turns out, had also come in for caustic comment. Presumably because the Bombacci made their money in the silk trade, another nun had once called donna Lucrezia's aunt Flaminia Bombacci a "silk spinner, [one] of the worst affronts she knew, because she was a relative of merchants," as Ruggeri put it. Ruggeri was also careful to point out, of course, that madre donna Flaminia reacted with patience and humility.[15] The incident reveals just how powerful and potentially divisive a force family status must have been in the social dynamic of the house.

The nuns' opinions delivered to the visitors in 1622–23 offer striking testimony to the expertise with which donna Emilia had implemented her invidious stratagem. But, although this scheme served to consolidate Grassi's political position, at least for a time, the long-range effect proved devastating. A primary source of the convent's alliances with the outside world—its links to powerful patrician families at the very highest level—had been severely weakened. Santa Cristina never really recovered from the blow.

"A Lost Soul"

The more immediate impact of this defeat concerning *educande*, which seems to have eclipsed earlier musical rivalries as a contentious issue, was to provoke Cecilia Bianchi's alleged epistolary campaign against the convent, prompting the visitation of 1622–23. As Ruggeri summed up Grassi and Bianchi's handiwork, "one provided the wood and the kindling, and the other, one might say, with her fiery rage, piled them in the form whence followed the conflagration."[16]

Thus it was that Cecilia Bianchi moves from archrival to archvillain. She remains a decidedly more elusive, enigmatic, and complicated figure than her enemy. On her arrival at Santa Cristina around 1590, Irenea Bianchi, the future donna Cecilia, already offered an interesting contrast to donna Emilia. The Bianchi were particularly ancient and distinguished among Bologna's hundred first families and were especially prominent in the neighborhood on nearby via Santo Stefano (though Cecilia's parents lived off strada Maggiore, to the north).

The family had acquired no particular status at Santa Cristina, however. Cecilia Bianchi thus was something of an outsider from the start. Despite the fact that her private annual income was among the largest at Santa Cristina, and substantially more than Emilia Grassi's, no evidence of any convent patronage has come to light. She may also have been dealt a severe psychological blow late in 1621, when an infamous dancer, acrobat, and fencing master slaughtered a Luca Bianchi, very likely Cecilia's brother and guardian, with thirty sword blows inside the church of San Martino.[17]

Both the abbess and Bianchi herself testified that Grassi frequently labeled Cecilia "un'anima persa," a lost soul. Bianchi also claimed to have been called "a hypocrite, a sham, a fake." The abbess repeatedly brought up Grassi's epithet, "hypocrite," and Grassi used it herself in front of the clerical visitors. In *hippocrita* Grassi had found an especially loaded word. For hypocrisy had come down as a favorite characterization of feigned religiosity and false sanctity. It flourished particularly in the late 1500s and 1600s, especially in association with religious women. In Antonio Pagani's widely read *La breve somma delli essercitii de' penitenti* (A brief collection of penitential exercises; 1587), for example, hypocrisy is a sin associated with "diabolical vainglory" and acts as "a cover-up for secret vices with deceits and simulations of virtue. Hypocrites are called dissemblers. Doing evil in secret, they make a show of doing good works in public." For Jean-Joseph Surin, who achieved notoriety as exorcist of the even more notorious sueur Jeanne des Anges and the possessed Ursulines of Loudon, hypocrisy represented "the detestable mask of those, corrupt to the core and leading a licentious life, who pretend to appear austere and modest and seek to attain a reputation for sanctity."[18] The shrewd donna Emilia could hardly have chosen a more effective epithet in mounting her counterattack.

"She Consorted with the She-Wolf and Learned to Howl"

To describe the transformation that Bianchi had worked on Maria Gentile Malvasia, who succeeded Grassi as Bianchi's closest friend, Ruggeri wrote "praticò cola lupa, imparò ad urlare" (She consorted with [played with, was on familiar terms with, dealt with, had intercourse with] the she-wolf and learned to howl). Ruggeri no doubt had in mind the Italian proverb whose modern equivalent is "Chi va col lupo impara ad ululare" (Whoever runs with the wolf learns to howl). He must also have been thinking of the biblical sheep/wolves paradigm when he coined this phrase, particularly since clerical superiors often referred to their female charges as sheep. Indeed, don Mauro had just likened the diocesan curia's betrayal of Santa Cristina to "the parable of the ewe told to King David by the prophet Nathan." Later he would compare secular priests' actions to "putting the poor lambs in the mouth of the wolf."[19]

Given Bianchi and Malvasia's false claims to pastoral visitors, he probably had in mind the following antiphon: "Attendite a falsis prophetis, qui veniunt ad vos in vestimentis ovium, intrinsecus autem sunt lupi rapaces, a fructibus eorum cognosceris eos" (Beware of false prophets, who come to you in sheep's clothing but inwardly are ravenous wolves, and by their fruits you will know them). It is even possible that Ruggeri was drawing upon the related traditional association of the wolf with hypocrisy. In the 1618 edition of Cesare Ripa's *Nova iconologia overo descrittione di diverse imagini cavate dall'antichità e di propria inventione* (New iconology or a description of diverse images drawn from antiquity or his own devising), "Hippocresia" appears as a woman in religious garb, carrying a rosary and a prayer book, but with the legs and paws of a wolf (fig. 20).[20]

But wolves and dogs also commonly symbolized what the nuns saw as the primary aspect of Cecilia Bianchi's behavior: thirst for revenge and uncontrolled vengeance. Ruggeri's analogy resonates with a long Renaissance tradition of dogs or wolves as symbols of treason, of quarrelsomeness and envy, of the fury of the vendetta. Ruggeri's words "imparò ad urlare" likewise recall descriptions of rioting north-Italian peasants as "barking dogs" or of vengeful Hecuba, who, after the death of her children, barked like a dog.

According to biblical tradition wolves were nocturnal animals, likely to get at the fold after dark, while dogs or she-wolves could also be symbols of promiscuity or wild sexuality.[21] Pastoral visitors' constant preoccupation with what the convent "sheep" in their care did at night suggests a negative significance not only for Ruggeri's noun but also for his verb: instead of the modern "va col lupo," we find *"praticò cola lupa."* *Praticare* could take on a pejorative implication, particularly in judicial contexts, as when the inquisitors at Santa Cristina asked, "Se nel Monastero, ò pure alle grade *pratichino persone sospette"* (If *suspicious people frequent* the convent or likewise the grates), or when Lucrezia Vizzana

FIGURE 20. Cesare Ripa, *Nova iconologia* (1618), "Hippocresia." The figure depicts a woman in religious garb, with the legs and paws of a wolf, holding a prayer book and a rosary.

responded, "non conosco che vi siano abusi nel convento *ne cattive pratiche*" (I do not know that there are abuses in the convent *or evil practices*). And *praticare* or *pratica* could also take on sexual connotations.

Could there possibly be some connection between Ruggeri's words to describe the relationship between donna Cecilia and donna Maria Gentile and the words of several sisters in response to a question that inevitably came up during pastoral visitations? Asked if all the nuns slept alone at Santa Cristina, some nuns responded vaguely that sisters occasionally slept *accompagnate* (in company) of necessity, for reasons of health or in the depth of winter—although donna Claudia Gozzadini admitted candidly that "some nuns sleep in company out of fear, as I do when one of the nuns dies." In those bitter winters, when the snow lay deep—so deep that in February 1615 the chapel roof at the convent of Sant'Agnese had collapsed under its weight—and when at Santa Cristina the primary heat came from the fire in a common room during the day, the nuns sensibly sought whatever warmth they could find in their frosty cells, in spite of clerical misgivings about the practice.[22]

But the most junior *professa* had also commented rather pointedly:

"Every nun sleeps in her own cell, and there are as many cells as nuns—and more. And two nuns sleep in the same cell, that is, donna Cecilia and donna Gentile—and in one and the same bed."[23] Half a dozen other sisters remarked upon the fact that Bianchi and Malvasia slept together, although the abbess suggested that they slept in separate beds, and another nun offered the justification that donna Gentile was often ill. The most senior nun, on the other hand, rather emphatically seconded the claim of her most junior colleague, that the pair slept *in uno solo letto* (in only one bed)—in contrast with the Vitali sisters ("but they have two beds").

Of the convent's two most assiduous critics, Maria Gentile Malvasia had nothing at all to say about convent sleeping habits, while Cecilia Bianchi's own testimony is notable for an uncharacteristic vagueness that rivals other nuns' evasiveness—and garnered an "X" from the visitors in the margin of the original transcript: "Every nun sleeps in her own individual cell, and some sleep in company [in the same cell or in the same bed?] on the pretext of illness; and in winter some nuns [which ones?] sleep in company in some [one? two?] beds; and in summer they sleep separately."[24]

What Bianchi's and Malvasia's sleeping arrangements actually were is impossible to say—but a follow-up, on-site inspection did reveal two beds in Bianchi's cell, as well as no fewer than four in Emilia Grassi's.[25] And the reality is less important than what the various testimonies suggest it was imagined to be, for that represents the reality that directly affected the social dynamic within the convent walls.

These ambiguities may also resonate with another of Bianchi's singularly vague answers about her relationship to her earlier friend turned enemy, a response striking for its circumlocutory character, which makes clear translation difficult:

La causa io non lo so investigare, se non che pare pretenda d'haverli io ad esserli sogetta particolarmente in più stretto modo di quello che sono con l'altre, et io pretendo non gl'esser' più obligata che sono con l'altre, et essa si lamenta sempre di me che la perseguito.

I don't know how to figure out the cause, if it isn't that it seems she would lay claim to have me in thrall to [also possibly "lying under"?] her particularly, in a more closely bound manner than I am with the others; and I claim not to be more bound to her than to the others. And she always complains that I torment her.[26]

Cecilia Bianchi's description of the breakup contrasts with the abbess's more matter-of-fact account of the same event:

Il che anco procede perche donna Cecilia lavorava insieme con donna Emilia et cono-
scendo essa donna Cecilia che non poteva soportare la sudetta donna Emilia, che
pretendeva fare la superiora adosso donna Cecilia, per ciò separandosi da essa diede
occasione d'acrescere sospetti et sdegni.

It also happens because donna Cecilia was working together with donna Emilia, and
when donna Cecilia realized that she couldn't bear the said donna Emilia, who insisted
on playing the superior on top of donna Cecilia's back, for that reason, in breaking
away from her, she created an opportunity to increase suspicions and anger.[27]

The contorted syntax of Bianchi's own recounting of the rift, with
its shifting, ambiguous pronouns, becomes a metaphor for their tor-
tured, ambivalent relationship. Could Bianchi's language be hinting
that Grassi had attempted one of those "particular friendships" that
nuns have been exhorted to avoid and that prelates have endeavored
to suppress for centuries? Isabetta Vizzana's opening description of Cecilia Bianchi (quoted in chapter 5) might suggest the opposite: "there's
one donna Cecilia by name, who is moved by a certain infatuation she
had with donna Emilia." Could the other nuns have hoped that their
testimony about Cecilia's sleeping arrangements would undermine her
credibility, would suggest the inner corruption beneath her mask of hypocrisy, by playing upon the imaginings behind their superiors' leading
question?

The Bolognese clergy's serious view of such transgression, real or
imagined, is clear from diocesan proclamations after a pastoral visitation to Santa Margherita in 1591: the vicar general threatened the nuns
with six months' imprisonment, deprivation of the veil, and no access
to the grates if they "should dare or presume in future to sleep together
in the same bed or in the same room." "Particular friendships" and their
potential physical component had long been seen as a threat even to
nuns' vow of chastity. Erasmus's Colloquy of 1523, *Virgo MIΣOΓAMOΣ*
takes the form of a dialogue in which one Eubulus attempts to dissuade
Catherine from the cloistered life by calling nuns' chastity into question
in just this way:

Eub.: Nothing's virginal among those virgins in other respects either.
Cath.: No? Why not, if you please?
Eub.: Because there are more who copy Sappho's behavior than share her talent.
Cath.: I don't quite understand what you mean.
Eub.: And I say these things in order that the time may not come when you do under-
stand, my dear Catherine.

In the sequel, "The Repentant Girl," a sadder but wiser Catherine, having quickly abandoned her hands-on experiments with convent life, darkly hints at horrors, which she refuses to reveal.[28]

Although these veiled hints directed back and forth by Bianchi, Ruggeri, and the other nuns said little or nothing about "sexual identity," they could raise the specter of "immodest acts" that might usefully call into question both the character of the dominating donna Emilia and the vaunted sanctity of the "lost soul," the "hypocrite," the *riformatrice* (reformer) Cecilia Bianchi. The possibility of some intensely emotional, psychosexual component to the original Bianchi-Grassi relationship gone sour would also go a way toward explaining the extraordinary and especially bitter playing out of this implacable enmity over two decades.

But the ecclesiastical hierarchy showed little interest in shared convent beds or in what some might have imagined went on in them—as long, that is, as all occupants were female. They probably chalked it up to another commonly perceived failing of female behavior, especially among nuns, articulated in a similar spirit by Cardinal Desiderio Scaglia in the mid-1630s, in discussing imputations of sorcery: "Since among them, women's wars and rivalries easily arise, it is thus quite credible that, should there happen to be among them some less loving person, and they make accusations about such things to their superiors, then all the others get in a fuss and have nothing to do with the accused. Whatever tiny wrong they hear about they attribute to her mischief, and blame her for it."[29] Like their colleagues at various other times and places, whose choice of penalties for female intimacies was generally moderate, the visitors to Santa Cristina simply reiterated the same, oft-heard threat of reprisals. They were exclusively concerned with the impact of the personal relationships on the good order of convent society as a whole. As we shall see, their reaction to the slightest hint of suspicious familiarity with *males* would be very different.

"All Stirred Up against Me because of Her Subornation"

The fact that her rival took refuge in intense sanctimoniousness and punctilious piety had abetted Grassi's campaign to isolate Bianchi. By her fault-finding, her inflexible calls for reform, and particularly by calling the honor of the convent into question, Bianchi had also alienated all but Maria Gentile Malvasia, who had become her new, and perhaps particular, friend. Much more startling and, by the standards of her time, unbecoming, Bianchi was even reduced to an alliance with a *conversa*, suor Ludovica Fabri, already judged "uppity for a *conversa*" by her betters. Suor Ludovica's pejorative nickname, "the theologian," also suggests that she displayed pretensions of religiosity similar to donna Cecilia's. Santa Cristina's blue-blood society of *professe* would still have seconded the remark of a fifteenth-century blue blood from Prato that "no gentleman who wants honor ought to be advanced by a merchant."[30] Cecilia Bianchi's even lower-class alliance was that much more dubious. Such an abandonment of her own class testifies to the extent of her alienation.

When Ruggeri and the nuns learned of the memorial Bianchi had handed to the pastoral visitors, in which she claimed all the troubles had begun because of music and where she raised the issue of Grassi's illegitimacy, they imagined it was filled with further calumnies. But the memorial turns out to contain nothing anyone really wanted to hear. Where almost everything else in the 110 pages of the trial transcript was intended to deflect attention away from the speakers, Bianchi's personal memorial turns obsessively inward. It witnesses eloquently to her painful isolation, her sense of persecution, and the destructive effect of ostracism within an institution whose very nature was intended to be intensely communal:

It has been eighteen years that I have endured this persecution, and it began because of music. Because we had words, I called her misbegotten, and she responded to me viciously. Thus, despite my conciliations and my other loving gestures, she has never wanted to believe me to be her true friend. Ever since then she has put me in disgrace before all our superiors and the confessors, and all the fathers of the congregation, and achieved my disgrace before all our superiors, to such an extent that they won't risk speaking to me or availing themselves of my services. At her command, I've also felt the great repugnance of many. Then she accused me, always saying her every torment was my fault and that I was the one who made her unhappy. She claims and preaches constantly to the other sisters that I am a lost soul. And by this and other fabrications she tries to make me loathsome to the whole world and even among the laity.

Well, if any may have gone to pay court to her—as many do—and because she sometimes may have said capriciously that what's white and black is black and white, now as a result those do the same thing. To revenge themselves against me, they claim that I've caused the convent to be reformed, pressing this matter so emphatically that they don't notice or don't care about committing perjury. If the superior reprimands her [for such acts] she says she commits no sin but rather is justified, because there could be no counterclaims.

But I can't do that, because we're different in our inclinations and dispositions. My inclination is to be retiring and mind my own business and to live as quietly as possible. I've said this little bit that I could remember, because I take no account of offenses, in order better to enjoy my soul's peace. For I take no notice of the rest.

I thought that we should be reformed in this and that we need no reform but our own consciences. There was no chance if not this one, so I wish to set my will free in that way permitted me, both for the honor of God and for the service and benefit of my convent. This is repugnant to her and I'm sorry it's that way. But, truly, I can do no other.

Since sometimes the mother abbesses, present and past, have employed me to compose some letter or petition on behalf of the convent, for that reason one might imagine that the statements and petitions sent to our superiors in Rome might have been my work. Especially because of that, she and her other allies made known that they want me tormented, even unto death.

Had Bianchi in fact written to Rome, provoking the investigation, as the nuns and Ruggeri were convinced she had? Bianchi claimed that "they're all stirred up against me because of her subornation, and because of her insinuation that I wrote to Rome. Now she's induced them all to commit perjury. She's made up the truth and concocted how they should answer questions—as she's now doing with the *converse*."[31] The diocesan curia, right up to Archbishop Ludovico Ludovisi himself, emphatically seconded Bianchi's denials. Ruggeri's case for the prosecution rests to some extent on convent gossip, although he makes the point that the conclusion to the August 1622 letter to Rome, "*supplico* di rimedio" (*I* petition for a remedy), demonstrates it had been a single author's work rather than representing the sentiments of many.

It seems quite certain that the defamatory letter had indeed been Bianchi's handiwork—just as it seems likely that Grassi coached various *professe* and *converse* before they testified. Archbishop Ludovisi's biographer affirms the fact when he comments that Bianchi and her cohorts became "repulsive to the nuns because they had informed their superiors about their failings." Furthermore, toward the end of a long second day of testimony, donna Cecilia remarked, "I was moved to write the petition sent to our superiors so that they would see to the disturbances among the laity, who had been told of these, our imperfections." Clearly, then, she had written some letter to the clerical hierarchy. In recopying his original transcript of her testimony for the archiepiscopal archive, the scribe first wrote "mandato à Roma" (sent to Rome), which he immediately crossed out and replaced with the original, vaguer "mandato à superiori" (sent to our superiors)—a natural slip if he had known the true destination.[32]

Phrases from Cecilia's testimony also echo the original defamatory letter's accusations: both specifically cite the wearing of illicit pleated veils (*velli stampati*), for example. Most striking, the lax nuns' alleged claim that "non è il tempo de santi" (it is not the age of saints) from the original letter of August 1622 becomes in Cecilia's testimony of four months later "è quasi una voce comune che *non è più il tempo di S. Benedetto*" ("They say as if with one voice that *it is no longer the age of Saint Benedict*").

The odd, irregular trio of donna Cecilia, donna Maria Gentile, and suor Ludovica had convinced the rest of the community that they had brought the authorities down upon them. Again and again the other nuns accused the three of bringing the house into disrepute. It also appears that Bianchi and her allies had made a practice of carrying tales for some time. An unnamed tertiary's denunciation to the Inquisition seems to have been among their unsavory acts. Donna Cecilia's claim during the investigation in 1623 that others had unjustly accused them of this betrayal was rather undermined by suor Ludovica's subsequent boast to the visitors that "donna Domitilla said to me lately that I did right in making an accusation to the Holy Office."[33] Thus it was that donna Cecilia earned for herself the title of *riformatrice*.

What Ruggeri saw as her envy, vanity, pride, and ambition, but which also emerges as her acute alienation and isolation, left Bianchi particularly susceptible to the influence of Giovanni Bondini, the perennial nuns' vicar of Bologna. While suffragan bishops and vicars general came and went, this archetypical ecclesiastical survivor, "don Gioanino," continued year after year to exercise various sorts of petty tyranny over the nuns. As the guardian of convent parlatorios, for example, he frequently made life difficult for those seeking permission to speak to the nuns. On one occasion he even refused to countersign an indult from the pope himself permitting the reunion of a brother and his cloistered sister at Santa Cristina, remarking that they would see each other in paradise.

One of the nuns revealed to Ruggeri the way around this particular problem: "The remedy turned out to be to send him a plate of toffee or apples with the license under a big toffee, and then the license was signed without further difficulty." This don Gioanino knew just how to play upon Bianchi's weaknesses. "He would promise her oceans and mountains, but in the end she would find herself hoodwinked," in Ruggeri's words. His was not the run-of-the-mill seduction that has commonly fueled popular imaginings about priests and nuns but an appeal to her lusts for revenge and power. As Ruggeri put it, "Donna Cecilia was moved to do this wrong to her convent by her old hatred of donna Emilia and by the hope that don Gioanino gave her that she would become abbess or reformer."[34]

Despite Ruggeri's pious claim that "nothing was ever heard about the convent of Santa Cristina that might have offended the pious ears of the Bolognese," Bianchi probably knew that the convent had long suffered from a somewhat-tarnished reputation. The defamatory letter of August 1622 included the remark, "The nuns of Santa Cristina need to be reformed as happened eighty years ago." In 1506 (to be more precise), because of a scandal brewing there since the late 1400s, Bologna's vicar general had transferred exemplary nuns from another Bolognese convent to Santa Cristina to reestablish regular observance. And as long ago as 1433, the Camaldolese prior general Ambrogio Traversari had been appalled by the claim that "in the convent of Santa Cristina I had not uncovered even a morsel of truth, because they were all whores." Looking back from the early 1700s, on the other hand, an anticlerical chronicler also commented, "It is quite true, in fact, that they were never looked upon with favor. But there is in them such a deep-rooted affection for friardom and monkery that the affection survives even to this day."[35] Bianchi need not have looked far for inspiration, and one can imagine why many in the outside world would have been inclined to believe her.

"Chastity—I Would Not Speak of It out of Respect"

The curious along via Fondazza may well have braved the cold, hoping for delicious gossip, as clerical investigators came and went between 20 December 1622 and 13 January 1623, first twice a day, then only once, because the light faded so quickly on those midwinter afternoons. The mortified speculations of the nuns' families and the prurient fantasies of the public at large in the meantime ranged free. They are unlikely to have strayed far from the inevitable theme whenever monks and nuns are the topic of conversation. If Ruggeri is to be believed, rumor said that as many as eight nuns were pregnant.[36]

Donna Cecilia Bianchi entered the parlatorio for what promised to be the visitation's most sensational testimony late on 22 December. It had been a comparatively uneventful and disappointing two and a half days. Apart from the many details of the Bianchi-Grassi feud, the previous twenty-one witnesses had revealed little beyond the sorts of accommodation to a convent lifestyle that would have turned up had the visitors gone snooping at other upper-class, unreformed convents.

The trial transcript simply does not bear out Ruggeri's claim that Suffragan Bishop Gozzadini had actually upset the prescribed order and called Bianchi early, impatient to get to the real scandals he hoped to hear. Unquestionably, however, Bianchi tried the visitors' patience, for her testimony dragged on for the rest of 22 December, for all of 23 December, and, after the holidays, for most of 28 December. She kept the notary scribbling for more than nineteen pages, compared to Emilia Grassi's eight pages of testimony. There was hardly any aspect of convent life in which Bianchi failed to ferret out some fault, however minor. And they all seemed minor.

But the critical issue on both sides of the convent wall was embodied in the cryptic phrase from the defamatory letter to Rome, "Castità non ne parli per riverenza" (Chastity—I would not speak of it out of respect). Its author had concocted it shrewdly, as Ruggeri recognized, since its ambiguity admitted either a positive or a negative interpretation. And, clearly, this was the issue that fired the wildest speculations among the populace, which imagined no fewer than one nun in five to be with child.

Castità was critical to *onestà* (decency) and *onore* (honor), in which any claims the nuns might have to authority were grounded. Nuns' traditional role as intercessors for their cities derived its particular efficacy from the chastity of the consecrated virgins, a purity rarely matched beyond their cloisters. One abbess claimed that her nuns' prayers were "more useful coming from persons of such great religion than are two thousand horses." It was their perfection that guaranteed them a hearing in heaven, and also in the world.[37]

Even if some no longer held this pious view by 1620, the common belief in the relationship between a daughter's chastity and her family's honor remained thoroughly intact. As Annibal Guasco warned his daughter in the 1580s, "there is no cure for the loss of chastity; it besmirches a woman even after her death." And it was not only her honor that remained at stake. Guido Ruggiero asserts that "the sexual honor of a woman was not only hers, I would say not even primarily hers; it was tied to a calculus of honor more complex, which involved both the family and the men who dominated it. . . . The honor of an entire family and of the men responsible for it revolved about the conservation of a daughter's virginity."[38]

That situation certainly did not change when daughters entered the cloister. Indeed, the surrogates who supplanted their fathers as their new guardians found their own honor also at stake in the maintenance of their spiritual daughters' virtue. And because of nuns' special role in ritually affirming the continuity of public life by their prayers, any violation of their *onestà* constituted a violation of the honor not only of the clergy and of their families but also of the entire city.

The dramatic turns in Ruggeri's account of Bianchi's interrogation, in which an impatient Bishop Gozzadini puts aside her written statement unread the second morning to "attack at the primary point, where the nail should be driven home," are scarcely evident in the original trial transcript. Sandwiched between an allegation that, contrary to their vow of poverty, the nuns grub for anything they can get and an accusation that three nuns owned their own farm animals, the long-awaited response finally appears, with nothing more remarkable to set it off than a full stop and the beginning of a new sentence: "And as for chastity, I deem everyone to be holy, as the sanctity of the place requires." Judging by the transcript, the notary did not even look up from his furious scribbling as Bianchi droned on for another full day. Ruggeri claims, however, that all were stunned at her crucial answer to the critical question. The timorous Camaldolese don Desiderio Bardelloni da Monza, who a moment before had been trembling with fear and dread, broke into a joyous grin.[39]

Even if Ruggeri may have been making a good story even better, as one suspects he was, his additional dramatic touches point up more clearly how crucial to the whole visitation this issue was seen to be. One can understand don Desiderio da Monza's misguided belief that the worst was finally over. The investigation dragged on for another three weeks. But with the chastity issue settled, diocesan representatives were chiefly going through the motions. Their most serious discovery about inappropriate shenanigans between the sheets turned out to be nothing more scandalous than a nun's hapless puppy, temporarily hiding out in the bed of a *conversa*. The suffragan bishop descended upon the *conversa*'s cell, exposed the interloper, and confronted its owner with his discovery. The nun claimed that the pup, which belonged to her sister-in-law, was just visiting and should have been sent home three days before. Since dogs could not be excommunicated for violation of *clausura*, the visitors had to be content with its banishment from the cloister. High clerical drama, it seems, had dipped dangerously toward farce.[40]

Don Mauro Ruggeri, the appointed guardian of the nuns' *onestà*, had reason to exult: "God Almighty, the Blessed Virgin, Saint Romuald, and

Saint Christina, to whom the nuns constantly commended themselves to sustain their innocence and defense, interceded so that donna Cecilia should answer truthfully and faintly, with these solemn words: 'In this I deem them holy.'"[41] This was not to be the end of the affair, however. Within two years, the efficacy of such heavenly intercessions would be much more severely tested.

SEVEN

Losing Battles with a Bishop: "We Cared for Babylon, and She Is Not Healed"

Cecilia Bianchi's anticlimactic declaration effectively ended the pastoral visitation. But it dragged on for another two weeks, as the visitors dutifully worked their way through the remaining *professe* and *converse*. At the end, the archbishopric imposed a string of familiar remedies with few surprises. Mass and Office should occur when there would be no distractions. To remove inappropriate socializing, services should be recited with the parlatorio grates shuttered. Chapel silver could no longer be borrowed from the sacristy; dogs were banned from the convent and cats from the chapel, where fans and alternative reading matter were also forbidden. There should be no more picnics at the portals. Nuns, forbidden mirrors, must limit themselves strictly to their regular habits—no jewelry, colored sleeves, pleated veils, or oversize collars. Sun hats were declared "unseemly virginal attire." Even on the sultriest August days, nuns should never go around with bare shoulders, with bosoms exposed, or covered only with "indecent" see-through veils. And no sister should set foot outside her cell in a state of undress.

The combat zone that the choir had become required more detail.

Correcting faults in choir falls to the mother abbess and not to others, except for singing mistakes, which fall exclusively to the choir mistress. That position should rotate as
do the other minor offices. It falls to the choir mistress alone to raise or lower the into-
nation of the antiphons sung in choir. No sister except the novice mistress is permitted
to teach singing to any novice. It is expressly forbidden to pay a salary or give other
gifts to a master of music or to a harpsichord teacher—seeing that they are prohibited.

As for Emilia Grassi and Cecilia Bianchi, the visitors suggested they
should be seated on opposite sides of the choir and declared propheti-
cally, "one can anticipate more of the same from them—and worse—in
future."[1]

At the publication of the decrees before the assembled nuns, Suffragan Bishop Gozzadini preached pointedly on the example of the harvest,
when even the highest fruit is cast down to earth. As he had implied,
donna Emilia was denied the post of bursar she coveted, while donna
Cecilia was passed over for the position she had set her hopes on, novice
mistress, in favor of donna Adeodata Leoni, the prominent patron of
convent music. Bianchi complained bitterly to Rome, citing her right of
seniority, but the Congregation of Bishops ruled against her.

Much to her dismay, the position of abbess fell to Lucrezia Vizzana's
aunt, the venerable Flaminia Bombacci. Donna Flaminia must have
mixed political acumen with piety. Perhaps she questioned her own ef-
fectiveness, given the Bombacci family's somewhat humbler origins by
Santa Cristina's exalted standards and in light of what she had witnessed
in convent government over many years. Donna Flaminia tried to decline in favor of the noble Cleria Pepoli, whose singularly illustrious and
noble lineage might check Cardinal Ludovisi and also restore important
political alliances close to the pope in Rome.[2] But Pepoli was much too
sickly to rule, a condition to which she had repeatedly testified in December. Then her shrillest complaint had been that convent toffee making monopolized the communal fire and prevented her from keeping
warm.[3] In the end donna Flaminia had no choice but to serve.

During Flaminia Bombacci's reign an unaccustomed, albeit superfi-
cial, tranquility settled within the walls on via Fondazza. But Bianchi
continued to conspire with archiepiscopal ministers, chiefly the nuns'
vicar don Gioanino, who fed her aspirations to become abbess and convent reformer. In the meantime Bianchi also acquired another, more
socially preeminent ally. Lucidaria Bolognetti, the niece of Cardinal Al-
berto Bolognetti (1538–85), hailed from one of the city's greatest families. She had also been Emilia Grassi's enemy at least since Grassi's reign

as abbess. In 1616 Bolognetti had complained to the Congregation of Bishops that Grassi and the convent father confessor were thwarting her efforts to obtain a substantial inheritance, and she alleged financial mismanagement by Grassi and the father confessor, "her counselor, secretary, and treasurer."[4]

Little by little, donna Lucidaria's dour manner left her friendless. Ruggeri claimed she became so ill-tempered that even her own kin wanted nothing to do with her. So inevitably she was drawn to the bitterly alienated and disaffected Cecilia Bianchi and Maria Gentile Malvasia.

Madre donna Flaminia, who reputedly prophesied the sorry outcome of this unholy alliance, did not live to witness their handiwork. Worn out by decades of fasting, discipline, and twenty-two years of perpetual prayer in chapel with only brief periods of rest on bare boards, she survived her election as abbess by only eighteen months. Continually glorifying God, donna Flaminia passed to a better life, assisted by Mauro Ruggeri at her bedside. On 28 September 1624, as first vespers sounded for the feast of Saint Michael, the archangel saw her safely on her way to paradise.

During 1625 the crisis escalated, as Archbishop Ludovisi worked to drive a wedge between Santa Cristina and the Camaldolese order. In February the Bolognese vicar general declined to confirm the Lenten preacher elected by the nuns and approved by their Camaldolese superiors; instead, he appointed a preacher himself. When the Camaldolese abbot general protested, Ludovisi responded that the nuns should in no way be permitted such a choice "because of the evil consequences that can result, since they can for various reasons elect persons who, instead of edifying, might destroy them with public scandal."[5]

Ruggeri repeatedly claimed that diocesan ministers' desire to lay hands on rich convent holdings motivated their attempts to subjugate Santa Cristina to archiepiscopal control. Nevertheless, Ludovisi's stated objective was quite in line with the goals of the post-Tridentine church, in whose eyes convent governance by regular clergy rather than by ordinaries had long impeded a uniform and well-regulated ecclesiastical system.

Hints of convent scandal offered the handiest means to justify changes in convent government. Following close on Ludovisi's innuendo, such an opportunity appeared early in 1626, when new defamatory letters—presumably from Cecilia Bianchi, Maria Gentile Malvasia, and Lucidaria Bolognetti—provoked the Congregation of Bishops to investigate alleged Carnival improprieties by various Camaldolese monks and nuns at Santa Cristina. According to Ruggeri, the new suffragan bishop Carlo Bovio was so completely in league with Cecilia Bianchi's faction that he sent Lucidaria Bolognetti a festive olive branch, not as a symbol of peace—but as a sign of impending victory.

Common wisdom dictated that, for the sake of charity and monastic reputations, any such investigations be carried out as circumspectly as possible. Neither secrecy nor discretion was a consideration in this visitation. For a month the Bolognese public, who had scarcely forgotten the sensational events of 1623, was treated to a new spectacle. Constables were posted around the convent and in the public parlatorio during daily interrogations. Servants hung about outside gawking and loudly discussing the case, "provoking such great scandal, and fostering such loathsome opinions," according to Ruggeri, "that there was no place in the city and throughout Italy—or, one might say, throughout Europe—that the sacred virgins were not spoken of as women of the greatest ill repute imaginable, a thing to make one weep tears of blood."[6] The crucial source of the nuns' influence, their virtuous reputation and honor, already under a cloud, continued to slip away.

Suffragan Bishop Bovio welcomed Bianchi, Malvasia, and Bolognetti ("the three furies," as Ruggeri calls them) to the parlatorio, one by one, with smiles and encouragement. "Don't tell me trivialities—tell me major matters that I can use to help you!" he exclaimed—at least according to nuns who had hidden themselves close by to eavesdrop.[7] In Ruggeri's account Bolognetti suborned the most junior member of the community to testify that the father confessor and the convent's Camaldolese procurator had illicitly attended an evening performance of a secular play put on by the nuns in the parlatorio during Carnival. But the young witness soon had second thoughts and retracted her testimony. She continued to maintain her resolve even after Bovio imprisoned her.

No matter. True or false, her allegation found its way into the summary of the investigation forwarded to Rome, which mentions the performance of a secular play entitled *L'ore mascherate* (Masking times) after-hours in the parlatorio:

All the nuns say it wasn't recited in the parlatorio except a novice, who says that it was presented at night in the parlatorio. But she didn't see any other audience but the bursar; and she seemed to make out a [man's] white hat in the said parlatorio. Two other nuns [Bianchi and Malvasia?] say they heard from the said novice that it was performed in the parlatorio. They believe this to be true, because the nun performers from that night didn't turn up for matins.

Suffragan Bishop Bovio claimed that the nuns had rehearsed their responses to his investigation in advance—all, that is, but the two most junior, whom he had taken by surprise:

The first confesses that the play was recited in the parlatorio at night in her presence, and that friars were there. The second doesn't dare deny it but says she can't remember. The play was not only secular but lascivious and included a role of a lady courtesan. As for the other charges, they have almost all been proven by the confessions of the monks themselves and of the nuns. From this sort of thing the Sacred Congregation will see the improprieties, the licentiousness, and the laxity of these monks.

"The other charges" that Bovio alleged in the summary suggest that the three malcontents had accepted his challenge to come up with major offences:

The father confessor is almost always hanging around the *ruota* in the sacristy, and most of the time he is chatting up the abbess's niece: and this according to three nuns [Bianchi, Malvasia, and Bolognetti?]. Another nun claimed that the said confessor told her that the first time he saw the abbess's niece, he went mad for her, exclaiming that she was his little angel and lamenting that he hadn't a lot of presents for her. And two nuns testified to having seen some of the same monks chatting with the nuns at the *ruota* with the door shut.[8]

Camilla Bombacci, who had succeeded her sister, was the current abbess. In that case the *angioletta* who had so won the father confessor's heart could only be Isabetta Vizzana or the younger Lucrezia Orsina. It appears the neophyte confessor don Giusto Bordino may have been every bit as young and foolish as Mauro Ruggeri claimed. Or perhaps one of the Vizzani sisters (by then closer to forty than thirty) still retained all her youthful charms.

There must have been at least a few grains of truth to these imputations, for Ruggeri's own account describes behavior that Bovio and the Bianchi faction could have doctored with a negative spin. Ruggeri was probably the monk who was observed in intimate conversation at the *ruota* and who, according to Bovio, had "confessed." During the *carnevalino* (mini-Carnival) celebrated at the convent on the days before Advent in 1625, Camilla Bombacci has summoned Ruggeri to Santa Cristina. As Ruggeri conferred with Bombacci at the confessional grate, Suffragan Bishop Bovio arrived unexpectedly. A nun who happened to be peering through the grilled window above the high altar spotted Bovio as he entered the public church and raised a commotion with the other nuns. The suffragan bishop may have suspected she was sounding an alarm when he discovered Ruggeri at the confessional. The next day the bishop summoned and severely chastised Ruggeri for compromising behavior with a nun at a secluded grate—he should have met her in the public parlatorio. Ruggeri retorted that convent superiors were permitted access to such grates. But Cecilia Bianchi was quick to divulge that by late 1625 Ruggeri's pastoral authority no longer extended to Bologna. Ruggeri barely left town in time to escape imprisonment by the bishop's chief constable, sent to arrest him.[9]

Bovio and Bianchi could hardly have wished for more. Their allegation gained authority simply by bringing together the threats to nuns' virtue that were habitually considered most grievous in the popular and ecclesiastical imagination: grates, parlatorios, seclusion, and confessors. These sites of potential worldly pollution remained the butt of anticlerical cynicism in pornographic images, prose, and poems such as the eighteenth-century *I costumi delle monache* (Convent manners):

Ad una grada un Cavalier in piede,
Finge con una di parlar segreto,
E mentre esser veduto non si crede,
Con allungar le man gli tocca il petto.
Anch'ella tocca ciò che non possede,
E va su e giu cercandogli diletto.
Suonano, e in consonanza, e per appunto,
Del Vescovo al venir giungono al punto.[10]

Before the grating a gallant is waiting,
Feigning in private to speak with a sister,
Thinking the chaperones sit unsuspecting,
Straining his fingers on bosom to touch her.
Faintly she fondles that thing she is lacking,
Sliding up, slipping down, thrilling together.
Fiddling in consort, to put it quite nicely,
By bishop's arrival, they've finished precisely.

The public's worst—or favorite—imaginings, fed by pornographic works like Pietro Aretino's *Ragionamento della Nanna e della Antonia* (A discourse between Nanna and Antonia) and periodically confirmed by complaints such as the following to the Congregation of Bishops in 1659, from the men of Bettona (Assisi), turned even innuendos of impropriety into serious concerns to be dealt with severely: "Don Giovanni Maria Penna, who serves the convent of Santa Caterina [as confessor], maintains an intimate friendship with suora Maria Fulvia, scandalizing nuns and laity alike. After he shut himself inside the communion closet, he was seen to put his member in her hands, and other actions. These [confessors] want to send the brides of Christ to the devil's domain!"[11]

The Bianchi bloc and their diocesan allies were maneuvering against those newly empowered at Santa Cristina. In this scenario, Camilla Bombacci, who had snatched the position of abbess from Cecilia Bianchi's faction, had been compromised by alleged improprieties with a senior Camaldolese official. One of her nieces had been implicated in unseemly behavior with the Camaldolese monk specifically mandated to guard the nuns' collective *onestà*. The plotters had chosen their targets well, for Camilla Bombacci and Isabetta Vizzana dominate the paroxysms of the next three years.

But the secretary of the Congregation of Bishops, deep in Archbishop Ludovisi's pocket (according to Ruggeri), still found Bovio's accusations insufficiently damning. In June 1626 he ordered the Bolognese papal legate to lay bare "the complete truth concerning the excesses allegedly committed in that convent of Santa Cristina, governed by Camaldolese monks." Not long thereafter, the legate descended on the convent, locked the nuns in the choir, confiscated all their keys, invaded the cloister with his men, and ransacked the place. According to Ruggeri, "not content to have searched the chests, they even tore apart the beds; and even though they had done so without warning, they found nothing to carry off." This extraordinary act—almost unparalleled in the convents of Bologna during the 1600s—represented a kind of ravishment, penetrating to the most private corners of the nuns' world.[12]

Thwarted in this third attempt to expose sufficiently damning evidence, the Congregation of Bishops had no choice but to write the legate and the nuns in April 1627, lauding "the good government and observance by which they live there under regular [Camaldolese] rule, and the good order that wafts from every corner of that holy place of purity and goodness."[13] As in 1623, it might seem that Santa Cristina had been vindicated.

But this letter was simply a sop to the nuns, designed to divert attention from the curia's larger scheme. A canceled draft from the Vatican record book, dated a month earlier but never sent, concludes, "Given this fine demonstration of the discipline in which they have lived until now under the governance of these [Camaldolese monks], [the cardinals] are led to believe that with each passing day they will profit in God's service under the salutary direction of the Illustrious Lord Cardinal Ludovisi, archbishop and ordinary of that city, to whose government they now find themselves subject." Two weeks before he canceled this draft, the secretary of the Congregation of Bishops had quietly notified the Camaldolese prior general of Pope Urban VIII's decision to transfer Santa Cristina to Ludovisi's control: "It will therefore be expedient, for the sake of your order's reputation, Most Reverend Father, that within three days at most you make a voluntary renunciation into the hands of His Holiness and give the appropriate orders for the release of control. Deliver them directly into my own hands, to be absolutely certain of their arrival." The nuns, who had got wind of what was afoot in Rome, implored Cardinal Barberini to intercede with his uncle, Urban VIII, "lest the reputation of the convent and of such high nobility that reside therein be tarnished." It was a waste of time—the pope acceded to Ludovisi's wishes.[14]

Peering out his window next door to the convent on 2 June 1627, don Vincenzo da Sant'Agata, Santa Cristina's confessor extraordinary, spied a crowd of the bishop's yeomen advancing on Santa Cristina with clubs, guns, and other weapons, "like an army of Turks, with screams, shouts, and clamor." The tumult so terrified don Vincenzo that he fled out the back of his lodgings and across a garden to a neighbor's, where he begged layman's clothes, then slipped away in disguise to take refuge at the Camaldolese monastery downtown.[15] Behind the fleeing monk, archiepiscopal forces seized Santa Cristina.

The nuns were fully aware that assurances about unsullied virtue framed in the most benignant pastoral rhetoric meant nothing if their Camaldolese superiors were banished. Among the nobility, where reputation meant everything, what *was* remained less important than what seemed to be. As Sherrill Cohen puts it, "*Onore* for a patrician woman or *onestà* (decency) for a plebeian woman was not so much a matter of actual behavior as one of what her community knew and said about her."[16]

Meekly to accept subjugation to the archbishop would prove that the nuns acknowledged their sullied *onestà* and their families' disgrace. So when the archbishop sent his secular priests to administer the Sacraments, the nuns sent them packing with threats and abuse. When Camilla Bombacci's term as abbess expired in the fall of 1627, the sisters defied Ludovisi's command to elect a successor. To preserve their reputation, under Bombacci's continued leadership, they swore a solemn oath early in 1628 to reject the archbishop's authority and to recognize no superiors but the Camaldolese. All of them swore the oath, that is, except Cecilia Bianchi and her two allies, and as Ludovisi later complained, "For demonstrating their readiness to obey or because of vain suspicion that they had made revelations against you, they had to be imprisoned within their own cells for the sake of their very lives." Ludovisi later alleged that the nuns even convinced a mortally ill sister that it would suffice to confess before a crucifix rather than resort to a secular priest.[17]

In May 1628 Ludovisi demanded appropriately harsh methods to curb the nuns' yearlong contumacy and disobedience. Within the month the Congregation of Bishops cracked down hard, ordering the papal legate to use any and all means at his disposal to bring the rebellious nuns to heel: to imprison the most recalcitrant, if necessary; to deny the nuns access to their administrators and lawyers until they recognized Ludovisi and elected a new abbess; to break the will of the renegade Camilla Bombacci if she refused to abdicate; to remove convent staff, who continued to make the nuns' case to the outside world.

In August a reluctant papal legate tried to comply. After he endured considerable difficulty and indignity even gaining admittance to Santa Cristina, Camilla Bombacci harangued him for so long that he had to return another day and then another over the following two weeks, to no avail. Even the legate's offer to oversee an election himself, in place of the deeply compromised Suffragan Bishop Bovio, only aggravated what the legate called "the nuns' willful contempt and the scandal of the city." The legate concurred with Bovio that transferring the six worst rebels to other monasteries would quell further tumults more effectively than their imprisonment. But he pointed out that their removal to another Camaldolese house outside the city would suggest they had won. And he doubted that acceptable convents could be found locally without provoking further uproar.[18]

The desperate nuns appealed to Cardinal Pietro Maria Borghese in Rome, as one of similarly noble blood who could not fail to come to the defense of the reputation and honor of the many nobles among them:

Our innocence is manifest from the investigations already carried out repeatedly, in multiple visitations. But as long as our honor is not restored, our families remain eternally defamed and we, therefore, remain abandoned by them. So we have almost reached the point of our own damnation. Prostrate, we implore your aid in the restitution of our honor and the welfare of our souls. The cruel threats are at hand, which like lions, seek to devour us. And truly, if that comes to pass, the whole world will hear of us.

Within ten days, Ludovisi's official auditor and ally on the Congregation for the Propagation of the Faith responded on Ludovisi's behalf that the nuns had no other alternative but to obey.[19]

Threatened reprisals became reality on 17 November 1628. To cu off further communication, the Congregation of Bishops ordered Ludo visi to seal up the parlatorio, blockade all the gateways, and provide the nuns with only starvation rations. Twenty beadles and workmen sneaked into the convent courtyard under cover of darkness, after the nuns had gone to bed. It took them several hours to wall up the parlatorio doorway. The next morning archiepiscopal authorities arrived to survey the results and presumably receive the miscreant nuns' inevitable capitulation. But the doorway looked absolutely normal, without a trace of bricks or mortar. An astonished Ludovisi rounded up the convent servants and threw them into prison for complicity in breaking open the doorway. There was no way such highborn ladies could be capable of the required hard physical labor. But, in the words of one Bolognese chronicler, that wall "could not withstand the fierceness of the infuriated sisters." By first light they had demolished all the new masonry themselves.[20]

The episcopal auditor returned in broad daylight with a full squadron of yeomen and stonemasons to wall up the main cloister doorway. The assault caught the nuns at prayer before the Blessed Sacrament. With one accord, they clambered to the upper reaches of the convent, whence they greeted these latest invaders with a dense shower of bricks, roof tiles, and stones, provoking their retreat out of range to the double gate on via Fondazza. As a call to arms sounded from the bell tower, donna Isabetta Vizzana broke off from the others, grabbed a crucifix, and headed for a window of the loggia above the courtyard (fig. 21). At the open window, with her face veiled and the crucifix in hand, she began a passionate harangue that lasted four hours, until after sundown. Some in the gathering crowds of sympathetic parishioners, their long-term loyalty sustained by regular, illicit handouts from convent gardens, were moved to tears. Before long verbal counterattacks assaulted archiepiscopal forces from the rear—"Long live the nuns of Santa Cristina!" All the while a cohort of neighborhood children mustered at a side gate, where they began gathering up stones and tossing them into the convent, just in case the nuns might run short of artillery. Faced with such overwhelming opposition from all sides, and with the real possibility of public insurrection, the members of the curia mustered what dignity they could and beat an indecorously hasty retreat back downtown.[21]

Having failed with physical methods, Archbishop Ludovisi next tried sending his notary to negotiate a truce with Camilla Bombacci and her nuns. After an indecorously long wait outside the wall, the notary is let inside the courtyard. His mustered dignity cannot entirely mask a

FIGURE 21. The restored public church and courtyard of Santa Cristina della Fondazza (2008), site of the nuns' battle with archiepiscopal forces in 1628. Isabetta Vizzana's oration occurred at a window above the portico. The original wall surrounding the courtyard was demolished in 1914. Photograph: Luca Salvucci, Bologna.

certain anxiety as his wait continues, and he keeps an uneasy watch for possible missiles from above. A nun appears at a window up near the roof (fig. 22): "Yes? What do you want?" "The mother abbess." "Come closer, so she can hear you." As the notary moves nearer the shade of the archway beneath the window, he can make out a shape appearing directly above. "Here's the mother abbess!" A great hunk of marble plummets toward him!

"If the poor man had not quickly jumped out of the way, he would have been overwhelmed and crushed by that blow!" exclaimed the sole chronicler who records this encounter.[22] The writer was not above making a good story even better. True or false, his extraordinary tale hints at an attitude that naturally arose after the several violent confrontations. For the Bolognese, the infuriated attempt against the notary symbolized

FIGURE 22. Santa Cristina della Fondazza (2011), window above the entry to the cloister; most likely to have been the site of the nuns' attack on the archiepiscopal notary in 1628. Photograph: Luca Salvucci, Bologna.

the potential havoc loosed if irrational female energies continued to run wild and uncontrolled. The nuns' subjugation to archiepiscopal government came to be seen as essential to a civil society.

The hierarchy eventually turned to less physically hazardous but ultimately more effective means to end the siege. They called upon Bologna's chief theologians, the university, and even the father inquisitor to rule publicly on the nuns' common oath of disobedience. With that ruling in hand, the diocesan curia proclaimed:

Be it known to all the nuns of Santa Cristina that their oath, together to stand united and to disobey their superiors' commandments, is false, void, and against the vow and oath they made in their profession, when they vowed obedience to their superiors. And therefore, whoever took that oath [of defiance] and whoever forced anyone to take it has committed mortal sin. This is the view of all the theologians of the city and of the University of Bologna. But because that oath should not be a chain dragging you all down to iniquity, for the greater peace of your consciences we absolve you of the said oath, which we proclaim null, void, and worthless.[23]

Now the archbishop's agents could more easily influence the nuns' families and noble sympathizers, their sole remaining source of any potential support, already undermined by gossip. Ruggeri claimed that the nuns' relatives finally convinced them to petition Ludovisi for forgiveness and for permission to be placed temporarily under Capuchin control. For his part, the archbishop could decry his own ministers' earlier unruly violence, which had occurred during his absence. On his return from Rome, Ludovisi visited Santa Cristina, said Mass, and expressed his conviction that the convent would return to Camaldolese rule some day. Having thus deluded the nuns about his good intentions, the archbishop and his agents continued to thwart them at every turn.[24]

Ruggeri suggests that the nuns' Roman advocates had temporarily persuaded Urban VIII to reconsider the matter and to place the nuns for the time being under Capuchin control; but Ludovisi's allies dissuaded the pope at the last minute. In a letter of 7 February 1629, the nuns gratefully acknowledged Ludovisi's aid in securing papal authorization of Capuchin confessors. Ludovisi's mild-mannered reply pointed out, however, that he had just received the Congregation of Bishop's contrary orders with "a decision very different from what you heard from your attorney." This decision, dated 1 February, which he enclosed with his response, left no room for maneuver:

In this matter one must in no way entertain treaties and compromises so prejudicial to the authority of this Holy See, so injurious to the state and health of the nuns themselves, and offering such a pernicious example to anybody else to attempt to oppose the execution of apostolic orders. Obedience must be exact, total, and undiminished. And it is no less scandalous than it is astonishing that nuns would dare to negotiate terms with the pope, their supreme lord. His Holiness granted [authority] to you so that you would be so kind as to exercise it—to crush once and for all such prolonged and obstinate impudence by these poor souls.[25]

Three weeks later the archbishop promulgated a decree bluntly rehearsing for the city's benefit the nuns' prolonged contumacy and his own forbearance and justifying his ultimate threat of excommunication if the nuns of Santa Cristina failed to capitulate:

You, donna Camilla Bombacci, sometime abbess of the convent of Santa Cristina in this city of Bologna, and you, professed nuns, and you, *converse* in the same convent, and all other members, we pray you, by the Holy Spirit, the gift and power of reason and counsel, to see to the salvation of your souls.

Although in the school of religion, the opinion of Saint Jerome should suffice, that the true reputation of religious persons consists in prompt obedience and in their right actions, and not in the praise or vain judgment of men, you, happily ignoring the ear of your own hearts, have not heard the salutary voices of the cardinal legates, of your fathers and pastors, of your ministers, of such learned and virtuous religious, and of your own relatives. We may therefore rightly exclaim, *curavimus Babylonem, et non est sanata* [we cared for Babylon, and she is not healed]. Thus, this convent is become nothing else but a Babylon, where most grievous disorder rules and holds sway. You put in manifest danger donna Serena Maria Celeste Terribili, to let her die without the Sacraments, rather than admit secular priests, to whom she might have confessed. You wickedly claimed she could have done so before a crucifix, an intolerable folly, since there are plenty of confessors and her soul was weighed down in mortal disobedience.

Lest the stench of such scandals spread, by order of the Sacred Congregation, your parlatorios were walled up. But you, with reckless audacity, had them torn open, throwing stones and wounding not only the beadles, agents, and notaries but even the auditor of the monsignor suffragan bishop himself. Your inconstancy and fickleness, first to accept, then to reject, secular priests as confessors, to promise, then refuse, to obey, your constantly growing hardness and contumacy offer the most patent proof that the spirit of all evil, the author and father of discord and disobedience, has always been your counselor, your companion, and your master.

After everything that we have done to restore you to sanity, from your vile intercourse with most obvious ingratitude and ungratefulness, all must recognize that *curavimus Babylonem, et non est sanata*. If there be no emendment, we are left, in our infinite sorrow, *derelinquamus eam* [to cast her away].

To this we are constrained by our conscience, after such forbearance, by human and divine law, by our fear—totally justified—that disobedience breeds with impunity.

Therefore, by our authority, we do order and command you, donna Camilla Bombacci, former abbess, and you other nuns, in virtue of Holy Obedience, within the next fifteen days, on pain of excommunication, to submit and subjugate yourselves to our authority.

Finally, because the wicked are never lacking, who *dicunt malum bonum et bonum malum* [say bad is good and good is bad], we command, on pain of excommunication, that no one dare give counsel, aid, or protection that might impede or delay the execution of the apostolic breve and of our orders. And if in the prescribed time the said monastery does not submit in due obedience to the Supreme Pontiff and to us, from that hour we cast out the said Babylon, most justly abandoned for pertinacious disobedience by God and His Church, which the excommunicant has not for mother, neither God for father, but Satan in place of father and mother.[26]

Formally under interdict, cut off from the world by Ludovisi's yeomen at the gates, rejected by their families because of their sullied reputations, which compromised the decency of family and city alike, provided with such meager rations that they may have been reduced to eating grass, having rejected the spiritual food of the Sacraments from the hands of secular priests for six months,[27] and finally faced with this ultimate threat of papal excommunication, which on 1 March 1629 was nailed to the cloister door, to the column in the episcopal notary's chamber, and to the cathedral door, with two extra copies thrown over the wall into the convent, twenty-two months after Urban VIII had removed them from Camaldolese jurisdiction, the sisters of Santa Cristina finally submitted to the authority of the archbishop of Bologna.

But they did not do so meekly. On 4 March, the full community of nuns (apart, of course, from Emilia Bianchi, Gentile Malvasia, and Lucidaria Bolognetti), ranging from the aged Lorenza Bonsignori and Junipera Fuzzi (who would both be dead before summer came) to twenty-year-old Elena Cristina Paracini, gathered in the parlatorio before a public notary. All affirmed the following official declaration, which claimed that their capitulation was technically invalid since they had been coerced and did not act of their own free will. As was customary, they signed in order of seniority. Donna Lucrezia Orsina Vizzana, now thirty-nine years old, appeared twenty-sixth out of thirty-five on the list.

We protest and emphatically reject the subjugation of ourselves and our convent by any act whatsoever, either public or private, that we may do. This will not be absolutely of our own free will, but in fear of these censures and so that our reputation will not suffer more than it has already suffered. Therefore, we wish that whatever we might do to the contrary should not be taken as fact, and that this same protestation should always remain secure. Nor can it be said that we ever departed from it.[28]

Four months later, "the three furies"—Cecilia Bianchi, Maria Gentile Malvasia, and Lucidaria Bolognetti—were removed from Santa Cristina, while Emilia Grassi and the other nuns handed over £3,000 to each of the three convents that had agreed to take one of them. "And the three—oh woe!—who were such friends and companions, from that day forward they never saw each other again: the price of their malevolence," as Ruggeri put it, with satisfaction barely disguised. Because of her illustrious lineage, Bolognetti rode in Marchioness Riaria's carriage to her new, humbler home, the Clarissan convent of San Bernardino, way across town. There she lived on inconspicuously for another thirty years in a crowd of more than 130 other nuns, most of the "ordinary sort." She outlived just about everyone at Santa Cristina who had participated firsthand in the events of the 1620s that she had helped to provoke.

According to Ruggeri, her former sisters in religion flatly refused donna Lucidaria's repeated pleas to return to Santa Cristina, sweetened with promises of lavish donations.

The other two had to settle for more common conveyance. Malvasia found her way to the humble convent of Sant'Agostino, among the city's poorest. Despite Ludovisi's personal insistence that she be granted the superiority due someone with thirty years of religion behind her, she formally renounced all rights to precedence in choir and in chapter, an act her new colleagues seem to have found entirely appropriate. Maria Gentile lived on at Sant'Agostino until December 1647.

The chief troublemaker, Cecilia Bianchi, after years of ostracism within the walls on via Fondazza, was packed off as far beyond the city wall as possible, all the way to the tiny Dominican convent of San Michele Arcangelo in the suburb of San Giovanni in Persiceto, twelve miles from Bologna. There she vanishes, virtually without a trace, though later Camaldolese historians hinted darkly that "she lost herself in evil." And, as Ruggeri put it, "thus ended their hopes of becoming abbesses and reformers."[29]

Ruggeri's account of the aftermath reveals a persisting trend of deception and demoralization. Ruggeri alleged that Ludovisi contrived to have a letter purportedly from the archbishop to the Roman curia, expressing sympathy with the nuns, dropped where it would be discovered and transmitted to Santa Cristina. Having thus convinced the nuns once again of his good offices, the archbishop continued to undermine them whenever he could. When three carriages of Camaldolese, with Ruggeri among them, stopped in Bologna on route to their general chapter in Rome, the diocesan curia dispatched a squadron of yeomen to stand guard at the convent, as if the monks might attempt a replay of Ludovisi's earlier tactics, to retake it by force.

In reality the Camaldolese appear to have abandoned their sisters. After Urban VIII's proclamation of a universal jubilee in October 1629, the nuns requested as their customary confessor extraordinary the Camaldolese curate of San Damiano. To their consternation, the monk claimed that he was too busy with parish matters, provoking the taunt from the archbishop's agents, "See how you are esteemed by your Camaldolese fathers, who decline to confess you during the jubilee." A few months later, the curate admitted to the general of his order that he had received nocturnal warnings from Ludovisi's emissaries not to risk the archbishop's displeasure by giving in to the nuns' request. Ruggeri's apologia for his order deflects the blame, of course. "If it be true that the nuns may call the Camaldolese fathers their betrayers (which is unbelievable), it is for no other reason than the evil notions that the agents and others of the archiepiscopate put in their heads."[30]

Ruggeri recorded without comment the curate of San Damiano's death shortly afterward, during the plague of 1630–31. He leaves no doubt about the appropriateness of the fates of Ludovisi and his accomplices. Prospero Fagnani, the secretary to the Congregation of Bishops and the archbishop's chief Roman ally, was struck blind, Ruggeri tells us. This seems to have left him unhindered, for "the sharp-eyed blind catechist," as he was known, later became an influential adviser to Pope Alexander VII and survived until 1678, when he died at a ripe old age variously reported as eighty or ninety.[31]

The conniving nuns' vicar don Gioanino went on to enjoy a canonry at San Petronio, unmerited in Ruggeri's opinion. But he eventually received his comeuppance. During Carnival, Ruggeri claims, an unknown band of maskers accosted Gioanino in the street and forced him to dress up in costume, took him with them to a convent, and made the sixty-year-old priest dance with the nuns across the grates of the parlatorio, with the priest on one side and the nuns on the other. Released with a warning to keep his mouth shut or regret it, don Gioanino never discovered his abusers' identities. Although Ruggeri only had the story on hearsay—from a very reliable source—he passed it on "so that it may be understood that nuns subject to [secular] priests are no better governed than those under regulars."[32]

As for Cardinal Archbishop Ludovico Ludovisi, Ruggeri claimed he was disgraced for complicity with a faction of Spanish cardinals in a plot to depose the pro-French Urban VIII for alleged mental instability. "Ludovisi left Rome as fast as his feet would carry him and returned to Bologna; filled with anguish, he passed to another life."[33] Although Ludovisi's collusion in any putative Spanish plot appears improbable, the archbishop was definitely implicated with Spanish cardinals whose open defiance of Urban VIII in March 1632 stunned the curia and Rome. Shortly thereafter, the pope gave Ludovisi ten days to return to his diocese or risk being run out of the city. On the morning of 27 March, Ludovisi, "more a breathing corpse than a man," departed the *caput mundi*. Nine months later he was dead in Bologna, aged thirty-seven.[34]

EIGHT

A Gentler Means
to a Bitter End

"They Have always Been
Betrayed by Secular Priests"

Archbishop Ludovico Ludovisi had scarcely been entombed at Bologna's cathedral of San Pietro (only temporarily, however, for his will required his eventual translation to Sant'Ignazio in the Eternal City) before the nuns of Santa Cristina again turned their attention to Rome. In 1633 Emilia Grassi, whom the nuns finally reelected abbess, may have convinced them to petition the pope to reconsider their case.[1] Perhaps they hoped Ludovisi's disgrace would win them a sympathetic papal ear. Donna Emilia's death within a year of her reelection spared her further disappointment, for Urban VIII ignored their plea. Another petition to the Congregation of Bishops three years later suggests the grim reality of the convent's continued decline:

Abandoned by our own families, although we personally have been lovingly consoled by Your Eminences' many declarations of our decency and innocence, the opposite impression thrives throughout the city. So much so that, not only are our reputations still torn to shreds, but we can find no one, even of the ordinary sort, who wishes to be accepted and to profess in our convent, where formerly places were granted only to members of the nobility. Now, with as many as fifteen places vacant, our convent's total destruction and annihilation may result.[2]

The decimation of the convent population owed as much to Grassi's elimination of *educande* in the early 1600s. The forty-nine *professe* of 1588 had dwindled to forty-three by 1606 and to thirty-five at the time of Ludovisi's ultimatum in 1629. Deaths continued to outpace professions, so that by 1639 only thirty professed nuns remained.

The nuns' petition of 1636 abandoned hope of full reunion with the Camaldolese. They "did not intend ever to be withdrawn on any account from the jurisdiction and good government of His Eminence the lord cardinal archbishop."[3] But they would simply like a token Camaldolese confessor. The Congregation of Bishops took a dim view of this symbolic gesture; Celestine monks continued to confess the nuns until 1638, when Olivetans succeeded them.

But in 1643 an aged convent cook, suor Francesca Malatendi, turned everything upside down. Faced with imminent heavenly judgment, whose torments she believed had already begun to afflict her (she died four weeks later), suor Francesca was moved to confession. During the scandals of the 1620s, she had whispered to Cecilia Bianchi's belowstairs ally, Ludovica Fabri, that a curious, intermittent indisposition affecting suor Cherubina Noci (presumably in the morning) must have been the unhappy result of suor Cherubina's amorous predisposition toward a certain convent gardener whose sudden, mysterious disappearance shortly thereafter proved it.

She now recognizes the immense damage that has befallen this convent and the nuns since 1626, above all with respect to their reputation, because they were subjected to formal investigation. And so the Camaldolese monks, their spiritual directors, were banished. Suor Francesca therefore desires to unburden her conscience. She recognizes that Our Lord in his just wisdom has laid upon her the very same infirmity that suor Cherubina once suffered. Lest she damn her soul, and to repair in the best way possible the reputations of the monastery and the nuns, she declares, confesses, and publicly acknowledges that the said suspicions and words she once implied were and are false and vain, with absolutely no basis in truth. And in affirmation of the truth, she has made a cross in the presence of witnesses, because she does not know how to write.[4]

Back in 1623, however, suor Francesca had offered investigators not the slightest hint of convent improprieties. She had corroborated the view that every *professa* treated the *converse* with the indulgence and forbearance appropriate to women of their station, and almost every *conversa* knew her place and valued her good treatment. Even Cecilia Bianchi's ally, the uppity *conversa* Ludovica Fabri, testified to no specific sexual indiscretions belowstairs. But Fabri's description of goings-on among the servants suggests between the lines that suor Francesca's calumnies just might have been taking their toll: "Two or three months ago suor Geronima knocked suor Dorothea in the head and blood flowed down to the ground. And she ripped suor Cherubina's cowl and left her all roughed up. This had something to do with this investigation, but I don't know the reason." Other servants also alluded to physical violence among the help. Many knew that this aggressive suor Geronima, a veteran of thirty-three years belowstairs, had long been possessed by the devil (after all, she refused to take Communion every month, insulted the abbess, and committed other acts of insolence). Suor Geronima had claimed self-defense: "She [suor Cherubina] grabbed me by the throat, and I wanted to defend myself. So I said 'I'll tear your veil,' and she didn't listen." Under interrogation, the maligned Cherubina had also proven singularly uncommunicative; the notary recorded less than a hundred of her words, which ended "I don't know of any wrangling in the convent, nor anything unusual, and I'm very well treated by the nuns, and as to why I'm here, I've never been offended by anybody, and I don't have anything to say."[5]

Suor Francesca Malatenda's imagined scandal may have kept the servant nuns in turmoil, but it remained largely beneath the notice of her betters, abovestairs or above the clouds. The archiepiscopal visitors did note, however, that "suor Geronima and suor Ludovico, the *converse*, both turn the convent on its head." Perhaps more significant, they noted, "Advise them not to appoint the younger *converse* as garden mistresses, and most assuredly not to send young *converse* with meals for the male gardeners, because of the dangers that could arise when they enter these gardeners' remote huts."[6]

Nevertheless, even the professed nuns seized upon Malatenda's deathbed confession as justification for another rehearing of their cause and for restoration to their pristine state. Led by a new abbess, Adeodata Leoni, and by Isabetta Vizzana, who had rallied the crowds during the nuns' last stand in 1628 and had since risen to the rank of bursar, the sisters began late in 1645 to bombard a new Bolognese archbishop, Cardinal Niccolò Albergati Ludovisi, and the Congregation of Bishops with requests for a return to Camaldolese rule: "All Your Eminences' suppliants unanimously desire to see redressed the damage that has resulted from [these calumnies] and above all daily affects their honor and the reputation of the convent, which consists of Bologna's principal nobility, and likewise finally to be freed from their continual distress. They therefore humbly beseech Your Eminences benevolently to deign to grant that the justice of their cause be reconsidered."[7]

Rome had heard quite enough of this. In August 1646 the Congregation of Bishops not only denied the nuns' request but also imposed perpetual silence upon them in the matter. They laid that long moribund issue of Camaldolese reunion to rest once and for all. Worse yet, the cardinals happened to notice that for twenty-five years, ever since the troubles of the 1620s, the nuns had been confessing to priests in regular orders rather than to the secular clergy dictated in the congregation's earlier decrees. Rome now insisted that the archbishop enforce the letter of the old law and replace regular confessors with secular priests.

So the issue of regular versus secular confessors displaced the lost cause of Camaldolese rule. But for the nuns the issue was much the same: their *libertà* and the maintenance of some measure of autonomy. Confessors appointed by the archbishop intruded in convent government as an instrument of diocesan control. Such episcopal appointees' potentially divided loyalties rendered them suspect, especially in the matter of confidentiality. These suspicions were not unfounded, for the inviolability of the seal of the confessional, much vaunted in the aftermath of Trent, was compromised as the seventeenth century wore on, especially in relation to investigations by the Inquisition.[8]

Three months after its first letter, an impatient Congregation of Bishops reiterated its command even more emphatically to a reluctantly dawdling archbishop of Bologna. This new and apparently rather reticent ordinary, Niccolò Albergati Ludovisi, was the cousin of the nuns' old adversary, Ludovico Ludovisi. Ruggeri suggests that Albergati Ludovisi's relations with the nuns were at first more than cordial and encouraging. "Such were the hopes that His Illustrious Eminence gave them that he seemed to them to touch heaven with his fingers." For Ruggeri, however, Albergati Ludovisi was cut from the same cloth as his namesake. By the time the nuns' campaign began in earnest, their former confessor claims, even Albergati Ludovisi's public attitude would change.[9]

Surviving documents suggest, however, that Niccolò Albergati Ludovisi was no carbon copy of Ludovico Ludovisi. This later Ludovisi appears to have had little faith in his late cousin's draconian measures. But his own initial, gentler overtures proved as ineffective as Ludovisi's harsher methods: the nuns flatly refused to accept secular confessors. One leader of the Bolognese senate, then another, stopped by the archbishop's palace: the nuns had begun to exploit the conflicting channels of influence that had mediated between them and episcopal authority in the past.[10] Alarmed at the sympathetic view of the nuns' plight circulating in the city, Albergati Ludovisi divulged what he called "the monstrous contumacy of the nuns, thus to arouse some shame in these disobedient souls." He hoped to prepare the ground so that if the sterner measures of the past were again required, his actions would not arouse further sympathy for the nuns and the people's additional disapprobation toward him.

To combat the nuns' latest epistolary public relations campaign, Albergati Ludovisi summoned their relatives, to whom, as he put it, "I expounded at length upon the nuns' obduracy." The archbishop carefully pointed out how the unhappy affair could affect them and their families personally. "They left universally edified, and there was no shortage of people who heartily despised the nuns' good-for-nothing correspondence"—or so he hoped.

Only after all these months of advance preparations did the cautious Albergati Ludovisi finally get around to presenting the August 1646 decrees of the Congregation of Bishops to Santa Cristina in January 1647. He sweetened them, however, by the concession of confessors from the regular clergy during a two-month grace period. The nuns promptly dispatched another mediator to request additional regular confessors at Christmas and Easter and a Benedictine confessor to administer the last rites. Albergati Ludovisi's justification to the Congregation of Bishops of his response to the nuns enumerates most of the informal sorts of influence that had long formed the basis of convent women's culture, probably suggesting to Rome that the sheep were still leading their pastor:

The extravagance of their whims (so difficult to control), the ease with which the public supports and sympathizes with the desires, right or wrong, of the weaker party, and the memory, still fresh, of their past rebellion counseled me not to promise more than the Sacred Congregation had authorized. But most of the city accepted the fragility of their sex, their condition as prisoners, and the quality of the women, deluded in their opinion. So that not to give in would have been interpreted as excessive rigidity. And the nuns' quite inevitable femininity of spirit—proud, alas, to be insubordinate and rebellious—therefore reduced me to the point of assuring them, by virtue of my authority from this Sacred Congregation, that they would be entirely satisfied.[11]

Predictably, Albergati Ludovisi's additional concessions failed to yield the desired outcome. When the grace period expired, the nuns simply requested an extension for all of Lent. But even this Ludovisi had his limits. After additional cajoling by their confessor and the cathedral's chief preacher proved fruitless, on 22 March the archbishop published a broadside, reminiscent of his late cousin's ultimatum of eighteen years earlier. It reproduced his own exhortation to immediate obedience and included the congregation's two most recent decrees, "so that their allies and their loved ones might see, from the very source, the paternal prudence so widely used by Your Eminences toward them for the space of twenty years."[12]

By contrast with Ludovico Ludovisi's stern commands and open threats of 1629, Albergati Ludovisi's ultimatum reads like an attempt at self-justification: less a demand than a plea for obedience. He offers no enumeration of the nuns' offences and hardly a hint at possible excommunication but chiefly reiterates the hierarchy's interpretation of what constituted nuns' true *imitatio Christi* (imitation of Christ):

To the nuns of Santa Cristina, most beloved in the Lord, true peace and health.

The natural piety and religious discipline, which we have clearly recognized and experienced in your persons, have never allowed us to doubt your souls' readiness to obey your superiors' holy decisions. Whence it has pleased the Congregation of Bishops and Regulars lovingly to hear during these past months your entreaties for restoration to the care and government of Camaldolese monks. They respond, in full agreement, that they cannot depart in any way from the most holy opinion of the supreme pontiff, whose decrees they do not arbitrate but enforce.

Most beloved, by the bowels of Christ and with all the power of our spirit, we pray you willingly to accept what God, by means of his supreme earthly ministers, so expressly reveals to you as his will! In true certainty that you do not err so long as you follow, not your own spirit, but that of Jesus Christ, your spouse. He came down from the throne of his majesty only to obey, declaring, *Veni ut faciam voluntatem meam, sed eius, qui misit me Patris* [I came not to do my own will, but his, the Father who sent me (John 6:38)]. While he never ceased to obey, so long as he lived. *Factus*, as the Apostle writes, *obediens usque ad mortem* [He became obedient unto death (Philippians 2:8)].

This is the true peace, the sole honor, and singular glory of religious persons: always to remain loyal and fixed in their desire for divine approval. May it please the Spirit of Truth to assist you with his clearest light, as we hope, that you may not err in the recognition and election of the good.[13]

Albergati Ludovisi's letter also represented, of course, a carefully articulated defense of episcopal policy to the public. In his report to the Congregation of Bishops, the ever-optimistic archbishop claimed to have undercut a primary source of the convent's strength: "Insofar as one can tell, this latest effort has succeeded most usefully among the people. It seems that not only the nobility but also the general citizenry and the common sort now betray their extreme distaste for such monstrous wrongheadedness."[14]

Albergati Ludovisi continued to underestimate his strong-minded (or "wrongheaded") opponents. Two days before the publication of his broadside, the thirty-seven professed nuns of Santa Cristina, including nineteen survivors who had made a similar gesture eighteen years before, with Lucrezia Vizzana, now fifty-six, as the eleventh on the list, gathered once again to proclaim:

Threatened with censures, excommunications, and other penalties if they choose not to obey, they therefore protest and protest again that, should they agree to receive secular priests for their confessors and chaplains, it would not be of their own free will but by force. For it seems to them that a regular confessor to quiet their consciences should not be denied them, because they had entered this convent under the rule and for the government of their souls by regulars. Otherwise, they would not have entered. Therefore, they once again protest and protest again that they would wish their rights always to remain safe and entirely unharmed, as they were before they were induced to agree to accept secular priests. They protest that they do not do so voluntarily but for fear of censure and penalties, resulting from the main force of him who can command. They do not act of their own will but under compulsion to escape the censure, punishments, and other charges with which they are threatened. And thus they protest, shall protest and declare, not only in the aforesaid manner and form but by any other better means that is rightfully possible.[15]

This official, notarized declaration, echoing the words with which they had capitulated in March 1629 but with the addition of a new breach-of-contract argument, heralded the beginning of a replay of the 1620s. But the nuns continued their new, less directly confrontational strategy. They agreed to obey the archbishop and the congregation in all matters but the crucial issue of secular confessors, who were "prejudicial to their statutes," words that became another rallying cry for decades. They promptly made a token confession to secular priests in sign of obedience but then immediately petitioned the pliant Albergati Ludovisi for another special, regular confessor for Easter. Many outside supporters seconded this request, "less suppliant than importunate," as the archbishop put it. "The demand struck me—and it really is—strange and astonishing," he remarked. "In any event, the torrent of prayers then swelled to the point that finally I was prevailed upon to consent." The archbishop then had to find regulars willing to assume the task, "since the Olivetans don't want to enter the place on any account."[16]

Late in April, Albergati Ludovisi expressed such satisfaction with the nuns' spiritual progress thanks to his latest concession that he warmly entreated the congregation to lift its decades-old ban on the acceptance of postulants, reassuring Rome that "one can find no more appropriate means to establish firmly the sisters' every perfect consolation and quiet in their new state." By the time the archbishop wrote a second time to affirm the nuns' full compliance, they had renewed their own barrage of petitions to Rome, even enlisting a member of the pope's own family to back them. No wonder, therefore, that in June the skeptical congregation demanded Albergati Ludovisi's absolute assurances of the nuns' full obedience before it lifted its ban on admission of new members.[17]

These he found he could not provide. After continuing to wheedle one extension after another, the nuns had finally begun to ignore the archbishop altogether. At last Albergati Ludovisi had been pushed to the limit. When he cracked down, the nuns rebelled, as their sisters had done in the standoff of the 1620s, absolutely refusing to confess to or communicate from the hands of secular priests. They claimed, as the archbishop put it, "that they can trust no secular priest, that they have always been betrayed by secular priests." The nuns' refusal of confession and Communion stretched on from Ascension to the solemn feast of Corpus Christi, then dragged on through the summer and into the fall, as the nuns continued unflaggingly to petition for regular confessors, since they "could not entrust their consciences to the secular priests assigned them, [who are] totally ignorant of their [Camaldolese] statutes."[18]

"They not only persist more than ever in their disobedience, but what is more, with detestable pertinacity, they willingly deprive themselves of the Sacraments, and of that celestial food that nourishes and maintains the religious in the spiritual life," the congregation fulminated in a letter of September 1647 intended to stiffen Archbishop Albergati Ludovisi's backbone once and for all. In a replay of their actions in November 1628, the cardinals authorized the harshest reprisals, again including the walling up of all the grates to cut off the nuns' access to the outside world. Ruggeri claims that they even threatened the nuns with Santa Cristina's dissolution and their dispersal among the convents of the city.[19]

Even now, never one to act precipitously, the archbishop dispatched his emissary to Santa Cristina with a further warning of this latest, impending ultimatum. The nuns immediately responded with a request for a fifteen-day delay while they petitioned the congregation yet again. As Albergati Ludovisi explained, "Repulsed at their first try, they responded more fervently with a second—in the face of which, to avoid departing from my usual gentle principles in these latest experiences, I thought it good to be indulgent. In fact, I did yield to them. Not content, the next day the nuns requested that if within such a brief time span they had not obtained the desired result, I would be content to postpone [the implementation of the decree] until its arrival." But even Albergati Ludovisi had his limits. "In the face of such a request I became totally inexorable, and that is where we stand."

He did not, however, dispatch masons to Santa Cristina to carry out their work, as Rome dictated. Within the week, the convent's other administrators reappeared at the archbishop's residence with a new request. The nuns, they reported, repented their hardness of heart and in future would maintain due obedience, which even now they hastened to embrace. But their souls remained so ill disposed toward the secular priests they had been defying these past five months that they could only unburden themselves properly to a confessor in regular orders. By now, the "totally inexorable" archbishop's reaction comes as no surprise. "As the loving father of the same nuns, I earnestly entreat that you deign to console them, for their convent (apart from this affair) is otherwise one of the most exemplary and most commendable in my jurisdiction." With this recommendation Albergati Ludovisi forwarded the nuns' latest petition to Rome—while the late Archbishop Ludovico Ludovisi (still waiting patiently to join his uncle, Gregory XV, at Sant'Ignazio in Rome) no doubt turned over in his temporary grave:

Never would we have thought, Most Eminent and Reverend Lords, that poor religious women, shut in between walls and bars, merely requesting most humbly a confessor of their rule, would so offend you that you would not only decline to permit one but would even order that we be walled in and severely punished according to canon law. Eminent Lords, we are innocent! We are discredited before this sacred tribunal! We are indicted as disobedient and contumacious because we would clash with our superiors! It is so false that we are horrified even to hear it! Prostrate before that Mother of Mercy, we humbly supplicate that you grant us the grace of a confessor of our rule, so that we may confidently purge our consciences. And remember, Fathers, that your sacred robes are dyed crimson in Jesus's blood, which dripped down from him to save souls, as it would be shed anew for a single soul. Pity us, imitating our Lord, whose ministers you are, before whom, humbly kneeling, we kiss your sacred mantles.[20]

Such eloquence, it seems, could soften even the calloused hearts of cardinals. Within the week, the congregation granted "for one single time" a confessor extraordinary in regular orders, with the stipulation, however, that from then on, without further discussion, the nuns must obey in full.

Albergati Ludovisi, cautious to the last, informed the nuns' emissaries that he was prepared to console the nuns—once they had provided some visible pledge to assure him of their obedience. The next day a go-between returned with word that the nuns had deputized him to take the pledge for them. A little wiser by then, the archbishop sent him back to via Fondazza to point out that, after the events of last Easter, another secondhand verbal assurance would not satisfy without some clearer demonstration of obedience. The emissary retraced his steps, this time to convey the nuns' "dumbfoundment to hear that one had so little faith in their solemn word" and to test the archbishop's mettle again by insisting that their verbal pledge alone should suffice. "But in spite of that, I remained adamant in my first response"—words greeted, no doubt, with relief (and perhaps with incredulity) in Rome. Twenty-four hours later the emissary reappeared finally to announce the nuns' capitulation, in confirmation of which they had at last confessed to secular priests.[21] The long process of their subjugation to archiepiscopal control, which had begun with the loss of their Camaldolese superiors and would end with the disappearance of one last, token regular confessor, was complete.

One cannot tell whether the nuns realized that prelates saw the alleged blots on their reputation that had so preoccupied them and their families these twenty-five years as a useful means to an end. For the ecclesiastical hierarchy, "moral" reforms, provoked by convent "scandal," had long provided an effective excuse for political reforms within the cloister, often to right internal imbalances of dynastic power carried over from the world. Most likely, the nuns did finally realize that, even with considerable outside sympathy and support within the city, even if they could manage to hold their own against the more malleable Archbishop Albergati Ludovisi, few women of any kind—and even fewer women religious—could realistically hope to prevail against the Roman curia.

"The Weight of Calamities, as if Fallen Straight from Heaven"

On 22 December 1647, the Congregation of Bishops commended Albergati Ludovisi's "paternal zeal," his "great prudence and pastoral solicitude," and his "gentle means in disposing the nuns to exact obedience." Rome therefore decreed that the convent of Santa Cristina could once again accept novices and *educande*.[22] By now, down in the crypt of the external church, Emilia Grassi, who had worked so hard against them forty years before, probably took no notice. It was twenty-five years, almost to the day, since the feast of Saint Thomas the Apostle in 1622, when Suffragan Bishop Angelo Gozzadini and the other visitors had begun their investigation into strife that, as Cecilia Bianchi had claimed "began because of music." By strange coincidence, Maria Gentile Malvasia, Cecilia's old ally, died that same December, across town and probably oblivious to it all, at the convent of Sant'Agostino. Donna Cecilia was also probably underground by then, miles from town and from Santa Cristina.

Donna Lucrezia Orsina Vizzana still survived. The composer whose *Componimenti musicali* had played a part in the earlier struggle was the first nun singled out by name at the opening of Mauro Ruggeri's long history of that turbulent quarter century, for the luster her talents had brought to the house. She reappears at the very end, as a living symbol of the toll those twenty-five years had taken: "So great was the terror that they suffered from this further blow [the final defeat of 1647] that, as I have been assured, one donna Lucrezia Vizzana, otherwise among the wisest, took a shock to the brain. And whenever she heard the cloister bell ring, her imaginary fears were so great that she would fall about, shaking."[23] The clangor of the bells, which had rallied parishioners in the battle of 1628 and for fifty years had marked the daily rhythms of her life, became the musical nun's undoing. With Ruggeri's last reference, Lucrezia Orsina Vizzana, who after her brief moment of renown in the 1620s vanished into the shadows of her activist aunt and older sister, disappears behind the wall into illness and the black hole of madness. Or as the convent necrologist put it, under "the weight of calamities, as if fallen straight from heaven."

Like the venerable madre donna Flaminia Bombacci, Lucrezia Orsina Vizzana increasingly took solace in her devotions, especially to the Mysteries of the Rosary. Perhaps she was drawn back to the solitary comfort of the narrow, little staircase near the refectory that she may have discovered as a child. Huddled on the landing halfway up, which had become a tiny chapel a few years before the crises of the 1620s (fig. 23), she may have rehearsed the Sorrowful Mysteries adorning its lunettes, above the Man of Sorrows and Our Lady of Consolation. Or perhaps she lost herself in the lofty Capella della Beata Vergine del Rosario, the chapel above the church doors, site of so much music and so much rebellion (fig. 24).

Lucrezia survived all her cloistered companions who had endured the visitation of 1622–23 except for two of the most junior *professe*. She outlived her more assertive sister, Isabetta, who died in 1653, and the apologist, Mauro Ruggeri, who died in 1660. After sixty-five years of religion, Lucrezia Orsina Vizzana passed to a better life on 7 May 1662, the eve of the Apparition of Saint Michael the Archangel, who had likewise seen

FIGURE 23. Santa Cristina della Fondazza (2011), chapel (1616) on the landing of the back cloister staircase. Photograph: Luca Salvucci, Bologna.

FIGURE 24. Santa Cristina della Fondazza, Cappella della Beata Vergine del Rosario (unrestored), the chapel above the church doors (c. 1988). Photograph courtesy of Ugo Capriani.

Flaminia Bombacci to paradise. Her body was removed for burial to the public church, where she joined the Blessed Flaminia, donna Isabetta, and her other cloistered relatives in a sepulcher beneath the floor before the side altar of Saint Christina.[24]

For the last forty years of her life, Lucrezia Orsina Vizzana never again ventured into print.

NINE

"Pomp Indecent for Religious Observance and Modesty"

In the late 1670s Lucrezia Orsina Vizzana's cousin madre donna Teresa Pompea Vizzana commissioned a new altarpiece for the side altar of Saint Christina, to the right of the high altar in the convent's external church. Domenico Maria Canuti's dramatic work (fig. 25) presents none of the common episodes from the saint's highly eventful passion.[1] Christina's cruel father, Urbanus, dominates the scene, his right fist clenched, as he grabs his daughter by the hair with his left, drives his knee into her side, and wrests her backward to the ground to bend her to his will, while astonished bystanders try to restrain him. Visitors with a sense of local history may have come away from the altar wondering whether the nuns of Santa Cristina intended a dark analogy between the classic artistic symbol of subjugation, grabbing the hair, and their own plight. Defeated in the 1620s by their policy of open confrontation, after a latter-day Urbanus, Pope Urban VIII, had subjected them to archiepiscopal control, then vanquished again in the 1640s in the matter of regular confessors, after decades of extraordinary resistance they had been subjugated totally to the diocesan hierarchy.

The nuns had lost the last direct link to the order that had governed them for five hundred years. But just as their new altarpiece could be read as a symbol of their oppression at the hands of powerful prelates, a single, ritual act remained to symbolize their former independence under

FIGURE 25. Domenico Maria Canuti, *Saint Christina* (c. 1680), public church of Santa Cristina della Fondazza, side altar of Saint Christina. Reproduced with permission of the Biblioteca Comunale dell'Archiginnasio, Bologna.

Camaldolese superiors. The ritual consecration of virgins following the Roman pontifical—the Sacra, as they called it—was a third ceremony in a nun's rites of passage, only permitted when she reached the age of twenty-five, after the rites of investiture and profession. We encountered it earlier in relation to Lucrezia Vizzana's life and her motet *Amo Christum*, probably composed for her own consecration. In this solemn ritual's periodic reenactment, the nuns of Santa Cristina may have recognized one of those "other better means" of protest cited in their proclamation of 1647. The Sacra represented an artistic, flexible, indirect means of public persuasion, which could reaffirm their *libertà*, their *onestà*, and their links to their old superiors. At the end of the 1600s, it also became a way to act out in some measure their independence from the usurping authority of the archbishop of Bologna.

Nuns' Rites of Passage

We can best understand the power of that ritual consecration of virgins against the background of a nun's more usual investiture and profession ceremonies, which were important in the social dynamic of convent, city, and curia. The rites focused symbolically upon the meeting—and the separation—of the cloister and the world, a symbolism intensified by the strict imposition of enclosure after Trent.[2] In the ecclesiastical view, the lavish rituals of investiture, which marked a girl's official acceptance, and profession, when she took her final vows, both traditionally under-written by her parents, represented a violation of the monastic ideal of simplicity—in the words of the Congregation of Bishops in 1677, "pomp indecent for religious observance and modesty." But they also re-affirmed the primary position of patrician families as mediators between the convent and the curia. Little wonder, then, that these ceremonies remained a source of tension among church authorities, the nuns, and their relations. Predictably, ecclesiastical superiors—whose contrasting double standard for their *own* lavish installations and opulent clothing ceremonies continues unchanged into the twenty-first century[3]—regu-larly attacked nuns' equivalent ceremonies. The nun's first rite of passage came after an indeterminate period as an *educanda*. For some girls, such as Lucrezia Vizzana, this prenovitiate preparation extended from early childhood. Only after age twelve, according to the Council of Trent, could a postulant officially enter the novitiate, an event marked by her acceptance into the convent and her reception of her habit in the cloth-ing ceremony.

Benedictines traditionally considered a year as the appropriate length of time for the novice's prayer, meditation, and study of the rules of monastic life and the constitutions of the order before profession. The Council of Trent made a full year's novitiate a general requirement, with profession to follow only after age sixteen. The nun's profession, when the novice was inscribed among the ranks of the religious, marked her second rite of passage. The solemn consecration of the nun's virginity, on the other hand, was a much rarer rite, which largely fell into disuse after Trent.

When it came to such ceremonies, post-Tridentine reformers attempted to restore monastic decorum and to enforce monastic enclosure. "Abuses" in the rites of investiture, profession, and consecration were among the many objects of Bolognese archbishops' reforming zeal. In 1580, Gabriele Paleotti addressed the issue of pomp and dynastic display by forbidding gatherings of onlookers and relatives in convent external churches and by specifically banning music during professions. In practice these attempts to promote austerity resulted in disparity, with the ideal frequently at odds with the reality.

For the nuns and their families, the accompanying festivities not only reaffirmed links between the nuns and their lineages in the world but also strengthened other informal social ties between convent and community, which remained primary forces in convent women's culture. Many of these social and festive aspects involved their female relatives almost exclusively.

It is unsurprising that although enclosure could be imposed rather easily upon the ritual features of investiture ceremonies and professions, it was more difficult to moderate the festive aspects, including music, which the nuns and their families had commonly observed (and enjoyed) for centuries. Ever since its creation, the Congregation of Bishops had attempted to reduce the indecorous spending at clothing ceremonies and professions and to enforce greater uniformity among richer and poorer houses in such rituals. In March 1592 Cardinal Paleotti's coadjutor and eventual successor, Alfonso Paleotti, effectively acknowledged the inefficacy of earlier attempts at reform by republishing a broadside whose bleakly precise prohibitions provide, between the lines, a sense of what the common practice in the city must have really been like.

On the day when the young girl is to enter the convent, she must arrive in the morning, without any sort of display, in simple dress, without ornament, frills, or train, dressed in white, black, or buff or purple. [Her hair should be] without buns, twists, flowers, or other adornments on her head. While she remains outside and otherwise at large in the city, she should not dare to go about in any other sort of dress but the above-named. Briefly, [she should arrive] unaccompanied by carriages but bringing with her only two or three of her closest relatives, who should accompany her only as far as the convent and then immediately withdraw. Only the superior and the doorkeepers will receive the girl at the door. Then, on the day when she receives her habit, any public gathering, music, and assembly should be excluded from the external church, while the church is kept closed. Only those ministers necessary to give the girl her habit or to administer the profession to the novice should be admitted, and no others.[4]

A wide implementation of the new austerity remained a vain, if abiding, hope, even during the Paleottis' own lifetimes, for the patriciate was unwilling to embrace it. Such family send-offs, the sacred equivalents of the secular nuptials for those few daughters who took earthly spouses, affirmed the dignity and social status not only of the families they left behind but also of the convents they were entering. A daughter's marriage to the Son of God rather than to the son of some noble family obviously complicates any comparisons with secular marriages. Yet, although details may be different, the parallels help to explain why the festive and social aspects of these espousals to Christ were as hard to control by episcopal decree as their worldly equivalents in some cities were by secular law.

The convent rites and festivities also renewed dynastic links, commonly extending back for generations to a time before Trent, when freer convent comings and goings had fostered more frequent reinforcements of family ties. With special license, or as best they could, the older convent brides of Christ, like equivalent matrons in the world, rehearsed the new alliance with the new bride who joined them, whose place in the convent "lineage" was thereby articulated. In the convent situation the social network also expanded informally to embrace the novice's female lineage, for whom gifts and honors from the nuns created a sense of obligation, comparable to those between families in the world.

From the beginning, such displays also acted as a way to articulate and emphasize an illustrious postulant's special place in the convent social hierarchy. For the first families of Bologna, these public rituals were almost as much an instrument of social promotion as their secular equivalents, a function they also served for the convents themselves, where the building of a strong network of family alliances was critical. For convent and family alike, it was important that these actions be performed in public view, not hidden away behind locked church doors, like some furtive clandestine marriage before an obliging friar.

Convents' presentation of plays before a select audience was a favorite adornment of profession celebrations that helped to balance the families' offerings. Such performances, which spotlighted the talents of the younger nuns and often acted out the internal hierarchies before an audience of senior nuns and, when possible, an exclusive company of female lay patrons, were particularly fascinating and attractive to outsiders—and therefore a constant source of archiepiscopal displeasure and vigilance. A Bolognese nuns' vicar's decree in 1650 against such productions differs from others regularly promulgated over the decades only in providing slightly more detail than usual:

It is the mind of the Sacred Congregation of Bishops and Regulars and of the most eminent and reverend lord cardinal archbishop that on the occasion when girls are accepted into the religious life or receive their habits, or at their profession, the nuns should perform no play at either the convent gateway or any place else where they can be seen or heard by the laity, even when they are simple dialogues for two persons only or soliloquies for one person.[5]

The fullest descriptions of such sumptuous superfluities tend to appear in this sort of prohibition intended to control them. The Bolognese nuns' vicar published one of the fullest in May 1677, singling out investitures and professions especially:

It is further ordered that at times when novices receive their regular habits or profess, on such occasions music, fireworks, shooting off firecrackers, playing of trumpets or drums, the handing out of flowers or things to eat in church or at doorways or in parlatorios is forbidden, either at the expense of the convent or of individuals or of the girls' relatives. It will therefore be the mother superior's responsibility, immediately upon receipt of the present letter, to have it read publicly, so that all may hear and observe it.[6]

Control of these festivities was a losing battle. A festival lasting more than a week, described in the records at San Guglielmo twenty-five years after the 1677 order, ignored most of the prohibitions and must have taken place by special license of the archbishop (whose direct participation demonstrates his own ability to turn a blind eye):

On 19 December 1703 the chapter's acceptance of the illustrious lady Giuliana Maria Banzi took place and was very beautiful. Then followed the ante-vigil of Christmas, which fell on Sunday; at her entry into the church, players performed a most beautiful sinfonia in the external church, with four trumpeters outside in the street, who played continuously until three hours after sundown. She then received her habit on the feast of Saint John [27 December]. She was vested to the accompaniment of music, with a general invitation [to the ceremony extended] to ladies. And it was Cardinal Giacomo Boncompagni who gave her the habit.[7]

No wonder, then, that in 1714 Bolognese lawyer Alessandro Macchia-velli exclaimed after an investiture at Sant'Agnese, "Every day people condemn the great sums spent to profess the nuns, but each one still wants to spend more than the next!" The following year, after a similar *festa* at Santissima Trinità, he observed, "The expenses required for these functions are unspeakable, and yet nobody attempts a remedy."[8]

In rare instances when voices within the convent speak essentially to one another, however, with no assumption that their words will carry beyond the walls, one also gets a sense of how nuns could perceive artistic adornment as more than the mere vanity prelates made it out to be. There is no reason to question the nuns' own brief, formulaic reactions to elaborate *feste* recorded by anonymous chroniclers at San Guglielmo over the years: "to the great contentment of all the sisters" (1644), "in sum, it was a thing of the greatest devotion" (1644), "to the spiritual pleasure of [us] all" (1656), "to our greatest consolation" (1692). For in these private, drabber worlds, cut off from the regular round of religious and secular festivals at San Petronio and elsewhere in the city, such rare display need not represent decadence or secularization, always suspect among the ecclesiastical hierarchy when nuns were involved. Within convent walls, even the most modest, unstaged adornment of a rite of passage could seem miraculous: "April 21, 1627. Let us remember how on this day madre suor Penelope Vizzana passed to a better life [at the convent of San Guglielmo]. And don Antonio Vanotti administered the Most Holy Sacraments to her. And as she died the birds came in great numbers to her window and sang their sweetest song, which inspired wonder and devotion in all those who were present."[9]

The Consecration of Virgins

It should come as no surprise that at Santa Cristina della Fondazza, nuns were accepted, received their habits, and professed with the customary, lavish festivities. In the 1400s a banquet for family and friends within the convent customarily followed the investing of nuns there. In 1663 the convent still received a daughter from the Zoppi family "with the greatest display and pomp," including a dramatic performance that evening at the Teatro di Zoppi, in the presence of the papal legate, vice-legate, and numerous other local worthies,[10] if not (obviously) of the girl herself. Clearly, at Santa Cristina, as elsewhere, sumptuary restrictions were more someone else's ideal than the convent reality.

What set Santa Cristina apart from all the city's other convents was its adherence for half a millennium to that additional rite, the consecration of virgins, following the Roman pontifical. Chroniclers variously described this solemn group ritual as lasting from four to six hours. It took place on an average of once every fourteen years. Affording special prominence to music, particularly performances by the nun consecrands themselves, the rite enacted the nuns' perception of their singular status, their relationship to the Camaldolese order, and their relative autonomy vis-à-vis the archbishop of Bologna.

The ritual unfolding of the ceremony grows out of the same spirit of theatricality that gave birth to medieval liturgical drama, which emerged concurrently with the rite. Such theatricality remained a primary aspect of seventeenth-century festivals and rituals. The consecration makes of the whole external church a stage, which extends to the cloister gate. In the course of the drama, the brides of Christ, like their secular equivalents in the world, are displayed publicly in the wedding finery with which the bridegroom adorns them, marking their final, full integration into the senior rank of their convent family.

In the midst of the pontifical High Mass, the archpriest interrupts with the chant "Wise virgins, prepare your lamps!" All heads turn toward the vestibule of the external church, where pairs of consecrands appear, lighted candles in hand, and begin to process slowly past the illustrious audience. They pause modestly until the bishop repeatedly exhorts them, "Come!" When they finally reach the high altar, they kneel before him, singing, "Receive me, Lord, according to thy word." After declaring their vows, hand in hand with the bishop as Christ's proxy, the consecrands prostrate themselves before the altar during the chanting of the litany.

As the consecrands retire briefly out of view, the officiant blesses their veils, rings, and crowns. In their newly blessed habits, they return to public gaze, singing, "The kingdom of this world and every trapping of the age have I despised." Pairs of sacred virgins then receive their veils as they sing, "I am Christ's handmaiden," then their rings as they continue, "To him I am betrothed whom the angels serve." After displaying their rings with additional songs, they finally receive their crowns and the bishop's blessing.

Then the lengthy solemn Mass continues. After its conclusion, followed by the ritual presentation of the breviary to the consecrands and the singing of a festive Te Deum, the consecrands retrace their steps past the congregation, out the church door, and onward to the cloister gate. There the bishop reconsigns them to the care of the abbess inside *clausura*.

Strictly speaking, this rare and particularly lavish liturgical drama was an extra ceremony, however. After all, as Lucrezia Orsina Vizzana had suggested to the Congregation of Bishops in 1607 when it served her own interests, "It is nothing else but a ceremony to confirm one's profession."[11] Particularly in light of post-Tridentine stipulations concerning monastic enclosure and the church's desire to moderate inappropriate pomp, for the curia the consecration of virgins became an increasingly inconvenient, expensive superfluity. For most convents of the Catholic world, it may not have seemed worth fighting for. As early as 1634 Agostino Barbosa, the voluminous writer on canon law, commented, "You may note that the custom of blessing virgins is no longer in use."[12]

The primary new post-Tridentine impediment concerning the consecration rite involved, of course, the imposition of strict enclosure, which should have prevented the public display of the brides of Christ in the external church. This essential feature of the rite remained the sticking point in the ceremony's subsequent history. In 1584, for example, the Congregation of Bishops informed the bishop of Cefalù (Sicily) that to consecrate nuns "the bishop should enter the cloister with his assistants and not have the nuns come outside," thereby obliterating a chief feature and a major attraction of the ceremony: the brides' public presentation. But two years later the pope ruled that the lesser evil was for the consecrands to exit rather than have the bishop and his entire entourage troop en masse into the cloister.[13]

Divergent interpretations would continue throughout the 1600s. In 1647, for example, the Congregation of Bishops agreed to the wishes of some nuns of Santa Chiara in Sora (Lazio) to have their consecration in the external church, provided that this had long been the custom—the force of tradition always remained a critical factor in the congregation's decisions. To meet the post-Tridentine requirements of strict enclosure, however, the cardinals added the further stipulation that the rite be performed at a window specially cut in the wall of the external church, then bricked up again immediately afterward.

In 1668, on the other hand, nuns from the convent of Santa Caterina in Rieti (Lazio) petitioned not only for a one-time relaxation of the local ban on elaborate convent music but also for permission to perform their consecration rite according to the Roman pontifical, with the promise that their parents would bear all extra expense and that the consecrands would "not take one step outside the cloister." They presumably planned somehow to get into their veils, crowns, and rings while huddled inelegantly around the cloister doorway.[14]

Such attempts to cope with restrictive post-Tridentine reforms suggest that the pontifical consecration of virgins may have lingered on in the form of exceptions to a pattern of general neglect. Fifty years after Barbosa's remark of 1634, the Oratorian and voluminous writer on theology and religious history Louis de Thomassin d'Eynac reconfirmed the earlier observation: "It is astonishing that the consecration of virgins by bishops, formerly so solemn and so celebrated among all the monuments of ecclesiastical antiquity, could have vanished in such a way that hardly any trace of it remains."[15]

Although the pontifical consecration of virgins may largely have faded into oblivion, one convent continued to maintain the tradition unbroken down to the Napoleonic suppression in 1799: Santa Cristina della Fondazza in Bologna.

TEN

Another Bishop, Another Battle, a Different Outcome

"But Surely, the Nuns Aren't Vile Strumpets!"

As the century closed, Bologna had not witnessed a pontifical consecration of virgins in almost twenty-five years. In 1696 the nuns of Santa Cristina approached reigning archbishop Giacomo Boncompagni to request that he consecrate twelve nuns, the largest group of the century. Boncompagni opposed the rite in the external church, however, and would only agree to perform it in the privacy of the small Communion closet near the high altar. For he was determined to avoid exposing consecrands to the curious gaze of throngs drawn to the ceremony, as he imagined, by the singular opportunity to gape at them during their exodus from the cloister. By now it comes as no surprise that for the nuns of Santa Cristina such half measures would not do. They refused to take the archbishop's no for an answer.

The sixty-four-year-old convent bursar, madre donna Luigia Orsina Orsi, who would marshal forces in the ensuing legal battle, turned for help to her brother, Ludovico Maria Orsi, prior of the Camaldolese hermitage of San Benedetto di Ceretola, five miles from town. He, in turn, promptly enlisted his former protégé, Giovanni Battista Sabbatini, conveniently up from Rome for Holy Week at the hermitage, "a learned and experienced fellow, a great head and an ample brain, so that he really knows how to manage things," as Ludovico Orsi put it. Because Sabbatini enjoyed Archbishop Boncompagni's particular favor, Orsi hoped that his mediations on the nuns' behalf might prove successful.[1] When Sabbatini's repeated pleas to his longtime friend failed to persuade the cardinal, Sabbatini cast his lot with the nuns and went on to pursue the campaign as their procurator before the curia back in Rome.

The resulting study in the ins and outs of curial diplomacy contrasts with the nuns' struggles and defeats over the previous seventy years, which neither side had forgotten. Profiting from their bitter lessons of the 1620s, 1630s, and 1640s and heeding their intermediaries' advice, the nuns avoided the direct confrontations of the past and remained more discreetly, patiently, and, above all, obediently behind the front lines. With their advocates' help, they quietly worked the networks of influential Bolognese and Roman friends, who might wield power they lacked.

Sabbatini decided to approach Pope Innocent XII first, once he had enlisted the aid of some of Bologna's favorite sons. Monsignor Alessandro Caprara, from an old Bolognese senatorial family, partially drafted Sabbatini's papal petition and promised his surreptitious support of the nuns' cause. As early as August 1697 Monsignor Ulisse Giuseppe Gozzadini, papal secretary of briefs and former Bolognese professor of canon law, privately vetted the petition as well. "The sisters of Santa Cristina are totally in the right—it's the rashest display of vainglory on Our Friend's part!" Gozzadini exclaimed (using Boncompagni's transparent code name). But Gozzadini insisted that his own name be kept as far from the affair as possible. Sabbatini requested the same of Orsi: "Never bring my name up in this business, because I don't want to show up in any of it—especially before his lordship. I've done what I've done out of love for you, Reverend Father. But let's keep it secret, between us."[2] At various stages in the proceedings the Bolognese ambassador in Rome also discreetly took the nuns' part.

But the pope declined to rule on the nuns' petition, insisting instead that it follow normal bureaucratic channels for such requests: he summoned Gozzadini from the papal antechamber and commanded him to forward the petition to the Congregation of Sacred Rites. Sabbatini therefore redirected all his energies to the cardinals of the congregation. To his considerable surprise and vexation, he learned after months of work that the nuns had already petitioned the Congregation of Sacred Rites on their own regarding the Sacra back in 1696. "But one must be patient," he gently chided, "because if nobody made mistakes in this world, it would be too great a lubberland." Sabbatini also reported back to Bologna that when "Our Friend" had responded to the Congregation of Sacred Rites' request for elucidation in July 1696, the archbishop had rehearsed the notorious history of Santa Cristina's removal from Camaldolese control and its subjugation to Archbishop Ludovico Ludovisi in the 1620s. Boncompagni had even dug up the Congregation of Bishops' old letter authorizing Ludovisi's harshest reprisals against the disobedient nuns and had forwarded a copy to the congregation. This time an exasperated Sabbatini exclaimed, "But what has that to do with our insistence that the consecration be performed in the external church in the form prescribed in the Roman pontifical?"[3]

The nuns' past history had everything to do with their latest petition, of course. Boncompagni had already hinted at the consecration rite's significance as a symbol of the convent's resistance to archiepiscopal control. The archbishop brought up the infamous visitation in 1622–23, which had resulted in the walling up of an old grate between inner and outer church, through which, he claimed, the nuns had customarily received their habits. That visitation, of course, had also provided Ludovisi with an excuse to oust the Camaldolese from control of Santa Cristina.

The Sacra's symbolic and historical implications become apparent when we look more closely at the relationship between the ritual, political events, and convent struggles since 1620. Our old friend Mauro Ruggeri reveals the connection. In the aftermath of the first visitation in 1623, which initiated Santa Cristina's decline, the nuns planned a consecration for 1624. This would have been an effective means to reaffirm their dignity and *onestà*, compromised in the eyes of the city, and also to reenact their links to Bolognese patrician families. Because the Camaldolese prior general would officiate, the Sacra would also point out most impressively the convent's place in the Camaldolese order.[4]

Ruggeri relates that Cecilia Bianchi let Archbishop Ludovisi know that he should come witness huge sums being squandered on luxury and ostentation. We have to take Ruggeri's word that Ludovisi, who believed the monks had usurped his authority, devised a way to humiliate the rival Camaldolese by sending don Gioanino, his scheming nuns' vicar, to forbid the ceremony at the very last minute. But when don Gioanino reached Santa Cristina on the morning of the rite, he found the ceremony already well under way, with such crowds outside and such a traffic jam of carriages in the streets that even the papal legate, arriving fashionably late, had to turn around and go home. After don Gioanino retraced his steps to inform Ludovisi of his failure, the cardinal hurried to via Fondazza himself, still hoping to have his way. By the time the archbishop managed to squeeze through the crowds and get inside the church, he beheld the consecrands already crowned and displaying their rings. In a fury, he returned to his carriage, where he reportedly exclaimed, "Friars! Friars! Even if I should lose the red hat, never again will you consecrate nuns in Bologna!"[5]

Seventy years later Cardinal Boncompagni explicitly articulated the connection between the consecration rite, the Camaldolese, and the nuns' disobedience:

I steadfastly want to believe that my predecessors as archbishop would have perse-vered [in outlawing the rite] if they had not been mindful of the survival of all or a faction of those nuns (none of whom is still living), who were bitterly tried by their removal from their regulars and by their subjugation to the bishop. I suspect they [the diocesan curia] considered it expedient not to object, lest they incite enduring extravagances. But since by now all the old ones have died off, as I said, one can hope for nothing else but the fulfillment of the good work, so strongly commended by these authorities, seconded by a decision by the Sacred Congregation, admitting no appeal.[6]

Behind-the-scenes machinations surrounding performances of this invariably controversial ceremony as early as the 1590s illuminate the nuns' basic strategy. They provide a particularly apt illustration of what we have seen from the beginning: how nuns worked within and around the restrictions created to control them. The sisters exercised influence through tactics of evasion and delay, the discovery of loopholes, the use of intermediaries, and patience.

Early in 1599, for example, Santa Cristina had petitioned the Congre-gation of Bishops on behalf of several potential consecrands. The nuns made no mention of the intended location for the consecration and the congregation's response overlooked the issue. The convent may also have benefited from the Roman bureaucracy's glacial pace, for the cer-emony must have taken place before another critical ruling by the con-gregation arrived in January 1601. It included the following stipulation: "The ceremony of the black veil as they required in their consecration must be performed within the cloister, at the grates, without permitting the nuns under any circumstances to enter the external church."[7]

The nuns, seconded by their Camaldolese superiors, chose simply to ignore this new stipulation at the next Sacra, in 1607. This consecra-tion followed the Congregation of Bishops' ban on the acceptance of *educande*, at a time when Santa Cristina had begun to feel an increasing neglect by the daughters of the highest nobility.

Repetitions of the consecration rite as the convent's decline continued largely coincided with later campaigns against archiepiscopal control. The nuns knew better than to repeat the consecration while Cardinal

Ludovisi was alive. They staged the next Sacra in 1636, with the participation of his successor, Archbishop Girolamo Colonna, who seems to have gone along with the nuns' desires. According to Ruggeri, Colonna was "charmed by the beautiful nuns' consecration he performed."[8]

Cardinal Antonio Barberini, the influential cardinal nephew and Bolognese papal legate, officiated at the next Sacra, in 1643. This Sacra set the stage for the nuns' subsequent attempt at reunion with the Camaldolese order, which Urban VIII's death in July 1644 may have disrupted. The campaign eventually ended, of course, in the confrontations of 1647 and the nuns' absolute subjugation to diocesan control.

It is unsurprising that talk of the next consecration began within months of Alexander VII's accession, in April 1655. In their petition to their old adversaries on the Congregation of Bishops, the nuns mistakenly mentioned the location for the rite. The congregation predictably stipulated that the ceremony must not take place in the external church. So the nuns simply postponed the ceremony for another two years. When they re-petitioned in 1657, they made no mention of the external church, and the Congregation of Bishops neglected to specify where the ceremony should occur.[9] So, naturally, when the nuns finally staged the Sacra in 1658, they considered themselves free to perform the ritual, as always, in the external church. The new archbishop of Bologna, Girolamo Boncompagni, apparently raised no objections, so things went forward in the time-honored way.

In 1698, while Sabbatini guided their latest case in Rome, the nuns continued to work behind the scenes to reinforce old lines of influence and establish new ones that they might use to their own advantage. Sabbatini urged that Cardinal Leandro Colloredo be named *ponente* (cardinal in charge) to oversee the case in the Congregation of Sacred Rites, since the prelate had married off one of his female relatives to a member of donna Luigia Orsina Orsi's family. Sabbatini also advised the abbess to make an ally of Cardinal Ferdinando d'Adda, Bolognese papal legate, who could mediate on the convent's behalf with cardinals in the congregation. Sabbatini further suggested that the nuns enlist other supporters to testify that previous consecrations had occurred without scandal. By then, the busy nuns had already secured testimonials from distinguished nobles, a senator, and a doctor of theology and canon of San Petronio that the consecrations of 1658 and 1675 had been models of modesty and decorum. And Sabbatini urged the nuns to appeal to their ultimate advocates in heaven: "Even with all our valid justifications, when dealing with an archbishop who is also a cardinal, one can lose, because in these cases it isn't enough to be in the right."[10]

As lobbying intensified, Sabbatini encouraged the mother superior, madre donna Maria Caterina Allé, to enlist the support of Count Paolo Bolognetti, who had witnessed the Sacra of 1675. "Because of the considerable esteem the count enjoys with many cardinals," he was in an excellent position to advance the nuns' cause. Soon the count became a key figure in the enterprise, and his intercessions played a primary role in subsequent political maneuvers.[11]

Even more intriguing are the subtler sources of influence among whom the nuns found sympathetic ears: networks of female relatives and friends and other women of their class active in the world. The proactive sisters had already approached "Princess Pallavicina"—the illustrious Flaminia Pamphili Pallavicina—when Sabbatini suggested the abbess write her in January 1698, because of the princess's considerable influence in the Congregation of Sacred Rites. In March, Sabbatini also advised that "it would not prove fruitless for the mother superior to write a letter to Princess Ottoboni [Maria Moretti Ottoboni, wife of Antonio Ottoboni, nephew of Alexander VIII] in Venice, requesting that she recommend the cause to her son, Cardinal Ottoboni [Pietro Ottoboni, papal vice chancellor and renowned patron of literature and music], and to some other cardinals in the congregation."[12]

The continuing correspondence also testifies to personal visits to Santa Cristina, discussions of family matters, and other written exchanges between donna Luigia Orsina Orsi and at least one female member of the nobility, a "Contessa Isabetta" (probably Count Paolo Bolognetti's daughter-in-law). All these actions affirm in a particularly intriguing way that social alliances with highly placed women within the Bolognese nobility, nurtured at convent festivities, could also be established with women much farther afield. In a later letter of May 1698, Sabbatini commented that "we found almost all the cardinals disposed to oblige the nuns, and Cardinal Grimani should also be nicely warmed up, especially to please the countess" (who remains unnamed). Ties of sisterhood, family, and class, powerful, if elusive, were obviously at work across great distances. Those slaving closer to home in the convent kitchen also quietly played their part. Early on the bursar ended a note to Ludovico Maria Orsi, "If you'd like any little tarts for Christmas, let me know so I can get busy on them and send them for you to have on Christmas Eve."[13]

Boncompagni's own strategy also followed the ingrained methods of his predecessors. Sabbatini informed the nuns that their archbishop had proposed to Cardinal Colloredo that the consecration be performed near the high altar, at the Communion window, or through a larger hole cut specially in the wall below the window and extended to the floor.

Colloredo's auditor had secretly passed along to Sabbatini the nature of the archbishop's justification for such discretion: "In his letter he again writes little good about the nuns, and about certain ones in particular, but I don't know which ones; and his justification of his conscience must rest upon this." The implications of these familiar old veiled hints about the nuns' *onestà* were not lost upon the nuns' lawyer and on their secret Roman supporter, Monsignor Caprara. Both crossed themselves in astonishment when they heard about Boncompagni's allegations. As Sabbatini put it:

By claiming he could not perform the ceremony in any other way for reasons of conscience, he is going to defame the whole convent, as much before the city as before all the other convents of the order. For if they saw the ceremony performed differently than on other occasions, they might rightly fear some great defect among the nuns, that among the consecrands there might be someone who might have amorous alliances outside the convent.

Many cardinals affirmed to Sabbatini and the nuns' lawyer that "the whole business was sophistry and a useless indiscretion on Our Friend's part." Indeed, the venerable (if doctrinally unorthodox) Cardinal Pier Matteo Petrucci exclaimed, "But surely, the nuns aren't vile strumpets— and he said that to me!"[14] The public consecration thus symbolized more than the nuns' independence; once again it had become an affirmation of their honor and good name, which were under episcopal attack in the usual ways.

But Boncompagni had miscalculated. This latest action only fed abiding noble-ecclesiastical tensions that characterized Bologna in the 1600s. From the 1650s to the 1730s the Boncompagni family monopolized the local archbishopric, while at the same time they rented out Palazzo Boncompagni to others and left their place in the senatorial ranks empty. So to their fellow Bolognese the archbishops' primary allegiances seemed to be to the curia and to Rome, where they had also acquired a palace on via Veneto—now home to the American embassy.

The mother superior had scarcely read Sabbatini's latest letter when she received another, reporting the archbishop's "accustomed slanders against the convent and the nuns—that he acted, not out of spite, but according to the dictates of his conscience." To the letter writer, Boncompagni's veiled hints redounded against him, inasmuch as the archbishop's remarks reaffirmed other rumors about his lack of charity. Boncompagni had "at other times contrived to write to the congregations in similar ways, and especially against the nuns of San Mattia and San Luca, discrediting them and slandering them as much as he could to achieve his objective, instead of concealing deficiencies, if such there may have been, as a charitable pastor should."[15]

Unfortunately for Boncompagni, Count Paolo Bolognetti's family had relatives among the slandered nuns at San Mattia. In reaction to this earlier affront to their honor, Bolognetti became an even more vigorous champion on Santa Cristina's behalf. (Ludovico Maria Orsi subsequently remarked that one of Bolognetti's letters was "nothing if not blessed.") The count personally lobbied almost every cardinal in the Congregation of Sacred Rites, extolling the nuns' good name and the decorum of the Sacra. As Sabbatini observed, "almost always [the cardinals] have resolved against him [Boncompagni]. Therefore, this, his disgrace, can only be good luck for the nuns." It is particularly ironic that the potent force of family honor, which had been a critical issue that had so preoccupied the nuns in earlier times, should have come back to haunt Ludovico Ludovisi's successor seventy years later.[16]

By pleading his conscience and by his latest imputations, Boncompagni had restored the old rhetoric and hints of scandal from that earlier era. Count Bolognetti strongly urged the nuns to inform the curia that their archbishop's rejection of a public consecration would so discredit the convent that Santa Cristina would no longer be able to attract girls to be educated and to profess there—precisely what the nuns had lamented to the Congregation of Bishops half a century before, when their removal from Camaldolese jurisdiction had provoked similar gossip. The mother abbess, madre donna Colomba Carrati, could not help remarking privately, "If we are all so wicked and scandalous, where are the scandals? In so short a time are we become such demons?"[17]

In May 1698 the nuns' lawyer tentatively hinted at the possibility of some compromise. But the sisters of Santa Cristina responded emphatically in words that echo the proclamations of their forebears:

Let it therefore please your lordship [Sabbatini] to believe and to make signor Zanelli [their lawyer] clearly understand that we would rather risk a negative verdict in the Sacred Congregation regarding the justice we desire than to stop short of the most just and justifiable plea set forth in our petition to the supreme pontiff. Our monastery is a holy receptacle of brides of Christ, where the veil is granted only to those from the ranks of ladies and gentlewomen. Here we live with sentiments of both nobility and piety, which is to say, of absolute honor and esteem. We have always lived with this respect, and at present our utmost esteem is more than ever at its height, by the grace of God. And whoever presumes to say or to make people believe otherwise had better produce, not airy imaginings, but specific, distinct examples. We tell your lordship this so you may realize that here we suppose that, to thwart our objective, someone in Rome might have presumed certain opinions against our esteem and reputation. But whoever has a clear conscience need fear nothing.

Then onward! We are resolved, either to lose everything and preserve that esteem which has always been proper to this convent or to obtain from the Sacred Congregation what those most eminent lords in so many years past and present have considered to be in agreement with the Roman pontifical.[18]

On 5 July the Congregation of Sacred Rites deliberated Zanelli's brief. Since precedents and established custom weighed at least as heavily as political influence for legally trained minds in the congregations of the curia, the lawyer's meticulously researched case marshaled numerous precedents for the nuns' claims. The Camaldolese may not have officiated at any Sacra at Santa Cristina in over seventy years, but in Zanelli's case, ancient links between Santa Cristina and its old superiors and the strength of centuries of tradition outweighed the apparent whims of the latest archbishop.[19]

Meanwhile, Sabbatini continued to work behind the scenes, finally winning over one inimical cardinal in the eleventh hour, for example, with the witty remark that Boncompagni's dangerous suggestion (that the nuns be consecrated through a hole cut in the ancient wall near the high altar) ran the risk "of making a spiritual pancake—and a clerically scrupulous one" (di fare una frittata spirituale, e religiosa). After weighing evidence and influence, the cardinals finally ruled that the consecration should be performed in the time-honored way. But the battle still was not over. The congregation left it to Boncompagni to see to the consecrands' modest and discreet egress from the cloister: "the means of egress [from the cloister] into the outer church [is left to] the judgment of the most eminent archbishop."[20]

Nuns were not the only ones adept at ferreting out loopholes in Rome's decrees. Loath to abandon the field, the archbishop chose an alternative attack plan: he took the ruling to mean that he could choose the actual point of entry into the external church. His partisans in the cardinalate in fact encouraged him: "If he wanted to have the nuns exit even from the rooftops he could do so." Boncompagni therefore reasserted his original proposal that a special doorway be cut between Santa Cristina's internal and external church, near the high altar.[21]

From behind the lines on via Fondazza, the nuns launched repeated sorties by the nobility against the archbishop's palace downtown. Boncompagni rebuffed further overtures from their patrician emissaries, with a specific command to the mother abbess and prioress to quit sending them—which provoked Count Bolognetti to remark "the lord cardinal can garner no praise by his chosen form, to decline to hear men of honor."[22] But the nuns continued to insist on the total observance of the Roman pontifical's rubrics.

In Rome, the cardinals remained divided. Shortly after the congregation's initial ruling, Count Bolognetti reported that one spoke in favor of the new door in the old wall, "as Our Friend wishes." But another responded forcefully, "As long as the Roman pontifical prescribes that the consecrands exit from the convent door, it is unnecessary to open up another one." The nuns also dispatched drawings to illustrate the hopelessly constricted location that Boncompagni proposed, together with the decorous, traditional route from the parlatorio through the courtyard to the vestibule, then into the external church. Faced with this latest evidence, even cardinals who wished to support Boncompagni acknowledged that his alternative proposal was impractical.[23]

On 27 September 1698 the Congregation of Sacred Rites took the decision out of Boncompagni's hands rather pointedly: "It was our wish that Your Eminence be informed that the Tribunal of Sacred Rites declared that the pontifical should be observed without any change whatsoever concerning their exit and return to the convent, in the precise manner prescribed by the pontifical: the consecrands may leave through the regular door to the convent and at the end of the ceremony reenter by the same door."[24]

A vanquished Boncompagni resigned himself to officiating at the consecration, as a stand-in not only for Christ but ironically also for the Camaldolese, who Ludovico Ludovisi had vowed would never consecrate another nun at Santa Cristina. A positively gleeful Count Bolognetti, after gently teasing the mother superior, "whom we should dub a doubting Thomas" for her earlier pessimism, went on to exult, "It now remains to behold the incompatibility of the cardinal and [nuns' vicar] Pini performing the ritual with all the constipation [*stitichezza*] their feigned zeal will fling at them." Ludovico Maria Orsi responded more decorously, "Divine Goodness has restored your convent to its pristine reputation and has closed the case on all those who cherished an evil opinion of your good name."[25]

Even as he sounded retreat, Boncompagni was not quite ready to strike the archiepiscopal colors. Although he would perform the consecration as the Congregation of Sacred Rites required, he declared a disinclination to sing the accompanying pontifical Mass. (Rome had not mentioned that.) For the dozen consecrands, exultation abruptly turned to consternation. In her usual way, tugging at the tangled ties of authority and influence within the ecclesiastical hierarchy, the convent bursar, madre donna Luigia Orsina Orsi, went quietly back to work to change his mind. Her first emissary, the master of ceremonies at the cathedral of San Pietro, returned five days later with an unpromising report—His Eminence was solidly dug in. So the bursar sought out a "more suitable" mediator. She called upon the chief chaplain to Cardinal Ferdinando d'Adda, the papal legate, to persuade the cardinal to act as intermediary. In the face of this latest, decidedly more powerful force, even Boncompagni recognized the unwisdom of his potential Pyrrhic victory.

D'Adda's chief chaplain hastened to Santa Cristina, arriving well after dark, just as the nuns were retiring. In the faint light of the reception room door he discovered the unsuccessful master of ceremonies, who had beat him to the gate with the welcome news. Following the rules of the game to the end, the convent bursar amply rewarded both for their good and discreet offices—though the legate's chaplain rightly received the greater gift, as the nuns carefully recorded.[26]

"To Him I Am Betrothed Whom the Angels Serve"

The year 1699 opened inauspiciously with bitter cold and unusually heavy snow, followed by severe flooding. But a little winter weather could not dampen enthusiasm on via Fondazza. On 11 January 1699, the long-fought-for ritual consecration of twelve nuns finally occurred, with Archbishop Giacomo Boncompagni officiating "in the amplest and most dignified form ever employed" (or so it seemed to the nun who recorded it, with, we may assume, the slightest smile of satisfaction). The celebration was largely consistent with former (and future) practice, though it undoubtedly seemed particularly significant in 1699. The inevitable published collection of laudatory verses, *La verginità consacrata*, presumably commissioned by the nuns, who are named as patrons, highlighted the 1699 event.[27] Such commemorations and other surviving descriptions of the ritual help us reconstruct the ceremony and its meaning. The modest 1699 publication aptly matches the modest talents of eighteen poetasters, one of whom wisely chose anonymity as "the unlucky one among the Arcadians." Their poetic effusions, though mediocre from a literary point of view, regularly return to images that suggest what public and patrons must have expected.

The dedication, for example, alludes elliptically to recent archiepiscopal turbulence: "Your preeminent shepherd now acknowledges you wholly as that flock whose spirit embodies fidelity to its Lord" (not quite true of either party, of course). Learned Latin couplets, which compare the nuns' veils to the helmet of "the high-minded warrior, about to endure the arduous battle, managing to carry back the palm from his vanquished foe," hint discreetly at the nuns' recent victory over a vanquished archbishop. Such martial language echoes earlier, less public communications. In the uncertain days before the final victory, Ludovico Maria Orsi had consoled his sister: "Even if everything should turn out worse and you don't at least obtain the favorable decree, you will always be esteemed as such Amazons, for taking up the sword in defense of your arguments in such an improper and difficult molestation." After the final victory, another admirer wrote the convent bursar to compare recent events to Alexander the Great's victory over Rome (!) and to suggest that although she might not be an Amazon in war, she had had the stout heart to sustain the entire enterprise.[28]

The spectacular aspects of the Santa Cristina consecration took no notice of all those sumptuary laws, from Gabriele Paleotti's to Innocent XI's, and set out to dazzle eye and ear with splendor unmatched by any other convent in the city. Particulars from consecrations between 1624 and the landmark event of 1699 are consistent with the most detailed account—from the 1711 Sacra—on which we can rely heavily for a sense of the spectacle. This effusive description ignores little about the ritual, though the author's overabundant enthusiasm obscures much of the detail.[29]

Santa Cristina created many additional features that were unspecified in the Roman pontifical and were designed to enhance the rite's drama, splendor, and political utility. During the chanting of the litany, for example, the consecrands, prostrate before the high altar, were all covered by a single, giant black pall, starkly representing not only their death to the world but also their symbolic sacrifice on the city's behalf. This traditional theme of oblation echoes throughout *La verginità consacrata*. Its dedication speaks of "heroic confirmation of such a sacrifice: by such a generous act you reveal a heart worthy of God." One sonnet opens with an image of virginal tribute: "Behold us, O God, little virgins united at thy feet, to offer up to thee our heart, together with our soul." Another is more explicit: "A holy zeal destines you as sacrificial victims to God," (ignoring the reality that insistent fathers rather than pious zeal brought many consecrands to the altar).[30]

The singular moment that Boncompagni found so disquieting, when the consecrands stepped forth from the cloister into the public gaze, escaped few commentators. The procession from cloister gate to church portal, appropriately led by the nuns' ally Count Bolognetti, must have been as brisk as solemnity would allow, given the unusually frigid temperatures in January 1699. To heighten the solemn moment when pairs of consecrands, robed in white, each with a candle in hand, reached the doors of the public church and emerged into view, a seminarian as well as a *paranympha* (lay matron godparent) accompanied each consecrand to assist her at her entrance and throughout the rite. In 1711, when the number of consecrands had dropped from twelve in 1699 to eight, a squadron of another twenty-five seminary alumni joined eight seminarian escorts, for a total of thirty-three, one for every year in the life of the nuns' heavenly spouse.[31] For the 1699 ceremony, the twelve consecrands paid out eighty lire apiece for the remarkable transformation of the interior ritual space, created especially for their benefit. Both sides of the external church were fitted out with steeply raked bleachers with railings to protect the patrician audience of lords, ladies, and clergy, who thus had the best possible view of the consecrands, venturing forth from the cloister into public view for the first—and last—time. Rich festoons, gathered in clusters, hung down from near the ceiling, decorated with red banderoles ornamented with arabesques. Large medallions bearing gilded Latin inscriptions were also affixed near the vaults, which had been freshly whitewashed for the occasion. Below the windows, colored bunting garnished with white taffeta draped the wide cornice molding to form a loggia, from which twelve monumental statues representing the fairest virtues (with their nudity discreetly draped for the occasion, of course) observed the proceedings. These virtues of faux marble, highlighted with gold and rented for the occasion from a local sculptor, matched the scale of the eight stucco saints in niches below them.[32] Between the sculptures stood eighteen vases filled with laurel and cypress, symbolizing the consecrands' honor and victory but also their death to the world. Red and yellow streamers further embellished the pseudo-loggia, below which hung damask in similar colors. All the columns and pilasters of the church and the high altar were resplendent from floor to ceiling with the customary draperies of crimson damask.

The high altar shone with silver. In addition to silver vessels, seven candlesticks, and other permanent furnishings, two stepped credenzas flanked the altar and displayed over a hundred pieces of silver and silver gilt, most on loan from the flower of the nobility. Large salvers contained the consecrands' habits, which were to be blessed by the archbishop. Also on display were the renowned bridal crowns, the rings, and other regalia. So much for Alfonso Paleotti's old prescription of a simple, unornamented dress of white, black, buff, or purple for any would-be nun and a ceremony conducted in an empty church, behind closed doors.

But music captured as much or even more attention than the visual spectacle. Convent confessor Mauro Ruggeri remarked that consecrations ran five to six hours, "depending on whether the music took more or less time."[33] It seems no coincidence that all five of the music collections dedicated to the nuns of Santa Cristina in Ruggeri's day (in 1599, 1601, 1606, 1613, and 1623) appeared within a year or two of a ritual consecration of virgins, at which some of the music was probably heard. Indeed, Adriano Banchieri's *Messa solenne* (1599) was especially well suited to that purpose, since it included not only a double-choir setting of the Mass Ordinary (the portion Boncompagni initially declined to perform in 1699) but also a festive, double-choir setting of the Te Deum, also an essential part of the rite. Motets from Banchieri's collection such as *En dilectus meus loquitur mihi* (Behold, my beloved speaks to me; *SMSM*, track 9) also speak directly to the relationship of Christ and his brides in the language of the Song of Songs.

Virtually every subsequent commentator made some reference to the music. Musical themes also run through the commemorative verses of *La verginità consacrata*, in which the nuns compel even the rival celestial choirs to join the applause. An anonymous sonneteer exclaims:

Fulfill that great Desire! Those teardrops wringing
From inmost heart no more signify sorrow.
But subtle breezes sweeten at thy singing.

Music regularly caught the attention of diarists and chroniclers, too. One account from 1699 merely remarks that the Mass began "with the greatest constant rumbling of fireworks, drums, and trumpets." Convent account books confirm payments for no fewer than eight trumpeters and six drummers, plus twelve hundred fireworks and seven hundred rockets. Another chronicler claimed that the ceremony ran for five hours (still another commentator claimed that it lasted as long as six) and lauded the "innumerable and most exquisite voices," including, apart from trumpets and drums, a choir of extern musicians brought in for the occasion, who sang terce (the appropriate service from the Divine Office), the Mass Ordinary, the Veni Creator Spiritus, and the Te Deum, directed by the illustrious Giacomo Perti, *maestro di capella* of San Petronio.

The 1711 descriptions are even more effusive. One diarist recorded only the inevitable "resounding of trumpets, drums, timpani, and the shooting off of a sizable quantity of fireworks." These included four trumpeters to play before and after the consecration, as well as the archbishop's two trumpeters, and six drummers and timpanists; the evening before the ceremony a hundred rockets and a thousand firecrackers started things off with a bang, while a barrage of a hundred mortars immediately followed the ritual. Expenditures for fireworks even surpassed the cost of the extern musicians in 1711, again led by Giacomo Perti as *maestro di cappella*, who provided music for triple choirs.[34]

But the primary musical focus was on the consecrands, who accompanied virtually every ritual action with songs of their own. On receiving the veil they "sang certain motets with great applause from the people and cardinals present." They received the rings "with various songs." They donned their crowns "with other songs, always accompanied by their instruments." After the Communion, "two of the nuns sang the most beautiful motet possible, accompanied by the organ and instruments." Some of the music must have been traditional plainchant, whose stark purity would have set off the real musical highpoints, involving polyphony.

One writer in 1711 attested that "each of the eight nuns sang a motet." Another confirmed enthusiastically that "during the ceremony they also sang one motet apiece, with voices as if of angels." This writer may not have been the most impartial judge, however, since he had a relative among the consecrands. Unfortunately, when it came to the nuns' singing, the most meticulous witness to the 1711 consecration expended more of his creative energies on ecstatic rapture than on precise description. He indicates that an alto and a soprano sang *Suscipe Domine secundum eloquium tuum* (Receive me, according to thy word) on behalf of their fellow consecrands, who were lying prostrate before the archbishop. But then he lapses into another of his typical effusions: "Rightly might the spectators exclaim with the great Seraph [Saint Francis] of Assisi, '*satis est*, no more, no more,' as everyone remained as if in ecstasy of love for the great God of most excellent mercies because of the sweetness of the melodious voices."[35]

The singing consecrands who thus took center stage most effectively conveyed the immediate and broader resonances of the ritual. To be sure, the trumpeters and drummers, the double or triple choirs of extern musicians who performed the imposing, impersonal elements of the Ordinary, amid volleys of pyrotechnics, may have enhanced the splendor and solemnity of the rite. But the ritual words of the consecrands themselves, whether in ancient plainchant accompanied by the organ or in polyphony, articulated the more direct and particular meanings of the rite by affirming their own singularity and virtue (recently called into question yet again by the archbishop):

The kingdom of this world and every trapping of the age have I despised, for the love of our Lord, Jesus Christ. To him I am betrothed whom the angels serve, whose beauty sun and moon do wonder at. With his ring has my Lord Jesus Christ betrothed me and with a crown, adorned me as his bride. The Lord has wrapped me round with cloth of gold, and with countless gems he has adorned me. Behold, that which I have desired, now I behold, that in which I hoped, I now hold fast. To Him am I joined in heaven, whom yet on earth I have, with all devotion, loved.[36]

Of the large cast of characters in this sacred drama, therefore, those in the starring role most persuasively encouraged the audience to unite in affirming their virtue and esteem. The same had been the case 250 years earlier, when Ambrogio Traversari officiated at the reception of a novice in 1433. It was "above all, [the nuns'] scruples and their uncommon knowledge of divine worship and of the sacred liturgy" that had persuaded the Camaldolese prior general to reject current rumors about the nuns' *onestà*.[37] In 1699 the congregation and the city could join with the archbishop—in the words of Revelation, which also inspired many of the sonnets of *La verginità consacrata*—to pray God's grace upon "your handmaids, who have vowed to serve you with a pure mind and spotless heart; that you may think them worthy to be numbered among the one hundred and forty-four thousand who have remained virgins and have not debased themselves with women, in whose mouth no guile is found. So likewise you cause these your handmaids to remain spotless to the end" (cf. Revelation 14:4–5).[38]

Other sorts of ritual stagecraft, elaborating upon the Roman pontifical's stipulations, also acknowledged and reinforced affiliations to the urban patriciate, reestablishing old social patterns of clientage and creating new ones, winning support where it was likely to matter. The flower of the nobility were there to see, to be seen, or, indeed, even *not* to be seen—but as ostentatiously as possible. In 1699 no chronicler failed to note the fashionably late arrival of the papal legate and protector of the Camaldolese religion, Cardinal Ferdinando d'Adda, robed in black, ringed by his personal security, having stopped on route to pick up Monsignor Grimani, the vice-legate, and the visiting Cardinal de' Medici. The illustrious trio swept in to observe "incognito" from a prominent spot near the high altar, but behind gilded screens. Surely some must have recognized how deliciously appropriate it was that the papal legate, whose aid behind the scenes the mother abbess had enlisted early in the struggle and who, at the behest of the mother superior, had later secured Boncompagni's grudging participation in the rite, should also witness the fruits of his influence "behind the scenes" but known to be present.

The flower of the nobility from other cities enhanced the luster of the local nobility in fuller view. In 1699 Cardinal de' Medici and other dignitaries made a special detour to Bologna en route to Modena to pay court to Amalia of Brunswick, then proceeding to Vienna to wed Joseph of Hapsburg, king of Hungary. In 1711, from behind similarly gilded screens, members of the illustrious Borghese family, up from Rome, likewise added special excitement and discreet brilliance to that consecration.[39]

The nuns also devised ways to draw the cream of local society into a more active role than simply as viewers. At Santa Cristina the ritual crowns that played a central part in the rite were not the simple garlands depicted in some pontificals. Figure 26, from the Roman pontifical of 1595–96, illustrates the usual crown (note also other nuns inside *clausura*, watching the rite through an open door). Santa Cristina's crowns became a dazzling focus of attention. *La verginità consacrata* draws liberally on jewels, crowns, and garlands to represent literally the bridal accoutrements and, metaphorically, the consecrands themselves. For one poet the heavenly and earthly treasures were inseparable:

> Go, plait ye
> Thy crowns of innocence, lilies, and roses.
> You, diamonds most select, make haste! Fly quickly
> To throat, to breast of divas here espousèd.
> Hasten, gems refulgent, entangle tightly
> These iv'ry hands 'midst golden bands concealèd.

These jewels represented, literally and figuratively, the wealth of Bologna, embodied in its illustrious citizens.

This preoccupation with gems and jewelry was understandable, for the crowns, first prominently displayed beside the banks of borrowed silver and silver gilt, then worn by the brides during the ceremony, were hardly simple coronets. In 1711 they were "interlaced with gems, quantities of the finest pearls and diamonds, and with as many necklaces." In 1699 the crowns "were set with the most beautiful and rich jewels of all the nobility of Bologna"; Ruggeri had also carefully made clear that at the 1624 Sacra the jewels were all borrowed. Thus, the convent enlisted the help of the wealthiest ladies of the city by raiding their jewel boxes, then permitted them to bask in the reflected splendor of their own generosity at the ceremony. Almost a century earlier, Lucrezia Orsina Vizzana had also acknowledged these jewels in the conclusion to her consecration motet *Amo Christum* (*SED*, track 13): "He has adorned me with countless gems and with a crown he has adorned me as his spouse."

By their loans of jewelry and silver, the Bolognese nobility not only symbolically joined the family of the heavenly bridegroom, clothing these brides of Christ, but were also assumed into the convent family, initiating or reviving systems of mutual obligation to be tended carefully in future. This incorporation is implicit in one sonnet from *La verginità consacrata*, which opens by playing upon the enactment of the Sacra within the octave of the Epiphany, as Bologna's generous nobles become the Magi:

Golden diadems this earthly sovereignty,
Prostrate before an infant God, now proffers.
These tributary crowns, in turn, he offers,
Gifts unto his brides, signs of love's certainty.[40]

Following the time-honored method of choosing godparents, the nuns sought out the pinnacle of Bolognese society to join them on the stage of the consecration rite as *paranymphae*, the consecrands' female escorts, prescribed by the Roman pontifical. These matrons served partly to effect the ritual transfer of the brides from their families to their heavenly spouse. Figure 27, from the 1595–96 Roman pontifical, illustrates an elderly, kneeling *paranympha*, acknowledging her relationship to a kneeling consecrand, who receives her ring from the bishop. In 1598 Alfonso Paleotti had stipulated that a postulant be attended by "only two or three of her closest relatives" at her reception at the convent door. The glittering list of matrons for the 1699 consecration, however, reads like a Bolognese "Who's Who" (Names in small capitals represent nobility of the highest rank; those italicized are of the second rank; asterisks indicate senatorial families):[41]

MATRONS
Countess Elena PEPOLI* ALDROVANDI*
Countess Laura *Conti* BONFIGLIOLI*
Maria Angiola MARESCALCHI* *Zanchini*
Marchioness Costanza SCAPPI* SAMPIERI*
Marchioness Camilla CAPRARA* BENTIVOGLI*
Ginevra FAVA SAMPIERI*
Countess Flavia Fasoli BOLOGNETTI*
Marchioness Isotta ERCOLANI* BUOI*
Countess Anna BOLOGNETTI* LEGNANI*

FIGURE 26. *Pontificale Romanum editio princeps* (1595–96), p. 214. Consecrands receive their crowns during the ritual consecration of virgins; other nuns, inside *clausura*, observe through an open doorway at right.

FIGURE 27. *Pontificale Romanum editio princeps* (1595–96), p. 212. A kneeling *paranympha* acknowledges her relationship to a consecrand, who receives her ring from the bishop during the ritual consecration of virgins.

Francesca BOVA *Ferri* BANZI
Countess Anna BOLOGNETTI* *Bombaci*
Countess Bulgarini ROSSI*

CONSECRANDS
Maria Teresa Diamante Brighenti
Maria Marsibilia Vittoria BOLOGNINI*
Maria Romualda Teresa Diamante Lucchini
Maria Diletta Vittoria *Muzzi*
Florida Rosaura *Garzaria*
Teresa Madalena Liberata MORANDI
Maria Angelica Teresa Geltruda Gaetana Riguzzi
Maria Christina Teresa Prudenza Deodata Cavazza
Maria Emilia Chiara Antonia Vittoria *Vittorii*
Maria Giuditta Carla Carrati
Maria Giuditta Ginevra BOLOGNINI*
Barbara Teresa BOLOGNINI*

Everyone on the matrons' list had been born or married into one of Bologna's hundred best families. Only three were not countesses or marchionesses. More significant, none of the matrons on the list was directly related to a consecrand in an immediately obvious way.

The consecrands themselves are less distinguished. The list includes only four from first families (three of them from a single senatorial family); three others were from families that were at least mentioned in Pompeo Dolfi's catalog of the Bolognese elite. There were five, however, from families that Dolfi does not mention at all, even though some of the families (e.g., Cavazza, Carrati) achieved distinction in Bologna.[42]

The unimpressive pedigrees of many nuns consecrated in 1699 may in part reflect the declining demographic fortunes of the old families, many of whom became extinct in the early 1700s. It likewise may reflect the middle classes' eclipse of the patriciate in convents generally.[43] Whatever the explanation, this cohort of consecrands stands in marked contrast to its predecessors. Of the four identifiable consecrands from the modest group of five in 1675, all had come from the first families; of nine in the 1650s, five were of the first rank, one of the second rank, and only one a social nonentity. And, of course, the social profile of Santa Cristina at the turn of the seventeenth century bears little resemblance to that of a century earlier, before Emilia Grassi's campaign against *educande*. Then at least half the *professe* had hailed from the very highest echelons of the Bolognese élite.[44]

Thus, at the end of the 1600s, the nuns of Santa Cristina managed to retain an illusion of venerable nobility, which had been real before the crises of the early 1600s. To compensate for social decline they managed to forge ritual family ties between the consecrands and their aristocratic *paranympha* godparents, with an eye toward future financial and political utility. The choice of matrons in 1699 also betrays sweet but subtle revenge, for at least three families active behind the scenes in the suit against Cardinal Boncompagni are represented. It is especially fitting that the matrons also included Countess Anna Bolognetti Bombacci, a last link to the family central to Santa Cristina's spiritual, political, and musical life a century earlier.

The end of the consecration did not mark the end of hostilities. "As a sign of gratitude for the service he had performed majestically with the true zeal of a loving pastor," the nuns sent Boncompagni a huge bouquet of silk flowers, several large candles of the purest white wax, and a beautiful and costly silver crucifix, with a pair of statues at its base. But the archbishop sent it all back, saying that he would accept nothing: a last, parting shot to cover his defeat, with pique masquerading behind a punctilious sense of ecclesiastical propriety—accompanied, Count Bolognetti would probably suggest, by another bout of *stitichezza*.[45]

Boncompagni had pointed out in 1696 that the Vizzani, the Bombacci, and the others from the 1620s and 1630s were long dead. The very last of them, Lucrezia Orsina Vizzana's niece, madre donna Clorinda Vizzana, had died just the previous year, in fact, at age seventy-seven. Boncompagni was also more or less correct that the troublemakers who had fomented the protests of the 1640s had exited the stage. But witnesses to past troubles were not quite all gone. Seventy-five-year-old madre donna Maria Caterina Allé, who as mother superior courted Count Paolo Bolognetti and Princess Ottoboni in the campaign of 1698, and the prioress, madre donna Geltruda Malvezzi, had both been present in Santa Cristina's parlatorio on 20 March 1647 to be counted in the nuns' last official protest. Madre donna Maria Colomba Carrati, the sixty-nine-year-old abbess who managed the campaign of 1698 "with clever and mature discretion," had, at age eighteen, been the most junior signatory to that protest of half a century earlier.[46]

Among the male protagonists of this long tale, Mauro Ruggeri had fought the battles of the 1620s and 1640s chiefly on paper after they were over and the damage was done. At that time, the nuns' Camaldolese superiors stood rather helplessly by, leaving the nuns to fight their own battles alone—or so the surviving documents seem to indicate. But

in the 1690s Cardinal Ferdinando d'Adda, protector of the Camaldolese religion, atoned for the earlier inactivity of his predecessor of the
1620s. Don Ludovico Maria Orsi, prior of the Camaldolese hermitage of
San Benedetto, worked tirelessly on the convent's behalf throughout the
campaign of 1698. More important, he recruited his protégé, Giovanni
Battista Sabbatini, who, in the words of one observer, "has had fourteen
months of agitation for the Camaldolese nuns' suit, has lost the cardinal
archbishop's favor and much more, and has incurred the wrath of His
Eminence. He thus merits substantial recognition and therefore should
receive no less than ten doubloons, which is very modest, as the recognition is very modest."[47] Primarily the potent ties of family loyalty and
honor had compelled Orsi, Sabbatini, and Count Paolo Bolognetti to
action. Ironically, it seems to have been largely among the nuns of Santa
Cristina, not their male superiors, that Camaldolese loyalties burned
most brightly. It had been the nuns' own *onore* and *onestà*, after all, that
were chiefly at stake.

The wider implications of the Congregation of Sacred Rites' decision
were not lost on a later generation of nuns. Not so long thereafter the
sister designated as convent archivist made her way to the small, corner
room on the ground floor, adjoining the main staircase and the parlatorio where the bursar and the nuns customarily gathered to transact
business and sign contracts. This archive preserved all the records of
Santa Cristina's six-hundred-year history. After unlocking the grille, she
retrieved a fresh pasteboard carton from among several ranks of similar
boxes, all shaped like large, bound books and each marked with a large
black letter. She placed the Sabbatini and the Orsi letters, already carefully bound, inside the carton, together with every other document from
this latest battle. At the end she noted, "Finally, all the nuns of our convent of Santa Cristina have worked in support of this consecration." She
must have smiled at this affirmation, a fitting complement to another,
opening inscription, penned earlier to commemorate

our superior, the most reverend mother abbess donna Colomba Carrati; the prioress,
the most reverend donna Geltruda Marsibilia Malvezzi; the bursar, the most reverend
donna Luigia Orsina Orsi; who, working together with skillful and mature wisdom, had
the victory, to the glory of His Divine Majesty and the honor and dignity of the entire
Camaldolese order, as commemorated in our convent archive, in perpetual memory
of those who had a part in it.[48]

The archivist closed the carton, tied its ribbons, and scanned the shelves
for the appropriate spot. She pushed open a gap and inserted the carton

beside an identical box—the one she knew to contain the original trial transcript and all other memorials from the crises of the 1620s.

This was madre donna Columba Carrati's last battle; she died in March 1702, at age seventy-three. The 1700s were barely under way, however, before her surviving companions in arms, Geltruda Marsibilia Malvezzi and Luigia Orsina Orsi, would skirmish one last time against an old, familiar adversary. Like the earliest struggles almost a century before, this one, too, would begin because of music.

ELEVEN

A Last Battle and an Uneasy Peace

In January 1684, as my usual and habitual bad luck would have it, it fell to me to go to Bologna by stagecoach, with great inconvenience and exorbitant expense, because of the cardinal, my uncle's illness, who then died of it. And it turned out to be a very unlucky business for me, as everybody knows. Spring of the same year brought me back from there to Rome. And I arrived at the beginning of Holy Week,
   Yet Do I Flee the Memory of Bologna's Every Horror.[1]

A most unpromising recollection for a prelate sent back there six years later as archbishop. When Giacomo Boncompagni was tapped to lead the archdiocese in April 1690, he returned to a see that had remained effectively vacant since the death of his uncle Girolamo Boncompagni in 1684. Girolamo's successor, Angelo Maria Ranuzzi, had never even set foot in the city. Instead, Ranuzzi spent several eventful years in Paris as papal ambassador extraordinary, some of the time under arrest by order of Louis XIV.[2]

Bologna had not seen the likes of Giacomo Boncompagni for generations. In a manner reminiscent of Gabriele Paleotti, the thirty-seven-year-old prelate promptly (if perhaps reluctantly) fulfilled the post-Tridentine requirement of episcopal residency that his immediate predecessor had neglected. Indeed, Giacomo Boncompagni placed as the cornerstones of his reign the Tridentine decrees, Carlo Borromeo's model Milanese diocesan reforms, and the treatise on episcopal government *Episcopalis sollicitudinis enchiridion* (Manual of episcopal care; Paris, 1668), which held up Gabriele Paleotti as the paradigmatic *bonus pastor* (good shepherd). "Musical abuses" had been a prime target of Paleotti's monastic house-cleaning. For all the same reasons, convent music would preoccupy Boncompagni's attention 150 years later.

"Ever watchful, ever sleepless, everywhere present, visiting with restless feet, he climbed the lofty, precipitous heights of mountains, and descended into the deepest valleys, where waters inundated open fields." There is only slight hyperbole in this contemporary characterization of the earnest archbishop's determination to carry out Bologna's first pastoral visitation in decades. Boncompagni's suspicion of nuns' music emerges during visits to twenty-nine diocesan convents, which began within months of his elevation and continued for much of 1691. In some he reiterated all too familiar commands that the view through organ windows be obscured. At four convents he also inquired whether nuns or *educande* were receiving music lessons from outsiders—this at a time when the Congregation of Bishops in Rome temporarily liberalized its attitude toward the admission of music masters.[3]

Unsurprisingly, Boncompagni's archdiocesan synod of 1698 (the first in forty years) reconfirmed decrees from synods under Girolamo Colonna in 1634 and Girolamo Boncompagni in 1654, which had denied nuns all song except plainchant and all instruments but the organ and harpsichord, except by special license from the curia. As Santa Cristina's lavish Sacra the following year demonstrates (with Giacomo Boncompagni's grudging participation), the revived decrees were not observed to the letter initially.

Boncompagni fretted especially about the dangers of indiscriminate crowds in all churches. He tried separating men and women during sermons, but that innovation failed. He fixated especially on lavish music that attracted throngs to convent ceremonies. As he reported to Rome in 1704:

The frequent irreverence committed in nuns' churches when they celebrate their festivals was relentlessly increasing, to the great dishonor of the house of God. All the same, not only preachers' and confessors' edicts and admonitions about appropriate respect for the church proved futile, but, what is more, the order in His Holiness's last edict as well. I thus saw the scandals as unavoidable if music continued there. The resulting assembly of people is so congested, with men and women irresistibly intermingling together in the continuous crush, that great improprieties and tumults result, with less respect than if it happened in a public square or open marketplace. The most licentious types congregate there to take advantage of the opportunity that the confusion of such throngs usually lends to their evil ends.[4]

Not since Archbishop Alfonso Paleotti's day had the rhetoric against convent festivals sounded so shrill.

The archbishop's worries were not chimerical. Teeming throngs presented more concrete problems than the sexual improprieties that obsessively preoccupied Boncompagni. During San Pietro Martire's titular festival in April 1691, a year after the new archbishop's elevation, Girolamo Zanchetti challenged Carlo Marescalchi for insults to his family honor, then took a sword blow to the head and was run through before he could even unsheathe his sword. Zanchetti managed to hold off Marescalchi at gunpoint long enough to flee San Pietro Martire, pursued by a screaming crowd to the convent of Sant'Omobono, where he escaped into the house of the nuns' confessor. In July 1700 throngs lured to the convent of Santa Maria Maddalena by music for a particularly lavish festival were so large that a sepulcher in the floor collapsed, swallowing up a child and burying an eminent senator up to his shoulders.

In January 1703 the crush literally went too far. As Boncompagni told it:

In the church of the nuns of Sant'Agnese (governed by the Dominicans), they not only perpetrated the usual immodesties, but second vespers could not be completed because the crowds reached all the way to the high altar. During the singing of the Magnificat, the priest, vested in his cope, and his other two assistants could not possibly proceed to cense the altar, so they had to retreat to the sacristy. The extern musicians also started leaving—they could not perform their music because all the noise prevented their hearing the voices.[5]

This latest tumult provided Boncompagni with the perfect excuse to ban music from all the convents in the city. Three weeks later, on the feast of Saint Matthias, the nuns of San Mattia were the first to pay the price for the uproar at Sant'Agnese. On 9 March, even Blessed Catherine Vigri, patroness of the city, received no immunity to the ban. One chronicler's remarks could well reflect general disapproval of the archbishop's inflexibility:

The festival was not celebrated with all that pomp commonly practiced in tender devotion by her affectionate devotees. Because they are barred from providing the music; and the same prohibition likewise extends to all other nuns' churches on their feast days. This by order of the archbishop. Apart from the displeasure it causes these poor religious, this decree reduces musicians, one might say, to beggary, since we see them everywhere denied the chance to support themselves by their virtuous profession. It removes the crowds from the same churches and prejudices not a little the services and attendance at the same.

Licenses for music at special feasts during the early 1700s, carefully preserved in the archive of the convent of Santi Vitale et Agricola, also break off abruptly after 1702, testifying to the enforcement of Boncompagni's interdict.[6]

The archbishop's crackdown was thus widely known and widely observed. But when it came time for the feast of their patron saint in May 1703, the independent-minded nuns of Santa Cristina, fresh from their victory over the archbishop in 1699, chose to ignore it. One chronicler, commenting upon their disobedience, points out that they celebrated lavishly with music but declined to invite their clerical superiors, "remarking that they had been forbidden to make merry, and all other convents should have done likewise, saving themselves the lavish gifts they give their superiors."[7]

Three weeks later, at the vesting of a novice, the nuns even sang the Mass in the presence of the officiating nuns' vicar of Bologna ("simply to do him honor," the nuns later claimed; "to his astonishment," according to Boncompagni). It is unclear what actually transpired the following day when the archbishop's official deputy from the cathedral arrived at Santa Cristina to convey archiepiscopal displeasure; it would remain a bone of contention in subsequent litigation. This time, however, Boncompagni chose to let them off with a warning.

But on the feast of Santa Cristina the following year, the emboldened nuns ignored him once again and once too often. On 21 May 1704, donna Maria Giuditta Ginevra Bolognini, donna Maria Christina Teresa Prudenza Deodata Cavazza, and donna Maria Diletta Vittoria Muzzi (three of the consecrands from 1699) sang first and second vespers and Mass in polyphony, accompanied by organ and cello. "Anyone who attended this feast could attest that not a whisper could be heard, and that we all stood back from the grates and doorways, as is customary at our monastery," the singing nuns were careful to point out. The archbishop countered, "When the nuns sang first vespers, few attended because people were unaware of it, since the prohibition to the contrary is well known in the city. But on the following day the throng was immense and raucous because there are some fine voices in this convent."[8]

Three days later Boncompagni promulgated a fresh ban on convent music, to be hung in the choir of every nunnery, though he may have formally presented it only at Santa Cristina. He further decreed that, for permitting the latest singing, Santa Cristina's abbess was suspended

from office for three days (one for each singer?), while the three vocal-
ists were denied active and passive voice (the right to vote in convent
elections or be elected to office) and forbidden access to the grates, to
their families, and to the outside world at the archbishop's pleasure. In
an extraordinary scene on 27 May, the aging prioress refused to accept
the archbishop's decrees against the abbess and the three singers from
the messenger dispatched to deliver them. So the archbishop's deputies
"tossed the decrees into the tube or trumpet through which one speaks
to the prioress, who had injured her hearing many years ago."[9]

It comes as no surprise that the nuns launched a counterattack. After eighty years and more than fifty petitions to the Congregation of
Bishops, however, and after their successful strategy of 1698, they had
learned something about the realities of ecclesiastical politics. The abbess
and the three singers, in sign of obedience, promptly accepted Boncompagni's punishments. But then, employing a tactic reminiscent of those
used back in 1647, they sent the convent's noble governors to plead their
case before the archbishop. As the nuns put it in a letter to the Congregation of Bishops, which they wisely decided never to send (presumably
when they recognized it was indecorously blunt), "succumbing to raging
passions, Boncompagni refused to hear them, with the retort that if the
nuns felt aggrieved, they could have recourse to the Sacred Congregation, as was their accustomed practice." They took him at his word. And
thus it was that for the second time in barely five years, the nuns of Santa
Cristina found themselves "amid a tempest of calamities," as the abbess
put it. They were led into the fray by their abbess, "an honest person and
a lady of advanced age, timid, and of feeble constitution," and by their
prioress—perhaps flourishing her ear trumpet.[10]

In July 1704, letters, memorials, affidavits, claims, and counterclaims
once again clogged the mails between Bologna and Rome. The nuns'
first (and rather thin) defense insisted that neither the abbess nor the
singing nuns could have violated the archbishop's command because
no formal, written legal document declaring the prohibition of convent
polyphony had ever been served upon the abbess but had been delivered only verbally as an "insinuation" (*insinuazione*)—Boncompagni's
very word in his rebuttal to the Congregation of Bishops, as the nuns
carefully pointed out shortly thereafter. To support their assertion, the
nuns submitted the abbess's sworn affidavit that she had never received
such a document. Exploiting the old, informal network among local
convents, they also provided notarized testimony from witnesses to performances of polyphony at the convents of Santi Naborre e Felice and
Sant'Omobono during the period of the alleged ban. Cheekiest of all,

they even presented sworn confirmation that they themselves had sung no fewer than ten times in 1703 and 1704. Had they known of any such ban, they audaciously claimed, of course they would never have sung. And if such a ban had really existed, of course they would never have gone unpunished.

Both sides spilled considerable ink confronting this point. The archbishop's repeated attempts to discredit the nuns' claims suggest that he recognized that they had discovered another legalistic loophole. Those with a little more distance and clearer heads saw through this litigious hairsplitting. As the nuns' lawyer conceded, "even if there were no concrete decree or order, there is at least a certain, sure knowledge that they should not have been singing." Chroniclers' comments cited above, as well as the actions of more compliant nuns at San Mattia and Corpus Domini, affirm the lawyer's assessment. Cardinal Leandro Colloredo seconded the lawyer. After his appointment as *ponente*, or overseer of the case, Colloredo advised the nuns to eschew this line of argument: "Moreover, do not get yourself especially entangled in the issue of your unfamiliarity with the lord cardinal archbishop's known order."[11]

Behind such niggling, which the nuns of Santa Cristina, like their cloistered sisters elsewhere, had learned over the years in order to work around the regulations imposed upon them from without, and behind the curia's attempts to plug such loopholes lingered the familiar issues of independence and obedience. The nuns repeatedly emphasized that any episcopal prohibitions should refer only to music by outsiders in the exterior churches and not to the nuns' own music in the inner chapel. Strictly speaking, they were right: Boncompagni's 1698 synod had reconfirmed the musical ban from the synod of 1654, which in turn had cited the Congregation of Bishops' rulings in 1584 and 1593. Those took aim strictly at extern musicians and had quite specifically declined to touch the nuns' own music. More important than this latest legalistic subtlety, the nuns claimed that their own Camaldolese constitutions had permitted polyphony at Santa Cristina. The archbishop had no authority to override that constitution. Such music was a convent tradition, going back for centuries, with the force of law.

So music, which had helped provoke the crises of the 1620s and had figured in the legal battles of 1698 concerning the Sacra, which in turn had whetted the nuns' appetite for battle and the archbishop's appetite for revenge in 1704, reemerges as the clearest symbol of the nuns' Camaldolese heritage and of their independence from the long-contested control of the archbishop. The nuns' indignation at the public manner

in which Boncompagni's emissary had presented his latest decree, supposedly defaming them in the eyes of the city, recalls the impugning of
their *onestà* and their families' *onore* in the notoriously public visitations
of the 1620s. Their repeated, more sinister suggestions that the archbishop might have suborned their confessor recall the nuns' demands
of the 1640s for Camaldolese confessors because they could never have
faith in any appointed by the diocesan curia. They complained to the
Congregation of Bishops in 1704 that "if any assert that our confessor
acts as accuser for the archbishopric against our convent, our trust will at
once be wounded and the secret of our consciences put in doubt," which
implies the fulfillment of their own prophecy of sixty years earlier "that
they can trust no secular priest, that they have always been betrayed by
secular priests."[12] And their closing plea in their petition of 1704, not for
permission to sing but for "the continuance of what our Holy Founder
permitted us in his deeply considered statutes," focuses upon their original superior, Saint Benedict, whose authority in their view superseded
that of any local archbishop. Indeed, every time they had sung, they had
acted out their allegiance to that superior and their perceived independence from episcopal control.[13]

Particularly interesting are further remarks that articulate awareness,
never before voiced so clearly, of their marginal place as women in the
Catholic order of things. The exorbitant penance Boncompagni had imposed—stripping the abbess of her office, a penalty appropriate only for
mortal sin—was magnified, they argued, by the fact that "removal from
executive power is one of the greatest penalties that can be meted out to
heads of religion, and above all when one considers the dignity of the
office of abbess, which is the highest of all in the ecclesiastical hierarchy
that pertains to the female sex." Their several comments about scandalous crowds insist that convent churches should be treated no differently
from other churches, suggesting a rejection of the isolation imposed specifically upon nunneries ever since Trent:

His Excellency's motive, to remove scandals that lurk in the crowds in churches, does
not undermine our arguments, because these scandals wait in all other churches,
too. But music is not forbidden there, even though those churches may be subject to
the archbishop. There are a hundred other more universally applicable and therefore
better means to remove these abuses without penalizing cloistered religious women
for the misdeeds committed by laymen, of which the nuns are completely innocent,
above all those in this most holy house. Or if one must remove all causes, even laud-
able ones, that produce evil effects, it would be necessary henceforth to change the
entire system, not only ecclesiastical but temporal as well.[14]

Boncompagni must have been smarting from the slap at his authority implicit in the Sacra affair of 1698–99. But evidently he, too, recognized the connection between singing at Santa Cristina and the weight of history and interpreted the nuns' challenge as just the latest example of the same disobedience that the curia had faced since the 1620s. Lest the link escape the Congregation of Bishops, Boncompagni searched out and sent along to Rome yet another fresh copy of Archbishop Ludovisi's final threat of excommunication against an earlier generation of recalcitrant nuns back in 1629, as he had also done in 1698. An intact copy of the eighty-year-old letter survives in the Vatican documents from the 1704 dispute.

In the weeks before the case was to come before the Congregation of Bishops, maneuvering on both sides intensified. As early as 7 September the nuns' Roman lawyer passed on suggestions from the newly appointed overseer of the case, Cardinal Leandro Colloredo, who had similarly overseen the nuns' successful suit regarding the Sacra six years before. Colloredo urged them to compose a letter of compromise to Boncompagni, whose possible contents he outlined in detail. The lawyer tactfully indicated certain weaknesses in their case and realistically pointed out that "a congregation that takes the side of bishops will very likely support all the more readily even what the lord cardinal has done." In addition, the lawyer warned that in the congregation's critical deliberations, the cardinals whose opening votes would set the pattern for those to follow included especially scrupulous (*delicatissimi*) ones, who easily could and probably would carry the day. One convent ally, commenting that Boncompagni was "harsh, and inimical to song in nuns' churches," seconded Colloredo's suggestion about compromise, pointing out the precariousness of the political realities.[15]

Willingness to compromise had rarely been the nuns' way. In the same spirit as their predecessors in earlier generations, they responded to Colloredo with a detailed list of their grievances and the legal bases for their defense. The reluctant congregation tabled the case repeatedly during the rest of the summer and through the fall, as the nuns' advocates continued to urge compromise. Buoyed by the happy outcome in 1698, the nuns attempted a replay of the strategy that had worked for them then. They prepared a meticulously documented defense, probably modeled on the one from six years earlier. Indeed, their lawyer seems to have cribbed several details of his own Latin brief of 1704 from the legal citations in the nuns' petition.

They failed, however, to recognize the particular social and political realities of the current case. The Sacra at issue in 1698–99 not only had an unbroken history, backed by traditions including those of the Roman pontifical, which weighed heavily in decisions of the congregations of cardinals: as a ritual, it incorporated the city's powerful families, who could therefore be drawn into the convent's defense. In contrast, nuns' singing—often touched by hints of impropriety, real or imagined—had an ambivalent history at least since Trent. The clear hints of disobedience at Santa Cristina in 1703 and 1704, which had not escaped notice in the city, exacerbated a somewhat-embarrassing situation in which the nuns were unlikely to find much support, even from politically dispassionate cardinals or patricians who otherwise might have been able to help them.

What finally happened in the Congregation of Bishops is not entirely clear. At the end of November the nuns still doggedly refused to settle. "Your lawyer prepared very beautiful briefs. Our most illustrious ambassador spoke to more than one cardinal on the nuns' behalf, and especially to your cardinal *ponente*," noted an eleventh-hour letter from a Roman supporter. A scribbled note on the cover of the sheaf of congregation documents reveals, however, that "this case had been placed on the docket for the meeting on 5 December 1704 and then was settled amicably by His Eminence [Cardinal Colloredo]."[16] On the day the suit was to be discussed, Colloredo took matters into his own hands. Rather than risk a vote that could only embarrass either the Bolognese archbishop or the nuns and their families, at the last minute he suspended the case.

When he informed the nuns of his decision the next day, Colloredo tried sweet talk: "I would malign not only your daughterly discretion but also that good and prudent wisdom God has granted you were I to doubt that you would all approve my judgment and recognize how it serves your advantage." The cardinal also sent along a tactfully composed petition for the singing nuns to copy out and sign, with assurances that Boncompagni would readily reconcile them to "his paternal esteem and affection." It took two weeks for the nuns to swallow this bitter pill. On 13 December, the anxious Colloredo wrote again, urging the nuns to "embrace my counsel, to get out of such a quandary with your reputation intact."[17]

Finally, on 22 December 1704 (ironically enough, the anniversary of their defeat in 1647, and within a day or two of the anniversary of the 1622 investigation), the abbess and the three singers signed Colloredo's ghostwritten petition, affirming

that although they are unaware of the same, ever to have disobeyed the most reverend commands of Your Excellency—just as they would be incapable of such an error—nevertheless, having heard that it was variously represented to Your Excellency on occasion that this past May the nuns celebrated the solemnities of Santa Cristina with polyphony, they do not try thereby consciously to displease, and even less to see themselves deprived for that reason of the honor of your most prized grace. In order to merit that grace they have fulfilled with due promptness the penance which it pleased you to impose. They thus submit themselves forever as daughters and most obsequious subjects in obedience to Your Eminence.[18]

The archbishop received the letter "with sentiments of paternal love," as Colloredo had predicted and as the nuns later acknowledged. Boncompagni must have deemed it prudent to accept this carefully composed declaration, which openly admitted to no wrongdoing but only to having provoked his displeasure. He wasted no time in responding:

Considering that the nuns have punctually observed, as they declare, the penance imposed by us, we kindly grant them the grace they requested [had they in fact requested one?]. But the synod's prohibition, expressed in our obvious order, which they must observe inviolably, remains in force—not to sing in polyphony, song mixed with organ, or any other concerted music. They are permitted only ecclesiastical song, which they call plainchant, and likewise not to have others perform music in their external church.[19]

This was not quite what the nuns had been led to expect. The disappointed sisters reported the outcome to Colloredo in an icy flow of polite negatives, passives, and subjunctives: "But one cannot help protesting, with the requisite reverence for Your Eminence, that in general this did not quite appear to have corresponded to the graces that were hoped for through Your Eminence's beneficent intercession." In an equally polite response, Colloredo firmly shut the door they tried to nudge open for further recourse to the congregation. Presenting Boncompagni's ruling in the best possible light, he closed the matter with the inevitable exhortation that the nuns "resign themselves with good cheer to God's ordering of things, as made manifest through their superiors. And be convinced that the true glory and reputation of good religious women consist in always making their obedience shine forth amid all their other Christian virtues."[20] For women, and women religious in particular, obedience outweighed all other concerns.

But Colloredo may not have had the last word, after all. The nuns quietly turned from those who unconvincingly claimed to have their best interests at heart to other channels of influence: those more potentially like-minded advocates who had also served them in 1698. A

New Year's Day letter to the convent bursar reveals the gentle intercessions of Countess Orsi, who with her family had played central roles in the suit of 1698 and who would march among the *paranymphae* at the Sacra in 1711. Particularly intriguing, the letter is signed by Ippolita Ludovisi Boncompagni. Wife of Gregorio Boncompagni, Duke of Sora (great-great-grandson of Gregory XIII), and sister-in-law to Archbishop Giacomo Boncompagni, this Ippolita (1663–1733) was the last survivor of the Ludovisi line that had produced the nuns' adversary of the 1620s, Archbishop Ludovico Ludovisi.[21] Once again the ties of sisterhood among women of similar social strata, embodying flexible, reciprocal patron-client relationships, assiduously cultivated by the nuns, may have transcended the cloister to balance even powerful family ties.

The initial results were less than the nuns desired, however. The lady Ludovisi Boncompagni reported with regret:

As regards the matter it pleased you to communicate to me, I attempted to mediate most zealously with the lord cardinal archbishop. But I did not meet with all that [positive] inclination that I had hoped for in serving your illustrious ladyship; I left the response to the lady Countess Orsi, because he has communicated [the response] to her. I therefore pray you to reward my mortification with the favor of your further commands.

But it appears that the "zealous mediations" of Countess Orsi and Duchess Ludovisi Boncompagni eventually bore at least a little fruit. On an unsigned, undated slip of paper enclosed with the other documents from the case in the convent archive, we read: "We concede to the nuns of the convent of Santa Cristina in Bologna license that in future they can practice the use of mixed or altered song [canto misto o alterato], only in ecclesiastical ceremonies, after the method and manner that the other convents of this city use, notwithstanding the order they have to the contrary."[22]

Thus it was that Giacomo Boncompagni apparently saved face. The nuns had to be satisfied with a private, partial, somewhat ambiguous, but thoroughly characteristic sort of vindication. After more than eighty years of periodic petitioning and protest, the waves of documents from "those nuns of Santa Cristina," as the Congregation of Bishops had come to call them, seem largely to recede. After 1704 Santa Cristina della Fondazza did have dealings with the congregation, but not about music or communal misbehavior. The long struggle testifies to the independent spirit passed from one generation to another within a female institution striving to preserve traditions that provided its identity and offered some measure of self-direction. They had doggedly and—in the eyes of the church hierarchy—exasperatingly persisted in taking their case to Rome. They had exploited indirect means of influence, extending beyond their own families in the urban patriciate to informal links between one woman and another. Such actions reveal the continuation into the eighteenth century of methods of maneuvering that extend back before the Council of Trent and well into the Middle Ages.

Recourse to Rome had been a primary means to guard some measure of autonomy for fourteenth- and fifteenth-century religious women, too. As Katherine Gill puts it, "[Medieval] women's communities had no reason to believe they should apply to themselves the ideas of every bishop, ordinary, or monastic superior who set himself up in their diocese."[23] Such a view may have become considerably less realistic after Trent, but it was one that the nuns of Santa Cristina continued to hold throughout the 1600s. The case of Santa Cristina indicates that within the more highly regulated post-Tridentine church, supported by various congregations of cardinals in Rome, persistence, patience, and political maneuvering might occasionally bring some small measure of success in a world where the rights of religious women still depended on their petitions being granted.

The frail mother abbess at Santa Cristina did not long survive the struggles of 1704; she died of cancer in 1708. One of the miscreant singing nuns, Maria Giuditta Ginevra Bolognini, lived on into her eighties. A "pillar of the choir," she also served three years as bursar, six as novice mistress, fifteen as prioress, and nine as abbess before her death in 1762. Her piety and a particularly good death earned her a place, alongside the Venerable Flaminia Bombacci, in the Camaldolese calendar of the sainted and blessed, where she is remembered to this day every 16 January.[24] Maria Diletta Vittoria Muzzi also went on to hold high office and to become a patron of the arts.

The subsequent career of the third singer, Maria Christina Cavazza, soon took a less illustrious turn. In July 1708, disguised as an abbot, she was caught sneaking out of the convent once too often to attend the opera. Sentenced to a decade of imprisonment at Santa Cristina for violations of *clausura*, she repeatedly petitioned for transfer until 1719, when she was moved to the country convent of Lateran canonesses, Sant'Agostino at Lugo. Instead of making her repeat the novice year as the Congregation of Bishops required, the nuns of Sant'Agostino, supported by Santa Cristina's old ally of 1698, Ulisse Giuseppe Gozzadini, by then titular archbishop of Imola, elected her abbess instead. When Rome discovered this egregious violation of its decrees fifteen years later and deposed her, ex-abbess Cavazza fled the convent in Lugo, in violation of *clausura*, back to Santa Cristina in Bologna, where in 1735 she was reluctantly received. When she died of apoplexy in 1751, the convent necrologist discreetly chose to remember only her musical talents.[25]

Archbishop Boncompagni did not live to witness the end to this final embarrassment, though he lasted into the 1730s, possibly wondering whether his reforming efforts had done much good. On 21 January 1705, within a month of his settlement with Santa Cristina, a Bolognese chronicler recorded the performance of elaborate music, "in spite of the archbishop's prohibition," at the convent of Sant'Agnese, where all the trouble had started two years earlier.[26] In February 1706, the nuns' vicar of Bologna once again began to sign annual licenses for lavish music at Santi Vitale et Agricola, which continued in a largely unbroken stream into the 1720s. This did not prevent the nuns' vicar's self-satisfied, disingenuous response to a universal letter from the Congregation of Bishops in February 1708: "One may reflect upon the fact that here in Bologna music making in nuns' churches has in fact already been forbidden. Here they don't sing to the organ, nor at the grates in any way whatsoever, as they do elsewhere. In this city we don't have that practice of laypeople hanging around the nuns, as in Ferrara and in all the other surrounding territories."[27] Just three weeks later, another scandal during Carnival contradicted this pious picture of strict observance:

When the nuns of San Guglielmo performed a spiritual play in their internal church, their father confessor removed the Blessed Sacrament and the tabernacle from the altar in the external church and installed a bench, which filled up with outside spectators, who enjoyed the performance through the grated window [above the altar]. When word of this reached their superiors, it led to the suspension of the priest, pending further orders from Rome.[28]

And precisely then Christina Cavazza began her series of nights at the opera. The following year, chroniclers recorded a new stream of at least ten musical *feste* at the convents. The number of lavish convent celebrations rose to as many as thirty in 1712, when Bologna's Catherine Vigri finally achieved sainthood. From then on, despite the nuns' vicar's claims or prohibitions to the contrary, nuns' churches were rarely silent for long. And sometime around midcentury, with little apparent fuss, the nuns of Santa Cristina were restored to communion with the Camaldolese order.[29]

On 11 September 1729, toward the end of his life and exactly a century after the nuns' bitter subjugation to episcopal control, Cardinal

Archbishop Giacomo Boncompagni found himself at Santa Cristina one more time, for a ritual consecration of ten nuns. Bursar's accounts record that the seventy-seven-year-old archbishop was played into and out of the church by four trumpets, hunting horns, and the resounding reports of the obligatory five hundred firecrackers. No fewer than forty-eight extern musicians accompanied him during the ceremony, with lavish music yet again by Giacomo Perti as *maestro di capella*. Rivaling the angelic voices of the singing nuns, a singer to His Majesty of Sardinia sang a special motet.[30]

One can but wonder whether, as the musicians washed down 112 pastries with wine at the lavish reception after the ceremony, His Eminence, nearing the end of his forty-year reign but probably still "harsh and inimical to song in nuns' churches," ate crow in silence.

Coda

Finale Primo (1995): "An Ancient Church Gone Wrong and Waiting to Fall Down"

In the spring of 1796 Napoleon's armies broke into Italy. The Piedmont and the Po fell in April; by mid-May Napoleon had reached Milan. In the evening on 18 June, an advance guard of French soldiers passed through Porta San Felice into Bologna. A few days later Napoleon entered the city and laid down the terms for a new order. With the Peace of Tolentino in February 1797, Pope Pius VI formally ceded Bologna and the church's northern holdings to France. Within the month Napoleon created the first of his new states, the Cispadane Republic, and made Bologna its capital. The entire province became part of the republic the following year. Nuns would have little place in this new regime.

As the French armies continued southward, Santa Cristina and the city's other religious houses began to confront the imminent abolition of monastic enclosure. The mammoth task of inventorying convent property dragged on through 1798. In October, occupying forces hauled off the great table from Santa Cristina's refectory for their own use. Four months later, in early February 1799, thirty-one male monasteries and thirty-eight convents in and around Bologna were officially suppressed. As for the nuns, a final entry in a chronicle from Santa Maria Maddalena records that "all the poor religious women were constrained to put off their sacred habit and withdraw to God knows where."[1] At Santa Cristina, the last of the nuns had scarcely ventured back into the world, pensioned off with a stipend matching her original dowry, before the sale of convent furnishings got under way.[2] The volume of material was so vast that the auction stretched on from February into April. A month later occupation forces bartered away the orchards, icehouse, and part of the cloister in trade for rice to feed the troops. The following year some of those troops moved into the unsold cloister wings. On and off for most of the next two centuries Santa Cristina would serve chiefly to house military personnel. It was a slightly more dignified fate than awaited some religious houses, such as the Bolognese male monastery of San Giovanni in Monte, which became the city prison. In March 1805 Napoleon had himself crowned king of Italy. The following year, church officials formally incorporated the old parish of Santa Cristina into the adjoining parish of San Giuliano; two years later Santa Cristina's external church reopened for services.

After Napoleon's fall, the Congress of Vienna restored the city to papal control in 1815. Shortly thereafter, a few sisters began to find their way back to via Fondazza, joining a trickle of nuns from other orders with nowhere else to go. In all, twenty-two sisters, unprepared for a more modern world, sought refuge in their old way of life. The archbishop of Bologna reacquired portions of the convent from the family that had bought them in 1799. The convent flock grew to thirty over ten years, not many fewer than in times past, though the women who lived in the formerly Camaldolese house now represented an array of monastic traditions, which the authorities united under the rule of Saint Augustine. In 1827 only two Camaldolese lived among them: Maria Claudia Dotti, who had joined Santa Cristina half a century before, and one who had scarcely entered the convent before the Napoleonic suppression— Countess Barbara Malvasia, a final link to the family that helped create the crises at Santa Cristina exactly two centuries earlier. For another thirty-five years, the mixed community of women lived quietly and inconspicuously on via Fondazza. But in May 1862 church and convent were closed once again, and the military entirely took over the cloister buildings. The church alone was reopened in 1896, still as part of the parish of San Giuliano. As a convent, Santa Cristina had closed for good.[3]

For well over a century the cloister served as a military barracks, the Caserma Pietramellara. Outbuildings became stables and haylofts, while the venerable *chiesa vecchia* (old church) was turned into a warehouse. By World War I, Lorenzo Costa's Saint Benedict, Saint Romuald, and Saint Christina looked down from the vaults upon tangles of bicycles, which would remain there for decades. In the final stages of World War II, the former convent became a refuge for evacuees and their livestock, which the fighting had driven from the surrounding countryside and into the city, as generations of country folk before them had been during similarly hard times. After the war, Italy continued to call its youth for obligatory military service; some of them would live and exercise within the convent walls over the ensuing decades. The regular troops gave way to sharpshooters (*bersaglieri*), who were replaced in turn by the fire brigade and other sorts of military personnel. Only in 1982 did the military sound its final retreat. Officials had the last antiquated army vehicle towed away in 1985, and the convent was completely abandoned.[4]

Not so long thereafter, in June 1989, I moved for the summer into an apartment block at the intersection of via Fondazza and via del Piombo, just across the street. My corner apartment, three or four stories up, looked out onto the abandoned church and its former courtyard, where, in 1628, nuns had held diocesan ministers and beadles at bay with bricks and stones. Long after those dramatic events, and long before my arrival, the demolition of the convent wall at the intersection in 1913–14 transformed the old courtyard into the unprepossessing Piazzetta Morandi. The throngs of onlookers, which the papal legate's Swiss guard formerly barred from the courtyard during periodic reenacts of the Sacra in the 1600s and 1700s, by the late 1980s had given way to a few cars and motorbikes that perpetually packed themselves into every inch and angle of the piazzetta and even crept up onto the curb. Only spiked iron gates that never opened kept vehicles from commandeering the church portico.

From my apartment windows, I tried to peer into the abandoned Cappella del Rosario above the church doors, its gloom briefly and faintly illuminated by the midafternoon sun. The chapel, where on feast days choirs of nuns once had sung through grated windows into the public church, stood desolate, its grates walled up long ago, with only scars in the plaster to mark their locations and the site of its altar. The chapel's lofty west windows, through which in 1628 an eloquently defiant donna Isabetta Vizzana rallied parishioners and neighborhood children to the convent's defense, had been filled partway down with masonry during some past refurbishment and now resembled oddly drooping eyelids. They stared darkly onto the piazzetta, open to the elements and flocks of pigeons that were transforming the derelict chapel into an increasingly squalid dovecote.

From high above the truncated, unimposing old convent wall, I could observe remaining portions of the old convent gardens beyond the piazzetta–turned–car park. The eastern edges had been nibbled away little by little until 1958 to make way for Piazza Carducci and for blocks of housing built in the 1920s and 1930s. What was left opened every morning as a congenial and pleasantly kept public park. Beneath tall trees planted long after the nuns' last exodus, the very young would wear themselves out every day under the watchful eyes of the very old. On the grass, teenage couples, presumably constrained by circumstances to live at home, found in the shadow of the wall a kind of public privacy for experiments with earthly delights that earlier occupants, monastic and military, would likely have experienced within these walls only in their imaginations.

Even from upper-floor windows across the street, I could not see over the church's massive bulk into the hidden cloister, which remained as much a mystery as it had always been to the outside world. Surrounded by makeshift wire fencing that was posted with stern warnings of falling masonry to keep back the curious, the monastery buildings continued their unobtrusive decline. It took a year or two to wheedle my way past the chain-link barrier and through a cloister side door. The resident caretaker and his family, who occupied the nuns' old laundry and common rooms of the east wing, kept less determined intruders, as well as vandals, graffiti artists, and drug addicts, at bay. But they could not hope by themselves to stay the natural forces of decay and dilapidation. On a sweltering July day in the early 1990s, the cloister's central courtyard, still dominated by Bibiena's elegant campanile, remained almost as whitely bright and open to the sky as when nuns passed along the cooler, more shadowed stillness of its shaded arcades. But the caretaker's kitchen garden that had taken root since the late 1980s (fig. 28)—a weedy tangle of squash vines, peppers, stick tents for runner beans, a jungle of clotheslines, fig trees that overtopped the second story, and a fir tree beginning little by little to challenge the bell tower—called to mind less an *hortus conclusus* from the Song of Songs than *God's Little Acre*.

The *Crocifisso di pietà* that had miraculously appeared around 1613 in the cloister's upper gallery, where Lucrezia Vizzana and the other nuns commemorated Christ's Passion every Friday, and grudgingly said grace after meals at Emilia Grassi's insistence, was long gone, of course. Perhaps it was obliterated by the July 1745 lightning bolt that blasted the weathervane depicting Saint Christina off the top of the bell tower and brought part of the campanile tumbling onto the roof and down into the cloister. Since then, most other depredations were acts of men, not God. Only in 1978 did the state officially recognize the artistic and historical importance of the site (though nothing much was set in motion to preserve it at that time).

FIGURE 28. Santa Cristina della Fondazza, the decrepit, overgrown cloister (c. 1993), prior to restoration. Photograph: Craig Monson.

In the meantime, the refined detail in terra-cotta and sandstone on the fifteenth- and sixteenth-century corbels, capitals, and doorways to the nuns' inner chapel, the *chiesa vecchia*, and the infirmary had largely disappeared beneath thick layers of battleship gray paint. My guide on that July afternoon, Signora Giovanna, the caretaker's wife, pointed to the lintel above the most elaborate doorway and explained to me that the carving of this particular ornamentation incorporated eradications and alterations that sixteenth-century nuns had made after they discovered the donor's pregnancy and banished her from the cloister. I could not spot any alterations—perhaps the gray paint obscured them. Or perhaps Signora Giovanna, like generations of the laity before her, was just ringing the changes on a favorite, old convent theme.

The nuns' private chapel—where Cecilia Bianchi and Emilia Grassi's quarrels regularly disrupted services in the 1620s, where Pantasilea Tovagli kept one eye on inappropriate reading matter hidden in her prayer book, and where the nuns' feline and canine companions, wandering in and out, distracted worshipers from higher things—by the 1990s was simply unrecognizable. Sometime before 1920 the chapel had been transformed into a parish theater for activities of the Associazione Leone XIII, which periodically closed and reopened, depending on good or hard times. After the war it became the Cinema Leone XIII, which lasted a few seasons before closing its doors for good by 1970.[5]

In the still dimness of the former inner church, simultaneously fetid and chilly even at midsummer, feeble light filtered through gaps in sagging and moldering black drapes that effectively shut out the sun that otherwise might have invaded the space through four great windows. Dim light revealed no trace of the frescoes of the Madonna and saints that I was told could still be seen as late as the 1930s above the altar (also long gone by the time of my visit). A looming, abandoned proscenium stage cramped the once lofty space. As the chapel's dominant focus, the stage's yards of gold-fringed, musty red curtain, hanging at half-mast, and, most incongruously, a dark-green, winged lion guardian emblazoned up above supplanted the vanished fragment of the True Cross, the head of one of Saint Ursula's martyred companions, the bodies of Saints Felice and Lucio,[6] and other relics of the religious house that used to pray here. Like the spirits of those departed women, any ghosts of comfortable, neighborhood intimacy as depicted in Salvatore Tornatore's *Cinema Paradiso* or any amiable chaos like that offered in the variety theater of Fellini's *Roma*, although they may have briefly flourished there in the days of the Associazione Leone XIII, by the 1990s resisted conjuration. Herded in disarray into a corner, a jumble of upturned, rickety, and fractured straight chairs opposed the broken ranks of wooden theater seats that had replaced the nuns' choir stalls, all awaiting some eradicating bonfire.

But high above the chaos at floor level, the ancient vaults still rose largely unaltered. Not far below the vaults an ancient catwalk still hugged the wall, linking the two original organ rooms, up near the ceiling, from where choirs of disembodied voices once sang through grated windows. Only a basketball goal mounted underneath the catwalk, its orange, netless hoop mysteriously slam-dunked flat against the wall, marred the lofty image that floated above the theater wreckage.

To pass from the oppressive, perpetual dusk of the unrecognizable interior church on that July day into the bright expanse of the external church was to enter quite a different world. Recalling their fifteenth- and sixteenth-century predecessors who devotedly tended Santa Cristina di Settefonti long after it too had effectively been abandoned, one or two late-twentieth-century caretakers tended the locked-up outer church on via Fondazza so faithfully that I could imagine that the feast of Saint Christina had been celebrated only a day or two before. Rich and festive crimson damask, faded and beginning to split here and there under its own weight as testimony to its age, still adorned every doorway and the impressive length of every pilaster. Streaming shafts of light from north and south windows high in the vaults flooded the airy space and struck upon the imposingly gilded side altars, whose startling brilliance belied the passage of four centuries.

The eight monumental stucco statues still stared just as intently down from their niches, but they looked across the open space above an empty, crumbling floor, gesturing to one another and to no one else. The eagles, boars, and wild goats from the coats of arms belonging to families of illustrious nun benefactors had been obliterated from the altars these women had donated. Otherwise, the church might well have convinced me that little had changed.

Given the Napoleonic depredations and decades of abandonment, I sensed an anachronistic yet appealingly modern austerity about the place. Relics of Saint Christina and others languished behind a grille above the side altar of Saint Romuald, but miraculously they were still there, though they had spawned no silver encrustations of ex-votos of the sort that to this day continue to creep up the walls of a living parish such as Santa Maria dei Servi a few blocks west. At Santa Cristina the few altar furnishings surviving into the 1990s betokened an ascetic sparseness and hermetic simplicity that Saint Romuald, surveying the church from his niche in the north wall, would no doubt approve.

Offering a final link to earlier, more vital times, six silver candlesticks still stood amid the general anonymity on the high altar, their tall candles listing like the Torre Garisenda downtown. On looking closely, one could make out the date 1730 and the name of the donor, Diletta Vittoria Muzzi (1670–1748).[7] She had to be among the last of the many convent benefactors who left their marks in the church, and the date confirmed that her donation had been placed here long after she had marched down its nave among the twelve consecrands at the victorious Sacra of 1699. In 1704, with two other nun musicians beside her, Muzzi performed in defiance of Cardinal Archbishop Giacomo Boncompagni and, in so doing, provoked what would be the last struggle of the singing nuns of Santa Cristina.

For a moment in this space one could imagine how it must once have been almost three centuries earlier and overlook the telltale signs of darkening damp, creeping across the vaults above and spreading a

FIGURE 29. Santa Cristina della Fondazza, deteriorated vault of cloister staircase in west wing (c. 1988). Photograph courtesy of Ugo Capriani.

haze up the marbling of the altars below. Disregarding the incursions of pigeons looking to extend their empire beyond the adjoining Cappella del Rosario above the doors, one could almost forget the ever-deepening tide of their crusty droppings, which already carpeted the floor of that derelict chapel where—in the emotional disorder of her final years—Lucrezia Vizzana may have knelt and lost herself in special devotions to the Mysteries of the Rosary. For a short while, one could not think about the collapsing roof above the cloister staircase (fig. 29), ascending to the nuns' cells. But such an imaginative leap would be impossible in a few years. For once the roof begins to go, a building's back will break.

The majority of Bologna's renowned convents and convent churches have disappeared or been remade in an image that better fits the more modern world. The covered market between via Ugo Bassi and via San Gervasio supplanted Santi Gervasio e Protasio. Santa Maria Nuova had first become a tobacco-processing plant, then Allied bombing largely reduced it to rubble during World War II. More recently the Cineteca di Bologna has risen on the spot. San Giovanni Battista became a psychiatric hospital in 1869. Santa Maria Maddalena, its inner and outer churches combined into a barn for hay in 1798, had its other buildings partly knocked down in 1810 to make way for the Arena del Sole. The military demolished the church of Sant'Agnese after 1819 and refurbished its cloister as the Caserma Minghetti. Corpus Domini survived a devastating direct hit by an Allied bomb that dropped through the dome and into the nave in October 1943. It has managed to rise again, thanks perhaps to the abiding influence, spiritual or otherwise, of Bologna's *santa cittadina*, Saint Catherine Vigri, who still keeps company there with a handful of her Clarissan disciples, as they continue their cloistered life together even into the twenty-first century.

Across town at Santa Cristina, a few fragments of Blessed Lucia of Settefonti long lay forgotten, as they had been once before in another, older Santa Cristina—"an ancient church gone wrong and waiting to fall down." That is how Bedinus Marzochi described the situation back in 1571,[8] shortly before laborers pulled down most of Santa Christina *vecchia* in the hills outside town. At that time Lucia's remains made their peregrination from Settefonti to Sant'Andrea di Ozzano, and in the 1640s some of them came to rest in Bologna. By 1990, with every grate bricked over, and every door locked, barred, or walled up, stricter *clausura* than even the most reform-minded prelate had ever envisioned descended upon church and convent alike at the "new" Santa Cristina on via Fondazza, where some of Lucia's fragments had rested for 350 years. Where *clausura* once held the corruptions of the world at bay, since 1986 the enclosing walls shielded the world outside from the quiet corruption and slow decay that proceeded largely unnoticed within.

Santa Cristina della Fondazza, among the last largely intact witnesses of the bounded world in which thousands of Bolognese women made lives for themselves as best they could over the centuries, faced a threat more ultimate than those posed by Cardinal Archbishop Ludovico Ludovisi in the 1620s or by Napoleon and the Directory in the 1790s. The convent's fate depended, as it always had, upon the mediation of outsiders. But old patterns of clientage and influential links to prestigious families and the broad community had vanished long ago with the unremembered nuns who once nurtured those connections. Only a handful of the old names were still mentioned in the neighborhood: Albertazzi, Cavazza, Malvezzi, Panzacchi.

During the fifty years since World War II, the communal, provincial, and regional administrations of Bologna and Emilia-Romagna, aided by various banks, undertook—more vigorously and successfully than most other administrations in Italy—the daunting task of preserving their region's artistic and architectural patrimony. Yet, as one city resident remarked during another visit to Santa Cristina in 1993, "They can't save everything."

Finale Secondo (2011): "Ornaverunt Faciem Templi"

But, in reference to Santa Cristina, he spoke just a little too soon.

At Christmastime in 1992, Monsignor Niso Albertazzi, *abate-parroco* of the parish of San Giuliano, and architects Glauco, Giuliano, and Roberto Gresleri presented a proposal for the restoration of Santa Cristina's inner and outer churches to the local civic administration. In 1996 church and civic authorities mounted a campaign to save the entire structure, including the cloister. The Cassa di Risparmio di Bologna underwrote the enterprise with generosity rivaling—indeed, surpassing—that of Santa Cristina's occupants during the convent's last architectural Renaissance in the late 1500s.

It took three years to consolidate the timber and masonry structure of roof, walls, vaulting, and ceilings, as well as to clear away two centuries of encrustation and reconfiguration. The objective: return the ancient edifice as much as possible to its original form.

I found my way back to Santa Cristina in December 2000, together with participants at a conference on early-modern convents as centers of culture—almost exactly four centuries after Lucrezia Vizzana became a novice there. We confronted a worksite not so different from the way it must have appeared to her in 1600. Amid excavations and piles of building materials, the exciting results of so much expense and labor were sufficiently advanced that the end seemed tantalizingly close. But it would take three further years to accomplish the painstakingly meticulous work of salvaging and restoring endless expanses of surface ornament on wall after wall. How many in the world beyond the convent's wall that borders via Fondazza (in either the seventeenth or the twenty-first century) would have imagined such extensive and opulent decoration within a center of monastic simplicity and sobriety? But given what we now know of its aristocratic inhabitants from centuries past, perhaps we should not be too surprised.

Clerical visitors—whether archbishops, their representatives, or the Camaldolese—had given us hints of the artistry displayed on these walls hidden inside *clausura*. Even when the cloister went public, its conversion into the Caserma Pietramellara kept the secret of these frescoes still concealed—this time under whitewash, dropped ceilings, and regimental inscriptions. Only in the twenty-first century can any outsiders experience the artistic richness and visual excitement of the secret world that Lucrezia Vizzana and her sisters in religion inhabited. Some details, such as frescoed lunette after frescoed lunette in the delicately vaulted

FIGURE 30. Santa Cristina della Fondazza, the restored frescoes (1645) of the atrium to the refectory (2011). Photograph: Luca Salvucci, Bologna.

convent reception room and along some corridors, now offer only dim shadows of their original appearance, though the lessons they were intended to teach cloistered women are still not hard to discern. Others, most notably the gloriously frescoed antechamber to the nuns' refectory (fig. 30), with its side walls populated by favorite male saints and its ceiling crowded with a veritable "Who's Who" of female monastic worthies who look down from trompe l'oeil balconies, continue to capture viewers' imaginations as vividly now as they must have done in 1650.

On the wall below, Christ still welcomes a chosen bride into this heavenly Jerusalem. On a branch behind her, the phantom cat, which to a modern viewer in 2011 bears a striking resemblance to a distant relation from Cheshire in *Alice in Wonderland*, still looks back impassively, perhaps remarking, "We're all mad here."

Just as Lucrezia Vizzana may have done, the especially lucky and observant visitor may stumble upon the tiny staircase nearby that leads mysteriously and dimly upward (fig. 5). Any visitor fortunate enough to discover that its gate has mistakenly been left open and bold enough to risk its perilously worn stairs may recapture in a quiet moment the look and feel of the hollows within the walls as they would have been in

Vizzana's time. Such a daring intruder will very unexpectedly discover the miniature but delicately frescoed chapel of Our Lady of Consolation and the Man of Sorrows. Since at least 1616, these figures have graced the tiny landing halfway up the cramped, forgotten stairwell (fig. 23), and they may still gladden—perhaps even console—a calloused, cynical postmodern heart.

The rickety theater seats that, in the early 1990s, remained stacked in the nuns' chapel across the cloister, have been carted off long ago, of course, together with the yards and yards of moldering black drapes and the red velvet theater curtain. Demolition of the proscenium stage and the guardian green lion of the erstwhile Cinema Leone XIII revealed original, imposing expanses of bare plaster wall rising to delicate vaults. They now betray a rather stark, modernist aesthetic whose austerity might coax a nod of begrudging approval even from the dour Archbishop Alfonso Paleotti.

Beneath the delicate vaulting, just under the inner chapel's old catwalk that joins paired organ rooms, restored frescoes of the Madonna and saints that had vanished by the 1930s (fig. 31) now displace the flattened orange basketball goal from the early 1990s. These remnants of the nuns' private altar, now restored to life and displaying their original shades of iridescent lavender, pale green, and golden yellow, afford some impression of the visual opulence that must once have rivaled what has been more fully recoverable in the adjoining cloister.

Santa Cristina's public church survived time's (and man's) depredations much better than the rest of the monastic complex. Now spectacularly restored, with its original artistic and architectural treasures enhanced by twenty-first century renovation and lighting, it has become a showplace for the city. Only rows of concert hall seating in the nave and a hulking concert grand piano strike a somewhat discordant, if thoroughly practical, note. The church's excellent acoustics make it a favorite concert venue—though a self-absorbed performer there may worry that the artistically dazzling interior might distract audiences from the musical offerings.

Convent sisters who walked the cloistered arcades were supplanted in the 1800s by army recruits; these were displaced in turn by the aging *partigiani* (partisans) of the early 1990s, and all have given way to the current occupants, more in tune, perhaps, with times past. The south cloister wing now houses offices, meeting rooms, and halls of the University of Bologna's Department of Visual Arts. Outside the *aula magna* (great hall, formerly the nuns' refectory, with its early-sixteenth-century frescoed Crucifixion; fig. 15), Saints Veronica, Gertrude, Barbara, Scholastica, Caterina, Francesca Romana, and, of course, Christina look down

FIGURE 31. Santa Cristina della Fondazza, restored frescoes above the altar of the nuns' inner chapel, with the catwalk and entrances to the choir lofts above (2011). Photograph: Luca Salvucci, Bologna.

benevolently from within the newly revealed ceiling fresco that represents one of the cloister's artistic treasures (fig. 30). How do these academics ever get any work done, amid such visual distractions?

Upstairs, beneath original massive, wood-beamed ceilings, a great, barnlike space has become the thoroughly modern reading room of the art library and the Fondazione Federico Zeri, whose 85,000 volumes and 290,000 photographs were transferred here in 2007. The foundation welcomes scholars, individually and in groups, who are interested especially in interdisciplinary aspects of the arts.

Perhaps most appropriately, one of the particularly ancient portions of the cloister, Santa Cristina's *chiesa vecchia*, which predates even the monastic reconfigurations of the late sixteenth century, has become home to the Centro delle Donne. The Associazione Orlando, which sprang up in the late 1970s as part of an especially vital Italian feminist movement, continues to administer the center's library, the Biblioteca Italiana delle Donne and its Sala da The Internet.

Through the especially elaborate cloister doorways that Lucrezia and her sisters once passed, feminist scholars can access the center's collection of some 30,000 volumes. From a vantage point much less precarious now than it was twenty years ago, Saints Christina, Benedict, and Romuald, who have observed this space from its vaults for five centuries,

FIGURE 32. Santa Cristina della Fondazza, the restored remains of the *chiesa vecchia* (c. 1500), subsequently the nuns' chapter room, now the Biblioteca Italiana delle Donne (2011). Photograph: Luca Salvucci, Bologna.

might well marvel at cleverly engineered metal spiral staircases, narrow catwalks, and ranks of bookshelves that hug the ancient walls (fig. 32). Although barred railings vaguely reminiscent of convent grilles keep browsers safe today, researchers may yet occasionally require scholarly determination to keep acrophobia or vertigo at bay.

We can be quite certain that Archbishops Paleotti, Ludovisi, and Boncompagni would take a dim view of the ordinarily steady trickle and occasional stream of scholars, conferees, and feminist dignitaries lured to the center—in violation of now obsolete commandments about monastic enclosure. After all, for many in the church hierarchy, regardless of the century, time stands still. The spirits of generations of nuns (well, perhaps not Cecilia Bianchi, Lucidaria Bolognetti, or Maria Gentile Malvasia) might approve of these new female networks that still draw women into Santa Cristina's cloister as effectively as the older and time-honored methods of former centuries. Thanks to the center's access to the World Wide Web, interested parties can now form new, virtually real alliances without even setting foot inside the walls. The shades of Paleotti, Ludovisi, and Boncompagni almost certainly would disapprove of that, and such disapproval might prompt the once-cloistered spirits of these prelates' former charges to consider one last round of petitions to Rome.

Lingering shadows of past occupants might also marvel to hear music regularly echo from both church and cloister, even motets by their sister, donna Lucrezia Orsina Vizzana. During crises of former centuries it was the echo of disembodied voices that breached the walls of *clausura* to catch the ear of a concerned community. Today, Lucrezia Orsina Vizzana, who four centuries ago turned her back on the world and passed within these walls, speaks to a far wider world through the music she left behind. The eloquence of her voice, "sweeter than honey and the honeycomb," which once touched seventeenth-century Bologna from "within the hollow of the walls," reaches out to a far-flung world but may move new generations to reaffirm the value of a fragile, hidden past.

Ornaverunt faciem Templi coronis aureis, et dedicaverunt altare Domino; et facta est laetitia magna in populo. . . . Et victoriam dedit illi Dominus. Et facta est laetitia magna in populo.

They adorned the front of the temple with wreaths of gold, and dedicated the altar unto the Lord. And there was great rejoicing among the people. . . . And the Lord granted unto her the victory. And there was great rejoicing among the people. (Lucrezia Orsina Vizzana, 1623)

Notes

1. Craig A. Monson, *Disembodied Voices: Music and Culture in an Early Modern Italian Convent* (Berkeley and Los Angeles: University of California Press, 1995). This book made it into print only months before Robert L. Kendrick's highly influential *Celestial Sirens: Nuns and Their Music in Early Modern Milan* (Oxford: Clarendon Press, 1996). Several other recent works related to convent music appear in the bibliographical listing "Further Reading and Listening" supplied at the end of the present book.

2. Cappella Artemisia's *Canti nel chiostro* (Tactus 600001) was released in 1994. Musica Secreta recorded Vizzana's motets on the CD *Songs of Ecstasy and Devotion* (Linn CKD 071). See also "Further Reading and Listening," below. For a recent discography of no fewer than forty-one recordings of convent music released before 2008, see Chiara Sirk, "*Sonet vox tua in auribus cordis mei*: Discografia della musica composta da monache tra cinque e seicento," in *Soror mea, sponsa mea: Arte e musica nei conventi femminili in Italia tra cinque e seicento*, ed. Chiara Sirk and Candace Smith (Padua: Il Poligrafo, 2009), 147–83. Seven Vizzana motets, edited by Craig A. Monson, appear in Martha Furman Schleifer and Sylvia Glickman, eds., *Women Composers: Music through the Ages*, vol. 1 (New York: G. K. Hall, 1996); the series also contains works by other convent composers. For additional scholarly editions of nuns' music, see "Further Reading and Listening," below. Artemisia Editions makes available a substantial list of convent music as well: http://www.cappella-artemisia.com/.

3. Elissa Weaver, "Review: *Disembodied Voices: Music and Culture in an Early Modern Italian Convent*," *Renaissance Quarterly* 51 (1998): 974.

PRAELUDIUM

1. James McKinnon, *Music in Early Christian Literature* (Cambridge: Cambridge University Press, 1987), 133.
2. ASV, VR, posiz. 1593, B–C.
3. BUB, MS It. 3856, 138.
4. Elissa Weaver, "Spiritual Fun: A Study of Sixteenth-Century Tuscan Convent Theater," in *Women in the Middle Ages and the Renaissance*, ed. Mary Beth Rose (Syracuse, NY: Syracuse University Press, 1986), 173.
5. ASV, VR, posiz. 1625, A–B.
6. On the silk industry, see Ludovico Frati, *La vita privata in Bologna dal secolo xiii al xvii*, 2d ed. (Bologna: Nicola Zanichelli, 1928; repr., Rome: Bardi Editore, 1968), 184–85. On Bologna's porticoes, see ibid., 4.
7. For a summary of religious life in Bologna, see Gabriella Zarri, "Istituzioni ecclesiastiche e vita religiosa a Bologna (1450–1700)," in *Storia illustrata di Bologna*, vol. 2, ed. Walter Tega (Milan: Nuova Editoriale AIEP, 1989), 161–200. On Bolognese women religious, see Gabriella Zarri, "I monasteri femminili a Bologna tra il XIII e il XVII secolo," *Deputazione di storia patria per le province di Romagna: Atti e memorie*, n.s., 24 (1973): 133–224.
8. Mario Fanti, "Le classi sociali e il governo di Bologna all'inizio del secolo xvii in un'opera inedita di Camillo Baldi," *Strenna storica bolognese* 11 (1961): 148.
9. Ibid., 144.
10. Population figures recording 2,480 nuns and 1,127 friars are from BCB, MS B3567, entry for 30 September 1595. See Zarri, "I monasteri femminili a Bologna," esp. 144–45.
11. In discussing women's reactions to similar clerically imposed restrictions under the postrevolutionary Iranian regime, Erika Friedl observes: "Subversion, in the form of minimal compliance with controversial rules or the outright subversion of such rules, is at once a form of testing the limits of the rules and the tolerance of the rule-makers and thus is an expression of one's dissatisfaction with them." See Erika Friedl, "Sources of Female Power in Iran," in *In the Eye of the Storm: Women in Post-revolutionary Iran*, ed. Mahnaz Afkhami and Erika Friedl (Syracuse, NY: Syracuse University Press, 1994), 156.
12. For the present edition, I have broken the original transcript's lengthy and complex sentences into shorter units, deleted repetitive phrases, and trimmed text that was inessential. I have suppressed ellipses that, in more scholarly discourse, would signal omissions from citations. I have also simplified original syntax here and there. If the reader wishes to see the original Italian for quotations, it appears in notes to the earlier edition, *Disembodied Voices*.

13. For an overview of the archive, see Leonard E. Boyle, *A Survey of the Vatican Archives and of Its Mediaeval Holdings* (Toronto: Pontifical Institute of Mediaeval Studies, 1972). To visit the archive in virtual reality, see http://asv .vatican.va/home_htm.

14. For convent chronicles, see K. J. P. Lowe, *Nuns' Chronicles and Convent Culture in Renaissance and Counter-Reformation Italy* (Cambridge: Cambridge University Press, 2003).

15. CDs are listed in "Further Reading and Listening." Most directly relevant are Musica Secreta's *Songs of Ecstasy and Devotion* (hereafter *SED*) and Cappella Artemisia's *Canti nel chiostro* (hereafter *CNC*) and *Soror mea, sponsa mea* (hereafter *SMSM*).

CHAPTER 1

1. Italian family names for early-modern women sometimes end in *a* (e.g., Lucrezia Vizzana) instead of the usual, modern *i* (e.g., Ludovico Vizzani, Lucrezia's father). Some family names always have *i* endings, regardless of gender (e.g., Grassi, Bombacci). In the plural, the *i* ending is most commonly used (e.g., Lucrezia and Isabetta Vizzani, the Vizzani sisters). In this book, I have tried to follow contemporary usage, and thus some family names end in either *a* or *i*, depending on the person's gender.

2. A complete copy of Vizzana's publication is preserved in the Civico Museo Bibliografico Musicale, Bologna. A second copy, missing the *canto secondo*, survives in the Biblioteka Uniwersytecka, Wrocław. The entry on the composer in Stanley Sadie, ed., *The New Grove Dictionary of Music and Musicians* (London: Macmillan, 1980), 13: 874, appears under "Orsina, Lucretia." Donald J. Grout and Claude V. Palisca, *A History of Western Music*, 6th ed. (New York: W. W. Norton, 2001), first discussed Lucrezia Vizzana and her publication on 290.

3. BUB, MS It. 3856, 133–36. To this day the menology of the Camaldolese order remembers Flaminia Bombacci on 28 September. See Anselmo Giabbani, *Menologia camaldolese* (Tivoli: De Rossi, 1950), 59. The decorated necrology, Bologna, Biblioteca Arcivescovile, Libreria Breventani MS 64, seems to have disappeared from the Biblioteca Arcivescovile early in the twentieth century. An eighteenth-century transcription by Baldassare Antonio Maria Carrati appears in BCB, MS B921. See also Camaldoli, Archivio del Monastero, MS 1087.

4. On the most distinguished branch of the Vizzani family, see Alessandro Longhi, *Il Palazzo Vizani [sic] (ora Sanguinetti) e le famiglie illustri che lo possedettero* (Bologna: Zamorini & Albertazzi, 1902). For additional details of the Vizzani family, see Pompeo Dolfi, *Cronologia delle famiglie nobili di Bologna* (Bologna: G. B. Ferroni, 1670; repr., Bologna: Forni, n.d.), 710–711; ASB, Giuseppe Guidicini Alberi genealogici, 123; BCB, MS B700, no. 150. On Obizzo Vizzani's interment in the so-called Tomba di Rolandino Passeggeri, see Longhi, *Il Palazzo Vizani*, 84.

5. Camillo Baldi is quoted in Mario Fanti, "Le classi sociali e il governo di Bologna all'inizio del secolo xvii in un'opera di Camillo Baldi," *Strenna storica bolognese* 11 (1961): 152. Bombacci: BUB, MS It. 3856, 144.

6. BUB, MS It. 3856, 98, 103, 122. On the Bombaccis' noble Venetian connections, see BCB, MS B3758.

7. Bombacci family details from BUB, MS It. 3856, 75–76, 122, 133.

8. The dowry contract survives in ASB, Demaniale 9/2870 (Santa Cristina), no. 47/I. The record of their marriage appears in BCB, MS B901, 373.

9. For the sons' births, see BCB, MS B860, 76, 132; BCB, MS B861, 198. Since the legitimation of Dionigio's son in 1628 (see below) stipulates that, apart from Dionigio, Ludovico's only other surviving children were two daughters, and since Verginia and Lucrezia subsequently claimed an inheritance through Mario (see below), he must have died between 1598 and 1628. Verginia Vizzana's birth is recorded in AAB, Reg. Batt. 1587–88, fol. 10v. Lucrezia's name appears in AAB, Reg. Batt. 1590–92, fol. 74v.

10. These details are gleaned from petitions in ASV, VR, posiz. 1607, A–B. Lucrezia's entire memorial appears in BCB, MS B921, 50–51.

11. For the listings of 1574, see ASV, VR, posiz. 1588, A–B. For convent incomes in 1614, see ASV, Sacra Congregazione del Concilio, Visite ad Limina 136A, fol. 55r.

12. ASV, VR, reg. regular. 21 (1618), fol. 242v.

13. The Vizzani sisters' dowry agreement survives in ASB, Notarile, Belvisi Giulio, Prot. 8, fol. 379r. Other details on the Vizzani sisters' earliest years at Santa Cristina derive from ASV, VR, posiz. 1607, A–B.

14. In a list of nuns dated 10 December 1603 the sixteen-year-old donna Isabetta Vizzana is the most recent *professa*; Lucrezia's name does not yet appear. See ASB, Demaniale 7/2868 (Santa Cristina), no. 30/G. For the dowry arrangements, see ASB, Demaniale 51/5009 (Santa Cristina), fols. 1v, 2v; and ASB, Notarile, Belvisi Giulio, Prot. 8, fols. 378r, 379r.

15. For Ludovico Vizzani's remarriage, see BCB, MS B700, no. 150; and ASB, Notarile, Sturoli Ventura, Prot. 1, fol. 2r, dated 21 October 1610. For the deaths of Ludovico and Dionigio Vizzani, see BCB, MS B913, 254.2. For Angelo Michele's legitimation and the subsequent litigation with Lucrezia and Isabetta Vizzani, see ASB, Famiglia Banzi, busta 8, nos. 104–8.

16. Maria Clorinda Vizzana's dowry contract survives in ASB, Demaniale 20/2881 (Santa Cristina), no. 15/V; ASB, Demaniale 2/2863 (Santa Cristina), B/no. 25; and ASB, Demaniale 12/2873 (Santa Cristina), no. 2/L. The convent's attempts to obtain back support are described in ASB, Demaniale 35/2896 (Santa Cristina), no. 4/H.H.

17. For Teresa Pompea Vizzana's dowry agreement, see ASB, Demaniale 51/5009 (Santa Cristina), fol. 9r. After her death on 13 June 1684, she was remembered as *in cantu peritia* (skilled in song) (BCB, MS B921, 256); in 1666, she had compiled a 552-page book of plainchant for the choir's use (formerly in the Biblioteca Ambrosini, it is now lost).

18. Corrado Ricci and Guido Zucchini, *Guida di Bologna: Nuova edizione illustrata* (Bologna: Edizioni Alfa, 1968; repr., Bologna: Edizioni Alfa, 1976), 48, 60.

19. *Ambrosii Traversarii generalis Camaldulensium aliorumque ad ipsum, et ad alios de eodem Ambrosio latinae epistolae*, ed. Pietro Cannetti and Laurence Mehus (Florence: Typographio Caesareo, 1759; repr., Bologna: Forni, 1968), 2: col. 561.

20. On the campanile's negative reception, see Ugo Capriani, "Chiesa e convento di Santa Cristina della Fondazza in Bologna: Ipotesi di ricerca e recupero" (degree thesis, University of Bologna, 1987–88), 91; on the weighty bells, see CDSC, fol. 12r.

21. On the decoration of the refectory, see Capriani, "Chiesa e convento," 76; on precociously literate convent ten-year-olds, see ASV, VR, sez. monache, 1710 (gennaio–febraio).

22. On convent baked goods, see Mario Fanti, *Abiti e lavori delle monache di Bologna* (Bologna: Tamari Editori, 1972), 52.

23. The two-story cells are described in CDSC, fol. 11v. Emilia Grassi seems to have had one of these, for in 1623 she remarked to pastoral visitors, "I freely confess to having a lower closet, with the blessing of the mother abbess." See processo 2, fol. 11r.

24. The possible furnishing of the cell has been re-created from typical convent inventories in BCB, MS B450, no. 7; ASB, Demaniale 43/2904 (Santa Cristina); and ASB, Demaniale 18/2879 (Santa Cristina). Colomba Glavarini's furnishings are listed in ASB, Demaniale 18/2879 (Santa Cristina), no. 19/S.

25. Inventories from Santa Margherita survive in ASB, Demaniale 51/3918 (Santa Margherita). The specific prohibition against mirrors and jewelry at Santa Cristina after the visitation of 1622–23 confirms the presence of similar "vanities" there. See AAB, Misc. Vecchie 820, no. 2.

26. On processions to the chapels, see CDSC, fol. 11r.

27. Details on the convent grounds appear in Capriani, "Chiesa e convento," 73, 81–85, 121–22. On Flaminia Bombacci's menagerie, see processo 2, fol. 6v.

28. The bishop of Bologna's license, dated 9 March 1245, to erect the convent in Bologna appears in ASB, Demaniale 12/2873 (Santa Cristina), no. 25/M.

29. On the early-fifteenth-century remodeling, see Giovanni Benedetto Mittarelli and Anselmo Costadoni, *Annales Camaldulenses ordiniis Sancti Benedicti*, vol. 5 (Venice: Aere Monasterii Sancti Michaelis de Murano, 1760), 340 and appendix, cols. 476–77; Ricci and Zucchini, *Guida di Bologna*, 60.

30. ASB, Demaniale 51/5009 (Santa Cristina), fol. 11. On the nuns' complaint of 1529, see Giuseppe Guidicini, *Cose notabili della città di Bologna*, vol. 5 (Bologna: Giuseppe Vitali, 1873; repr., Bologna: Forni, 1972), 32. On complaints at San Lorenzo, see Craig A. Monson, *Nuns Behaving Badly: Tales of Music, Magic, Art, and Arson in the Convents of Italy* (Chicago: University of Chicago Press, 2010), 45.

31. Capriani, "Chiesa e convento," 81.

32. On the scaffold accident, see Giuseppe Guidicini, *Miscellanea storico-patria bolognese*, ed. Ferdinando Guidicini (Bologna: Monti, 1872; repr., Bologna: Forni, 1972), 74. See also Carlo Cesare Malvasia, *Le pitture di Bologna 1686*, ed. Andrea Emiliani (Bologna: Edizioni Alfa, 1969), 266–68 [181–83].

33. These details appear chiefly in Malvasia, *Le pitture di Bologna*, 266–68 [181–83]; and in Capriani, "Chiesa e convento," 125–39. For biographical details regarding Maura Taddea Bottrigari, named as donor of Carracci's painting in an inscription, see BCB, MS B921, 13.

34. Ottavia Bolognetti died aged sixty-four in 1612. See BCB, MS B921, 4. Costanza Duglioli died in her sixties in 1614 (ibid., 28).

35. Margherita "de Javerinis" died in February 1619 (BCB, MS B921, 8). Angela Maria Zambeccara died in 1645 aged sixty-six; her memorial also recognizes her lavish donations of "gold, silver, and silk" (ibid., 50).

36. On the sculpted niches, see Capriani, "Chiesa e convento," 50–51. On Mary Magdalene and music, see H. Colin Slim, "Music and Dancing with Mary Magdalen in a Laura Vestalis," in *The Crannied Wall: Women, Religion, and the Arts in Early Modern Europe*, ed. Craig Monson (Ann Arbor: University of Michigan Press, 1992), 139–60. Two additional statues by Giuseppe Mazza were added in niches cut in the east wall, flanking the high altar, in 1688 (Capriani, "Chiesa e convento," 27): Saint Joseph (right) and Saint John the Baptist (left).

37. Gabriella Zarri points out that the seven convent churches that, like Santa Cristina, also served as parish churches tended to be more elaborate. Four of these had more than five altars. See her "Recinti sacri: Sito e forma dei monasteri femminili a Bologna tra '400 e '600," in *Luoghi sacri e spazi della santità*, ed. Sofia Boesch Gajano and Lucetta Scaraffia (Turin: Rosenberg & Sellier, 1990), 394n32. Santa Cristina had a total of nine altars in its external church.

CHAPTER 2

1. Paolo Prodi, *Il cardinale Gabriele Paleotti (1522–1597)*, vol. 1 (Rome: Edizioni di Storia e Letteratura, 1959), 44–45, 230. On San Vitale, see Craig Monson, "Molti concerti, poca concordia: Monache, parrocchiani, e musica nella chiesa e convento dei SS. Vitale e Agricola, 1550–1730," in *Vitale e Agricola: Il culto dei protomartiri di Bologna attraverso i secoli nel xvi centenario della traslazione*, ed. Gina Fasoli (Bologna: EDB, 1993), 195.

2. The various convent "abuses" are cataloged in AAB, Misc. Vecchie 808, fascs. 6, 13, 23.

3. Original Italian cited in Craig Monson, "La prattica della musica nei monasteri femminili bolognesi," in *La cappella musicale nell'Italia della Controriforma*, ed. Oscar Mischiati and Paolo Russo (Cento: Centro Studi G. Baruffaldi, 1993), 145–46.

4. Alfonso Paleotti's comment appears in ASV, VR, posiz. 1607, A–B, letter dated 31 January 1607. The remark of Geronimo del Trombone appears in ASV, VR, posiz. 1609, A–M.

5. BUB, MS It. 206/2, no. 5, a memorial commenting on Gozzadini's ban, a copy of which is included with it. Other copies of Gozzadini's decree survive in ASB, Demaniale 48/4891 (Sant'Agostino), no. 23/1622; ASB, Demaniale 104/3472 (San Lorenzo); ASB, Demaniale 84/3233 (Santi Vitale et Agricola). Ludovisi's printed broadside survives in ASB, Demaniale 84/3233 (Santi Vitale et Agricola); and in ASB, Demaniale 48/4891 (Sant'Agostino), no. 22/1621. Ludovico Ludovisi's biographer described the archbishop's ban on convent music as a chief aspect of the cardinal's conventual reforms. See BAV, Cod. Boncompagni-Ludovisi B8, fol. 15r.

6. Gabriella Zarri, "Monasteri femminili e città (secoli XV–XVIII)," in *Storia d'Italia, Annali 9: La chiesa e il potere politico dal Medioevo all'età contemporanea*, ed. Giorgio Chittolini and Giovanni Miccoli (Turin: Giulio Einaudi, 1986), 386–87.

7. Quoted in Craig Monson, introduction to *The Crannied Wall: Women, Religion, and the Arts in Early Modern Europe* (Ann Arbor: University of Michigan Press, 1992), 2–3. For *ruota*, see the glossary.

8. Craig Monson, "Disembodied Voices: Music in the Nunneries of Bologna in the Midst of the Counter-Reformation," in *The Crannied Wall*, 191–94.

9. ASB, Demaniale 48/4891 (Sant'Agostino), no. 22/1621; ASB, Demaniale 84/3233 (Santi Vitale et Agricola), order of 27 June (the date is partially illegible—1646?); cf. ASB, Demaniale 84/3233 (Santi Vitale et Agricola), order of 24 December 1642.

10. ASV, Legazione di Bologna, vol. 3, fols. 19v, 51v. See also ibid., vol. 182, fols. 128r, 293r, 363r.

11. For San Pietro Martire, see ASV, VR, posiz. 1585, A–B. For the reference to the nuns of Santissima Trinità, see ASV, VR, posiz. 1586, A–C; ASV, VR, reg. episc. 12 (1586/III), dated 2 May. Paleotti's comment appears in Bologna, Archivio Isolani-Lupari, Fondo Paleotti, cartone 62, F32/5, lettere VIII (1586), fols. 135r–135v (badly burned and incomplete).

12. AAB, Misc. Vecchie 808, fasc. 2.

13. ASV, VR, reg. regular. 3 (1600–1601), fol. 93v, dated 2 May 1601.

14. For Isabella d'Este's letter, see William Prizer, "Una 'virtù molto conveniente a madonne': Isabella d'Este as a Musician," *Journal of Musicology* 17 (1999): 24. For the remarks regarding Ludovisi's prohibitions see BUB, MS It. 206/2, no. 5. For Vittoria Pepoli's letter, see ASV, VR, sez. monache, 1662 (aprile–giugno), first read 3 February, rejected 16 March, then in packet dated 23 June left to the vicar general to decide.

15. Quoted in Monson, "Disembodied Voices," 202–3.

16. ASB, Demaniale 120/1460 (San Giovanni in Monte), letter dated 3 August 1583 from don Theodosio di Piacenza to don Arcangelo, abbot of San Giovanni in Monte.

17. The viol document survives in ASB, Demaniale 83/3232 (Santi Vitale et Agricola). The copy of Paleotti's rules and the inventories at Santa Margherita survive in ASB, Demaniale 51/3918 (Santa Margherita). A suor Angela Maria Rugieri brought a trombone and a bass viol with her to Santa Caterina in 1618 (ASB, Demaniale 95/4021 [Santa Caterina]). Isabella Trombetta brought her trombone with her to Santi Gervasio e Protasio in 1576 (ASB, Demaniale 32/6061 [Santi Gervasio e Protasio], record book, opening 48 and coverless record book, fol. 60). In 1600, in requesting license for outside trombone lessons from the Congregation of Bishops, the nuns of San Giovanni Battista claimed that they had customarily used various instruments and recently had introduced the trombone into their ensembles (ASV, VR, posiz. 1600, A–B).

18. Jane Bowers offers comparative examples in support of this view in "The Emergence of Women Composers in Italy, 1566–1700," in *Women Making Music: The Western Art Tradition, 1150–1950*, ed. Jane Bowers and Judith Tick (Urbana: University of Illinois Press, 1986), 124, 151n49.

19. Ambrogio Traversari, letter no. 73 to his brother, 1433, in *Ambrosii Traversarii generalis Camaldulensium aliorumque ad ipsum, et ad alios de eodem Ambrosio latinae epistolae*, ed. Pietro Cannetti and Laurence Mehus (Florence: Typographico Caesareo, 1759; repr., Bologna: Forni, 1968), 2: col. 555.

20. Camilla Bombacci's necrology: BCB, MS B921, 50. For Camilla Bombacci's nomination as *maestra del choro*, see processo 2, fol. 14r. Petition from Catanzaro: ASV, VR, sez. monache, 1710 (gennaro–febraro), dated 21 February 1710.

21. For the ten-year-old at Santi Gervasio e Protasio, see ASV, VR, sez. monache, 1668 (giugno–luglio), packet dated 8 June 1668. See also *Ambrosii Traversarii . . . latinae epistolae*, 2: col. 561.

22. Paula Dorothea Vitali, processo, fol. 19v.

23. In Bologna, Anna Maria Cavalazzi, who joined Santi Bernardo ed Orsola as organist in 1644, was taught by her aunt, the current organist, whom she succeeded in that post (ASV, VR, sez. monache, 1644 [gennaro–maggio], packet of 18 March). A similar relationship may have existed between Marsibiglia Maria Vittoria Bolognini, musician and organist, who professed at Santa Cristina in 1683, and Maria Giuditta Ginevra Bolognini, a singer and future mainstay of the choir, consecrated there in 1699. Examples from outside Bologna include an Anna educated in singing and organ playing by her aunt and accepted at the convent of Sant'Anna in Senigaglia in 1685 (ASV, VR, sez. monache, 1685 [gennaio–marzo]) and several women from Milanese convents, such as the musical Cozzolani at Santa Radegonda. On Milanese musical dynasties both within and across convent walls, see Robert L. Kendrick, *Celestial Sirens: Nuns and Their Music in Early Modern Milan* (Oxford: Clarendon Press, 1996).

24. Adriano Banchieri, *Messa solenne a otto voci* (Venice: Ricciardo Amadino, 1599), fol. A1v.

25. For Emilia Grassi's tenure as *maestra del choro*, see processo 2, fol. 14r; BCB, MS B921, 5. Ruggeri's comments appear in CDSC, fol. 12v.

26. Gabriele Fattorini, *Il secondo libro de mottetti a otto voci* (Venice: Ricciardo Amadino, 1601). A copy, missing the *canto primo* part, survives at the Archivio del Duomo in Vercelli; another copy of the *canto secondo* survives in the Biblioteka Jagiellónska in Kraków. Giovanni Battista Biondi (alias Cesena), *Compieta con letanie che si cantano nella casa di Loreto, et motetti a otto voci* (Venice: Giacomo Vincenti, 1606).

27. ASV, VR, posiz. 1607, A–B.

28. The movable screens in the organ lofts are mentioned in AAB, Misc. Vecchie 820, fasc. 2, document dated 27 April 1623. Ruggeri, CDSC, fol. 11v.

29. Ann Rosalind Jones, *The Currency of Eros: Women's Love Lyric in Europe, 1540–1620* (Bloomington: Indiana University Press, 1990), 28, 205n41.

CHAPTER 3

1. ASV, VR, posiz. 1606, A–C.

2. ASV, VR, sez. monache, 1652 (gennaio–maggio): "soto pretesto di q[ues]ta dottrina si fà la scaletta co[n] altra chiave che di .b. molle e .b. quadro, p[er] natura acceta."

3. See Craig Monson, "Disembodied Voices: Music in the Nunneries of Bologna in the Midst of the Counter-Reformation," in *The Crannied Wall: Women, Religion, and the Arts in Early Modern Europe*, ed. Craig Monson (Ann Arbor: University of Michigan Press, 1992), 191–209.

4. AAB, Misc. Vecchie 820, fasc. 2, "Visitatio localis Ecclesie et Monasterij Monialiu[m] .S. Christine. Bonon." The remedies demanded after the visitation of 1623 were only partially successful; after Archbishop Girolamo Boncompagni's pastoral visitation of 1654, he decreed, "The screens should be removed from the organ windows and permanent covers should be installed." BUB, MS It. 231/1, fols. 8r–8v; see also AAB, Misc. Vecchie 262.

5. For the inventories from Santa Margherita, see ASB, Demaniale 51/3918 (Santa Margherita); for the musical bequest at San Guglielmo, see ASB, Demaniale 80/814 (San Guglielmo), entry no. 21.

6. For Alfonso Ganassi, see Gaetano Gaspari, *Musica e musicisti a Bologna* (Bologna: Forni Editore, n.d.), 170–75. For Alfonsina, see ASB, Demaniale 31/2892 (Santa Cristina), fol. 128r. See also BCB, MS B921, 46. For laxity in the parlatorios, see processo, especially fol. 11r.

7. For Porta's license, see ASB, Demaniale 26/7756 (San Michele in San Giovanni in Persiceto). For the abbess's testimony, see processo 2, fol. 15r. On the number of organists, see processo, fol. 39r.

8. Processo 2, fol. 15r.

9. *Adriano Banchieri: Conclusions for Playing the Organ (1609)*, trans. Lee R. Garrett, Colorado College Music Press Translations, vol. 13 (Colorado Springs: Colorado College Music Press, 1982), 50–51.

10. For performances at Banchieri's academy, see Denis Stevens, *The Letters of Claudio Monteverdi* (Cambridge: Cambridge University Press, 1980), 211 (emphasis added), which also summarizes the Monteverdi-Banchieri contacts.

11. See Margaret Ann Rorke, "Sacred Contrafacta of Monteverdi Madrigals and Cardinal Borromeo's Milan," *Music and Letters* 65 (1984): 175. See also Robert L. Kendrick, *Celestial Sirens: Nuns and Their Music in Early Modern Milan* (Oxford: Clarendon Press, 1996), 229–33.

12. See Giuseppe Vecchi, *Le accademie musicali del primo seicento, e Monteverdi a Bologna* (Bologna: A. M. I. S., 1969), 73–92, for a discussion of Banchieri's academy and Monteverdi's contacts with it. See also Stevens, *Letters of Claudio Monteverdi*, 211–12. The anniversary of the translation of Saint Romuald's body to Fabriano was 7 February. A "Libro, nel quale vengono notate diverse Memorie attinenti al Camerlingato," dated 1728, includes the note "February 7. The feast of our father Saint Romuald. The convent has High Mass sung" (ASB, Demaniale 26/2887 [Santa Cristina]). The same expense book also includes a feast of Saint Romuald on 19 June.

13. As mentioned in chapter 1, Santa Cristina's necrology, which lauds Vizzana's musical accomplishments, exists only in later copies.

CHAPTER 4

1. Jean Leclercq and Jean-Paul Bonnes, "Lettre a une Moniale," in *Un maître de la vie spirituelle aux xie siècle Jean de Fécamp* (Paris: Librairie Philosophique J. Vrin, 1946), 206.

2. On donna Flaminia's talents, see BUB, MS It. 3856, 134; see also CDSC, fols. 19r–20r. On Lucrezia Vizzana, see BCB, MS B921, 50–51.

3. The festival was celebrated in May, not on 24 July, as in the modern calendar.

4. Quoted in Margaret L. King, *Women of the Renaissance* (Chicago: University of Chicago Press, 1991), 93.

5. For the Vizzani sisters' requests regarding the Sacra, see ASV, VR, posiz. 1607, A–B; posiz. 1613, B–F; reg. regular. 8 (1607/8), fol. 55v; reg. regular. 14 (1613), fol. 132r.

6. Helen Hills comments on "heaping up the virile attractions of the Christ Spouse" in *Invisible City: The Architecture of Devotion in Seventeenth-Century Neapolitan Convents* (New York: Oxford University Press, 2004), 59–61.

7. On Flaminia Bombacci's Eucharistic piety, see BUB, MS It. 3856, 134; CDSC, fol. 19r. On the nuns' renewed sacramental devotion, see processo, fol. 20r.

8. See Carolyn Bynum, "Women Mystics and Eucharistic Devotion in the Thirteenth Century," in her *Fragmentation and Redemption: Essays on Gender and the Human Body in Medieval Religion* (New York: Zone Books, 1991), esp. 129–34; see also Carolyn Bynum, "The Female Body and Religious Practice in the Later Middle Ages," in ibid., 192.

9. Elizabeth Alvilda Petroff, *The Consolation of the Blessed* (New York: Alta Gaia Society, 1979), 172.
10. Bynum, "Women Mystics," 129; Bynum, "The Female Body," 206 and fig. 6.8, 211.
11. Ugo Capriani, "Chiesa e convento di Santa Cristina della Fondazza: Ipotesi di ricerca e recupero" (degree thesis, University of Bologna, 1987–88), 142, 145. For the attribution to Timoteo Viti, see http://www.giulyars.net/timoteo_viti/ viti_roio.htm. On the miraculous image, see processo 2, fols. 10r, 19v.
12. On sweetness in the mouth and Agnes Blannbekin, see Bynum, "Women Mystics," esp. 126 and 129.
13. See Jane Bowers, appendix to "The Emergence of Women Composers in Italy, 1566–1700," in *Women Making Music: The Western Art Tradition, 1150–1950*, ed. Jane Bowers and Judith Tick (Urbana: University of Illinois Press, 1986), 162–64.
14. On Clement's interpretation, see Robert A. Skeris, *CHROMA THEOU: On the Origins and Theological Interpretation of the Musical Imagery Used by the Ecclesiastical Writers of the First Three Centuries, with Special Reference to the Image of Orpheus* (Altöting: Verlag Alfred Coppenrath, 1976), esp. 54–65.
15. Barbaro is quoted in Ann Rosalind Jones, *The Currency of Eros: Women's Love Lyric in Europe, 1540–1620* (Bloomington: Indiana University Press, 1990), 21. Barbo is quoted in Margaret L. King, "Thwarted Ambitions: Six Learned Women of the Renaissance," *Soundings* 59 (1976): 284.
16. Karma Lochrie, *Margery Kempe and Translations of the Flesh* (Philadelphia: University of Pennsylvania Press, c. 1991), 25.
17. James McKinnon, *Music in Early Christian Literature* (Cambridge: Cambridge University Press, 1987), 32, 35.
18. Ibid., 81.
19. Quoted in Ronald E. Surtz, *The Guitar of God: Gender, Power, and Authority in the Visionary World of Mother Juana de la Cruz (1481–1534)* (Philadelphia: University of Pennsylvania Press, 1990), 72–73. Bonaventure's use of the word *chorda* probably involved an anatomical and musical play on words but not one involving the anachronistic meaning of several simultaneous pitches in the sense of the modern "chord."
20. Gasparo Bombacci on Flaminia Bombacci: BUB, MS. It. 3856, 133. Vizzana on her illness: processo, fol. 9v. Santa Cristina necrology: BCB, MS B921, 51.

CHAPTER 5

1. A summary of the letter, including the statements "Castità non ne parli p[er] riverenza" and "Esaminare senza scomunica papale non servirà niente," appears in CDSC, fol. 15v.
2. Processo, fols. 1r (Gozzadini), 38r–38v (Angela Cherubini), 37r (Verginia Fuzzi), 33r (Ortensia Bombacci), 19r (Paula Vitali).
3. Ibid., fol. 9r.

4. Ibid., fols. 10r–11r (emphasis added) and 10r (original emphasis), respectively.

5. Ibid., fol. 15r.

6. Ibid., fols. 14r, 12r, 19r, 32r, 47r, respectively.

7. Processo 2, fol. 4r.

8. Ibid., fols. 1r–1v, 8r; processo, fols. 23v–24r.

9. In 1635, for example, the nuns of Santa Maria della Regina in Naples had informed the Congregation of Bishops that bans on dogs applied only to male dogs (ASV, VR, sez. monache, 1635 [marzo–dicembre]), which apparently was confirmed in 1638 (see BAV, MS Borg. Lat. 77, fol. 23v: "Small female dogs permitted to cloistered nuns"), though it would be overturned at other times and places (e.g., at Genoa in 1683; see ASV, VR, reg. monial. 30 [1683], fol. 197v).

10. Processo 2, fol. 16v; Lorenza Bonsignori's testimony appears on fols. 13r–20v, as well as in processo, fols. 39v–47r.

11. Processo 2, fol. 9v; processo, fol. 33v.

12. Processo 2, fols. 12v–13r.

13. ASV, VR, posiz. 1600, A–B.

14. ASV, VR, posiz. 1593, B–C.

15. ASV, VR, posiz. 1602, A–C.

16. The complaint against the convent procurator survives: ASV, VR, posiz. 1599, A–C. The Congregation of Bishops' order for an investigation, which was unusually slow in coming, appears in ASV, VR, reg. regular. 3 (1600–1601), fol. 43. In July 1600 there had also been difficulties and misunderstandings between Archbishop Alfonso Paleotti and the convent regarding the admission of an unauthorized barber. See ASV, VR, posiz. 1600, A–D. The congregation's follow-up orders of January 1601 appear in ASV, VR, reg. regular. 3 (1600–1601), fols. 60r–60v.

17. In the visitation of 1622–23 the abbess confirmed that Adeodata Leoni, as well as Flaminia Bombacci, had been called on to reconcile the rivals as recently as Lent of 1622 (processo 2, fol. 10r).

18. *Il secondo libro de mottetti a otto voci di Gabrielle Fattorini da Faenza* (Venice: Ricciardo Amadino, 1601).

19. Prohibitive licensing fees to reproduce images from the Museo Internazionale e Biblioteca della Musica di Bologna prevented the inclusion of the dedication dated 1 January 1623. Reproductions of the 1623 title page, dedication, and index can be found at http://badigit.comune.bologna.it/cmbm/images/ripro/gaspari/BB063/BB063_C_00.asp.

20. The resulting reform decree was dated 27 April 1623. See AAB, Misc. Vecchie 820, fasc. 2. The music texts of the two surviving copies of *Componimenti musicali* are identical apart from a wrong note or two in the 1622 copy of the bass part of *Veni dulcissime Domine*, which appear to have been corrected during printing.

21. The insertion of the symbols <> indicates an omission from the original psalm.
22. ASV, VR: posiz. 1616, A–C; reg. regular. 19 (1616), fol. 162r; posiz. 1619, A–C; reg. regular. 21 (1618), fol. 242v; posiz. 1620, A–C.

CHAPTER 6

1. Ruggeri's account is preserved in Camaldoli MS 101 and CDSC. I have relied on the latter, slightly more legible copy. Ruggeri's characterizations appear in CDSC, fols. 12v–13r.
2. Details in CDSC, fols. 18r–18v, quotations from fols. 11r, 21v.
3. See Ecclesiasticus 25:23: "And there is no anger above the anger of a woman." The verse continued to be paraphrased down through the centuries. E.g., "Anyone seeking to restrain an angry woman wearies himself with wasted effort. . . . Moreover, the anger of any woman is aroused at the slightest, most unsubstantiated remark" (Andreas Capellanus, *De amore*, c. 1185); "But it is also true, without fail, that a woman is easily inflamed with wrath. . . . And thus she remains a very irritable animal. Solomon says that there was never a head more cruel than the head of a serpent and nothing more wrathful than a woman" (Jean de Meun, *Le roman de la rose*, c. 1275). Both quoted in Alcuin Blamires, ed., *Woman Defamed and Woman Defended* (Oxford: Clarendon Press, 1992), 121, 163.
4. BUB, MS It. 3856, 134.
5. CDSC, fols. 18r, 19r–20r.
6. Processo 2, fol. 4r.
7. Guido Ruggiero, *The Boundaries of Eros* (New York: Oxford University Press, 1985), 40, 55.
8. Attilio Gnesotto, "Francisci Barbari De Re Uxoria Liber," *Accademia Patavina, Atti e memorie della R. Accademia di SLA in Padova* 32 (1916): 41.
9. For Laura Bovia, see Craig A. Monson, *Nuns Behaving Badly: Tales of Music, Magic, Art, and Arson in the Convents of Italy* (Chicago: University of Chicago Press, 2010), 30–32. For the Congregation of Bishops' rulings, see BAV, MS Ferrajoli 612, fols. 41r, 54r.
10. Adriano Banchieri, *Messa solenne a otto voci* (Venice: Ricciardo Amadino, 1599).
11. Allegations against Grassi appear in processo 2, fol. 14v. For Ruggeri's explanation, see CDSC, fols. 13r–13v.
12. Mario Fanti, "Le classi sociali e il governo di Bologna all'inizio del secolo xvii in un'opera inedita di Camillo Baldi," *Strenna storica bolognese* 11 (1961): 154; ASV, VR, reg. regular. 5 (1604), fol. 149v.
13. Processo 2, fol. 7r–v.
14. See BCB, MS B922, 259.
15. CDSC, fol. 19v.
16. CDSC, fol. 12v.

17. On Luca Bianchi's murder, see Ferdinando Guidicini, *Miscellanea storico-patria Bolognese tratta dai manoscritti di Giuseppe Guidicini* (Bologna: Giacomo Monti, 1872), 284–85.

18. Pagani's treatises of 1587 and 1638, including the quotation, are discussed in Gabriella Zarri, "'Vera' santità, 'simulata' santità: Ipotesi e riscontri," in *Finzione e santità tra Medioevo ed età moderna*, ed. Gabriella Zarri (Turin: Rosenberg & Sellier, 1991), 20–21. Surin's characterization of hypocrisy is quoted in Giuseppe Orlandi, "Vera e falsa santità in alcuni predicatori popolari e direttori di spirito del Sei e Settecento," in ibid., 437.

19. CDSC, fol. 11r (a reference to 2 Samuel 12:1–13), fol. 23r.

20. Zarri, "'Vera' santità, 'simulata' santità," 11.

21. For an illuminating discussion of the dog, the wolf, the vendetta, and promiscuity, see Edward Muir, *Mad Blood Stirring: Vendetta and Factions in Friuli during the Renaissance* (Baltimore, MD: Johns Hopkins University Press, 1993), esp. 222–31. Hecuba took revenge by killing the children of Polymester, who prophesied that she would turn into a bitch before her death.

22. C. Gozzadini's remark appears in processo, fol. 17v; for Sant'Agnese, see BCB, MS B3595, 26.

23. Processo, fol. 4v.

24. Processo 2, fol. 6r; processo, fol. 27r.

25. AAB, Misc. Vecchie 820, fasc. 2.

26. Processo 2, fol. 4r. John Florio's *Queene Anna's New World of Words* (1611) includes "put or lying under" as one meaning of *soggetto*.

27. Processo 2, fols. 16r–16v.

28. For Bolognese clerical responses to convent sleeping arrangements, see ASB, Demaniale 51/3918 (Santa Margherita). *The Colloquies of Erasmus*, trans. Craig R. Thompson (Chicago: University of Chicago Press, 1965), 108.

29. Quoted in Albano Biondi, "L'inordinata devozione' nella *Prattica* del Cardinale Scaglia (ca. 1635)," in Zarri, *Finzione e santità*, 317. For another case of shared beds and interpersonal conflict, see Monson, *Nuns Behaving Badly*, 125–51.

30. Richard C. Trexler, *Public Life in Renaissance Florence* (Ithaca, NY: Cornell University Press, 1991), 139.

31. Cecilia Bianchi, processo 2, fols. 4r–5r.

32. Ludovisi's biographer's comment appears in BAV, Cod. Boncompagni B8, fol. 100. Ruggeri's observation regarding the wording "supplico di rimedio" appears in CDSC, fol. 15v. Cecilia Bianchi, processo, fol. 28r. The version with the copying slip survives in processo 2, fol. 7r.

33. Ludovica Fabri, processo, fol. 48v.

34. CDSC, fols. 31r, 14v, 15r, 16r.

35. CDSC, fols. 12v, 15v; BCB, MS Gozz. 132, entry under 1506. See also AAB, Misc. Vecchie 820, fasc. 2, "Ristretto di ciò, che si contiene nell'Instromento della Riforma del monastero delle Monache Camaldolensi di S. Cristina della fondazza" (misdated 1499, however). [Ambrogio Traversari], *Hodo-*

eporicon, ed. Vittorio Tamburini (Florence: Felice le Monnier, 1985), 116. Antonio Francesco Ghiselli's comment: BUB, MS It. 770/26, 295.

36. CDSC, fols. 16r–16v.

37. The abbess's remark appears in Trexler, *Public Life in Renaissance Florence*, 35.

38. Guasco is quoted in Ann Rosalind Jones, *The Currency of Eros: Women's Love Lyric in Europe, 1540–1620* (Bloomington: Indiana University Press, 1990), 16. Ruggiero's comment appears in Margaret L. King, *Women of the Renaissance* (Chicago: University of Chicago Press, 1991), 29.

39. CDSC, fol. 16v. Cecilia Bianchi, processo 2, fol. 6v.

40. The incident is described in processo, fols. 50r–50v.

41. CDSC, fol. 16v. The orthography of the final adverb is unclear: "intrepidam[en]te" or "intepidam[en]te."

CHAPTER 7

1. AAB, Misc. Vecchie 820, fasc. 2, "Ordini che si devono dare p[er] rimediare alle cose ritrovate nella Visita di Santa Xpina" and "Ord.ni del suffrage.o fatti nella visita di s.ta xpina." Ruggeri provides a less detailed summary in CDSC, fols. 17r–17v.

2. On the election and its aftermath, see CDSC, fols. 17v–18r; ASV, VR, sez. regolari, 1626 (febbraio–settembre); ASV, VR, reg. regular. 35 (1626), fols. 161v–162r; and BUB, MS It. 3856, 135.

3. Processo, fols. 23r–23v.

4. The petitions appear in ASV, VR, posiz. 1616, A–C.

5. ASV, VR, posiz. 1625, A–C. Other copies appear in ASV, VR, sez. monache, 1627 (gennaio–novembre).

6. CDSC, fol. 23r.

7. The commission of the Congregation of Bishops to Bishop Bovio survives in ASV, VR, reg. regular. 35 (1626), fol. 53. For Ruggeri's account, see CDSC, fol. 23r.

8. Summaries of the investigation are preserved in AAB, Misc. Vecchie 820, fasc. 2, "somario del p[ro]cesso delle Monache di s[an]ta Christina"; and ASV, VR, sez. regolari, 1625 (febbraio–settembre).

9. CDSC, fols. 22r–22v.

10. Venice, Biblioteca Correr, MS Cicogna 1863.

11. ASV, VR, sez. monache, 1659 (novembre–dicembre).

12. For the command to the papal legate, see ASV, VR, reg. regular. 35 (1626), unnumbered folio inserted before the fascicle dated 5 June. Ruggeri's remark appears in CDSC, fol. 23v. In the middle of the night in December 1649 the nuns of San Lodovico e Alessio in Bologna were subjected to a similar invasion, provoking a vitriolic letter to the Congregation of Bishops rivaling some from Santa Cristina in its language. Their reaction offers further insight into how the nuns of Santa Cristina would have reacted to their own invasion. See ASV, VR, sez. monache, 1650 (gennaio–febbraio).

13. ASV, VR, reg. regular. 36 (1627), fols. 195v–196r.
14. The canceled draft appears in ASV, VR, reg. regular. 38 (1627—minute). For the message to the Camaldolese prior general, see ASV, VR, reg. regular. 36 (1627), fols. 52r–52v. The petition to Barberini appears in ASV, VR, sez. monache, 1627 (gennaio–novembre).
15. Details from CDSC, fol. 25r.
16. Sherrill Cohen, *The Evolution of Women's Asylums since 1500: From Refuges for Ex-Prostitutes to Shelters for Battered Women* (New York: Oxford University Press, 1992), 121.
17. The nuns' petition and oath survive in ASV, VR, sez. monache, 1628 (febbraio–maggio). Ludovisi's accusation and his claim concerning the nuns' refusal to confess appear in ASV, VR, sez. monache, 1704 (agosto); other copies in AAB, Misc. Vecchie 880, fasc. 2; BUB, MS. It. 770/26, 297–316; CDSC, fols. 26r–29v.
18. ASV, Sacra Congregazione del Concilio, Visite ad Limina 136A, fols. 67r–67v; another copy in BUB, MS It. 206/2. The orders to the papal legate appear in ASV, VR, reg. regular. 39 (1628—minute). The legate's letters expressing his reluctance to accept the commission and repeated doubts about the efficacy of his participation survive in ASV, Legazione di Bologna, vol. 4A, fols. 239–41.
19. The nuns' letter is in ASV, Segretario di Stato, Lettere di Particolari, 11, fol. 108r; the response to their letter is in ibid., fol. 110r.
20. The orders of the Congregation of Bishops survive in ASV, VR, reg. regular. 39 (1628—minute). Various accounts of the walling up of the doorway, each offering different details, appear in CDSC, fol. 25v; BUB, MS It. 3856, 137–38; BCB, MS Gozz. 185, fol. 142v; BUB, MS 770/26, 292–93.
21. Details from BUB, MS It. 3685, 138; CDSC, fol. 25. Ludovisi's final ultimatum also confirms many of the details, as does his biography in BAV, Fondo Boncompagni-Ludovisi, Codex B8, fol. 99r
22. BUB, MS It. 770/26, 294.
23. Undated, unsigned letters in ASB, Demaniale 48/2909 (Santa Cristina), one beginning "Se bene si maravigliaranno" and the other beginning "Si notifica à tutte le Monache di S[an]ta Christina, che il giuramento fatto da loro."
24. CDSC, fol. 26; see also BUB, MS It. 3856, 138.
25. The nuns' letter of 7 February and Ludovisi's reply survive in ASV, Demaniale 48/2909 (Santa Cristina); the decision of the Congregation of Bishops appears in ASV, VR, reg. regular. 40 (1629—minute).
26. ASV, VR, sez. monache, 1704 (agosto). Other copies in CDSC, fols. 26r–29r; BUB, MS It. 770/26, 297–316.
27. The details of the nuns' plight, including the eating of grass and their families' urging them to give in to Ludovisi, appear in CDSC, fols. 25r–25v. The nuns' claim to have been abandoned by their families appears in ASV, VR, sez. monache, 1636 (gennaio–maggio), quoted at the beginning of the next chapter.

28. ASB, Notarili, Belvisi, Giulio, Prot. 18 (1628–30), fols. 133v–135r. Rough copy in ASB, Demaniale 43/2904 (Santa Cristina).

29. Details from CDSC, fol. 29v; Bianchi's presence at San Michele Arcangelo by 30 June 1629 is confirmed by ASV, Misc. delle Corporazioni Religiose Soppresse 43, 59; and by ASV, Demaniale 3/7733 (San Michele Arcangelo di San Giovanni in Persiceto), no. 159. For details of Malvasia's career at Sant'Agostino, see BCB, MS B922, 158–59, 175; ASB, Demaniale 7/2868 (Santa Cristina), no. 38/G. For the Congregation of Bishops' stipulations of December 1629 regarding the reception of Malvasia and Bolognetti in their new convent homes, see ASV, VR, sez. monache, 1629 (settembre–dicembre). See also ASB, Demaniale 11/4854 (Sant'Agostino), L. no. 354; ASB, Demaniale 14/2925 (San Bernardino), nos. O/12, O/22; ASB, Demaniale 4/7734, 5/7735 (San Michele Arcangelo di San Giovanni in Persiceto); Giovanni Benedetto Mittarelli and Anselmo Costadoni, *Annales Camaldulenses ordiniis Sancti Benedicti*, vol. 8 (Venice: Aere Monasterii Sancti Michaelis de Murano, 1764), 285.

30. Various details of Santa Cristina's relations with the Camaldolese appear in CDSC, fols. 30r–34v.

31. Ludwig Pastor, *The History of the Popes*, trans. Ernest Graf (St. Louis, MO: B. Herder, 1952), 31:127 and n. 2.

32. CDSC, fol. 31r.

33. Ibid.

34. Cardinal Domenico Cecchini's description of Ludovisi's departure appears in BAV, MS Vat. Lat. 12174, fol. 78r. Ludovisi's biographer, Lucantonio Giunti, cited the cardinal's struggle with Santa Cristina as primary among the four most notable events of his reign. See BAV, Fondo Boncompagni-Ludovisi, Codex B8, fols. 98v–100r. On Ludovisi's fall, see Ludwig Pastor, *History of the Popes*, trans. Ernest Graf (St. Louis, MO: B. Herder, 1952), 28:290–93.

CHAPTER 8

1. The 1633 petition is printed in Giovanni Benedetto Mittarelli and Anselmo Costadoni, *Annales Camaldulenses ordiniis Sancti Benedicti*, vol. 9 (Venice: Aere Monasterii Sancti Michaelis de Murano, 1773), appendix, col. 324.

2. ASV, VR, sez. monache, 1636 (gennaio–maggio).

3. Ibid.

4. Francesca Malatendi, ASV, VR, sez. monache, 1646 (gennaio–marzo). She had confessed on 10 September. The convent necrology recorded her death on 8 October (BCB, MS B921, 37).

5. Processo, fols. 48v (suor Ludovica), 49v (suor Geronima), 52r (suor Cherubina). The nuns' reactions to suor Ludovica appear in processo, fol. 20v; and processo 2, fol. 12r.

6. For episcopal visitors' observations, see AAB, Misc. Vecchie 820, fasc. 2, "Ordine che si devono dare p[er] rimediare alle cose ritrovate nella visita di Santa Xpina."

7. Nuns of Santa Cristina, ASV, VR, sez. monache, 1646 (gennaio–marzo).

8. Giovanna Paolini, "Confessione e confessori al femminile: Monache e direttori spirituali in ambito veneto tra '600 e '700," in *Finzione e santità tra Medioevo ed età moderna*, ed. Gabriella Zarri (Turin: Rosenberg & Sellier, 1991), 366–88; Ottavia Niccoli, "Il confessore e l'inquisitore: A proposito di un manoscritto bolognese del Seicento," in ibid., 412–34.

9. CDSC, fols. 31v–32r.

10. Among the documents in the convent archive regarding the convent's removal from Camaldolese jurisdiction is an undated letter, "Agl'Ill[ustrissi]-mi S[igno]ri li S[igno]ri di Regimento," which, although its content suggests that it pertains to the tumults of the 1620s, reveals that the nuns had appealed to the senate in the past in combating the incursions of the diocesan curia. See ASB, Demaniale 48/2909 (Santa Cristina).

11. Albergati Ludovisi's remarks in the preceding paragraphs all come from the same letter dated 30 January 1647: ASV, VR, sez. monache, 1647 (gennaio–marzo).

12. ASV, VR, sez. monache, 1647 (aprile–maggio).

13. Ibid.

14. Ibid.

15. Nuns of Santa Cristina, ASB, Notarile, Belvisi, Giulio, Prot. 23 (1646–52), fols. 105r–106r. Another copy in ASV, VR, sez. monache, 1647 (aprile–maggio).

16. ASV, VR, sez. monache, 1647 (aprile–maggio).

17. Albergati Ludovisi, ASV, VR, sez. monache, 1647 (aprile–maggio). The petition from the pope's relative appears in ASV, VR, sez. monache, 1647 (giugno–agosto). The congregation's request for assurances appears in ASV, VR, reg. monial. 2 (1647), fol. 328r.

18. Albergati Ludovisi, ASV, VR, sez. monache, 1647 (giugno–agosto and settembre).

19. Albergati Ludovisi, ASV, VR, reg. monial. 2 (1647), fols. 521r–521v. For Ruggeri's claim, see CDSC, fol. 34r.

20. These various exchanges survive in ASV, VR, sez. monache, 1647 (novembre–dicembre).

21. ASV, VR, sez. monache, 1647 (novembre–dicembre); the Congregation of Bishops' response can be found in ASV, VR, reg. monial. 2 (1647), fol. 555r.

22. For the congregation's final letter, see ASV, VR, reg. monial. 2 (1647), fols. 576v–577r.

23. Ruggeri's description of Vizzana's madness appears in CDSC, fol. 34r.

24. On the sepulcher, see Ugo Capriani, "Chiesa e convento di Santa Cristina della Fondazza in Bologna: Ipotesi di ricerca e recupero" (degree thesis, University of Bologna, 1987–88), 86–89.

CHAPTER 9

1. Marcello Moscini points out the unusual subject matter of the altarpiece at Santa Cristina in *Cristina di Bolsena: Culto e iconografia* (Viterbo: Agnesotti, 1986), 196.

2. Gabriella Zarri suggests how certain aspects of the ritual in the seventeenth and eighteenth centuries were specifically intended to emphasize this separation. See her "Recinti sacri: Sito e forma dei monasteri femminili a Bologna tra '500 e '600," in *Luoghi sacri e spazi della santità*, ed. Sofia Boesch Gajano and Lucetta Scaraffia (Turin: Rosenberg & Sellier, 1990), 385–86.

3. ASV, VR, reg. monial. 24 (1677), fols. 15r–15v. For ostentatious twenty-first-century male clerical fashion, see, e.g., http://www.tridentinum.com/en/homepage.html.

4. Gabriele Paleotti: Bologna, Archivio Isolani-Lupari, Fondo Paleotti, cartone 33, 40; some of the beginning pages survive in cartone 25. *Episcopale Bononiensis civitatis et diocesis* (Bologna: Alessandro Benacci, 1580), fol. 188, "Modo da osservarsi nel fare la professione." Congregation of Bishops: ASV, VR, reg. episc. 1 (1573–76), 847–48. Alfonso Paleotti: Archivio Isolani-Lupari, Fondo Paleotti, cartone 25, E68/4.

5. ASB, Demaniale 48/4891 (Sant'Agostino). For a similar prohibition from 1608, see ASB, Demaniale 51/3918 (Santa Margherita). On traditions of convent drama, see Elissa B. Weaver, *Convent Theatre in Early Modern Italy: Spiritual Fun and Learning for Women* (Cambridge: Cambridge University Press, 2002).

6. ASB, Demaniale 48/1817 (Sant'Elena); other copies in ASB, Demaniale 17/4798 (Santissima Concezione) and Demaniale 84/3233 (Santi Vitale et Agricola).

7. ASB, Demaniale 80/814 (San Guglielmo), unnumbered entry.

8. BCB, MS Gozz. 358, 12; BCB, MS Gozz. 359, 9.

9. ASB, Demaniale 80/814 (San Guglielmo), entry no. 156.

10. BCB, MS Gozz. 328, entry for "11 Giugno [1663]." Compare also "On 20 June 1720 a daughter of Senator Beccadelli became a nun at Santa Cristina with an invitation to all the nobility, with solemn music" (BUB, MS It. 225/2, fol. 49). "On 29 November 1726, in the morning, the lady Marchioness Margherita Bolognini Amorini took the habit at the convent of Santa Cristina, with a great concourse of the nobility; and the king [i.e., the Stuart Pretender] attended with his eldest son" (BCB, MS B3667, 107).

11. ASV, VR, posiz. 1607, A–B.

12. René Metz, *La consécration des vierges dans l'église romaine: Étude d'histoire de la liturgie* (Paris: Presses Universitaires de France, 1954), 340–41.

13. BAV, MS Ferr. 612, fol. 12r.

14. ASV, VR, reg. monial. 2 (1647), fol. 245v; ASV, VR, sez. monache, 1668 (giugno–luglio).

15. Metz, *La consécration*, 341. On continued use of the ritual consecration in Siena, see Colleen Reardon, *Holy Concord within Sacred Walls: Nuns and*

Music in Siena, 1575–1700 (Oxford: Oxford University Press, 2002), 58–60. A discussion of similar practices in Venice will appear in Jonathan Glixon, *Mirrors of Heaven or Worldly Theaters? Venetian Nunneries and Their Music* (in preparation).

CHAPTER 10

1. Ludovico Maria Orsi's assessment appears in a letter of 15 March 1696 in SACDOC.
2. SACDOC, letter dated 1 January 1698. This Gozzadini, as titular archbishop of Imola (1710–28), would prove a sympathetic and practical ally of the nuns of Sant'Agostino in Lugo and of Christina Cavazza, a consecrand in the 1699 Sacra, whose adventures and misadventures (including illicit trips to the opera in Bologna) are described in Craig A. Monson, *Nuns Behaving Badly: Tales of Music, Magic, Art, and Arson in the Convents of Italy* (Chicago: University of Chicago Press, 2010), 153–96. Sabbatini's request appears in SACDOC, letter dated 28 August 1697.
3. SACDOC, letter dated 11 January 1698 and letter dated 18 January 1698, containing the two quotations.
4. A petition requesting age dispensations for the youngest consecrands survives in ASV, VR, posiz. 1624, B–F.
5. Ludovico Ludovisi quoted in CDSC, fols. 20v–21r.
6. Giacomo Boncompagni, BUB, MS It. 3897/39. The document is unsigned and undated and contains no overt links to Boncompagni, but it clearly refers to the suit involving the archbishop and nuns of Santa Cristina in the 1690s.
7. 1599 petition: ASV, VR, posiz. 1599, A–C. 1601 ruling: ASV, VR, reg. regular. 3, fol. 60v.
8. CDSC, fol. 31v.
9. ASV, VR, sez. monache, 1655 (settembre–dicembre). The response appears in ASV, VR, reg. monial. 7 (1655), 306–7. ASV, VR, sez. monache, 1657 (gennaio–aprile).
10. SACDOC: a letter from a "don Agostino" dated 11 January 1698 mentions Colloredo's relationship to the Orsi; see also Sabbatini's letters of 1 and 18 January.
11. Bolognetti's role: SACDOC, letters dated 18 March and 14 May.
12. On Princess Pallavicina's intercessions, see SACDOC, Sabbatini's letter of 11 January 1698. The remark regarding Princess Ottoboni appears in a letter dated 18 March 1698.
13. On exchanges with Contessa Isabetta and on Christmas tarts, see SACDOC, letters dated 20 December 1697 and 1 January, 18 March, and 23 March 1698. The quotation from Sabbatini appears in a letter dated May 1698.
14. SACDOC, letter from Sabbatini dated 14 May 1698. Petrucci's comment, "Ma le Monache non sono già Puttanaccie e lo disse à me," appears in

another Sabbatini letter from May 1698. Cardinal Petrucci had been investigated by the Inquisition and many of his writings placed on the Index a decade earlier.

15. SACDOC, unsigned letter dated 14 May 1698.

16. Lodovico Maria's comment appears in an undated letter in SACDOC that also speaks of "his sisters at San Mattia." Another unsigned letter, dated 14 May 1698, apparently from a Bolognetti, remarks, "I had two sisters there [at San Mattia]." Sabbatini's comments on Bolognetti's lobbying and the quotation appear in a letter dated 12 June 1698.

17. Bolognetti's suggestion appears in SACDOC in an unsigned letter dated 14 May 1698. The remark by the mother abbess, Colomba Carrati, appears in a letter dated 23 May 1698.

18. SACDOC, letter to Giovanni Benedetto Sabbatini, 28 May 1698.

19. For Zanelli's brief, see BUB, MS It. 770/61, fols. 28ar–28hv.

20. For Sabbatini's quip, see SACDOC, letter dated 6 July 1698. *Queene Anna's New World of Words* (1611) includes "scrupulous in conscience to do amisse" and "a Clergie-man" among the definitions of "religioso." The congregation's ruling is published in *Decreta authentica congregationis sacrorum rituum ex actis eiusdem collecta . . . sub auspiciis SS. Domini Nostri Leonis Papae XIII,* vol. 1 (Rome: Typographia Polyglotta, 1898), 437, no. 2001; and in Aloisi Gardellini, *Decreta authentica congregationis sacrorum rituum,* 3d ed., vol. 2 (Rome: S. Congregatione de Propaganda Fide, 1856), 168.

21. The roof exit is mentioned in SACDOC, Sabbatini's letter dated 2 August.

22. SACDOC, undated letter from Count Bolognetti to the bursar, Luigia Orsina Orsi.

23. SACDOC, Paolo Bolognetti's letter dated 9 July 1698.

24. *Decreta authentica . . . Leonis Papae XIII,* 440–41, no. 2012; see also Gardellini, *Decreta,* 172–73.

25. SACDOC, Paolo Bolognetti's letter dated 2 October 1698.

26. Ibid., "Piena e distinta Informatione del fatto occorso in occasione della Lite."

27. The nuns' comment appears in ibid. A copy of Giovanni Pellegrino Nobili, *La verginità consacrata* (Bologna: Eredi del Sarti, 1699), survives in BUB, MS It. 770/61, between fols. 28iv and 29r.

28. Nobili, *La verginità consacrata,* 3–4. Francesco Ferrari, in ibid., 21, misbound after 4. SACDOC, letter from Ludovico Maria Orsi dated 4 August 1698. The signature of the other letter, dated 11 October 1698, is illegible.

29. Antonio Morazzi's full description appears in BUB, MS It. 4/22.

30. Nobili, *La verginità consacrata,* 3, 13, 19.

31. The seminarians are mentioned in BUB, MS It. 770/61, 21. For the analogy to Christ's thirty-three years on earth, see Morazzi's description in BUB, MS It. 4/22, fols. 204v–205r.

32. Ugo Capriani, "Chiesa e convento di Santa Cristina della Fondazza in Bologna: Ipotesi di ricerca e recupera" (degree thesis, University of Bologna, 1987–88), 139.

33. CDSC, fol. 20v.

34. Nuns' singing: Nobili, *La verginità consacrata*, 4, 19. Convent pyrotechnics: BCB, MS Gozz. 184, fol. 65v. 1699 extern musicians: BUB, MS It. 770/61, 17–27. 1711 music and fireworks: BUB, MS 225/1, fol. 58; another, similar brief entry appears in BCB, MS B83, 473. See also BCB, MS Gozz. 184; BUB, MS It. 4/22, fol. 204r.

35. 1699 consecrands' singing: BUB, MS It. 770/61, 23–25. 1711 consecrands' singing: BUB, MS It. 225/1, fol. 58; see also BCB, MS B83, 473; BCB, MS B3666, 369; BCB, MS Gozz. 355, 25. 1711 enthusiastic descriptions: BUB, MS It. 4/22, fol. 203r.

36. The complete text appears in René Metz, *La consécration des vierges dans l'église romaine: Étude d'histoire de la liturgie* (Paris: Presses Universitaires de France, 1954), 430, 440–43, 445.

37. [Ambrogio Traversari], *Hodoeporicon*, ed. Vittorio Tamburini (Florence: Felice le Monnier, 1985), 116.

38. Metz, *La consécration*, 444.

39. For 1699: BCB, MS Gozz. 185, fol. 65v; BCB, MS Gozz 331, entry for 11 January 1699; BUB, MS It. 616/7, 21; BUB, MS It. 770/61, 19; ASB, Demaniale 49/2910 (Santa Cristina). For 1711: BUB, MS It. 4/22, fol. 202r.

40. Poetic description of jewels in 1699: Girolamo Azzoguidi, in Nobili, *La verginità consacrata*, 16. For 1711, 1699, and 1624 comments on jewels: BUB, MS It. 4/22, fol. 203r. SACDOC, "Piena e Distinta Informatione." CDSC, fol. 20v. 1699 Bolognese nobles as Magi: Fernando Ghedini, in Nobili, *La verginità consacrata*, 20.

41. The 1699 list derives from BUB MS It. 770/61, 20–21.

42. Pompeo Dolfi, *Cronologia delle famiglie nobili di Bologna* (Bologna: Giovanni Battista Ferroni, 1670; repr., Bologna: Forni, n.d.).

43. Alfeo Giacomelli, "La dinamica della nobiltà bolognese," in *Famiglie senatorie e istituzioni cittadine a Bologna nel Settecento: Atti del colloquio Bologna 2–3 Febbraio 1980* (Bologna: Istituto per la Storia Bolognese, 1980), 71. Gabriella Zarri suggests the possibility that the number of noble *professe* was on the wane. See her "Monasteri femminili e città (secoli XV–XVIII)," in *Storia d'Italia, Annali 9: La chiesa e il potere politico dal Medioevo all'età contemporanea*, ed. Giorgio Chittolini and Giovanni Miccoli (Turin: Giulio Einaudi, 1986), 423.

44. BCB, MS Gozz. 329, entry for 27 January 1675. For 1655: ASV, VR, sez. monache, 1655 (settembre–dicembre), letter registered 17 December 1655.

45. The quotation is from the nuns' description of the whole affair in SACDOC, added at the end of "Piena e distinta informatione" by a different hand. The details of the gifts appear in BUB, MS It. 770/61, 27.

46. The few details of the nuns' individual histories have been retrieved from Carrati's transcript of the convent necrologies in BCB, MS B921.

47. Alessandro Caprara, SACDOC, inclusion at end of book of Sabbatini letters.

48. On the convent archive, see Capriani, "Chiesa e convento," 77. The relevant documents survive in SACDOC.

CHAPTER 11

1. Undated, unsigned memorial marked "Jacobus Boncompagni Card. Archiepiscopus Bononiae" in BUB MS It. 79/3.
2. See Ludwig Pastor, *The History of the Popes*, trans. Ernest Graf (St. Louis, MO: B. Herder, 1952), esp. 32:387–92, 405,525n2.
3. For Boncompagni's reform efforts and the anonymous, contemporary quotation, see Umberto Mazzone, "La visita e l'azione pastorali di Giacomo Boncompagni, arcivescovo di Bologna (1690–1731)," *Cristianesimo nella storia* 4 (1983): esp. 343–45, 352n38. For details of Boncompagni's *visita pastorale*, see AAB, MS 70.H.562, esp. fols. 110v, 123v, 211v, 224v. For licenses to music teachers, see ASV, VR, sez. monache, 1697 (aprile–maggio and luglio–agosto) and 1698 (gennaio–marzo and agosto–settembre).
4. For Giacomo Boncompagni's ban on the mixing of sexes, see Corrado Ricci, *Una illustre avventuriera (Cristina di Nortumbria)* (Milan: Fratelli Treves, Editori, 1891), 116. Boncompagni's quotation survives in ASV, VR, sez. monache, 1704 (agosto); and ASB, Demaniale 48/2909 (Santa Cristina).
5. Scandals in nuns' churches: BUB, MS It. 616/4, 66–67 (1691); BUB, MS It. 616/7, 296 (1701). Giacomo Boncompagni's description of the service in Sant'Agnese: ASB, Demaniale 48/2909 (Santa Cristina), "Risposta dell'Em. Arcivescovo alla Sacra Congregatione."
6. BCB, MS B3666, 213–14 (on San Mattia); BUB, MS It. 770/65, 22 (on Corpus Domini); BUB, MS It. 616/8, 628 (on Corpus Domini); ASB, Demaniale 84/3233 (Santi Vitale et Agricola), no. 22, "Licenze diverse per le funzioni della chiesa."
7. Antonio Francesco Ghiselli, BUB, MS It. 770/65, 40.
8. ASB, Demaniale 48/2909 (Santa Cristina), "Primo ricorso dalle M.M. alla sacra congregatione" and "Risposta dell'Em. Arcivescovo alla sacra congregatione."
9. Ibid., "Primo ricorso."
10. Ibid., "Lettera o Memorial da presentare alla sacra cong. che poi non vi si mandò."
11. Ibid., "Lettera del n[ostr]o avocato Narici"; ibid., letter dated 19 November.
12. Ibid., "Primo ricorso"; ASV, VR, sez. monache, 1647 (giugno–agosto).
13. ASB, Demaniale 48/2909 (Santa Cristina), "Primo ricorso."
14. Ibid., "Raggioni sopra il fondamento della nostra causa." The penance imposed by Boncompagni was not entirely out of line. Alexander VII's *pro comissio* of 27 September 1667, which the nuns had quoted in their own defense because it allowed music in the inner chapels of Roman convents, had also stipulated deprivation of office for any convent superior and of active and passive voice for any nuns who permitted performances by extern

musicians. See Fiorenza Romita, *Ius Musicae Liturgicae* (Taurini: Officina Libraria Marii e Marietti, 1936), 63n3.

15. ASB, Demaniale 48/2909 (Santa Cristina), "Lettera dell' n[ostr]o avocato Narici," dated 6 September 1704; ibid., letter dated Rome, 6 September 1704, from "Camillo Bologneti sen[ator]e de Bologna."

16. Ibid., letter dated 9 December 1704; ASV, VR, sez. monache, 1704 (agosto).

17. ASB, Demaniale 48/2909 (Santa Cristina), letter dated 6 December 1704.

18. Ibid., petition dated 22 December 1704.

19. Ibid.

20. Nun's protest: ibid., copy of undated, unsigned letter. Colloredo's final message: ibid., letter dated 7 January 1705.

21. See U. Coldagelli, "Boncompagni, Gregorio," in *Dizionario biografico degli italiani*, vol. 11 (Rome: Istituto della Enciclopedia Italiana, 1969), 693–94; Coldagelli, "Boncompagni, Antonio," in ibid., 679–81.

22. ASB, Demaniale 48/2909 (Santa Cristina), letter dated "Roma p[ri]mo del 707 [*sic*]"; ibid., unsigned, undated slip of paper.

23. Katherine Gill, "Scandala: Controversies concerning Clausura and Women's Religious Communities in Late Medieval Italy," in *Christendom and Its Discontents: Exclusion, Persecution and Rebellion, 1000–1500*, ed. Scott Waugh and Peter D. Diehl (Cambridge: Cambridge University Press, 1996), 187.

24. Biographical details from BCB, MS B921, 266. Anselmo Giabbani, *Menologia Camaldolese* (Rome: S. Gregorio al Celio, 1950), 5.

25. Craig A. Monson, *Nuns Behaving Badly: Tales of Music, Magic, Art, and Arson in the Convents of Italy* (Chicago: University of Chicago Press, 2010), 153–96.

26. BCB, MS B3666, 243.

27. AAB, Misc. Vecchie 820, fasc. 17.

28. Quoted in Craig Monson, introduction to *The Crannied Wall: Women, Religion, and the Arts in Early Modern Europe* (Ann Arbor: University of Michigan Press, 1992), 4.

29. Giovanni Benedetto Mittarelli and Anselmo Costadoni, *Annales Camaldulenses ordiniis Sancti Benedicti*, vol. 8 (Venice: Aere Monasterii Sancti Michaelis de Murano, 1764), 343.

30. ASB, Demaniale 49/2910 (Santa Cristina), "Conto Generale di tutte le spese . . . 11 settembre 1729."

CODA

1. For a summary of the Napoleonic era in Bologna, see Angelo Varni, "Il periodo Napoleonico," in *Storia illustrata di Bologna*, ed. Walter Tega, vol. 2 (Milan: Nuova Editoriale AIEP, 1989), 341–60. The departing nun's comment appears in BCB, MS B3283, final entry. The number of suppressed convents appears in Corrado Ricci and Guido Zucchini, *Guida di Bologna:*

Nuova edizione illustrata (Bologna: Edizioni Alfa, 1968; repr., Bologna: Edizioni Alfa, 1976), 231.

2. Nuns' pensions are mentioned in Roberta Zucchini, "Santa Cristina della Fondazza: Storia architettonica e storico artistica" (degree thesis, University of Bologna, 1987–88), 110.

3. For the reacquisition of convent property, see Ugo Capriani, "Chiesa e convento di Santa Cristina della Fondazza in Bologna: Ipotesi di ricerca e recupero" (degree thesis, University of Bologna, 1987–88), 41–42. The surviving pair of Camaldolese nuns appears in a listing of nuns with their various orders in AAB, Misc. Vecchie 262. For their original entries into Santa Cristina, see ASB, Demaniale 21/2882 (Santa Cristina), nos. Y/23, Y/43, Y/44.

4. On the conversion of the *chiesa vecchia* into a bicycle warehouse, see Zucchini, "Santa Cristina della Fondazza," 78; Capriani, "Chiesa e convento," 43. On the usages of the convent during World War II and its later abandonment, see Zucchini, "Santa Cristina della Fondazza," 24; Capriani, "Chiesa e convento," 44.

5. I am grateful to signor Luciano Malossi, secretary for the surviving members of the Associazione Leone XIII for details about the uses of the *chiesa interiore* in the twentieth century. I am pleased to report that the Coro Leone, a male chorus that first performed at the Teatro Leone XIII in 1967, continues to perform today.

6. Capriani, "Chiesa e convento," 246.

7. Ibid., 198.

8. The description of Santa Cristina *vecchia* appears in Giovanni Benedetto Mittarelli and Anselmo Costadoni, *Annales Camaldulenses ordiniis Sancti Benedicti*, vol. 9 (Venice: Aere Monasterii Sancti Michaelis de Murano, 1773), appendix, col. 161.

Glossary

AL SECOLO (IN THE WORLD): Term used with reference to a nun's time before entering the convent, particularly associated with her secular name.

ANTIPHONAL: A book of plainchant consisting of chants of the Divine Office; also a style of musical performance in which different groups answer one another.

ANZIANI: Eight aldermen elected from the upper classes by the Bolognese senate for two-month terms; by 1600 the *anziani* retained little authority beyond rendering judgments in minor civil and criminal cases.

BASSO CONTINUO: The underlying harmonic accompaniment, consisting of chords played chiefly on organ or harpsichord, almost invariably present in musical works of the 1600s and 1700s.

CANTO FIGURATO: As opposed to plainchant (*canto fermo*); refers to more elaborate music such as polyphony.

CHOIR (*CORO*): A term applied to a group of singers, to the place where they sing, and frequently to the place where religious recite the Divine Office ("nuns' choir," "internal church").

CHURCH—INTERNAL/EXTERNAL: The double church of a female monastery or convent, consisting of an internal sanctuary, inside *clausura*, for the nuns and an external church accessible to the public and outside *clausura*; the two are generally separated by a wall, most commonly behind the high altar and frequently pierced by one or more grates.

CLAUSURA (ENCLOSURE): The physical separation of nuns from the world, legislated by the Council of Trent and enforced in 1566 by

Pope Pius V; violation of *clausura*, either by nuns setting foot outside the convent or by outsiders setting foot inside, resulted in excommunication.

COMMUNION WINDOW: A secluded window covered with a grate, generally near the high altar of a convent church, through which Holy Communion was passed to the nuns by the priest during Mass.

COMPLINE: The last of the eight canonical hours of the Divine Office, originally celebrated after dinner.

CONCERTO: Term used to describe various combinations, alternations, or interactions of voices and instruments in music of the 1600s and 1700s.

CONFESSOR EXTRAORDINARY: Confessor specially appointed at times such as Lent or during jubilees to confess nuns.

CONVERSA (PL. CONVERSE): A servant nun, admitted for a smaller dowry, who did not profess final vows and was not required to recite the Divine Office.

DIVINE OFFICE: The eight canonical hours, consisting of prayers, readings, and psalms that, in most major religious orders, must be recited daily by those who have professed.

DONNA: The title adopted for a *professa* in Benedictine and Camaldolese religious houses such as Santa Cristina della Fondazza.

EDUCANDA (PL. EDUCANDE): A girl permitted to reside in a convent to be educated (*in educazione*), on the assumption that she will become a novice.

ELEVATION MOTET: A motet whose text adores Christ, present in the consecrated bread and wine of Holy Communion, through the miracle of transubstantiation; performed during the Elevation of the Host at Mass.

FALSOBORDONE: Simple polyphony in which a text is chanted in hymnlike, chordal harmony; frequently harmonizing Gregorian chant.

GRATE: The iron grille that covers the windows facing the world in convents; found chiefly in the *parlatorio*, on the Communion window, and on the window above the high altar of the external church, through which the nuns adored the consecrated Host at the Elevation during Mass.

INVESTITURE (CLOTHING CEREMONY): The rite of passage in which a postulant is accepted into the convent, receives her habit, takes her religious name, and becomes a novice.

JUBILEE: A year in which remission of sins is granted on confession, repentance, and the carrying out of prescribed religious acts. Although jubilees customarily fell every twenty-five years (1600, 1625, etc.), the pope could declare additional jubilees at critical times (e.g., 1629).

LEGATE: A papal appointee of cardinal rank who governed a papal state such as Bologna.

LICENSE: Special permission granting exemption, in a single instance or for a prescribed period, to some ecclesiastical law. A license was necessary for laypeople to visit cloistered relatives, for doctors or barbers to enter *clausura*, and for organ tuners, music teachers, and outside musicians to work in convents.

MADRIGAL: A work of polyphony, commonly secular, often of a worldly, at times lascivious, character.

MAGNIFICAT: The canticle of the Blessed Virgin Mary, recited at vespers, frequently sung in polyphony, even in convents.

MATINS: The first of the eight canonical hours of the Divine Office, customarily performed at midnight or dawn.

MELISMA: A type of musical word setting in which several musical notes are assigned to a single syllable of text.

MENOLOGY: A listing of saints and religious of particular merit, arranged according to the calendar.

MISTRESS OF NOVICES: The *professa* who teaches novices the rules of the order, how to recite the Office, and, at convents such as Santa Cristina della Fondazza, the elements of reading and music.

MONODY: A type of music involving a single singing voice; the term is used even if the single voice is accompanied by the basso continuo.

MOTET: A musical setting in polyphony of a Latin text, in the 1600s and 1700s normally of sacred character.

NECROLOGY: A list of deceased convent members, including not only their vital statistics but also their meritorious acts and talents.

NOVICE: A woman who has gone through the rite of acceptance and investiture at a convent and is undergoing a period (normally one year) of prayer, meditation, and instruction in the rules of the order.

ORDINARY: A bishop, archbishop, or his deputy serving as an authority.

PARANYMPHA (PL. PARANYMPHAE): A secular matron who assists a nun at the consecration of virgins.

PARLATORIO: The parlor in which nuns meet outsiders, consisting of an interior chamber for the nuns, separated by a grate from an exterior chamber for visitors; a convent frequently had several *parlatori*.

PLAINCHANT: The traditional single-line melodies to which texts of the Catholic liturgy were sung; during the 1600s and 1700s they were frequently accompanied by the organ.

POLYPHONY: Music involving several independent musical voices or parts of varying complexity performed simultaneously.

PONENTE: A prelate appointed to supervise the presentation of a suit before a curial body; a cardinal was appointed *ponente* to shepherd a petition through the Sacred Congregation of Bishops and Regulars, for example, particularly when no prelate directly involved seemed sufficiently impartial.

PONTIFICAL: A book containing liturgies performed specifically by bishops.

PROFESSA (PL. *PROFESSE*): A nun who has professed final vows, is required to recite the Divine Office, and usually has a voice in convent government. The *professa* normally paid a full dowry, unless granted a special reduction by the Sacred Congregation of Bishops and Regulars for special reasons (e.g., because she would become convent organist).

PROFESSION: The rite in which a novice professes her final vows of poverty, chastity, and obedience and is admitted to full rights in her religious order.

REGULARS: Religious subject to a religious rule or monastic order (e.g., Benedictine, Camaldolese, Franciscan), in contrast to seculars (secular clergy).

R(U)OTA (PL. *RUOTE*): A rotating device shaped like a barrel with a section cut out; it was fixed in a convent wall, and items could be introduced into the convent through it without the necessity of direct contact with the nuns inside.

SACRA: Consecration of virgins; a nun's final, particularly solemn rite of passage, to be performed only after age twenty-five. At convents such as Santa Cristina della Fondazza, it enabled her to serve in the highest monastic offices.

SECULAR CLERGY: Clergy not belonging to a religious order (cf. "regulars"); subject to the authority of a local bishop or archbishop.

STILE MODERNO: The musical style(s) introduced around 1600 that involved freer use of solo voices, instruments, more unusual or irregular harmonies, and a generally more variegated, overtly dramatic character.

SUFFRAGAN: An auxiliary bishop appointed to assist an archbishop, who is his superior.

S(U)OR(A) (SISTER): The customary title for *professe* and *converse* in most religious orders (Franciscans, Augustinians, etc.). In Benedictine and Camaldolese houses the term was generally reserved for *converse*.

SUSPENSION: A musical device in a piece of polyphony in which one or more voices or parts hold a note over from one sonority to the next; in the second sonority the suspensions commonly clash with other voices of the new sonority, which usually pause while the suspensions resolve to consonant notes.

VESPERS: The penultimate of the eight canonical hours of the Divine Office, customarily recited in the late afternoon or evening.

VICAR GENERAL: A high official of the diocesan curia who oversees the functions and discipline of the diocese.

VICAR OF NUNS: The diocesan official appointed to oversee the convents of the diocese, sign licenses, grant most exemptions, etc.

VIOL: A bowed stringed instrument particularly common in the 1500s and 1600s, usually with six strings and frets on its fingerboard, held between the legs when played. Although, like instruments of the violin family, viols came in various sizes, the bass viol was most common and was frequently used to support the bass line in a piece of convent polyphony.

VISITATION: Periodic or special investigations of convents by the bishop of a diocese or his deputy, by regular superiors, or, in cities under papal control, sometimes by the papal legate or vice-legate, to monitor their good order or look into possible improprieties.

Further Reading and Listening

Selected Bibliography

Baernstein, Renée. *A Convent Tale: A Century of Sisterhood in Spanish Milan*. New York: Routledge, 2002.

Blamires, Alcuin. *Woman Defamed and Woman Defended: An Anthology of Medieval Texts*. Oxford: Clarendon Press, 1992.

Bornstein, Daniel, and Roberto Rusconi, eds. *Women and Religion in Medieval and Renaissance Italy*. Chicago: University of Chicago Press, 1996.

Bowers, Jane, and Judith Tick, eds. *Women Making Music: The Western Art Tradition, 1150–1950*. Urbana: University of Illinois Press, 1986.

Brown, Judith. *Immodest Acts: The Life of a Lesbian Nun in Renaissance Italy*. Oxford: Oxford University Press, 1986.

Burke, Peter. *The Historical Anthropology of Early Modern Italy: Essays on Perception and Communication*. Cambridge: Cambridge University Press, 1987.

Bynum, Caroline Walker. *Fragmentation and Redemption: Essays on Gender and the Human Body in Medieval Religion*. New York: Zone Books, 1991.

———. *Holy Feast and Holy Fast: The Religious Significance of Food to Medieval Women*. Berkeley and Los Angeles: University of California Press, 1987.

———. *Jesus as Mother: Studies in the Spirituality of the High Middle Ages*. Berkeley and Los Angeles: University of California Press, 1982.

Cohen, Sherrill. *The Evolution of Women's Asylums since 1500: From Refuges for Ex-Prostitutes to Shelters for Battered Women*. New York: Oxford University Press, 1992.

Dolfi, Pompeo. *Cronologia delle famiglie nobili di Bologna*. Bologna: Giovanni Battista Ferroni, 1670. Reprint, Bologna: Forni, n.d.

Dunant, Sarah. *Sacred Hearts: A Novel*. New York: Random House, 2009.

Evangelisti, Silvia. *Nuns: A History of Convent Life, 1450–1700*. Oxford: Oxford University Press, 2007.

Ferrante, Lucia, Maura Palazzi, and Gianna Pomata, eds. *Regnatele di rapporti: Patronage e reti di relazione nella storia delle donne*. Turin: Rosenberg & Sellier, 1988.

Frati, Lodovico. *La vita privata in Bologna dal secolo xiii al xvii*. 2d ed. Bologna: Niccola Zanichelli, 1928. Reprint, Rome: Bardi Editore, 1968.

Gaspari, Gaetano. *Musica e musicisti a Bologna*. Bologna: Forni Editore, n.d.

Harline, Craig. *The Burdens of Sister Margaret: Inside a Seventeenth-Century Convent*. Abridged ed. New Haven, CT: Yale University Press, 2000.

Hills, Helen. *The Invisible City: The Architecture of Devotion in Seventeenth-Century Neapolitan Convents*. New York: Oxford University Press, 2004.

Jones, Ann Rosalind. *The Currency of Eros: Women's Love Lyric in Europe, 1540–1620*. Bloomington: Indiana University Press, 1990.

Kendrick, Robert L. *Celestial Sirens: Nuns and Their Music in Early Modern Milan*. Oxford: Clarendon Press, 1996.

King, Margaret L. *Women of the Renaissance*. Chicago: University of Chicago Press, 1991.

Laven, Mary. *Virgins of Venice: Broken Vows and Cloistered Lives in the Renaissance Convent*. New York: Viking, 2003.

Lowe, K. J. P. *Nuns' Chronicles and Convent Culture in Renaissance and Counter-Reformation Italy*. Cambridge: Cambridge University Press, 2003.

Malvasia, Carlo Cesare. *Le pitture di Bologna 1686*. Edited by Andrea Emiliani. Bologna: Edizioni Alfa, 1969.

Matter, E. Ann, and John Coakley, eds. *Creative Women in Medieval and Early Modern Italy: A Religious and Artistic Renaissance*. Philadelphia: University of Pennsylvania Press, 1994.

McKinnon, James. *Music in Early Christian Literature*. Cambridge: Cambridge University Press, 1987.

Meluzzi, Luciano. *I vescovi e gli arcivescovi di Bologna*. Bologna: Collana Storico-Ecclesiastica, 1975.

Metz, René. *La consécration des vierges dans l'église romaine: Étude d'histoire de la liturgie*. Paris: Presses Universitaires de France, 1954.

Mitchell, Katrina. "'Reading between the Brides': Lucrezia Vizzana's *Componimenti musicali* in Textual and Musical Context." PhD diss., University of Kansas, 2011.

Mittarelli, Giovanni Benedetto, and Anselmo Costadoni. *Annales Camaldulenses ordinis Sancti Benedicti*. 9 vols. Venice: Aere Monasterii Sancti Michaelis de Murano, 1755–73.

Monson, Craig, ed. *The Crannied Wall: Women, Religion, and the Arts in Early Modern Europe*. Ann Arbor: University of Michigan Press, 1992.

———. *Disembodied Voices: Music and Culture in an Early Modern Italian Convent*. Berkeley and Los Angeles: University of California Press, 1995.

———. *Nuns Behaving Badly: Tales of Music, Magic, Art, and Arson in the Convents of Italy*. Chicago: University of Chicago Press, 2010.

Muir, Edward. *Mad Blood Stirring: Vendetta and Factions in Friuli during the Renaissance*. Baltimore, MD: Johns Hopkins University Press, 1993.

Pastor, Ludwig. *The History of the Popes*. Translated by Ernest Graf. 34 vols. Reprint, St. Louis, MO: B. Herder, 1952.

Petroff, Elizabeth Alvilda. *Medieval Women's Visionary Literature*. Oxford: Oxford University Press, 1986.

Pomata, Gianna, and Gabriella Zarri, eds. *I monasteri femminili come centri di cultura fra Rinascimento e Barocco*. Rome: Edizioni di Storia e Letteratura, 2005.

Prodi, Paolo. *Il cardinale Gabriele Paleotti (1522–1597)*. 2 vols. Rome: Edizioni di Storia e Letteratura, 1959–67.

Reardon, Colleen. *Holy Concord within Sacred Walls: Nuns and Music in Siena, 1575–1700*. Oxford: Oxford University Press, 2002.

Ricci, Corrado, and Guido Zucchini. *Guida di Bologna: Nuova edizione illustrata*. Bologna: Edizioni Alfa, 1968. Reprint, Bologna: Edizioni Alfa, 1976.

Rosenberg, Margaret F. *The Honest Courtesan: Veronica Franco, Citizen and Writer in Sixteenth-Century Venice*. Chicago: University of Chicago Press, 1992.

S. Giuliano S. Cristina due chiese in Bologna storia arte architettura. Bologna: La Fotocromo Emiliana, 1997.

Scaraffia, Lucetta, and Gabriella Zarri, eds. *Women and Faith: Catholic Religious Life in Italy from Late Antiquity to the Present*. Cambridge, MA: Harvard University Press, 2001.

Schutte, Anne Jacobson. *Aspiring Saints: Pretense of Holiness, Inquisition, and Gender in the Republic of Venice, 1618–1750*. Baltimore, MD: Johns Hopkins University Press, 2001.

———. *By Force and Fear: Taking and Breaking Monastic Vows in Early Modern Europe*. Ithaca, NY: Cornell University Press, 2011.

Sirk, Chiara, and Candace Smith, eds. *Soror mea, sponsa mea: Arte e musica nei conventi femminili in Italia tra cinque e seicento*. Padua: Il Poligrafo, 2009.

Surtz, Ronald E. *The Guitar of God: Gender, Power, and Authority in the Visionary World of Mother Juana de la Cruz (1481–1534)*. Philadelphia: University of Pennsylvania Press, 1990.

[Traversari, Ambrogio]. *Hodoeporicon*. Edited by Vittorio Tamburini. Florence: Felice le Monnier, 1985.

Weaver, Elissa. *Convent Theatre in Early Modern Italy: Spiritual Fun and Learning for Women*. Cambridge: Cambridge University Press, 2002.

Zarri, Gabriella. "Istituzioni ecclesiastiche e vita religiosa a Bologna (1450–1700)." In *Storia illustrata di Bologna*, vol. 2, edited by Walter Tega, 161–200. Milan: Nuova Editoriale AIEP, 1989.

———. "I monasteri femminili a Bologna tra il XIII e il XVII secolo." *Deputazione di storia patria per le province di Romagna: Atti e memorie*, n.s., 24 (1973): 133–224.

———. "I monasteri femminili benedettini nella diocesi di Bologna (secoli xiii–xvii)." In *Ravennatensia ix: Atti del convegno di Bologna nel xv centenario della nascita di S. Benedetto (15–16–17 settembre 1980)*, 333–71. Cesena: Badia di Santa Maria del Monte, 1981.

———. "Monasteri femminili e città (secoli XV–XVIII)." In *Storia d'Italia, Annali 9: La chiesa e il potere politico dal Medioevo all'età contemporanea*, edited by Giorgio Chittolini and Giovanni Miccoli, 359–429. Turin: Giulio Einaudi, 1986.

———. "Recinti sacri: Sito e forma dei monasteri femminili a Bologna tra '500 e '600." In *Luoghi sacri e spazi della santità*, edited by Sofia Boesch Gajano and Lucetta Scaraffia, 381–96. Turin: Rosenberg & Sellier, 1990.

———. *Le sante vive: Profezie di corte e devozione femminile tra '400 e '500*. Turin: Rosenberg & Sellier, 1990.

———. "'Vera' santità, 'simulata' santità: Ipotesi e riscontri." In *Finzione e santità tra Medioevo ed età moderna*, edited by Gabriella Zarri, 9–36. Turin: Rosenberg & Sellier, 1991.

Selected Scholarly Editions of Music

Aleotti, Raffaella. *Sacrae cantiones: Quinque, septem, octo & decem vocibus decantandae*. Edited by C. Ann Caruthers. Introduction by Thomas W. Bridges. New York: Broude Trust, 1994.

Cozzolani, Chiara Margarita. *Motets*. Edited by Robert Kendrick. Recent Researches in the Music of the Baroque Era, vol. 87. Madison, WI: A-R Editions, 1998.

Leonarda, Isabella. *Selected Compositions*. Edited by Stewart Carter. Recent Researches in the Music of the Baroque Era, vol. 59. Madison, WI: A-R Editions, 1988.

———. *Twelve Sonatas, Opus 16*. Edited by Stewart Carter. Recent Researches in the Music of the Baroque Era, vol. 113. Madison, WI: A-R Editions, c. 2001.

Schleifer, Martha Furman, and Sylvia Blickman, eds. *Women Composers: Music through the Ages*, vols. 1–2. New York: G. K. Hall, 1996.

Selected Discography

Cappella Artemisia:
Canti nel chiostro (Tactus 600001).
Chiara Margarita Cozzolani: I vespri natalizi (1650) (Tactus TC 600301).

Piangere e gioire: La Settimana Santa nei conventi (Tactus: forthcoming).
Raphaela Aleotti: Le monache di San Vito (Tactus TC 570101).
Rosa mistica (Tactus TC 600003).
Scintillate, amicae stellae: Il Natale nei conventi Italiani tra cinquecento e seicento (Tactus 280003).
Soror mea, sponsa mea (Tactus TC 560002).
Sulpitia Cesis mottetti spirituali (1619) (Tactus TC 572801).

Magnificat Early Music Ensemble:
Chiara Margarita Cozzolani: Messa Paschale (Musica Omnia MO 0209).
Chiara Margarita Cozzolani: Vespro della Beata Vergine (Musica Omnia MO 103).

Musica Secreta:
Alessandro Grandi Motetti a cinque voci (1614) (Divine Art dda 25062).
Dialogues with Heaven (Linn CKD 113).
Sacred Hearts, Secret Music (Divine Art dda 25007).
Songs of Ecstasy and Devotion (Linn CKD 071).

Useful Websites

http://www.artemisiaeditions.com/.
http://www.cappella-artemisia.com/.
http://www.linnrecords.com/artist-musica-secreta.aspx.
http://musicasecreta.com/.

Index